GUL GULSHAN GULFAM

Born in 1925, **Pran Kishore** is one of the pioneers who brought cultural renaissance in Kashmir during pre- and post-Independence period. A prolific dramatist and novelist, Pran Kishore brought modernism to the theatre of Jammu & Kashmir. His productions *Jheel Bula Rahi Hai, Vitasta, Himala ke Chasme, Piya Baj Pyala, Tipu Sultan* have been staged across the country. As the senior producer of All India Radio, he has produced more than two thousand plays and documentaries during his long tenure in Broadcasting. His productions of *Aur Vitasta Bahti Rahi* and *Aab Ta Hayat* received the Akashvani Annual Award for Drama and the Akashvani Annual Award for Features. The latter was All India Radio's entry to Prix Italia. Credit of directing the first ever feature film *Mainz-Raat* in Kashmiri, which won the President's Silver Medal as the best regional film in 1965, goes to him. He wrote, along with Balraj Sahni, the feature film *Shair-e-Kashmir Mehjoor* and directed its Kashmiri version. Pran Kishore received the Sahitya Akademi Award for his novel *Sheen Ta Vatapod*. Recipient of the prestigious State Award for outstanding contribution to performing arts from the Government of Jammu & Kashmir, Pran Kishore has been bestowed with robes of honour from the J & K Academy of Art, Culture & Languages and the University of Kashmir (Urdu Department). He was nominated as International Jury Member for Prix Italia XXX and Jury Member for Indo–African Short Film Competition. He has scripted nearly a dozen very popular T.V. serials like *Junoon, Ghuttan, Noor Jehan, Saye Deodar Ke, Manzil*.

Poet, fiction writer, linguist, translator and literary critic **Shafi Shauq** has over forty-five books in Kashmiri, English, Urdu and Hindi to his credit. He has received several awards like the Best Book Award (1982), Sahitya Akademi Award in Creative writing (2006), Bharti Bhasha Saman Award (CIIL, 2007), Sahitya Akademi Translation Award (2007) and Ahad Zargar Award (2011). He is also associated with several national academic projects like Encyclopaedia of Indian Literature, Medieval Indian Literature, and Oxford Companion to Indian Theatre.

Praise for *Gul Gulshan Gulfam*

Gul Gulshan Gulfam (the rose, the rose garden, and the rose personified), the three houseboats owned by the protagonist Malla Khaliq, a character larger than life, his wife, his sons, their families and his neighbourhood living in the waters of this queen of the lakes are portrayed with such honesty that you love them, hate some, yet they remain there, in your mind, asking questions hard to answer. The characters, their definition spread over nearly a thousand pages is a glorious display and aroma of the saffron in the vast saffron fields of Pampore, the land that gave birth to the legendary poet Lalleshwari and the Romantic poet, Queen Habba Khatoon.

      – Ghulam Nabi Gauhar, poet, novelist and critic

We the simple 'hanjis' of the Dal Lake [are] indebted to you, Pran Sahib, for writing such a true to life novel on our life, our struggles, and our aspirations with such honesty and sympathy.

      – Abdul Samad Kotroo, former president, Houseboat Owners' Association

Though adapting a novel for a film or television sitcoms takes away lot of the substance of the novel, and shrinks its canvas, *Gul Gulshan Gulfam*, that started with a whimper, caught the fancy of the nation to become a rage and a sitcom smash and gave the viewers an idea how fascinating this Kashmiri novel must be that has become a valuable contribution to indian literature.

      – Sumit Rawal, film and TV critic

In these turbulent days when Kashmir is burning, this serial evokes hope and convinces us that the mornings of Kashmir still bloom into a smile and the evenings still hum the songs of love. How moving the original novel must be.

      – Gopal Das, former dy. director general, Doordarshan

A devoted lover of Kashmir and a regular visitor to the heaven on earth, I had never got an insight into the life of boat dwellers of the lovely Dal Lake. The fact that my Kashmiri friends are emotionally moved as me, vouches for the authenticity of this serial."

      – Amita Mallik, film, radio and TV critic

A good film is always based on great literature and *Gul Gulshan Gulfam* was no exception. The script was brilliant and true to life. I had spent my childhood fathoming the waters of this lake along with my dad but had not imagined that i will have the honour of becoming one of its habitants and present their ups and downs in life so faithfully portrayed.

      – Parikshit Sahni, who played Malla Khaliq for the TV serial

Gul Gulshan Gulfam is a brilliant adaptation of great piece of Indian literature. It portrays life as it. It is the story of every family. What a spontaneity! I just walked through the role.

      – Radha Seth, who played Aziz Dyad for the TV serial

GUL GULSHAN GULFAM

PRAN KISHORE

Translated from the Kashmiri by

SHAFI SHAUQ with **PRAN KISHORE**

HARPER PERENNIAL

NEW YORK · LONDON · TORONTO · SYDNEY · NEW DELHI

HARPER ⬤ PERENNIAL

First published in India in 2017 by Harper Perennial
An imprint of HarperCollins *Publishers*

P-ISBN: 978-93-5177-777-9
E-ISBN: 978-93-5177-778-6

2 4 6 8 10 9 7 5 3 1

HarperCollins *Publishers*
A-75, Sector 57, Noida, Uttar Pradesh 201301, India
1 London Bridge Street, London, SE1 9GF, United Kingdom
Hazelton Lanes, 55 Avenue Road, Suite 2900, Toronto, Ontario M5R 3L2
and 1995 Markham Road, Scarborough, Ontario M1B 5M8, Canada
25 Ryde Road, Pymble, Sydney, NSW 2073, Australia
195 Broadway, New York, NY 10007, USA

Typeset in 11/14 Bembo Std by
Jojy Philip, New Delhi 110 015

Printed and bound at
Nutech Print Services - India

This book is Dedicated to that Valley of the Rishis
that gave me birth,
that Valley of the Rishis
whose soul has been blessed
with immortality by The Almighty,
that Valley of the Rishis
which has re-emerged from the most trying times
with never-withering blossoms of celestial light.

GUL GULSHAN GULFAM

PART 1

'Don't be clumsy! This is not the way you use the brush to rub dirt off the wood panels of a houseboat. See, you are simply concealing the natural grains of the wood.' Snatching away the brush from Razaq's hands, Malla Khaliq himself started removing dust and fungus from the outer sides of his houseboat.

'Come closer and watch how the brush is moved over the surface of wood. When you rub the surface vertically, there won't be any scratches on the wood, nor will it diminish its beauty. But if you apply the brush horizontally, it may erase all the grains of the wood … Now take the brush and dip it afresh in soap water. Shabaash!'

Razaq immersed the brush in the tub containing soap water and began wiping the panels of the houseboat.

Malla Khaliq sat on the prow of the boat, took out a pack from the deep pocket of his phiran and lit a cigarette. After taking a long puff, he stood up and sat on the uppermost step of the wooden Jacob's ladder used for entering a houseboat from the ferry boat below. He looked all around. The little ripples on the wide expanse of the lake shimmered like flecks of gold in the afternoon sun. A smile bloomed on his lips. His eyes lit up at the feeling that the chilly winter was now in its last throes. He was convinced that life was again going to win over death and spring was approaching to shower its love over this valley of the rishis. He thought how only a couple of weeks ago, this Dal Lake had frozen into one solid sheet of ice and how their lives, too, had frozen with it. Moving even the smallest boat around had become almost impossible then.

Malla Khaliq, while ferrying people to and fro, mixing his sweat with the waters of the lake had watched this grand panorama. For seventy long years, he had borne witness to the changing nature of the Dal Lake. Sitting at the Boulevard that skirted the lake in the south, one could have a full view of the peaks of the Harmukh mountain far up in the north. He remembered how crystal clear and clean the water of the lake was in his childhood. The reflection of the surrounding mountains created a breathtaking wonderland in it. Alas! Now algae had ensnared the entire Dal and weeds had overtaken its argentine water.

Malla Khaliq was lost in such thoughts when he was startled by a distant call. 'Haji Sahib! *As-salaam-alaikum.*' Malla Khaliq saw Rahim Shoga approaching in a small boat, bearing all manner of merchandise to sell to the owners of the houseboats and the barges connected with them. A floating departmental store.

'Is it a party of Europeans or local tourists arriving?' Rahim Shoga asked Malla Khaliq halting near the stairs.

'Who knows who is destined to be my guest. It is rather early for the tourists. But why do you ask me?' Malla Khaliq asked, throwing the stub of his smouldering cigarette into the water.

'Seeing you tidying the boats I thought you must be expecting someone. Other houseboat owners haven't even begun thinking of putting out their carpets in the sun to dry.'

'I have no interest in what other houseboat owners do.'

'The turmoil in Punjab is abating now, they say. It may mean a good tourist season this year.'

'Yes, if God wishes so. God alone decides what is good or bad for us,' Malla Khaliq said, wanting to end the conversation there.

He abhorred Rahim Shoga for being so nosy, but he was helpless as his wife Aziz Dyad trusted this talkative vendor; she was convinced that whatever he sold was of the best quality. Besides, Rahim Shoga was the only one who carried news from the city to them. News such as who was doing what and who was saying what, who was born to whom, who fought with whom, or what sort of a daughter-in-law or mother-in-law one was. Only Rahim Shoga could collect such gossip and ferry them between housewives.

'I wish we get a good party of European tourists this year so that we are rid of all our wretchedness,' Rahim Shoga continued.

Malla Khaliq thought it wise to keep mum and stood up. Seeing this, Rahim Shoga perceived Malla Khaliq's disinterest and changed the topic.

'Is Aziz Dyad in?'

'She is waiting for you,' Malla Khaliq replied curtly.

'That is fine. *Salaam-alaikum!*' Having said this, Rahim Shoga paddled his boat towards the *doonga*, the barge anchored to the small isle between two houseboats, where Malla Khaliq had his kitchen and pantry. While rowing to the *doonga*, Rahim Shoga noticed Razaq cleaning the houseboat with utmost care and called out to him, 'Hooray, my boy! If you keep on like this, I am sure you will be rewarded well by Malla Khaliq. I advise you to persist.'

Hearing this Malla Khaliq was livid. He shouted, 'Will you mind your own job? The lady of the house is waiting there in the kitchen.'

But Rahim Shoga still could not contain himself and said while moving on, 'This lad of yours seems to be quite skilful. That is why I'm egging him on. Rahim Shoga, is generally least interested in others' affairs. *Salaam-alaikum!*' Saying so he began to paddle fast.

Malla Khaliq had three houseboats: Gul, Gulshan and Gulfam.

The smallest one was Gul, which his father had got made after much hard labour. It was originally a *doonga*. Khaliq's father had got it renovated. Malla Khaliq was born in this very boat, and naturally he was very fond of it. He, along with his wife Aziz Dyad, lodged in it. Considering it a precious heirloom, he always maintained it with his own hands.

The second one was Gulshan, which he had made from his own earnings during the years of the German war when European tourists thronged the city.

After the Second World War, when the British left India, tourism suffered tremendously because of the aggression of the tribesmen sent by Pakistan immediately after Independence, to let loose a reign of terror in Kashmir. Though their designs were defeated by the unity of the people and the defence forces, the lives of Kashmiris had been shattered. People who were directly connected with tourism, like the boatmen, suffered the most. Their entire livelihood depended on tourists. Many houseboat owners abandoned the occupation. Some of them decided to live on dry land and many sold their boats for paltry sums. But Malla Khaliq was a prudent man; he purchased a big houseboat that had been reduced to its keel from neglect.

And when the political conditions improved, he engaged carpenters and erected his third houseboat. He named it Gulfam. Not knowing the meaning of the word, his wife Aziz Dyad asked him, 'What does "Gulfam" mean?'

'Gul means a flower, you know that,' Malla Khaliq explained, casting a loving glance at her. 'Gulshan stands for a garden, isn't it so?'

'That much I know, but what is this Gulfam?' she asked.

'Gulfam connotes a lover of flowers, or someone very handsome wearing an attire made of flowers. Thus Gul, Gulshan and Gulfam together mean our entire world.'

Malla Khaliq took out one more cigarette from his pocket and looked at his three houseboats. He heaved a deep sigh and put the cigarette back into his pocket. He walked over to Razaq and rubbed the cedar planks of the boat with his hand to check the smoothness achieved by Razaq's toil. 'Well done. Give the brush to me, I will show you how to clean the carvings of the wooden pillars.'

He had hardly touched the brush when his daughter Parveen came in running. She snatched the brush away from his hands, threw it into the tub, and holding his arm, tried to pull him towards the isle complaining, 'Must Amma come and implore you to have lunch? For half an hour she has been waiting with food laid out in plates. If we are to work ourselves, what is the point of getting this clumsy boy from the village?'

Malla Khaliq guffawed. 'Don't you see that I am walking with you? Oh God! Don't drag me like that. Release your hold on my arm, please. If you take a wrong step you'll stumble and fall. You, a grandma of a daughter, do you hear?'

'Moej sent you four messages that the food is ready, then why didn't you come? I can't let you go now.'

'Okay, see, here I am going to the pantry straight away, I promise. You just release my arm.'

'That's like a good father. I shall meanwhile go call my brother. He too behaves like a prince; he wants ten people to invite him to meals.'

Parveen let go of her father's arm and hurried towards the next houseboat. Razaq watched her with a bewildered expression and that annoyed Parveen.

'Why are you staring at me like a deer? Pick up the brush and finish the job!'

Razaq started. He quickly took the brush from the tub. Parveen leapt like a gazelle to the next houseboat and Malla Khaliq fondly watched her go. He walked back to Razaq. 'You too come with us to have lunch. You must be hungry. Come on, my son.'

Razaq looked immensely grateful. Malla Khaliq laid his hand warmly upon his shoulder and said, 'Don't be frightened – this crazy daughter of mine is wont to govern all of us like that. Being the youngest, she is the most beloved of all.' In the meantime, Parveen was heard saying at her highest pitch: 'No more envoys will come to call you! You hear me, my brother?' Hearing her angry voice, Malla Khaliq also started. 'Now I shall have no excuses. She cannot pardon me further,' Khaliq said to himself as he quickened his pace to the pantry. His second son, Ghulam Ahmed, also came out of the houseboat and walked towards the pantry. Razaq, who was following Malla Khaliq, stood close to the wall to make space for Ghulam Ahmed, and raised his hand to him in salute. Seeing Ghulam Ahmed's eyes flash in anger at the gesture, he put his hand down, and followed him meekly.

No sooner had Malla Khaliq entered the kitchen than his wife unleashed her anger on him. 'So finally you have found the time to be kind enough to come for lunch!' Sitting down beside Malla Khaliq, she began putting rice into bowls for her daughters-in-law, and continued saying, 'If they want the rice to go cold in their vessels, I won't be cooking for them henceforth. I shall ask them to arrange for a chef to serve them according to their whims.'

'But how can a chef know how to make minced kale and onion paste like you?' Hearing Malla Khaliq's words, the daughters-in-law, already assembled there, could hardly stop tittering. Malla Khaliq nestled closer to his wife and tried to calm her down with his praises. 'No, I am not flattering you. If you go on strike, this Malla Khaliq of yours shall die of hunger.'

'Now stop it. Do not enrage me further. You are a completely shameless fellow!'

'Yes, I always was.' Saying so, he laughed boisterously. He stopped short and morosely pulled both his ears to beg for pardon. The daughters-in-law struggled to suppress their laughter.

Snapping at them, Aziz Dyad said, 'Stop giggling and pass on these bowls of rice!'

This was the routine lunch hour when Malla Khaliq's whole family came together.

Malla Khaliq had three sons and one daughter. All the sons were married. His eldest son was Noor Mohammad and his wife was Mukhta. The second son was Ghulam Ahmed and his wife was Zoon. The youngest one was Ghulam Qadir and his wife was called Zeb. Parveen was the only daughter. The siblings were very different from each other, especially in their temperaments. The eldest son, Noor Mohammad, was a replica of his father – the same seriousness, the same honest dealings, the same demeanour and the same humility. He was fortunate to have found a wife who was compatible with his nature. Noor Mohammad, like his father, had great pride in belonging to the Mir Bahris caste – sons of the waters. But his second son, Ghulam Ahmed, was not interested in the business of houseboats. He was impatient to be affluent and occasionally bid for and purchased fruits from the orchards to sell later on and make some money. And when he wasn't satisfied with the harvest, he dreamed of shifting trades and becoming a wholesale merchant. But it was his misfortune that any business he ventured into did not do him any good. Whenever he would get into trouble, he coerced his wife to go and beg for money from her father, Naba Kantroo.

Naba Kantroo was also a boatman by profession, but when he abjured this vocation and decided to dwell on land, he prospered within a few months. There were many rumours about his success. Some believed that he prospered from illegal trafficking of hashish, but many others believed that he had won a big lottery from some agency outside the valley. The real story of his success was shrouded in mystery. In order to display his virtue and put a stop to the rumours, he opened a shop with a large and gaudy signboard bearing the name 'Kantroo and Sons: Developers and Builders' in bold letters. All this notwithstanding, Malla Khaliq never liked having any association with his second son's father-in-law. His son would have never married his daughter if she wasn't related to Malla Khaliq's wife, Aziz Dyad. Nevertheless, the girl was fairly modest.

Malla Khaliq's youngest son, Ghulam Qadir, was a novice in the trade; romantic and mischievous, he was a graduate by education and had a close association with boys from affluent families. He nursed an intense desire to be rich, that too quickly. It was during his days in college that he seduced a pretty girl from a respected family. Malla Khaliq then had no option but to inquire into the girl's family background, character and moral demeanour. Satisfied with what he found out, he sought his wife's consent and proceeded to have Ghulam Qadir married to her. Within one year of their union, a lovely baby boy was born to the couple and Malla Khaliq fondly christened him Bilal. Malla Khaliq was already a grandfather to Nisar, Noor Mohammad's son, who was studying medicine. Ahmed, too, had a son, but he had been coaxed into living with his maternal grandfather, Naba Kantroo, much to Malla Khaliq's chagrin.

When Malla Khaliq squatted to have his meals, he happened to glance at Razaq who was standing near the water tap. He called out to Razaq, 'Why are you still standing there? Why don't you come in and have your food?'

Aziz Dyad got irked and said, 'Why should he come in? Parveen, take this bowl of rice and hand it over to him.'

Parveen took the aluminium bowl filled with food, daintily ambled out and gave it to Razaq. She came back into the kitchen, took her own bowl of food from her mother and nestled close to her father.

Malla Khaliq fondly cast a glance at his family. He noticed with a furrowed brow that his youngest son, Qadir, was not there. 'Where is Qadir? Was he not supposed to be here for lunch?'

'Yes, of course he was. God knows where he has gone,' Aziz Dyad replied.

Malla Khaliq asked Qadir's wife, Zeb, 'Did he not tell you where he was going?'

'He said that he was to go to the airport.' Saying this, Zeb immediately hung her head and feigned mixing some curry with the rice on her plate.

Upon her response, an incredulous Ahmed exclaimed to his father, 'As if visitors are waiting in queues for us at the airport. Not even a mongrel is visible there, or at the Tourist Reception Centre.'

Hearing this Aziz Dyad retorted, 'No one appreciates his efforts here.'

'What feat has he accomplished so far, that we do not appreciate his efforts?' Ahmed said sarcastically.

Hearing this, Malla Khaliq sharply responded, 'Yes, you alone have many achievements to your credit. We all know how you repaid every penny of the bank loan!'

'Had the hailstorm not hit the orchard in the spring bloom, I would certainly have repaid the whole loan in just one instalment.'

'Are you talking of debts of the bank or what you owe your father-in-law?' Saying this pejoratively to Ahmed, he looked at Zoon who bent her head. A strained silence prevailed for a few minutes.

Aziz Dyad caught sight of Razaq, who was following the conversation. She broke the silence by loudly asking her husband, 'Have you finished or you want some more rice?' Razaq started, red-faced and hurriedly swallowed his last morsel and went outside.

Aziz Dyad chided her husband, 'You have no limits! You never think about the people around you before you speak. Are you not ashamed of revealing our family's problems in the presence of a servant who has come only recently?'

'The poor urchin is caught up in his own problems! Why should he pay attention to ours?'

'Come, come! He is not a poor waif. The brute looks downwards, but his ears are always perked up this way.'

Malla Khaliq ordered Razaq who was waiting outside, 'Go now, my dear son.'

Razaq left his bowl near the threshold and walked away towards the houseboat. Aziz Dyad was still enraged by her husband's words and burst out, 'You never care about your own sons, but you are keen to bring street waifs into our home and treat them like your sons! Do what you like, but I must tell you that they are not to stay here for long. They shall collect their month's dues and the bundle of clothes that you give them, and leave the house like night burglars, without letting anyone know.'

'But this boy is a different sort. I assure you, he is certain to continue here.'

'How is he different?' retorted Aziz Dyad.

Noor Mohammad, who was silently listening, turned to his father and said, 'I too feel that this chap is quite gentle and thorough.'

'Oh, not you too! You are sure to defend what your father says,' said Aziz Dyad.

Noor Mohammad did not deem it proper to give any reply to his mother, and Malla Khaliq, too, ended the argument there.

Malla Khaliq had brought home Razaq from the streets. One day, he had gone to Narayan Joo's travel agency on Kothi Bagh street to find out when he was to return from Bombay. There he caught sight of Razaq who was imploring Narayan Joo's manager for a job. Mohammad Sidique, the manager, was a God-fearing man who was always ready to help the needy. But he was helpless as tourism that season had been badly hit by the turmoil in Punjab. There was hardly any work to do – how could he provide this poor fellow with a job?

'Please make him understand,' Mohammad Sidique said to Malla Khaliq who was sitting there, so that he could be saved from the obstinate boy's pleading. 'I don't even have a little space to shelter anyone here, how can I offer him a job!'

But Razaq started crying piteously and this melted Malla Khaliq's heart. He cast a deep look at Razaq. He saw honesty in the boy's wet eyes. Without asking him anything, he said to Razaq, 'My dear son, wait in the adjacent room. Let us see what destiny has allotted to you.'

Razaq offered his salaam to Mohammad Sidique and went to the waiting room. Mohammad Sidique turned to Malla Khaliq. 'He seems to be a gentle boy. But I'm helpless. If the Pandit Sahib were here, he could have engaged him in some of his orchards.'

'You still have not told me when he is to return.'

'After a week or so. You should have received his letter.'

'Yes. But he hasn't mentioned any dates.'

'Has he mentioned anything about the situation in Punjab?'

'Yes, he says that the turmoil has abated to a large extent and he expects a good season of tourists this year.'

'Oh, would our benevolent saint, Peer Dastgir, heed our call.'

Saying 'Amin!' Malla Khaliq took his leave. As he walked towards the door, Mohammad Sidique told him, 'Appoint the boy only after carefully assessing him.'

Malla Khaliq's experience spanned over seventy years. He had assessed Razaq with just one look at him. He brought the boy to his houseboats.

It had been two weeks since and Razaq had been serving at their house. Malla Khaliq's wife was yet to approve of this boy and Ghulam Ahmed disapproved of every decision his father took. As far as his third son, Ghulam Qadir, was concerned, he considered every person other than himself, particularly the servants, nothing but offal.

The three daughters-in-law were happy that there was someone in the house to help them with washing the utensils. Parveen was happy to have found someone to carry out her orders. She even took pity on the boy when any member of the family addressed him with a volley of abuses.

Squatting under the shade of the willow tree that grew in the lawn of the little isle just outside the pantry, Malla Khaliq was enjoying his hookah. Noor Mohammad and Ghulam Ahmed were also there, basking in the warm spring sunshine. Their nap was disturbed by Zoon's shrill voice. 'Why are you idling there, Razaq? Don't you see a heap of utensils lying there to be washed?' Hearing this, Razaq ran to the pantry.

Malla Khaliq was outraged, and told Ghulam Ahmed, 'When will you teach this haughty woman some manners?' Ghulam Ahmed turned his head away as he had nothing to say in response. Zoon was the daughter of a wealthy man. Ahmed was always under the burden of his debts. He scowled at Razaq who had put all the unwashed utensils in a basket made of steel mesh, and was walking towards the water tap outside the kitchen.

When Malla Khaliq had smoked all the tobacco in the chilam of his hookah and the chilam itself had turned hot with cinders, Noor Mohammad walked up to him.

He sat next to Malla Khaliq and took out a letter he had received from the bank. Opening the letter, he asked his father, 'What should our reply to this letter be? We failed to repay the instalment yet again, and if it continues this way, they may confiscate our new houseboat.'

Ahmed grabbed this opportunity to rebuke his father. 'I think that time is already in the offing. Why can't we discern the exigency of the time? Had we invested the same money in some other business, we would have doubled it by now. We were so quick to change the matting of this new houseboat, Gulshan, as though there were tourists queuing up to stay in it. There was nothing wrong with the old carpets. How can we rely on this tourism business? We should have abjured this old occupation, and settled somewhere on land to start a new career. We should have been wise enough to ape others.'

'They have been unfaithful to the waters of this lake. They do not know that the sweat of their forefathers is mingled this water,' Malla Khaliq retorted in his rage.

'Abba, water is after all water, always there to change its ways. It has no solid basis. I think we must consider better options.'

While Ghulam Ahmed continued, Malla Khaliq's hookah-puffing became faster and faster. When he lost control, he kept his hookah aside and stood up. His face looked like a bowl of burning cinders and he roared, 'Are you telling me that the legacy of Khizr and Noah is an idle pursuit? Do you mean to say that we too should indulge in accruing illicit wealth like others who have settled on land? I am not so foolish that I don't understand who is behind this Satan's brain of yours.'

Hearing her husband's angry voice, Aziz Dyad came out of the room. Zoon, Mukhta, and Zeb watched from behind the door. Parveen, who was placing the washed utensils in the basket, stood up and ran to her mother. Noor Mohammad doused the fire of this perpetual dispute between father and son.

'Now end this shouting, Abba. See how terrified Amma stands there.'

But the spark had started a wildfire and it would not be extinguished easily.

'How dare he brag like that! I am well aware of the people who are misguiding him.'

'No one on this earth can mislead Ghulam Ahmed. Yet if you think I have no right to utter a word in this house, then hang me.'

Aziz Dyad rushed to her husband. 'What has happened to you all? What kind of rivalry is this? I cannot understand what estates are to be divided among you. I have been watching both of you seeking excuses to quarrel with each other.'

'Ask this darling son of yours. He tells me to auction the heritage of our forefathers and, like his father-in-law, seek lodging in a stranger's house.'

Zoon, who had been silently listening to all this, now came out and argued with her father-in-law. 'Abba! His father-in-law owns as many as four bungalows; who says he lodges himself in others' houses?'

This made Ahmed angry with his wife. 'Shut up! Who has

taught you to meddle in the affairs of men?' Zoon was about to retort, but Ahmed cut her off saying, 'Go in! I am warning you. Don't you hear me?'

Parveen dashed to her brothers, pointing towards a speeding boat. 'Will you please stop it now? Look, Qadir is escorting someone here in that boat there.'

They stared at the boat approaching the landing ghat. Aziz Dyad turned to Malla Khaliq and said, 'See how this vagabond son of yours is bringing us the very first tourist of the season, and that too a *firangi* memsahib.' She looked at Ahmed next as her statement was also directed at him. Parveen hurried to the anchor end of the houseboat Gulshan which was assigned to Qadir by his father. Qadir's wife, Zeb, too rushed to Parveen to watch the approaching boat. But when she saw Qadir jumping out to the anchor end of the boat and stretching his hand out to help the mem, her heart sank. An autumnal pallor overtook her face. She caught Parveen's hand, held it tightly, and whispered to her, 'This is the same wretched and shameless Jane who came last year. Isn't it her?'

Parveen, too, recognized the lady. 'Couldn't my brother find anyone else other than this she-monkey?'

Jane stood on the porch of Gulshan. Looking all around, she stretched herself, making her ample bosom more pronounced.

Qadir, who was retrieving Jane's suitcase, moistened his lips and remained transfixed, watching Jane's enticing stretch. She took a deep breath inhaling the air of the Dal Lake. 'Oh, how soothing!'

In the meantime, Malla Khaliq reached Gulshan. While Jane was about to enter the houseboat, she saw him and waved to him in greeting. 'Hi Haji Sahib! See I'm back! Everything okay?'

Malla Khaliq did not like Jane's demeanour, but could not do anything; she was a guest after all. He responded to her greetings half-heartedly, 'Yes, by God's grace.'

Qadir came out of the houseboat and said to Jane, 'All set!' Jane went into the houseboat and Qadir followed her.

Malla Khaliq started ambling back towards the isle when Qadir came running to him and took out a bundle of ten thousand rupees from his pocket and put it in his father's coat pocket. Malla Khaliq looked at him in amazement. 'What is this?'

'Ten thousand rupees exactly. This is the advance tariff from this mem. She is staying here for three full months. She will pay twenty thousand more tomorrow.'

Malla Khaliq had been averse to hosting Jane even last year. But he could not help it, for all tourists cannot be to one's liking. The repeated reminders from the bank about the loan did not make it easier either. He thought that God had ultimately come to know about his financial compulsions and sent this Mem. He asked Qadir, 'Had she informed you about her arrival that you went to the airport to receive her?'

'Oh no, Abba. It was Ghulama of Malla Subhan who had told me that a big party of tourists was expected. That is why I went to the airport to see if our destiny was to have something good for us. There I met Jane.'

On observing a deep crease appear on his father's forehead, Qadir changed the subject. 'Abba, if you allow me, I will instruct Razaq to attend to Jane.'

'As you wish.'

Zeb had been hiding behind the willow grove observing all this. As soon as Malla Khaliq was near her, she said to him, 'Abba, this Mem is not a good woman. I entreat you that she not be provided with lodging in our houseboat. She will pollute the boat. Please return the money to her.'

Aziz Dyad heard this, and came out and said to Zeb, 'What nonsense are you talking? Don't jinx this! Should we reject and turn away the very first tourist of the season? Come in, it is already teatime. Come in.' Zeb cast a piteous glance at Malla Khaliq and followed her mother-in-law to the pantry.

Malla Khaliq called Razaq who had engaged himself wholeheartedly in cleaning the houseboat. He dropped his brush in the tub and came running. Malla Khaliq told him, 'Listen! As long as this Mem is here with us, you will work in Qadir Sahib's boat, Gulshan. But I warn you, be careful. I should not hear any complaint against you. Do you understand?'

'Yes, sir.' Saying this Razaq walked towards Gulshan. As he was about the step up to the porch of the houseboat, Qadir, who was paying the shikaarahwala, asked him angrily, 'What the hell are you going to do there? Come here and carry the rest of the luggage inside.'

Razaq stood stunned. Qadir shouted at him again, 'Are you deaf? Don't you hear what I said?' Hearing this, Razaq went running and started carrying Jane's belongings one by one. Qadir lashed out at Razaq again, 'Are you paralyzed? Don't you have the energy to take everything in one go?'

'I was wondering, where exactly should I place all—'

'What a blockhead of a servant our Abba has appointed! Go and keep everything in the circular room, I mean in the drawing room. Do you follow me?'

'Yes, sir.'

Malla Khaliq entered the *doonga*, the small kitchen-boat, and handed over the bundle of ten thousand rupees to Aziz Dyad who was busy tidying clothes in the cupboard. Taking the money from her husband, she asked him, 'What am I supposed to do with this money?'

'You just keep it. He says that this Mem will pay us twenty thousand more tomorrow. If she does so, I will go to the bank the day after tomorrow and deposit the loan instalment that is overdue.'

'And what will you expend on the Mem's food?'

'You need not worry about that. I have reserved some money that will last more than a week. Narayan Joo shall return in the meantime and I am sure he must have arranged some business for us.' Saying this Malla Khaliq propped himself against a pillow, and after a little reflection, added, 'I wonder why Zeb asked me not to house this Mem in the houseboat.'

'She is a child after all. She must be worried that the Mem might seduce her husband.'

Malla Khaliq heaved a deep sigh. 'I do not know why I too was not pleased to see this *firangi* girl. She was here only a few months ago. I wonder what made her return so soon.'

'Do not house baseless premonitions in your mind. Why should we bother about that? This Zeb of ours is apprehensive and suspicious by nature. If she could have her way, she would not allow Qadir to speak even to her sisters-in-law.'

Malla Khaliq stopped there. 'All right, hand over the hookah to me.'

Parveen stepped inside Zeb's room. She found her sitting woefully in a corner. Parveen sat beside her and, laying her hand on her shoulder, tried to reassure her. 'Do not be so scared, my darling sister. If this Jane tries to spread her snare again as she did last year, I will drag her by her hair and throw her in the drain behind the mire.'

'This Mem is not to be blamed for anything. The fault lies in your brother. He neglects all the important chores of the house, but never fails to follow her wherever she goes.'

'But I can't advise him on such issues. I am younger to him after all.'

'I know. I don't want you to get involved.'

'If Abba was not so short on money, he would have never allowed her to step on our lawn, not to mention the houseboat.'

'When one's destiny has been decided, how can one blame others?'

'Allah shall protect you. You need not worry. Come, sit here. Let us watch what this she-monkey is doing.'

'No, I don't want to see her face, but please be careful not to say anything blunt to this whore. Your brother will be angry.'

'Don't worry, I won't even spit on her.'

It was already time for the afternoon prayers. Parveen quietly retreated when she saw Malla Khaliq offering his nimaz in the willow copse. She saw Razaq prostrating after him. Watching Razaq's elegance, she stood motionless for a moment. When Malla Khaliq turned his head side to side in salaam. Parveen suddenly felt as if she had been caught committing a crime. She quickly ran away to the pantry.

Malla Khaliq was still squatting in prayer, when a shikaarah stopped near the outer trellis of Gul. A tall man, dressed in a Jodhpuri suit, stepped out from the shikaarah. He was Narayan Joo, the proprietor of Kashmir Travel Agency. He was a few years younger to Malla Khaliq.

Narayan Joo's father, Madhav Kaul, earlier lived on the right bank of the river Vyeth, known to the world as the river Jhelum; the lifeline of the Kashmir valley, on whose banks lies the city of Srinagar. Madhav Kaul's three-storey house was on the waterfront and down below Malla Khaliq's father Samad Haji's barge was anchored in the river.

Narayan Joo was born a couple of years after Malla Khaliq. The two grew up together, spending their days on the riverbank playing hopscotch. It was Malla Khaliq who taught Narayan Joo how to swim. Malla Khaliq's mother, Maal Dyad, always visited Narayan Joo's mother, Dyaka Dyad, to seek her counsel on various household matters. Seeing the friendship between the two women, Malla Samad and Madhav Kaul also developed a close bond. There was another reason for their friendship. Khaliq's father was a God-fearing man, who could recite a large number of mystic poems of the Muslim saint poets of Kashmir, which he would recite with a purity of heart. This bridged the gap in their monetary status.

Madhav Kaul initially worked with Cock Burn's Travel Agency, but when the first German war began, the agency was closed. Madhav Kaul then established his own travel agency which he named Kashmir Travel Agency. God helped him and his agency prospered at the end of the war, when his business expanded.

Thus Madhav Kaul became a big businessman, by local standards. Having disposed of his house in the old city, he shifted to Wazir

Bagh in the new city. This separation was very painful for the two friends, but it did not last very long. Madhav Kaul advised Samad Haji to try his luck, too, in business. In the beginning, he was not strong enough to withstand the stress, but gradually he agreed to shift his barge from the old city to Gagribal in the Dal Lake, where the houseboats had started to do good business. Madhav Kaul used his clout in getting Samad Haji to erect a houseboat in the lake. That was how Gul came into existence.

Madhav Kaul sent Narayan to Bisco School which taught its students swimming and boating. This helped him develop a kinship with the waters of the Dal Lake. Narayan Joo and Malla Khaliq grew up, got married and became fathers themselves. Time's merciless wings snatched away their fathers from them and placed the burden of their families on their shoulders. They witnessed many changes in their lives. The changes in prosperity, adversities, nothing affected their friendship.

The Second World War was a boon to those who were connected with tourism. Narayan Joo remained engaged in booking accommodation for Western tourists, mostly comprising British soldiers who preferred to spend their furloughs in Kashmir than other resorts, and Malla Khaliq was there to extend his hospitality to them. The business expanded so fast that Malla Khaliq, like many other houseboat owners, had to construct his second houseboat – Gulshan.

Time flowed fast as a river of no return. The war ended. The surge of tourists waned. The freedom struggle of the country culminated in the independence of the country whose outcome was the Partition. The upheaval of 1947 that followed. It was the beginning of a very dark period for Kashmir. Pakistan sent hordes of savage tribesmen followed by its soldiers to capture Kashmir by force. All the routes were blocked. And with this, the whole tourism business collapsed. But even in that terrible crisis, the two childhood friends stood by each other.

Thus the times took a new turn. The frost thawed and spring filled the gardens with fresh flowers. New avenues opened and the joint business of Narayan Joo and Malla Khaliq flourished again. On his son Vijay Kumar's suggestion, Narayan Joo established an office of his travel agency in Bombay to attract visitors from other parts of the country, that way they would not have to depend only on foreigners. Since Narayan Joo's spouse Leelavati passed away, he spent the six winter months away from Kashmir with his son. He not only looked after the business there but also arranged for tourist parties for Malla Khaliq's houseboats. Thus with time, the number of tourists to this paradise on earth increased year after year. Even the forbidden land of Ladakh was opened to tourists which gave tourism a further fillip.

But Kashmir had always attracted misfortune; stability never lasted for long. After a couple of decades of peace and prosperity, the neighbouring Punjab was overwhelmed by a long period of turmoil. This affected Kashmir too. The number of tourists coming to Kashmir decreased day by day as the route to Kashmir was through Punjab and people did not want to take any risks. Malla Khaliq and Narayan Joo therefore had to rely on what they had earned earlier. By God's grace, the violence in Punjab subsided and everyone began to look forward to having a fruitful tourist season.

With this hope, Malla Khaliq finished his nimaz and was about to fold the prayer mat when Gula Chooncha's shikaarah stopped near the shore, and Narayan Joo came out of the boat and walked up the stairs leading to the isle. Narayan Joo was a graceful man – tall, bearing an almond-shaped saffron tilak, the sign of a devout Kashmiri Pandit, on his forehead. He looked as fresh and happy as a newly-wed groom.

'*As-salaam-alaikum!*'

'*Wa-alaikum-salaam,*' Malla Khaliq responded without turning.

'What! Are you now hesitant to even turn your face to me?'

Seeing his friend, Malla Khaliq flung the prayer mat on a branch of the willow tree, and gave him a tight hug. Aziz Dyad, who was walking over to the water tap, saw them. She left the basket of utensils there and rushed towards the two.

'Is it you, Narayan Joo? I can hardly believe my eyes!'

Hearing Aziz Dyad, the two friends let go of each other, and Narayan Joo turned to her.

'*Salaam alaikum!* I intended coming directly to you, my sister, but he held me back.'

'Come, come! I know how you cared about me all this year.'

'Why do you say that? I have always inquired about your health over the telephone from Khaliq.'

'He doesn't care about me while being here, how will he inform you in Bombay about me over the telephone?'

'No, no, you are absolutely wrong! Whenever I asked him anything about his health, his answer was that Azi was not well. That shows how worried he is about you. And when I asked him about his children, he said, "Narayan Joo, I am here just for name-sake. If my children are settled to some extent, it is all because of this sister of yours. If she were not there, I would have been worse than a farthing."'

'He said all this, because he knows that I am a dear sister of yours.'

Malla Khaliq was enjoying this tête-à-tête between the brother and sister, and he gazed at Aziz Dyad's face with an affectionate smile.

'Now, let us come to more important things. Tell me, why are you so late in coming this year? Is everything all right in Bombay? Is our dear daughter-in-law well settled? I think the baby must have grown big by now,' Aziz Dyad said.

'Thanks to the Almighty, she is in good health and has started to go to office, too,' replied Narayan Joo.

'I was worried about her. Your wife, peace be upon her soul, too, used to be worried about her ill health till her last breath.'

Malla Khaliq diverted his wife's attention from further mention of Narayan Joo's deceased wife and said, 'Do you mean to keep him standing over here? Let him have a little rest. Come, Narayan, let us go inside.'

'But I would really like to stay out here for a while. It is after six months that I have had the fortune to witness the Zabarwan mountain and its magnificent reflection in the calm waters of this

Dal Lake. Let us just sit here on this turf,' said Narayan Joo as he took off his shoes and sat down.

'Oh no! Please wait. I shall get you a sheet something to sit on,' Aziz Dyad said.

'Aziz Dyad! Won't you let me relish the soothing touch of this sod? In Bombay, we crave this!'

'All right, I will send you something to munch on.'

'Razaqa. Oh Razaqa!' Khaliq called out to Razaq who was wiping the glass panes.

'Yes, sir!' Razaq responded.

'Come here quickly.'

Malla Khaliq, too, took off his shoes and sat near his friend. 'Now tell me, why did you take so much time to return? Is it because of the situation in Punjab?'

'No, Punjab is quite calm these days. It was only for you that I took some more time. There is a big party arriving from Japan. The tourist officer asked me to stay for a month longer so that their schedule could be finalized. Some Japanese tourists plan to come to Kashmir after they finish with other places. I did not want to miss the opportunity of hosting them here.'

'So was the plan confirmed?' Malla Khaliq asked, desperate as he was for visitors. It was after three long years that he hoped to have a good number of guests. But Narayan Joo was being jovial. 'You are always in haste. Let me bake the news a little more and then serve.'

'All right, take your time,' remarked Malla Khaliq, turning his face away.

'So now you are sulking. I swear by God that I craved to see you sulk in this manner. Now, dear friend, look towards me.'

'Okay. What do you have to say?'

'They are sure to come. The boats will be occupied for not less than ten days. But it will take some time. Till then, I already have the booking of two to three local tourist groups for your boats.'

'This is great news! There are no affluent Western tourists anywhere. Of course some still do come, but they do not stay for more than a couple of days. In the past we used to get Western tourists who stayed for a fortnight to one month. Forget them. Now our own local tourists are better for us. They stay longer and spend freely, provided they are really rich, which quite a few are.'

'All of those whom we have booked are millionaires. By God's help all our toils will end.'

Malla Khaliq felt reassured.

In the meantime, Aziz Dyad sent Parveen with a platter filled with some apples and almonds. She greeted Narayan Joo with respect, '*Namaskaar, Mahara, Lala Sahib!*'

'*Wa-alaikum-salaam wa rahmatullahi barkaatahu*, Miss Parveen Sahiba, daughter of Haji Abdul Khaliq *daama iqbaalahu!*'

Parveen laughed boisterously on hearing such an exalted greeting. As she kept the platter before the guest, she said to him, 'Tell me, how did you fashion my short name Parveen into such a long sentence? I am the same old Pari of yours.'

Narayan Joo turned to Malla Khaliq. 'My Pari was as big as my thumb, but see she has suddenly grown so big and fast like a poplar tree. That is why I have added so many honorifics to her name.'

'Your hair is turning grey and yet you do not give up your buffoonery,' remarked Aziz Dyad who had joined them with a steaming *samovar* full of qahva.

'This is not buffoonery but liveliness. I hope you still remember my father. He used to say that every moment you live is precious, so one should spend every moment jovially.'

Narayan Joo turned again towards Parveen and completed his statement. 'So, my dear Parveen, you should always try to live happily and prosper. And you, my Haji Sahib, do not bother. God is always there to help us. Your memsahiba has brought you tea – enjoy a cup.'

Holding a cup in her hand Aziz Dyad said to Narayan Joo, 'I entreat you, my brother, give up your orthodoxy and accept a cup of tea from my hand. Times have changed. Don't you see, now all eat from the same plate.'

'It hardly matters whether you share the same plate. What matters is that all should be united in their souls.'

'Yes, you are right there,' Malla Khaliq concurred. 'You pour tea into my cup, and I shall peel an apple for him,' he said turning to his wife.

Parveen extended her hand towards the apples, 'Let me do it.'

'No, my darling, you go and send me a couple of plates.' Aziz Dyad held her back.

Parveen went to the pantry. Aziz Dyad offered her husband a cup of tea, stood up and said to him, 'I will leave the samovar here. You may have some more tea. Razaq will take it away when you finish.' Then she left.

Narayan Joo took the apple from Malla Khaliq's hand. 'Give it to me, my friend, I still know how to peel an apple. You please have your tea. Why are you gazing at me like a gazelle?'

Malla Khaliq heaved a long sigh and took the cup to his lips.

Narayan Joo, while enjoying the juicy slices of the apple, watched the waves in the lake. The waves, he felt, were chasing each other like lovers. The two friends were lost in their own thoughts, when Razaq's voice broke the silence.

'*Salaam alaikum!* Should I pour some more tea into your cup?'

'What? No, no, my dear son, you take this samovar away.'

Razaq took away the samovar.

'He seems to be a well-behaved boy. Where have you got him from?' Narayan Joo asked Malla Khaliq.

'I got him from your office.'

'Is he the boy who was hankering after Mohammad Sidique for a job?'

'Yes, this too is God's grace. Had I not visited your office to inquire about you, how could I have found this gem of a boy?'

'So now that you have found him, never let him go. Good servants are almost non-existent now.' Narayan Joo offered a slice of apple to Malla Khaliq. 'Here, you also have a slice.'

'No, I just had tea, it will cause acidity.'

'But it is a real Kashmiri *ambri* apple, not the American variety. It will not make your stomach sour. Taste a slice.'

'No. I am not in the mood.'

Putting a slice of the apple into his own mouth, Narayan Joo tried to read Malla Khaliq's face. Malla Khaliq sensed this and turned his face towards the barge where Parveen was playing with Bilal.

Diverting Khaliq's attention towards him, Narayan Joo said, 'You're not in your element, I can see that. What is the matter?'

Heaving a deep sigh again, Malla Khaliq replied, 'What shall I tell you, Narayan Joo ... I have received three successive notices from the bank; two instalments of Gulfam are still due, and our business is in a shambles, as you know. The interest on the loan, too, must have amassed. Since the last one month, I am persistently gripped by this anxiety.'

Narayan Joo, who was about to peel another apple, flung down the knife in anger, and turned to Malla Khaliq. 'Did you consider me dead? You speak with me every week on the phone. You could have given me a hint. You would not have been indebted to me. Keep aside our brotherly relations. We are engaged in the same business, if nothing else.'

'Don't be angry with me. Who else can I rely upon? I would never feel shy of approaching you for help. I thought you would come back in April as you always do and relieve me of the anxieties, but you took a very long time to come.'

'Just come to my office tomorrow and we shall go to the bank together. I too have some work there.'

At that moment, Qadir came out of Gulshan. He saw Narayan Joo with his father. Standing on the anchor point of the boat, he waved at him, 'Hi, Narayan Uncle, all well?'

Hearing this, both Narayan Joo and Malla Khaliq looked at Qadir. Hearing Qadir's style of greeting, Narayan Joo said, 'Ghulam Qadir, since when did your Lala Sahib change into "Narayan Uncle"?'

Qadir overlooked his sarcasm and began to talk to the boatman who had stopped his boat near the isle. Narayan Joo turned to Malla Khaliq. 'Qadir seems to be using more Western lingo now.' Malla Khaliq was already irritated with Qadir's newly adopted mannerisms. He said acidly, 'There is a firangi woman in his houseboat, which might be the reason.'

He had hardly said this when Jane, carrying a bag in her hand, came out of the houseboat, and holding its trellis for support, stepped into a decorated shikaarah.

Qadir helped her as she sat on the spring-seat of the small boat while he sat on the cushioned seat in front of her. The shikaarah left, and Narayan Joo, who was intrigued after seeing Jane, asked Malla Khaliq, 'Isn't this the same girl who came last year, paid an advance for three months and then after two months suddenly left for Delhi?'

'Yes, and I have no faith in her ways. It was because of my financial constraint that I allowed her to stay in the houseboat.'

'It is not always possible to get the tourist of your choice. You should be happy that the boat has been occupied at the very beginning of the season.'

Narayan Joo had been managing his travel agency since he was a teenager. During his college days, he helped his father during his free time. After completing his graduation, he took over the occupation wholeheartedly. He knew that one had to bear both savoury as well as noxious things in business. Malla Khaliq, too, knew this harsh reality. However, he, like his friend Narayan Joo, had resolved to always be honest in his dealings. He did not approve of Qadir's and Ghulam Ahmed's ways. He sighed again and said to Narayan Joo who was watching Qadir's boat speeding away, 'How can I tell you what a wayward son this Qadir is! He did not learn anything even after spending over fourteen years in school and college. The only thing he has picked up from the dandies is to massage his hair with scented oil twice a day and buy a pair of jeans every month. He never tires of beguiling me, saying he has the knack to expand his business and make big businessmen sink in the competition.'

'Has he started some business of his own?'

'Nothing – this is all idle prattle.'

Narayan Joo remembered that Ghulam Ahmed had taken some apple orchard on contract last year. He was about to inquire about it, when Malla Khaliq continued, 'I, nevertheless, am happy that he does not demand money as Ghulam Ahmed often does.'

'Did he profit last year in his apple business?'

'Nothing but grief. He never perseveres in any vocation. To add to my worries, he is hell-bent on getting rid of this tourist business that has come to us from our forefathers. He always tries to convince me that the waters of the lake are nothing but useless fluid, never to remain static.'

This long tale of woe from Malla Khaliq made Narayan Joo ruminate about his own situation. His condition had not been very different. Malla Khaliq continued to vent, not sensing the changing colours on Narayan Joo's face.

'The idiot tells me that I should abandon the legacy of our clan since the great Hazrat Noah. It is, in fact, his father-in-law Naba Kantroo who is trying to instigate him. He has no brain of his own in his skull.'

Narayan Joo heaved a long sigh but did not respond. He was lost in his own worries. Sensing this, Malla Khaliq asked him with concern, 'Are you well? You are not saying anything. Am I wrong in my apprehensions?'

'What shall I say when I am facing the same dilemma? You remember how my Vij Lal pestered me when he returned to Kashmir after completing his training course?'

Vij Lal, that is, Vijay Kumar, was Narayan Joo's only son whom he had sent to Bombay for a degree in travel management so that after his return he would expand the family business. Narayan Joo had decided that he would invest all his resources in establishing a large office on the shore of the Dal Lake. He was determined to capture the entire tourist market of Ladakh that was open to even the foreign travellers. When Vijay Kumar returned with his degree in travel management, his father placed his plan before him to consider. He wiped off all his hopes. 'I am not the one to remain confined within this huge fortress of insurmountable mountains. Dad, this world is not a handful of sky that you can see in this narrow valley; the sky is too vast to fathom. Why are you so determined to clip my wings? Dad, you must pay a visit to Bombay and see the inexhaustible scope for expanding business. Perhaps then you will understand.'

Narayan Joo recalled every word of his son's that had demolished the empire of his dreams inch by inch. Malla Khaliq's voice retrieved him from the vortex of bitter memories.

'I was born in these waters, and have grown up on the lake. Ask this blockhead why these myriad winged ducks, swans and grebes traverse thousands of miles to be here every year and weave their nests here with the weeds of the lake. It is because they know that the waters of the lake are their own world; they cannot survive on land.'

'And what about Noor Mohammad, what does he say?'

'He is also facing the same predicament. Only he is there to keep my name alive. You yourself witnessed Ghulam Qadir's ways. To be honest, he is my only worry; he is always trying to soar in the sky and never places his steps on the ground. He returns very late in the evenings, sometimes as late as ten or eleven in the night. Whenever I try to inquire about his engagements, his answer, "there was a meeting".'

'It may be that he has joined some political outfit.'

'Who knows? I do not dare ask him.'

'But I am sure he will not be so careless in returning late in the evening these days since his boat is engaged now. God will set everything right. You should always have faith in His mercy, as I do. So let me take leave of you now. I have an urgent piece of work to attend to. But remember to come early to my office in the morning tomorrow.'

Narayan Joo went near the barge and bid goodbye to Aziz Dyad. Then he walked to the ghat, the landing, to anchor the shikaarah, where Malla Khaliq was already waiting for him. He extended his

hand to Narayan Joo and helped him sit in the shikaarah. He sat
beside him, saying that he too had some work to do at the Dal
Gate market.

Qadir made the shikaarahwala row the boat fast through the
swamps in the backwaters of the Dal. Whenever he noticed any
other shikaarah approaching or passing by, he enthusiastically
pointed at the rushes or towards the diving pintails, as if he had no
other concern but to give this European woman a feel of the life
on the lake.

There was a group of hippies lodging in a dilapidated, still
houseboat, hidden in the thicket of willows at the far end of the lake,
posing as if they wanted to be away from the hustle and bustle of city
life. But their hidden activities were known to Jane and Qadir. Jane
had lured Qadir into her circle of friends by paying him pocketfuls
of money. Having seduced him with her beauty, she also taught
him the knack of acquiring easy wealth. Before leaving for Bombay
last year, she had paid him a sum of thirty thousand rupees extra as
commission for the year's business of drug trafficking. Though she
tried to give everyone the impression that she was dealing in carpet
exports, Qadir wasn't blind to her true intentions.

Malla Khaliq's business had totally collapsed last year and he
could not pay the instalments towards his bank loan. Qadir was
well aware of this. He had the money but no courage to hand it
over to his father. He had deposited it all in a different bank so that
no one in the family would know about it.

It was already afternoon when Qadir's shikaarah reached the
hideaway of the hippies. A frail man stood shirtless and in tattered
jeans, puffing on a cigarette on the deck of the houseboat. He
climbed down the stairs to the prow. As soon as the rowboat
touched the rotting staircase of the still houseboat, the hippie
extended his hand to Jane and pulled her into a hug. She freed
herself from his clasp and entered the boat. Before entering, she
sternly told Qadir to wait outside. The hippie cast a derisive glance

at Qadir, gave a boisterous laugh and offered him his cigarette.
Qadir refused. The hippie guffawed again and climbed up the stairs
to the deck of the boat.

'Why are you staring like a dumb deer? Keep the boat there
behind those rushes,' Qadir ordered his shikaarahwala. 'It might
take us over an hour here.'

The boatman calmly moved his boat away. Qadir sat on the seat
on the prow of the boat. His mouth had grown bitter. He took out
a cigarette from his pocket, but meanwhile the owner of this still-
boat, Sula Kava, came out and sat down beside him.

'Is Haji Sahib well, Qadir Sahib?' he asked.

'Thanks to Allah,' Qadir said curtly, trying to stop the
conversation there.

But Sula Kava was adamantly nosy. 'I have wished so many times
to have the luck to see him, but am always entangled in never-
ending work here. Besides, I was worried I might inadvertently
mention this Jane or you ... you know.'

Qadir got irked. He felt like knocking down this nasty fellow
and smashing his hooked nose flat, but he contained his anger and
said, 'You did the wise thing by not going there to see him. He has
not forgotten that moment when you caused an upheaval in the
Boatmen's Union.'

'That was a ruse of your brother's father-in-law, and I was
blamed for nothing. Forget about it and relax. I am not to see your
father. First tell me what kind of tea you would like to have. To be
honest with you, the guys sitting inside the boat are enjoying beer.
You too may go in, they have no inhibitions.'

Qadir put his cigarette back in the packet and entered the boat
cabin. The door to the bedroom in the extreme end was ajar and
he could see the bed through it. He saw Jane's friend Ruby, half-
naked, glued to the chest of George, the gang leader. Qadir turned
back, but George called him, 'Hey, Qadir. Come in.'

Qadir entered the room. He saw Jane sitting on the edge of
the bed on the other side of George holding his hand and he
was giving it a soft massage. Qadir was aflame with jealousy. Jane

noticed the colour of Qadir's face change. She freed George's hand and stretched it to Qadir. 'Come here, darling, sit awhile.'

'No, Jane, it is getting late.' Qadir wanted to catch Jane by her arm and drag her out of this den, but he stood helpless. He did not want to lose her trust in any case. Thus he told her, in a seemingly calm tone, to finish her job there, and that he would be waiting outside. When he stepped out, George and Ruby laughed rowdily. Jane stopped them by saying that Qadir, if irked, could report them. This warning angered Ruby, but George was prudent enough to stop her. 'It is after much effort that Jane has succeeded in ensnaring such a dependable broker here. If he is annoyed, he will see us all handcuffed.'

Qadir sat at the prow. Noticing this, Sula Kava came near him again and said, 'Should I get you a cup of qahva?'

'No thanks.'

'A cup of qahva would make you feel good. It is very cold here.'

'Please, for God's sake, do not bother me.'

Sula Kava had tried his hand at many trades, but nothing profited him. 'Kava', meaning 'crow', was not his caste but his nickname. He was not a houseboat owner by descent. He owned a dinghy. That dinghy was, in fact, an open boat that he had roofed with a few wood planks and thatched with a mat of rushes. They were essentially firewood vending boatmen. He helped his father in hewing wood for the fireplace of an aged European woman called Liza. With time he became the head of Liza's domestic servants. It is said that Liza traded in felt-mats. She was quite agile, even in her old age. But one day she had an unfortunate fall from the stairs of her houseboat and since then was confined to her bed. She survived for a full five years after that and Sula Kava never failed her. Before breathing her last, she bequeathed the old houseboat called 'Elizabeth' to him.

This shanty of a still-boat was now in poor condition. Located in the back end of the Dal, it attracted no tourists. Sula Kava, being penniless, might have died along with his family had he not consented to be a family servant to Malla Khaliq in his good days.

It was there that he developed an association with a few hippies whom he, with the help of Qadir, had taken to his out-of-business boat. The hippies in the group had made acquaintance with Qadir at Gulmarg when he was there with a group of German tourists interested in playing golf. Since then business in Sula Kava's still-boat had been in full swing.

Sula Kava knew why the hippies preferred to stop in his crumbling boat. They wanted to be away from prying eyes. He thought it wise to remain silent and paid some corrupt policemen bribes to shield himself. He too would have surely joined their illicit dealings if he were not scared of his wife. His wife, a God-fearing woman, visited all the shrines to seek absolution for all his sins. In spite of all this, he strongly believed that Ghulam Qadir was there to provide him with good opportunities of earning without his personal involvement.

It was he who had brought George and Ruby, who stayed in his boat for the whole of last year, and now with the advent of March, they were back. Besides, they got one more hippie this time, Tony, who remained busy writing till late into the night. Thus, the money was enough for Sula Kava to manage his family. Ghulam Qadir, too, would make him happy by paying him a few hundred rupees when he would come carrying his empty bag to visit the hippies. Sula Kava was aware of what Qadir and Jane carried in that yellow bag. Whenever George rowed his small trip-boat through the rush-covered swamps to shoot with his camera, Sula Kava wished to follow him stealthily to see where he went. But the fear of losing these visitors held him back. Whenever George went on his trips, the new hippie entered Ruby's bedroom and latched the door.

Qadir waited for Jane to come out. Every second of this painful waiting made the blood boil in his veins. In his frustration, he said to Sula Kava, 'Sula Sahib, will you please go in and tell Jane that the sun is about to set and the weather is taking a bad turn.'

'No, I cannot. I do not have permission to enter their bedroom.' Saying this, Sula Kava sat down in front of Qadir and looked at Ismaal, the shikaarahwala.

'It seems it is about to rain.'

'I don't think so. For the last three days, the sky is overcast with clouds in the evening, but there is no sign of rain. I wish it would drizzle.'

In the meantime, a bolt of lightning, and thunder made the lake quiver. Qadir was about to step inside the boat, but catching sight of Jane tidying her make-up before the mirror inside the chamber and combing her dishevelled hair, he stopped. He turned back and stood against the door of the drawing room, stewing in a furious jealousy.

Jane came out as if nothing had happened inside the room. She said aloud to Qadir, 'Let's go. It is getting late.'

Without saying anything in reply, he called out to the waiting boatman, 'Ismaal! Get your boat here.'

Jane fished out a hundred-rupee note from her purse and handed it over to Sula Kava. Sula Kava lost no time in accepting the money. Bowing his head in gratitude, he said to her, 'When are you going to visit us again?'

'I will come when your sir invites me again,' Jane said with a smile.

The shikaarah touched the staircase of the houseboat. Qadir caught hold of Jane's hand coldly and helped her into the shikaarah. He sat silently on the prow of the boat. Sula Kava offered salaam to him, but he did not reply. The shikaarah moved towards the water avenues and Qadir, with head turned away, remained gloomy.

Bending forward, Jane took his hand and made him sit beside her. Shrinking her whole frame, she nestled under his arm. 'It is quite chilly.' But Qadir sat like a statue and tried to free himself when a bolt of lightning flashed again. It made Jane jump up and hug Qadir. Then there was a rumbling of thunder and it seemed that there was a cloudburst somewhere. Jane was now really cowering with fright. Within a moment, Qadir was warm again and said to her, 'Do you know why this weather is so fierce? It is because you broke my heart.'

Jane consoled him by saying that she was solely his, and it

was only for his sake that she went to George and Ruby. This comforted Qadir. In order to reassure him and calm his burning ache, Jane took her lips closer to his. This made Qadir melt like wax. He touched his lips to Jane's and held her tight. He held her till the lights of the Boulevard became visible. The shikaarah turned towards Gulshan. Qadir let go of Jane and hastened to go sit on the prow.

When the shikaarah touched Gulshan, Qadir noticed Malla Khaliq standing on Gul. He quickly jumped up the stairs of the houseboat, thinking of some excuse to give to his father. But Malla Khaliq remained quiet and returned to the room. Qadir felt relieved. He held Jane's hand and helped her out of the shikaarah. It had already started drizzling. Jane hastily entered the houseboat and Qadir followed her. When he was in the drawing room of Gulshan, he looked through the window at his own room. He saw the dim figure of Zeb in the electric light there. He picked up a polythene bag lying on the sofa and, without waiting for Jane who had gone to the washroom, went out.

Aziz Dyad stood by the kitchen window in the dark, anxiously waiting for her son. When she saw Qadir rushing towards his room, she shut the window and went in. Malla Khaliq came in from the rear door and, while removing his cap, he flung a dart of sarcasm at his wife, 'Relaxed, that your darling son is home? Did you see his gait, walking as if he is already rolling in millions? I'm sure, he will make me parade in the market one day.' Aziz Dyad kept quiet, calmly handed over a kangri to him to warm his hands and crept into bed. There was a clap of lightning outside and the thunder made the windowpanes rattle. 'Oh merciful God!' Malla Khaliq uttered. 'Forgive all my sins.' He switched the light off and stretched himself by his wife's side and pulled the quilt up. Qadir's son Bilal, who loved to sleep in his grandfather's room, was fast asleep in a corner. The wind was howling outside.

Aziz Dyad could not sleep. She murmured, 'The quilt is not getting warmed up.' Khaliq did not respond.

Malla Khaliq had erected a shanty comprising three rooms on

the isle amidst the three houseboats, Gul, Gulshan and Gulfam. The pantry was still in the barge, and he and his wife lived in the room adjacent to it. He had allotted the second room to Ghulam Ahmed, the third one to Noor Mohammad and the last one to Ghulam Qadir.

Noor Mohammad and his wife were still awake. They had received a letter from their son Nisar, who was studying medicine in Jaipur. He had to deposit an instalment of the fees there. Noor Mohammad alone knew how his father was struggling these days to manage such a huge family. They had only one hope, and that was the help from Narayan Joo. They were talking about it when his wife Mukhta said, 'Be quiet. Listen. I think Qadir is driving his wife crazy again.' She was about to go near the door to eavesdrop, but Noor Mohammad stopped her.

'Sit down, I advise you not to poke your nose in others' affairs.'

'Do you call them "others"?'

'I do not mean to say that they are strangers, but sagacity demands that one should not meddle in the affairs of any married couple. See how they give vent to their rage. Relax, they shall get tired soon.'

'But I think this time the problem is rather grave.' Saying this she tried to get up again, but Noor Mohammad pulled her by the arm and made her sit.

And there, Zeb had let all hell loose on Qadir for being so late. Qadir had already thought of an excuse to placate her. 'We were marooned in an eddy in the deep waters of Sadra Khwon. Don't you see what a bad turn the weather has taken? You should be thankful to God that we survived; but instead, you berate me. Don't you see how this kind-hearted Jane is always thinking of our well-being? Had she not helped us in time, this boat would have gone. Abba can hardly manage meals for the family – how could he help us?'

Zeb could hardly digest any of these excuses. She pulled a quilt up to her knees. Qadir picked up the polythene bag lying by his side and walked to Zeb. He took the silken cloth out of the bag and placed it on Zeb's lap and, in a passionate tone, said to her, 'See what a fine suit of silk Jane has got for you. She felt shy giving this to you herself and sent it through me.'

This made Zeb flare up and she threw the cloth away, saying, 'There may be others who believe in your lies, but not this Zeb here. You should be ashamed of your vile deeds, but instead you purchase this piece of cloth from the market and tell me that that filthy woman has bought it for me! You are already in her snare and have forgotten your family. Aren't you ashamed?'

'I swear by God that this is a gift to you from her!'

Zeb picked up the piece of cloth from the floor and flung it in Qadir's face. 'Go now and return it to her. Tell her that when Zeb goes mad, and wants to kill herself by hanging, she will use her own headscarf, not this dirty cloth. Do you hear me?'

Qadir smacked his forehead and started moaning, 'Oh my God, come to my rescue so that I can convince this woman that I have no illicit relations with Jane.'

'I have been observing you around her since last year.'

'Why don't you trust me? We have nothing to gain from this old occupation. I intend on starting the business of exporting carpets to England, and Jane's help is a necessity. It is after all a new business.'

'If you were really serious about this new business of yours, you should have consulted with Abba or your brothers, not this witch of a woman!'

Qadir retorted, 'You say I should have consulted with my brothers! Ghulam Ahmed, who is already drifting after his father-in-law? And if I seek counsel from Abba or Noor Mohammad, they will silence me with their own logic. They hardly have any inkling of the changed world.'

'They are not fools to try to fly without having wings as you do. New business! My foot! You can beguile others with these fibs but not Zeb. I say, leave right now and dump this rag of silk on that fairy of yours. Otherwise I'll go myself and throw it at that monkey-faced slut.'

'If I had known that there was such venom in your head, I would never have married you.'

Zeb was beside herself with anger now. 'You have not burnt all your boats; she is there waiting, undressed for you in the houseboat. Go, what are you doing here?'

Qadir lost his patience. He stood up and slapped her saying, 'Shut up, you…'

She caught both his hands in her own and started hitting her head with them. 'Go on, hit me! Why don't you hit me? Come, come, kill me. All your hindrances will be removed!'

Qadir freed himself and sat down holding his head in his hands. Zeb flung the door open, went out and sat on the stairs of the veranda.

It was raining heavily and the intermittent lightning and thunder made everything shudder. Zeb sat weeping. Thunder struck somewhere in the city, and the power supply went off. Everything was engulfed in darkness, but Zeb remained unmoved. She prayed for a great thunderbolt to annihilate everything and relieve her of this agony. Had she not had her son Bilal, she would certainly have killed herself by jumping into the lake. The very thought of the boy made her body shudder. Bilal was fast asleep beside his grandparents. She cast a look at Malla Khaliq's room. Even the emergency light which Narayan Joo had got Aziz Dyad from Bombay had not been lit. With a sense of complete helplessness, Zeb looked towards the sky. It was pitch-dark, yet she could visualize the tall poplars that stood around the isle, swaying in the wind, casting serpentine reflections that stretched their fangs in the water below.

Inside the room, Qadir stood dumbfounded; all his rage had subsided. He now desired to go out of the room to bring Zeb back. But he could not muster up the courage to face her. He moved to the window and looked outside. In a flash of lightning, he saw Zeb sitting so still on the stairs that it was as if she was petrified. A shudder of fright ran through him. He thought that if anything happened to her, his father would inter him alive. He somehow gathered the courage and ventured out. He walked to Zeb and softly laid his hand on her shoulder. She was completely drenched in the rain. He held her arm and said, 'It is not advisable to sit like this in such a terrible downpour.'

'Do I look like a lump of salt that I will dissolve in water? Go, that harlot might get frightened in this dark, terrifying night. Do not touch me, I say, don't touch me!'

In spite of her continuous protests, Qadir lifted her in his arms and took her inside. He shut the door and tried to help her pull off her drenched clothes, but she pushed him away. She buried herself under the quilt, and Qadir wrapped himself in a blanket and lay in a corner.

With the morning prayer call, the night was over. The thunderstorm, too, had completely abated. The prayer call, as usual, made Malla Khaliq rise from bed. Aziz Dyad was still asleep. He quietly came out of the room and went to the quay for his ablutions. It was still dark and leaves and twigs of trees were strewn all around. He could see heaps of spring sprouts washed away by the storm as if they were the innocent dreams of Zeb. Zeb was also awakened by the prayer call, but she did not get out of bed. Every inch of her body ached. She shivered and her eyes burned. She raised her head and looked at Qadir. He lay on the carpet without a cover. She pulled her quilt up and turned on her side.

Malla Khaliq was rolling his prayer mat when Aziz Dyad came in hurriedly. 'Please take out the small boat and get the doctor. Zeb is burning with fever. Even covered with two quilts, she shivers as if she is in a tub of ice.'

'Oh God! Mercy!' Malla Khaliq placed the prayer mat in the almirah and wasted no time in going to fetch the small boat.

Meanwhile, Noor Mohammad had summoned Qadir to his room and was reproaching him. Qadir put forth all manner of excuses to defend himself. Noor Mohammad lost his temper, shut the door, and said, 'Do you never feel any shame at telling all these lies? My wife and I heard every word you uttered in your room. My wife was about to barge into your room, but I did not deem it proper…'

'But she drives me mad. She does not trust even a word of mine. What she wants is for me to abjure my business and sit brooding near her all the time.'

'Didn't you feel any pity for her? She sat helpless like a beggar on the stairs in torrential rain!'

'If you really saw her sitting in the downpour, then you must also have noticed how I carried her inside in my arms.' Qadir pleaded innocence but Noor Mohammad knew where the real problem lay. 'If Abba comes to know the real cause of your conflict ...' Qadir was enraged and he stood up to leave. Before going out he said, 'I fail to understand why everyone is against me. Why no one advises Zeb.' Having said this, he entered his room where he found all the members of his family assembled around Zeb.

Sitting near her pillow, Parveen was applying a wet cloth to her forehead, and Mukhta was rubbing her soles. Bilal stood nonplussed in a corner. Aziz Dyad came with a tumbler of hot water and told Zeb, 'Drink this hot water, my child. It will relieve you of cold. The doctor too has advised so. Your Abba must be coming back from the market with the medicine.' She held Zeb's head in her lap and made her sip the water. In the meantime Malla Khaliq returned. 'Did you get the medicine?' asked Aziz Dyad.

'No, I sent Noor Mohammad to fetch a taxi.'

The glass of water dropped from her hand. 'Oh my God, but why?'

Malla Khaliq consoled her. 'There is no need to be so alarmed. Doctor's advised that we should get her admitted to the hospital. She will get better treatment there. All the tests too shall be done there.' He went near Zeb and said to her, 'You need not worry.' Turning to his wife he said, 'Help her walk to the ghat. Meanwhile I shall unanchor the boat to ferry her across to the Boulevard, where Noor Mohammad will be waiting with a taxi.' Saying this he left the room. Qadir extended his hands to help Zeb get up from the bed, but Zeb pushed his hands away. This angered Qadir and he said to his mother, 'You see, I have never seen such a stubborn woman!'

Zoon, Noor Mohammad's wife, was already in a bad temper, and she yelled at Qadir. 'See how unabashed is he! You shameless man, how many women have you seen that you compare her with them?'

Qadir turned and walked away without saying anything. Zoon and Parveen assisted Zeb to the ghat. Malla Khaliq and Ghulam Ahmed were already there. Qadir, with his head hung low, sat on the prow of the boat.

Aziz Dyad held Zeb clasped to her breast and the boatman moved the boat towards the Boulevard. Razaq also stood near the ghat. Malla Khaliq said to him, 'Keep a watch.'

'Yes, sir,' said Razaq. When the boat drifted away, Razaq returned to the isle.

Jane was also looking out through the window of her houseboat. She called out to Razaq and asked him, 'What happened?'

'Ill, she very ill, taking hospital …' Razaq tried to communicate to her what had happened.

While he babbled these words, Parveen, flaring up with anger, shouted at him. 'What are you doing there?' She cast a furious glance at Jane. 'Come, let us go. Damn her! If I find you whiling away your time talking to her, I won't spare you!'

Like a mouse smoked out of its hole, Razaq fled to the wooden shed that Malla Khaliq had erected for him on the isle behind the houseboats. Parveen watched him till he was out of sight. She had somehow sensed that Jane was trying to keep Razaq near her while Qadir was not available. She feared that Jane might entice Razaq, too, as she had Qadir. Razaq was no less handsome than the great Hazrat Yousuf. Taller than Qadir, he had striking features. Parveen blushed when she suddenly realized that these days Razaq was always on her mind. But poor Razaq was oblivious to it all. He did not dare raise his eyes in her direction.

The senior doctor at the Drogjan Hospital said, 'Haji Sahib, you must be thankful to God. She would have contracted double

pneumonia if you had not got her here in time. Now there is no
need to worry, she can go home after a couple of days.'

Malla Khaliq said to Noor Mohammad, 'Narayan Joo has asked
me to see him at his house, but I don't think it proper to leave Zeb
here. Could you please go there on my behalf? He will take you to
the bank; he knows what to do.'

Noor Mohammad looked at his mother who was sitting on
a stool near Zeb's bed. With a nod she approved of what Malla
Khaliq had said. Malla Khaliq took out a letter from his pocket.
'Take this with you. Go, my son.' When Noor Mohammad left,
Qadir moved close to his father and said hesitantly, 'You too may
leave for home, I am here.' Hearing this, Malla Khaliq's forehead
wrinkled up in anger. He nevertheless said, 'No, you should leave
instead, you have your customer waiting there in the boat. Razaq is
not trained enough to attend to customers. By God's grace all will
be well.' Qadir was waiting for this consent from his father and left
as if in compliance to his order. He felt a sense of relief because he
was worried about the bag which Jane had given him to hide. This
was the bag she had received from the hippies, full of drugs.

Qadir was about to step onto the prow of Gulshan, when he
heard the sound of a motorboat. He stopped and looked back. It
was Karmakar, a Bombay-based broker. He came to Kashmir to
buy carpets, but under this cover managed the transactions of drug
smugglers. He had dealings with Jane too. Karmakar's presence
helped Qadir make Malla Khaliq and Noor Mohammad believe
that Jane, too, frequented Kashmir to procure carpets for export to
other countries and Karmakar was her agent.

As soon as Karmakar's motorboat stopped near the landing of
Gulshan, Qadir went down to greet him. Karmakar lifted the rolled
carpet lying in the boat and, holding Qadir's hand, entered the
houseboat. After a while he came out carrying a brown bag in his
hand instead of the carpet. Qadir escorted him to the ghat. After
shaking hands with Qadir, he sat in the motorboat which took a
sharp turn towards the rear of the lake. Qadir did not waste any
time in re-entering Gulshan, where he found Jane taking money

out of the bag that Karmakar had brought wrapped up in the carpet and counting it.

'Keep it under the bed,' she told Qadir, zipping up the bag.

While Qadir was taking the bag from Jane, Razaq appeared with a coffee tray. 'Memsahib, coffee!' he said timidly. He cautiously placed the tray on the table, but Qadir lashed out at Razaq like a rabid dog. 'You ill-mannered cur! How dare you enter without seeking permission? Did you want to check what we were doing here?'

'But, sir, it was your order that I should get her coffee at four o'clock.'

'How impudent you are! You, a brother-in-law of dogs!'

The blood in Razaq's veins boiled and he said in a defiant tone, 'Sir, do not hurl such names at me!'

Catching hold of Razaq's throat, Qadir dragged him out and threw him on to the isle. Razaq was about to say something in protest, but Qadir gripped his throat again. 'Keep quiet, you bastard! You should know that Qadir uses his tongue just once, then it his knife that talks. Understand? You are always around prying.' He started kicking him.

Seeing this from her boat, Jane rushed out to intervene. Parveen, who saw the scene from the pantry, also came running. But when she saw Jane holding Qadir's hand and taking him to the houseboat, she stopped. She did not think it proper to go near Razaq even though she felt pity for him. She continued gazing at him. Razaq dusted his clothes and cast a fierce glance towards Qadir's houseboat. He wanted to re-enter the houseboat, drag Qadir out and let him know that he was much stronger than him. It was his respect for Malla Khaliq that held him back. Parveen walked quickly to catch up with Razaq and when he raised his eyes, she saw the tears in his eyes. Without saying a word, he entered his shed and bolted the door.

Parveen was seized by a strong desire to walk into the shack and wipe his tears, but she did not have the courage. After all, he was the servant boy. For a little while she stood outside the door and then returned to the pantry.

In the houseboat, Qadir was still enraged. He was busy removing the planks from the basement store of the houseboat. Jane coyly tidied his dishevelled hair to calm him down. 'Relax, Qadir, enough now.' Then she told him that it was necessary to maintain calmness and a steady mind in the business they pursued. The key to success lay in keeping a smile pasted on one's lips while talking to others. That was the way to remain free from suspicion.

Qadir hid the bag in the drawers of the space under the floor, stood up and held Jane in an embrace. Jane was quite adept in seducing men, and each of them believed that he alone was the fortunate person to win her love. While she held Qadir, she imagined that it was Razaq she was holding. Her desire for Razaq had gained in intensity since the time she had seen him swimming naked in the Dal while she sat at the deck of the houseboat. She felt he was no less charming than Zeus, particularly when he rose from the water after swimming and started getting dressed. Then she released herself from Qadir's embrace, saying that somebody was coming. Qadir let her go and went out of the room.

Parveen was sitting on the steps of the ghat having finished her work in the pantry. She was, in fact, waiting for her father to return so she could narrate the whole incident to him. Seeing her there, Qadir went near her and said, 'What are you doing here?'

'Waiting for Abba,' she said.

'He need not be shown his way home, does he?'

Parveen cast an angry look at him. He quivered with the fear that she might have seen him hugging Jane. So he changed the topic. 'I mean to say that if Abba ...'

But Parveen did not let him complete his sentence and dashed to the pantry again. Now he was convinced that she had seen everything and was eager to report to Abba. He turned back and sat down on the steps of the houseboat.

Seeing Qadir move away, Parveen came out of the barge and sneaked to Razaq's shed. She raised her hand to knock at the door but failed in her courage. She propped herself against a wall of wooden planks. She surveyed the wall from top to bottom and detected a rent, a little above her height. She stood on tiptoe and peeped inside. Razaq was filling his bag with books and a bag of clothes was already packed. Parveen felt her legs tremble and her heart sink. She stood transfixed for a moment. She might have stayed there like that had Malla Khaliq's call not alerted her.

'Parveen, where are you?'

Shielding herself by the willow tree, she walked quietly and went and stood before her father near the barge. He bore a plastic bag in his hands. Seeing Parveen coming from behind him, he asked her, 'Where are you coming from?'

'It was Gil, Malla Subhan's daughter. She had come to ask after Zeb's health.' In order to divert his attention, she asked, 'What are you carrying in that bag?'

'Oh, I had ordered a uniform for Razaq. We are expecting a big officer and his family from Bombay – it wouldn't look nice if Razaq appeared in tattered clothes to serve them. Open it and see if it will suit him.'

Parveen took the bag from her father and entered the barge again. Malla Khaliq was sharp enough to guess that something untoward had happened; otherwise she would have opened the bag then and there. He followed her into the barge. The moment he stepped into the pantry, she asked him, 'Tea is already boiling, shall I pour out a cup for you?'

'First tell me what the matter is. You are wont to frisk all my pockets when I return home. Why didn't you open the bag today? It might contain something for my daughter, too.' Saying this Malla Khaliq sat down and stretched his hand towards Parveen and said, 'First get that bag here. Then we shall have tea.'

Parveen had no other excuse to keep from telling him. Handing the bag to him, she said, 'Abba, I think you will have to go back to the tailor and make alterations to the size.'

'What do you mean?' Malla Khaliq asked. Parveen revealed all that had happened there earlier. The bag fell from Malla Khaliq's hand. 'Qadir was about to kill the poor chap then and there, but it was Jane who came out running and almost dragged him back into the houseboat,' she said.

'Where is Razaq now?'

'He must be in his room. I don't think he will stay here after such humiliation.'

Malla Khaliq stood up, took the uniform out of the bag and went to Razaq's room. He also thought of teaching Qadir a lesson, but he did not deem it proper to insult him in Jane's presence. He knocked at the door of the shack. Razaq opened the door and, seeing Malla Khaliq in front of him, he said, 'Sir, in fact, I was waiting for you.'

'Why? Are you all right?' Malla Khaliq asked him, feigning ignorance.

'I request you to kindly let me go. It is enough now, I have already had enough food at this place. If I have unwittingly committed any mistake, I request you to forgive me,' he said and proceeded to lift his bag of books and the pouch of clothes.

Holding him by the arm, Malla Khaliq said to him, 'But is it proper that a father should let his son leave like this? Keep this bag down. What has happened to you? Look, my son, Parveen has already narrated the whole incident to me. This Ghulam Qadir ... he is, in fact, very worried about his wife's health. That is why he loses his temper so easily. Otherwise he is not so harsh.'

Razaq said in reply, 'No, sir, please forgive me for saying so, but it's not just him; others in the family are not polite to me either.'

Malla Khaliq sat down beside him and, keeping his hand affectionately on his shoulder, said, 'Am I not polite to you? Noor Mohammad is always all praises for you. And my wife is fonder of you than her own children.'

'Yes, sir, I know that. But the person I am attached to is not like that. He is constantly rude to me, calls me names while ordering me to sit or stand ... how can I pass my days here?'

Hearing this Malla Khaliq stood up and said, 'Let me see who insults you any more. You watch how this small world of ours shall prosper from tomorrow and, with that, you shall too. Everyone will be engrossed in his or her work and no one will have time to waste in such idle things. A big party is expected soon from Bombay, and I have decided that you alone shall be in charge of catering to them, that too in my houseboat Gul. We will have someone else assist Ghulam Qadir. Are you happy now?'

Parveen was keeping a constant vigil over the wooden shed. When she sensed that it was taking her father longer than expected, she stealthily walked behind the willow trees and reached the shed. She stood against the same wooden plank and peeped in. She saw Razaq with his head drooped, visibly cooled down.

While listening to Malla Khaliq, Razaq thought it would not be easy for him to find another good job. Also in his heart of hearts he had felt that even if no one else in the family bothered about him, Parveen would still care for him. Had it not been so, why would she report Qadir to her father?

Razaq raised his eyes to Malla Khaliq and said, 'Sir, whenever I see you, I am reminded of my own father. I remember how dearly he loved me while my mother lived. But when he remarried after my mother's death, he was under the spell of his new wife. He started believing all the lies she told him and would keep thrashing me. I got fed up one day and fled from my home and school.' He gasped for breath. Tears rolled down his cheeks and he fell at Malla Khaliq's feet. 'Please forgive me. I caused you so much worry.'

Malla Khaliq pulled him up and held him in his arms. 'My dear son, I am here with you. I will make sure that everyone treats you well. If you are interested in studies, I will get you books. But please persevere.'

Saying this Malla Khaliq picked up the attendant's uniform. 'Take it and see if it is your size. Don't be shy, put it on. I know you really wanted to wear this uniform. There is a belt, too, in the bag, a red belt with golden embroidery. See if the coat fits you.'

Razaq forgot everything on seeing the uniform. He had once seen Malla Subhan's son wearing a similar uniform when he appeared on the deck of the houseboat, Queen Margaret, far out near the shore, feeding the aged Mem who stayed there even during winters. The snow-white uniform and the red belt with golden embroidery had dazzled in the spring sun. Having seen this, he had asked Malla Khaliq when he would be fit for wearing a uniform such as that one. Now, holding this uniform in his hands, he felt as if he owned all the wealth in the world.

Parveen quietly watched all this and felt relieved that Razaq would not leave. She went capering to the barge as if her entire being was filled with a strange ecstasy. Malla Khaliq made Razaq wear the outfit of a houseboat butler and then, casting a joyful glance at him from head to toe, he said, 'Malla Subhan's son is no match for you, I am sure. Now you should try the pants also. Remember to wear this uniform when the tourists arrive the day after tomorrow. In Malla Khaliq's houseboats, the butlers have never served the guests without wearing a uniform. I shall get you another set soon and I should never find your uniform dirty. Do you understand?'

'Yes, sir.'

'Now relax.' Saying this, Malla Khaliq left and was soon in the pantry again. Parveen was waiting there for him with a steaming samovar of tea. Entering the pantry he told her, 'He was really about to leave!'

Parveen asked, 'And now?'

'What now? Your Abba was by no means ready to let this gentle, wise and honest boy go away.' Taking the cup of tea from her, he said in a tone of great accomplishment, 'Now there is only one more task to be done and that is to find another assistant for Qadir.'

'Let him do it himself. You should have seen how brutally he kicked Razaq, only because he was appointed by you.'

'Now no one can dare touch him. You go and bring Qadir here.'

Parveen quivered with fear. 'No, Abba, please do not mention anything about the incident to him.'

'But today or tomorrow he has to understand that his hooliganism will not be tolerated in my house.'

Suddenly Parveen heard her name being called. 'Parveen!' She looked through the window and saw Qadir with Jane on the isle. On seeing Parveen, he told her, 'Parveen, when Abba is home, tell him that we are going to meet Karmakar to see the new consignment of carpets.' He held Jane's hand and helped her into a shikaarah. Controlling his anger, Malla Khaliq said to Parveen, 'I don't know what he was so busy with that he did not even know that I am already home. If this she-monkey were not with him, I would have killed and buried him right there.'

Malla Khaliq had been at Narayan Joo's travel agency to convey the good news that Mr Bhonsley had confirmed his air ticket for day after tomorrow. Narayan Joo on his part had provided the Raja of Ranthambhor with all the details of his travel.

But the nasty incident at his home marred all Malla Khaliq's joy. He heaved a deep sigh, saying, 'God is all-prevailing!' Then he went over to Gul to see if all was neat and tidy there. He loved this houseboat more than any others not because of this one was bigger than the other two, but because it had been constructed by his father and had won him respect in the fraternity of houseboat owners. Whenever he received a rich guest from outside, he made them stay there.

Seated on the front prow of the shikaarah, Qadir was enjoying himself by ogling at Jane. She, on the other hand, was busy counting the currency in the brown bag. The boatman was paddling the boat towards the Kabootar Khana pier east of the lake, where the erstwhile Maharaja had built a bungalow amidst blooming lilies.

A boat full of policemen coming from the Bod Dal, the larger lake, was approaching their shikaarah. The head constable greeted Qadir aloud saying, 'I see! Yesteryear's Mem is back on the very advent of spring!' Qadir started. He began to stammer and his heart began thumping fast, he felt as if he had been caught red-handed committing a crime. But he mustered some courage and said, '*As-salaam-alaikum*, Mir Sahib!'

The boat was already quite close to their shikaarah. The head constable smiled, cast a penetrating glance at Jane, and said to her, 'Good day, madam. All well?' Jane replied with a charming smile, 'Yes, good day.' Then Mir Sahib asked Qadir, 'How is Haji Sahib?'

'By God's blessing, he is fine,' Qadir replied.

'Has any other boat been hired?'

'Not yet, sir,' Qadir said trying to be brief.

'No worries. It is still very early. They say it will be a good season.'

'Yes, they say so.' Qadir was as restless as if on pinpricks. He wanted this threat to go away as soon as possible.

Mir Sahib was wise enough to keep it brief. 'Carry on. Convey my greetings to Haji Sahib.' He ordered his team to return to the water gate.

Seeing the police boat drift away, Qadir said to his boatman angrily, 'Why the hell did you have to take this route?'

'But you did not tell me in which direction you intended to go,' the boatman responded in an equally harsh tone.

'Now listen, you turn the boat towards the place we had been to the day before yesterday.'

'You mean near Kava's houseboat?'

'No, no! Row towards the place where the rush-mat maker's statue is submerged. Where it is said that he was petrified for cheating his customers along with the fradulent milkman.'

'You mean where that European was busy catching fish with his line the other day?'

'Yes, you're right. Now paddle faster, we are already late.'

The boatman turned the boat towards the swamps. 'God! That was a narrow escape.' Qadir heaved a sigh of relief. Jane mocked him saying, 'Your face was worth watching. What a coward!' She told him that he was not mature enough to run this trade. Here one must have a heart of steel. Qadir, who considered himself no less than a don, felt like a frightened mouse. In order to change the topic, he started narrating the tale of the rush-mat maker and the milkman of yore. But Jane took out a book from her bag and busied herself with turning its leaves. Qadir left the tale unfinished and started staring at her again.

The shikaarah was now moving very fast and the paddling caused the scum of algae to give way towards the willow trunks. When the boat came out of the thickets and turned to the right, the boatman shouted, 'There he is.' Hearing this, Qadir saw the hippie he had seen in Kava's houseboat. He told Jane that he was not like George, who never trusted anyone in matters of money. But Jane told him that he was the main supplier, and it was he who would be receiving all payments. On hearing this, Qadir turned to the boatman, 'Stop here, Gula. You keep the boat anchored just there near that chinar. This memsahib wants to meet the Sahib. Hurry up.'

The boatman anchored the boat near the chinar tree. Qadir held Jane's hand and helped her step into the boat. She asked Qadir to wait and then walked over alone to the hippie who pretended to be absorbed in watching the float of the fishing line. He did not turn to Jane until she was quite near him.

This swamp belonged to Sula Kava's father-in-law. This was the reason they faced no hurdle in sitting there or catching fish. Charles had examined all the swamps and watercourses in the rear of the Dal Lake and selected many such swamps and watercourses for running his drug racket. This was how he escaped the gaze of the police. The strongest loop in this long chain of smugglers was Jane, who stayed in Bombay and supervised the supply of hashish collected in Kashmir and other neighbouring areas to other parts of the world. She also managed the trade of supplying drugs from foreign countries to the local customers. Whenever she felt any pressure from the Bombay police, she took refuge in Kashmir or Delhi. This time she was here with George and was carrying a big consignment of drugs. Since the stuff was valued in millions, this old European, Charles, had come in the guise of a hippie to handle the finances himself. He pulled his line out of the water when he saw Jane near him. There was a brown bag lying to his left, exactly like the one Jane carried. The hippie was busy handling his fishing line with one hand and biting into a sandwich with the other. Without uttering a word, he gestured to Jane to sit down as he noticed a couple of boats coming fast from the adjacent Nigeen Lake. Jane pretended as if she had met this hippie by chance and, while sitting near him, greeted him loudly, so that the people coming in the boats could also hear her. 'Hi Charles! What are you doing there?' The hippie was sharp enough to understand her design and said in an equally loud note, 'Don't you see I'm fishing?' Then he took out another sandwich from his bag and offered it to Jane. Meanwhile the boat was coming very close to them. There were some elderly foreign tourists in the boats, men as well as women – the women were wearing gaudy dresses and loud make-up. The hippie and Jane waved to them and they waved back merrily.

Qadir, for his part, was keeping a constant vigil over the opposite side of the swamp. Mir Sahib might have become suspicious and could be watching their movements from somewhere. He knew that Mir Sahib was a very shrewd person. He knew every detail about the activities on the Dal Lake; who came and who went in the houseboats, and which spots were the trysts of gamblers; he knew everything. He calmly received his share at his place; that was a known fact. But even then one had to be careful. Qadir was lost in such musings when the boatman got a simmering samovar of tea and placed it before him. 'Have a cup of tea to while away this arduous waiting. Who knows how long they will keep us here like this? I feel this hippie is after this algae scum. Take it from me, he cannot find even a little mud fry here.' This irritated Qadir, who said, 'Hey you! Gula Tancha, how many times have I warned you not to poke your nose in their matters.' But this shikaarahwala was always sniffing around inquisitively. He sat beside Qadir but secretly continued darting looks at the hippie and Jane. Qadir discerned this and gave him a good spank on his head. 'Why are you being so impish? Don't disturb them. Don't you see how I keep a distance from them? These European tourists do not like to be watched. Do you hear me?' While he was scolding the boatman, Jane called him. Qadir left his cup of tea and ran. Jane exchanged her bag with the hippie's and took leave of him. 'Okay, Charles, keep on fishing.'

Charles flung the fishing line and the rushes-stick into the water. Jane came near Qadir and asked him to move the shikaarah.

'All well?' Qadir asked her.

'Yes.' She handed over the bag to Qadir, and holding his hand, stepped into the boat. Qadir then said to the boatman who was placing the cups in the basket, 'Let us move on, dear friend. Start pedalling, hurry up.' Gula Tancha took the oar in his hands and as he pushed it against the swamp, the boat started moving like a dart in the water. Qadir handed over the brown bag to Jane and sat as usual on the prow.

The bag was stuffed with drugs. Qadir told Jane that they should not keep it in the houseboat. At her behest he had chosen a dilapidated hut that stood behind the water, shielded by thick willow trees in a small isle, as if it was lamenting over its destiny. Last year, too, they had hidden hashish in the same hut. Today the fear of the police was again causing him worry and therefore, he suggested they hide the stuff in the same hut and come back for it another day. Jane agreed. Gula Tancha, who was crooning a song of Rasool Mir's, '*Rinda pooshimaal gyindinyey draayiloploo*', in his raucous voice, started when Qadir called him, 'Gula!'

'Yes, tell me what to do.'

'The memsahib needs to relieve herself. Take the shikaarah to the mire behind the willow thicket.'

Gula Tancha, who was already irritated with the two said, 'That will be a much more longer course. We will pass some other swamp on our way. Please ask her to have a little patience.'

Qadir was furious to hear this. 'You are very discourteous. Why can't you do what you are asked to do?'

Gula Tancha did not want to argue, and said, while turning the shikaarah, 'I am least concerned. Tell me and I will keep rowing you in the lake from dawn to dusk.'

On reaching, Jane was on the mire in a quick jump. Gula Tancha was about to follow her, but Qadir held him back. 'Why should you go there?'

'I thought it proper to keep a watch so that nobody passes by her. She is a woman after all,' said Gula Tancha.

With a sharp pull, Qadir made him sit back in the boat. 'Oh, leave her alone. She has traversed seven oceans.'

Gula Tancha sat in a huff. Jane knew the most secure spot in the ruined hut. She removed the sodden wood splinters which were piled up in a corner and emptied her bag. She covered the little packets with the wood splinters again. Then she zipped the empty bag and returned to the boat.

Malla Khaliq had woken up at dawn and taken his rowboat to the dargah where he offered his prayers in gratitude. With full solace of mind he was now rowing back to Gagribal. He was quite fast in beating his oar in the water. The sound of water splashing was no less sweet to him than the melody of fairies. The sun was about to raise its head from the blanket of clouds behind the Zabarwan summits. The golden rays gave a fresh vitality to his face. He was sure that the day would augur well for his life. Zeb was getting discharged from the hospital, and the Raja of Ranthambhor was arriving along with his family. Malla Khaliq had seen this king, Raja Rathinder Singh, over thirty years ago when he had accompanied his father Raja Bhupinder Singh to stay in their houseboat. Remembering those old good days, Malla Khaliq heaved a deep sigh. Raja Rathinder may not even recognize me, he thought. But how does it matter. He is not to stay here for life. A tourist is after all a tourist – they come only to go back. The thought sent a tremor down his marrow. No, all tourists are not like that. If it were so, why would my father have kept the file of letters well preserved for all his ninety years? Then, this Raja Rathinder is not a stranger to us. Some of the letters of his father are also in that file. Every word of those letters is replete with love. Malla Khaliq consoled himself and his hands found more strength.

Malla Khaliq always went to the shrine of Makhdoom Sahib early in the morning and on his way back he would invariably bump into Narayan Joo. He, too, visited the temple of Sharka Devi every morning. But this time Malla Khaliq had informed his friend on the phone that he had decided to go to the dargah at Hazratbal, and would not meet him at the Parbat hills. Engrossed in such thoughts, he hardly knew how he reached the houseboats at Gagribal. The moment he looked up, he found two rowboats near the ghat and all his family members gathered there on the isle. He applied all his strength on the oars and, within no time, reached them. On seeing him, Noor Mohammad cried, 'Lo, Abba has also come.'

'Is everything all right? Tell me ...' he said gasping. 'What are you all doing here?'

'First of all, you take out eleven rupees from your pocket. Your daughter-in-law is home.'

Malla Khaliq came out of his rowboat and, in one jump, was on the isle. 'But where is Zeb now?'

'There is no need to make haste now, Abba,' said Noor Mohammad. 'Mukhta and Parveen just took her to her room.'

'But where is Qadir? Was he not accompanying you?' Malla Khaliq asked, looking in all directions.

'He came along with Ghulam Ahmed and got the taxi,' Noor Mohammad said, and then started picking up supplies from the rowboat.

'Are we to spend all our time here counting the waves in the water?' asked Aziz Dyad. 'Let us go in, your daughter-in-law must be waiting there with her steaming samovar.'

'No, let me first see Zeb. Where is Bilal?' asked Malla Khaliq.

'He is also inside, with his mother. But come soon.' Saying this Aziz Dyad and Zoon left for the barge.

Qadir sat beside Zeb with his head stooped. Bilal sat in his lap. As soon as Malla Khaliq stepped in, Bilal ran and hugged his legs. Malla Khaliq picked him up in his arms and kissed him. Then he sat down near Zeb. She greeted him with respect. Malla Khaliq reciprocated by keeping an affectionate hand on her head, and prayed for her well-being and long life. Then he turned to Qadir. 'I wish that you will always care more about your family while running your business. Then there will never be any clashes in our house. Did you get all the prescriptions and reports from the hospital?'

Qadir had visited the hospital only to make a show of his responsibility. He knew nothing about the reports and the prescriptions. Zeb, therefore, replied on his behalf, 'Abba, all the documents are with Noor Toth. Qadir had gone to fetch the taxi.'

'All right, I shall ask him if there is any medicine to be bought immediately.' Malla Khaliq left the room. Zeb's reply emboldened Qadir, and he stretched his hand to hold hers. But she freed her hand from his grip and said, 'I said that only to convince Abba that you really cared about me. I said it to save your credibility.'

'Do you mean I had not gone to get the taxi? Who else was there to do that?'

Zeb said, 'Go to the pantry, they are waiting to serve you tea. It will take all our life to settle such issues. Be kind and get me that tumbler of water. I am still very thirsty.' Qadir hastened to get her the tumbler of water and he also helped her drink. Zeb said again, 'Now please go, Amma is waiting for you.'

Qadir asked her, 'Should I send your tea here?'

'Parveen is there to bring me tea,' Zeb replied coldly. Qadir was about to say something more but held his tongue.

He was still afraid of entering the kitchen where the family had assembled, and he had no guts to visit Jane at the moment. He had forgotten she had not been served morning tea. But he relaxed when he saw Razaq entering the houseboat with a tray in his hands.

Razaq waited outside Jane's bedroom after having pressed the bell. When there was no response, he pressed the button again.

'Who is it?' came Jane's voice.

'Memsahib, your tea.'

Jane opened the door. She stood in her transparent nightdress. Razaq lowered his eyes and entered the room with the tray. Jane shut the door, sat on the sofa and continued staring at Razaq. Jane imagined his body in the nude just the way she had beheld him when he had been taking a bath in the light of the rising sun. Razaq was quick to pour out tea into the cup and offer it to Jane. He was about to go out of the room when Jane addressed him.

'I am really very sorry for that unfortunate incident. Did he hurt you?' Jane asked with mock concern.

'No, memsahib, no.'

'He hurt you, I know he did. Let me look where.' She stood up. But before Jane could touch him, Razaq managed to open the door and rush out of the houseboat.

While he was gasping for breath, Malla Khaliq saw him and called out. 'Why are you not in your uniform? I have already told you that we are expecting a rich party from Delhi today. He is a raja, a real raja.'

'I will, yes, I will wear it soon. I had gone to give tea to the memsahib,' he said. He noticed Aziz Dyad going to Zeb's room with qahva in the samovar. He ran to her and took the samovar from her hands, saying, 'Give it to me, I shall serve her qahva.' He followed her to Zeb's room. Zeb was tidying the room by placing the folded clothes into the almirah. Aziz Dyad entered her room and said, 'Why have you got out of bed? The doctor has strictly instructed you to rest.' Turning to Razaq, she continued, 'Now keep this samovar here and go attend to your work.' When Razaq left, Aziz Dyad poured the qahva into the cup and said to Zeb, 'Have this hot qahva. I will sort these clothes.' Zeb's eyes filled up with tears. She embraced Aziz Dyad and sobbed heavily. Aziz Dyad consoled her. 'This crying does not become you. Now we are in our own house, you just relax.'

'I don't know why I'm so restless. I feel like some monster is gnawing at my heart. Even in my dreams I see myself wandering in the mountains; I have strange premonitions,' Zeb said, her eyes brimming over with tears.

Aziz Dyad wiped her tears with her own headscarf and said, 'My dear daughter, I know well what fears haunt you. Don't despair, for your Abba has understood everything. I am sure he will resolve all your problems very soon. He is waiting for the advance paid by this wench of a Mem to expire and then he will never allow her to step with her dirty feet into his houseboats. Now sip this cup of qahva. But no, it might have gone cold. Let me refill the cup.'

Zeb could hardly stop her tears. 'Amma, I have caused you so much trouble all these days. If my own mother were alive, even she would not care so much for me.'

'But you are my daughter. I am not doing anything to oblige you. Promise me that you will drink one more cup, okay? Now let me see what they are doing over there. A group of visitors is coming today,' Aziz Dyad said as she left the room.

Narayan Joo had told Malla Khaliq that Raja Rathinder loved fish. He had fetched over four kilos of fish from the dargah. When Aziz Dyad came out of Zeb's room, she noticed Malla Khaliq sharpening a knife near the water tap. 'What are you doing here?'

'Darling, see how I have sharpened your knife. We can slaughter even a lamb with it now. Do send all the fish here. I will carve them with this knife.'

Aziz Dyad snatched away the knife from his hand, saying, 'As if you always clean fish for the family! Go change, Narayan Joo will be here any moment with the tourists.'

'Whatever you say, I'm at your service. Here's Parveen getting the basket of fish,' Malla Khaliq said as he went into his own room. Parveen placed the basket of fish near the water tap and said to her mother, 'Let me clean the fish.' But Aziz Dyad never trusted anyone with fish. However thorough they tried to be, she always complained that the fish stank.

While going towards the houseboats, Parveen noticed Razaq near Gul. He was in his new, snow-white uniform. The moment he passed her, she could not stop giggling. She said to him, 'Idiot! If you must wear this uniform, then you must learn how to keep the waist-belt tight. Come here. Come – I am not going to bite you.' Razaq hesitantly moved closer to her. She turned his waist-belt around.

She was yet to finish when Ghulam Ahmed happened to see them. Sitting on the deck of the houseboat, he thought that

Parveen was glued to Razaq's body. He jumped down and yelled at Parveen. 'You shameless girl!' Saying this he caught hold of her arm and almost dragged her to Aziz Dyad who was cleaning the fish. He pushed Parveen towards her and said in a rage, 'Take care of this darling daughter of yours! You should have seen how she held that village boy in an embrace! She isn't even bothered about her father's respect!'

Hearing Ghulam Ahmed's angry voice, Malla Khaliq came out almost running. 'What is the matter?' he asked Ghulam Ahmed.

'Please ask your daughter whom you have spoiled with all your pampering.'

'But tell me what happened?'

Parveen boldly stepped forward and said to her father, 'I will tell you, Abba. I did not commit any sin. I saw Razaq in his uniform, but he had worn his belt the other way round. So I taught him how to wear it.' Having said this, she moved towards the pantry.

This made Ghulam Ahmed angrier and he said to his mother, 'Do you see how cheeky she has grown?'

Malla Khaliq did not want to drag this trivial issue and said to Ghulam Ahmed, 'You see, my son, Parveen is a child after all. If we shout at her like this, she will be confused.'

But Ghulam Ahmed continued to fume. 'Yes, yes, she is still a toddler, and you are always mindless in your decisions. Whosoever comes to work here, you deem him fit for this kind of uniform within a few days. As if our business will fail without the damn uniform.'

Malla Khaliq lost his composure and said, 'You must remember that these houseboats belong to Malla Khaliq. It is not a commonplace motel where the attendants work with a smudged towel on their shoulders. This is a place where people like Sir Roberts and Raja Bhupinder have spent their holidays.'

The father and the son were yet to settle their argument when Noor Mohammad came running to them saying, 'Will you please keep quiet? Lala Sahib is escorting the guests in that shikaarah.'

Malla Khaliq and Ghulam Ahmed went to welcome the guests. Parveen took Bilal, who was playing outside, to Zeb's room. She saw Qadir combing his hair. He cast an angry look at her. This frightened her and she left the child near Zeb and left. He had sensed that it was she who had informed Abba about his misbehaviour with Razaq.

The shikaarah was yet to be anchored near the wharf when Malla Khaliq descended to the ghat and cried out, 'Welcome to my humble houseboats, sir!'

Raja Rathinder responded while he was still in his chair, 'How are you, Haji Sahib?'

'I am well because of your kindness,' said Malla Khaliq quite obsequiously. The shikaarah was anchored and Narayan Joo, who was sitting at the prow, caught hold of Malla Khaliq's outstretched hand and stepped over. Noor Mohammad helped Raja Rathinder's two grandchildren to step out. First his grandson, Narpaul Singh, who was seven to eight years old, and then his granddaughter, Maya, who was five to six years old. They came running to the isle. It was spring and Malla Khaliq's rose garden was in full bloom. The two children were giddy with joy upon seeing the roses. Raja Rathinder called out to them and told them not to pluck any flower.

Raja Rathinder stood on the stairs waiting for his wife, who was straightening the seams of her dress, to come out of the shikaarah. Then she extended her hand to her husband and he helped her step over to the isle. Narayan Joo introduced Malla Khaliq to her. 'Here is Haji Sahib, the proprietor of all three houseboats.'

She shook hands with him and said to Narayan Joo, 'Yes, Raja Sahib was all praise for Haji Sahib while we were on the plane.'

Placing his hand on his chest, Khaliq greeted her by bending forward in a courtly manner and said, 'He is very kind, madam.' He then escorted the guests to the houseboat Gul.

'Oh my good old Gul!' the Raja exclaimed. 'It looks just the same.' Then he looked around and said to Narayan Joo, 'I am happy that Malla Khaliq has not painted his houseboats as other houseboat owners have done.' He held his wife's hand and helped her climb up to the veranda. He let out a long sigh and told his wife that he had come over thirty years ago with his father. 'Much has changed in Kashmir since then,' he said, 'but these mountains, these waters of the Dal, and all these rows of houseboats have defied all change. A few boats are covered in paint, of course.'

Malla Khaliq said, 'But, I beg your pardon, the Dal, too, has changed a lot. Please come in, I think Rani Sahiba is quite tired.' He kept the curtains to the door of the rounded room held up with his hands until the raja, the rani and Narayan Joo entered the drawing room. Malla Khaliq enthusiastically described every element of his houseboat to Rani Ranthambore. 'Amazing!' she exclaimed, seeing the detailing of the wood carvings and ancient carpets. Malla Khaliq felt a sense of pride. He told the rani that craftsmen having such expertize in the art were no more found in Kashmir. He said that the carpets spread in the houseboats had been woven by the master weaver who had also prepared carpets for the royal palace of Sherghari.

They were busy recounting the glories of the past when the two children came running and romped about on the carpets. She tried to stop them, 'Easy, children, easy!'

'They're kids after all!' said Malla Khaliq. 'Madam, our houseboats are not made of cheap cardboard.' The children were fascinated by the carvings on the walls and touched them. They argued with each other whether the designs were made by Haji Uncle himself or someone else. Malla Khaliq loved children. Children were God's angels until they grew up to cheat. He forgot about the rani and began telling them about the quality of timber and how many artists had collaborated in giving the interiors the finishing touch.

Narayan Joo entered the room to tell Rani Ranthambore, 'Raja Sahib is waiting for you with your cup of coffee.' She called the children, 'Come on, little ones!' The children enjoyed Malla Khaliq's stories. They wanted to stay back and talk with Haji Uncle, but their grandmother gently said that they had many more days to spend with Haji Uncle.

Raja Rathinder was examining the file of old letters when his wife entered along with the children. Narayan Joo and Malla Khaliq followed them. The raja said to Malla Khaliq, 'I hope you will excuse me for having opened this file lying on the writing table without seeking your permission.'

'Sir, it is kept there for guests to read,' Malla Khaliq said and then went on to explain how painstakingly he had preserved every ebb and flow of time in that file. The rani, already very impressed with Malla Khaliq's personality, said to him, 'Nobody can compete with you in the way you hold conversations with people. I wish you were a poet.'

'Of course!' said Narayan Joo in consensus.

Raja Rathinder turned the leaves of the file. Meanwhile Razaq, like a seasoned butler, brought coffee for the guests. He kept the tray on the side table, but the rani said to him, 'Keep it closer.' Razaq obeyed and placed the tray on the table in front of her. 'You may go now.'

Rathinder Singh called the children near him saying, 'Look at this letter. It was written in 1907. See the date! You know how old this letter is?'

The children assessed the years gone by and said that it was written about eighty years ago. Malla Khaliq told them that Sir Roberts had stayed in that very houseboat in the waters of Nigeen Lake. Rani Ranthambore and the children were amazed and asked how a houseboat could be moved from its position. 'When a ship, a thousand times bigger than this, can sail from one country to another, why can't this houseboat move?'

'Haji Uncle, can you make this houseboat move around the whole lake?'

'There are motorboats available in the lake for that purpose,' Malla Khaliq said with a smile. 'Then there are also numerous shikaarahs adorned like brides. They move about the lake quite freely.'

Being absorbed in the chat, Rani Ranthambore had forgotten about the coffee placed on the table. She lifted the cover from the coffee pot. Malla Khaliq called Razaq in and said, 'Go and get fresh coffee in this pot. It must have gone cold. The rani said, 'It is all right. It is still very hot.' Razaq stood with his head bowed in respect and his two hands crossed near his chest. Malla Khaliq said, 'You may go now.' The rani started making coffee and Malla Khaliq and Narayan Joo took leave of them. But Narpaul Singh stood up and said to Malla Khaliq, 'Wait, Uncle, I will come with you. I want to see the lake.' While taking the cup from the rani, Raja Rathinder Singh said to him, 'Sit down. You will be able to see the lake every day now.' But a child was a child after all; how could he be controlled?

Malla Khaliq took Narpaul Singh to the prow of the houseboat and said, 'Look, this is our lake. It is called the Dal Lake. The lake that stretches from here to that road is called Lwaokut Dal and Gagribal. The lake beyond this part is called Bod Dal.'

Maya too came dashing to the prow, and was impatient to see how big the lake was. But Malla Khaliq was endowed with a knack of making obstinate children concede. He told them with affectionate assurance that he would take both of them along one of these days on a trip through the Dal and also show them the floating gardens. He talked to them about the milkman and the rush-mat maker of ancient times who froze in a corner of the lake. Narpaul and Maya ran in to narrate all this to their grandfather. Malla Khaliq smiled at Narayan Joo and said, 'This is called politics. They are happy and with them we are also happy.'

'But please spare some time tomorrow to take them on a trip,' Narayan Joo said in reply. 'Do not woo them just with words, as our politicians do.'

'Now let's move. Do not equate your friend Malla Khaliq with the politicians of our time,' Malla Khaliq said.

Narayan Joo took leave of Malla Khaliq and stood waiting near the ghat for the shikaarah. The boatman turned the boat and Narayan Joo set out for the Boulevard.

The sun was trailing down to the summits of the Apharwat mountain when Malla Khaliq, after having served lunch to Raja

Rathinder and his family, was returning to the pantry of the houseboat. He heard the rumbling of a motorboat and turned towards the ghat. Karmakar came out of the motorboat holding a rolled-up carpet in his hands. He asked the boatman to wait and entered the houseboat Gulshan.

Qadir was eating lunch at the time. He left his meal, washed his hands, and quickly entered Gulshan. Even in his hurry, he saw his father who had turned back to see who had come. Malla Khaliq had discerned that something not quite right was afoot, otherwise Qadir would have greeted his father when he passed him. He started ambling towards Gulshan to check, but something held him back.

Inside the houseboat, Jane and Karmakar were arguing. Karmakar had got her the bag of notes, but he was not ready to hand it over to her unless she cleared the outstanding dues. As soon as Qadir came in, he told Karmakar that the police had been seen patrolling the Dal the day before and so they were not able to get the consignment to the houseboat. He convinced Karmakar that it was hidden in a safe place and would be handed over to him the next day. Just then he noticed Noor Mohammad carrying vegetables from the rowboat to the pantry and started speaking to Karmakar in a loud tone, 'Why are you bringing this carpet after so many days? They are not ready to take it back.' Karmakar was puzzled by the switch but kept silent. Qadir stood on his toes to peep through the window, and saw that Noor Mohammad had entered the pantry. Heaving a sigh of relief, he said to Jane, 'Thank God!' Jane said to Karmakar, 'If we keep repeating the same old ruse of this folded carpet, we will be suspected soon.'

Karmakar left the bag as well as the carpet there and went away.

Meanwhile, Noor Mohammad called on Malla Khaliq.

'I heard noises. What is going on?' asked Khaliq.

'The farmers are fighting over something,' said Noor Mohammad. 'They are about to hack each other for a small patch of land.'

'Let them chop each other, I don't care. But using volleys of abuses against each other and creating a ruckus might frighten the tourists away. Come with me – I will resolve this issue once and for all.'

'Abba, it is not the right time to interfere in their dispute. They are possessed by the Devil. They will not pay any attention to us.' But Malla Khaliq was not about to listen.

'All right, you stay back near your mother!' he said sarcastically, and stepped into the rowboat. Noor Mohammad quietly followed him.

In the back portion of the Dal, there was a swamp, and over fifty people were gathered there. The two warring sides had raised a pandemonium. As soon as Malla Khaliq's boat approached the swamp, Ghana Batukh saw him. He went running to Swana Hakh. Swana Hakh, being unable to settle the dispute, had raised his spade and was about to hit Muji Dar. 'Haji Sahib is coming here. Let us entreat him to deliver justice.' Ghana Batukh was the only brother of Swana Hakh's wife. Swana Hakh was fuming with rage. He flung his spade away and started shouting. 'This high-handedness will not be allowed here, everyone follows the principle of "might is right"! I will request a full bench of the five elders. Swana Hakh is a slumbering dragon. Never shall this brother-in-law come to know how I can reduce him to trash along with this stolen patch of land!' Muji Dar was not one to get scared. All of a sudden he pounced over him. Had the others not intervened, something untoward was sure to have happened.

Meanwhile Malla Khaliq and Noor Mohammad had anchored their boat to the bank and were already on the swamp. Malla Khaliq roared, 'Aren't you ashamed of what you are doing? You fight like pimps and call each other names?'

All were struck dumb, except Swana Hakh who was still panting in anger. In one jump he came near Malla Khaliq and said to him, 'But tell me, Haji Sahib, when one is driven to committing suicide, what else can one do?'

Muji Dar also could not contain himself and said, 'Hey, listen, Swana Hakh! Your shouting shall not avail you anything. Haji Sahib knows all. He is not a stranger here.' Swana Hakh also started to swing his arms, but Malla Khaliq stopped him. 'What has come over you? What is the issue?' This very inquiry stirred a fresh tumult. This agitated Noor Mohammad who was watching the scene from a distance. He managed to silence them when he said, 'There are so many tourists in the nearby houseboats. What will they think of you? Please sit down and explain the problem to Haji Sahib so that he can come up with a solution.'

'Yes, he is right. Haji Sahib is not going to be partial in his judgement,' someone in the crowd said loudly.

Malla Khaliq requested them all to sit down peacefully. The two factions sat facing each other and Malla Khaliq and a couple of elders sat at the centre. 'Now tell us what happened, but calmly, please,' he said.

Before Muji Dar could utter a word, Swana Hakh began to shout. 'Every night this Muji Dar, along with his kith and kin, comes and slots logs and poles into the bottom of the lake to demarcate their territory and usurp long stretches of water from my possession.'

Muji Dar yelled out to clarify his position, 'Hear oh my God, hear! What false allegations! The truth is that you have already occupied my stretches of lotus-growing mires by dropping boats full of clay into them.'

'What lotus-growing mires? You yourself filled the waters around your shanty with truckloads of debris and clay and raised so much of land.'

'But the waters do not belong to you. It was my own area and I did whatever I wanted to do with it.'

'Yes, it was your father who bequeathed this area to you on paper!'

'Mind your tongue! If you name my father here again, I will mend your ugly mouth with my shoe!'

Malla Khaliq could no longer be a silent listener. 'Will you keep quiet or shall I call the police to silence you? First tell me why all of you are after occupying the waters of the lake. If all of you continue filling it up, the lake will turn into a network of sewers. And if this Dal dies, how are we going to live?'

An elderly person sitting beside Malla Khaliq said, 'But they are never bothered about that. They will lust after land even if all the water disappears.'

Ghana Batukh shouted this elderly person down saying, 'You, Rahim Wangnu! You cannot be a judge in this dispute. It hardly concerns you.'

Malla Khaliq said loudly to all, 'These allegations and counter-allegations will lead us nowhere. Whatever both sides are doing is illegal. However, there is a solution. Let's ask the land surveyor – he will check the maps.'

This irked Muji Dar, who stood up and said, 'What can the patvari do? His hunger for bribes is insatiable. His only job is to transfer one person's land to the other who feeds him more.'

Malla Khaliq stood up. 'When the two parties are unwilling to settle the dispute peacefully, legal action becomes inevitable.'

'Haji Sahib, do not threaten us. Did you not encroach upon and beautify the land that was around your boats?' Muji Dar shouted at Malla Khaliq.

Noor Mohammad came to his father's defence. 'But we used the land that was already there. Did we narrow down this lake with fillings?'

Noor Mohammad's allegation caused a fresh uproar. Malla Khaliq tried once again to make them understand how their greed was turning their paradise into hell by slow poisoning. But they were so blinded by greed that such calamities did not bother them.

Seeing that they were adamant to knock each other down, Noor Mohammad held Malla Khaliq's arm and said, 'Abba, let's move away. They won't understand.'

This comment irritated Muji Dar's son. 'Oh yes, Noor Mohammad, how can we understand, for we all are asses here, aren't we? Wisdom is your monopoly.'

Malla Khaliq could not control his anger and said, 'If only you had an iota of wisdom, you would not be committing such a blunder. If you people on both sides do not stop ransacking this Dal Lake, I will certainly sue you in the court of law.'

'No more of this browbeating! You may go to whichever court you please. We also know how to expose the misdeeds of others.'

Noor Mohammad led Malla Khaliq to the shikaarah. 'Idiots! Incorrigible brutes! Beggars! Always mooching for alms!' Uttering these words, Malla Khaliq stepped into the boat.

Swana Hakh said to his folks, quite loudly, so that Malla Khaliq could hear, 'I thought he had come to settle our dispute, but he opened up his own can of worms here.' Then he said to his brother-in-law, 'Ghana Sahib, get up and collect all those shafts they have pulled out.'

Muji Dar pounced upon him, saying, 'Listen, if you even as much as touch the shafts, I shall chop your hand off!'

Malla Khaliq felt as if he had venom in his mouth. He said to Noor Mohammad, 'You turn the boat towards the Boulevard. I will report them at the police station.'

Noor Mohammad tried to assuage his father's anger. 'Abba, how many reports can we file against such dishonest people? There is not one family that is not busy filling up the Dal … to not only create swamps, but also to raise solid land. When the government is not able to do anything, what can you do? Only God can help.'

Malla Khaliq had gone from office to office many times with the request that something be done to save the Dal, but the officials could not do anything for they had the backing of the politicians. They were all interested in extracting as much as they could out of this illegal activity. He looked round, heaved a cold sigh and said to Noor Mohammad, 'If we don't do anything about it, their filling will reach our isle. No, I think I must get them a stay order from the court.'

When Razaq went to serve afternoon tea to Raja Rathinder Singh, the latter asked him about the commotion in the neighbourhood. But Razaq had no information. Meanwhile, Malla Khaliq, now pacified, walked in, and Raja Rathinder Singh asked him, 'What can

I tell you, Raja Sahib? These fools, I mean the vegetable growers, have made our life miserable. They have turned on each other in their greed for the waters of the Dal. These brutes will certainly make the lake dry up very soon.'

Raja Rathinder remembered the Dal Lake of old when its crystal-clear waters stretched from Gagribal up to the hills in the north. He was pained to see how ignorant and greedy people had destroyed its natural charm by growing thickets of trees on swamps, and it appeared as if the lake had turned upside down. The dense habitation, stretched far and wide on these ugly marshes, looked like a vast jigsaw puzzle. The conglomeration of ugly huts, houses and shanties seemed to be waiting to expand and cover the remaining lake. Raja Rathinder Singh had witnessed the full glory of this lake as a child. It was after over thirty years that he was here again. He had read many reports about the lake dying, but his eyes could hardly believe that it was being devastated to this extent. Even God could not restore its lost beauty.

Raja Rathinder, like Malla Khaliq, was absorbed in these thoughts. It was Razaq who diverted his attention by offering him a cup of tea. He took the cup and casting a melancholic look at Malla Khaliq said, 'Haji Sahib, why are you standing? Please take a seat.' Malla Khaliq, wont to follow old values, hesitated to sit down in Raja Rathinder's presence. But on his insistence, he finally sat on the sofa. Raja Rathinder asked Razaq to make a cup of tea for him, too.

Razaq left and Raja Rathinder told Malla Khaliq that he grieved more than him when he was on the deck of the houseboat that morning, watching over the Dal Lake. 'Is the government doing nothing about saving the Dal? Are they unable to understand that if the famous lake dies, nothing of its natural beauty shall remain?'

Malla Khaliq knew that Raja Rathinder was a compassionate friend of Kashmir and the Dal Lake, and thus he unburdened his heart but he also knew that this tourist was there only to enjoy Kashmir for a few days and would then go back to America where he lived after having lost his royal status in India. Still, he hoped that God might send some angel in the form of a human being, who would save and restore this paradise on earth. Raja Rathinder told him that he had met the Minister of Tourism in America and shown him a report, published in an issue of the *American Travel* about the plight of the Dal Lake. The minister had said that the government had prepared a comprehensive programme for saving the Dal Lake. 'But five years have elapsed since then, and the Dal is still languishing in utter neglect,' Raja Rathinder said.

Malla Khaliq lost his temper and said, 'All this is idle talk. It's just a ruse to extract billions of rupees from the centre which reaches the pockets of very few.'

Raja Rathinder's wife and his grandchildren came into the drawing room. Their grandson was holding his grandmother's hand tightly. Freeing her hand, she said, 'Yes, I will definitely tell him.' Malla Khaliq asked her what the child wanted. 'The children are growing impatient to go on a trip of the lake with you.' Malla Khaliq promised them that he would certainly take them the next morning and said, 'I will also take you to the place where those people from our folklore got punished and changed into stone for cheating. I shall also show you the stretches that grew lotus flowers. You will see how the water strewn on the broad leaves gets divided into pearl-like droplets.' Having assured the children, Malla Khaliq took his leave of Raja Rathinder.

Just then, Noor Mohammad came. 'It is Haji Ramzan's wife again, with a proposal for Parveen. Amma is waiting for you.'

On hearing this, Malla Khaliq blankly stared at his son's face. Noor Mohammad nudged him. 'Are you well, Abba?'

'Oh yes!' said Malla Khaliq as if awakened from a dream. 'I was just thinking of our little Parveen, who until yesterday did not know how to tie her hair, being considered marriageable.'

Noor Mohammad burst into laughter. 'I don't know what you will decide. But if you are not willing, I will tell this wife of Haji Ramzan's that our Parveen is not yet—'

'No. That is not the issue. Haji Ramzan's family is very good and they are quite well off. Let's go and see which son she has brought the proposal for.'

The sun rose gloriously behind the lofty cliffs of the Zabarwan mountains, and spread its resplendence across the valley of the rishis. The hillock of Hari Parbat, far behind the lake, emerged from the mist. With this, the aarti to welcome the morning, coupled with prayers from numerous mosques and shrines resounded in the air, making the morning peaceful. Malla Khaliq had reached Makhdoom Sahib's shrine on the summit of Hari Parbat even before dawn. He had had a sleepless night thinking how time flew so fast that his dear daughter, whom he had raised with great affection, would be separated from him after her marriage. Haji Ramzan's wife had made Aziz Dyad accept the proposal. He knew well that Aziz Dyad was more experienced than him in such matters. Yet he could not ward off the fears from his mind and that made him go to the shrine early in the morning.

After the prayers, Malla Khaliq ran his hands down his face, and then stepped out towards the portico. There he hastily put on his shoes and took out the pocket watch which his father had bequeathed to him. He climbed down the stairs to the bottom of the hill and turned towards the Chakreshwari Asthapan which stood loftily at a higher summit of the same hill. The last sounds of the aarti had subsided. When Malla Khaliq reached the bottom of the stairs to the deity's asthapan, he heard someone saying to him, '*As-salaam-alaikum … jinaab … Haji Sahib!*'

It was none other than his friend Narayan Joo who was breathing heavily after having climbed down the stairs of the shrine. Malla Khaliq looked upwards and said, 'Wow! What timing! This is one of the most important qualities lacking in the youth of today; they are not punctual.'

Narayan Joo embraced his friend and said, 'Old is gold, my brother.'

Malla Khaliq was prompt in agreeing. He said, 'Yes. You deserve a kiss on your forehead, my dear friend.'

Narayan Joo bowed his head, saying, 'And who is going to say no to you?'

'My boss seems to be jubilant. I think you received some good news last night,' said Narayan Joo.

The two friends sat in the shade of a tree.

'There is a marriage proposal for Parveen.'

'Congratulations! Who is the lucky family?'

'Haji Ramzan. The proprietor of the Neelofer Group of Houseboats and a big carpet dealer.'

'Yes, I know him. Has he sent the proposal?'

'His youngest son is yet to be married. His name is Parvez, I think.'

'Yes, Parvez. He has his business in Delhi. It wouldn't be wise to lose this opportunity. He is a very gentle and honest young man.'

'I was intending to seek your opinion on this matter. It is my good luck that you met me here.'

'You are really fortunate that the proposal came from the boy's side.'

'I think so too.'

'There is no scope for thinking further in this regard. People get exhausted seeking good boys for their daughters.'

'But that is truer about our Hindu brothers because all good young men have fled the valley.'

'What else could they do? They prefer to live in the scorching heat of other parts of the country in order to make a living. Now leave this digression. I advise you not to delay in this matter. You go home and send them your consent.'

The good news had rejuvenated Malla Khaliq after yesterday's dismal fight in their neighbourhood. He narrated the incident to Narayan Joo. The very thought of that nasty event made his blood boil. 'You can imagine my position, Narayan Joo. Those guys had the cheek to confront me. They hurled all sorts of abuses at me. You wait and watch. If they are not stopped, they will soon encroach upon the lake till my houseboats.'

After reflecting for a moment, Narayan Joo said, 'It is not an issue to worry about. I shall get them a stay order from the court in just one visit. This is a belligerent act against the law.'

The spot where the two friends sat gave them a panoramic view of the whole Baharara Lake and a major part of the Dal Lake. Malla Khaliq was absorbed in that view, heart, mind and soul.

'Do you see how the lake of our childhood has shrunk?'

Narayan Joo cast a glance at his face and said, 'If you do not get annoyed by what I am to say, I will tell you that this is not a new thing. It has been going on for so many years. Why were you silent when it all started? Now when you feel that you are suffering from the malady, you get irked.'

'What could we do? We were engaged in the turmoil, and those selfish people continued bribing the authorities so that their plunder of the Dal remained unhampered.'

'They are going to do the same again, mind it.'

Malla Khaliq burst out. 'This is not the time to lecture as our politicians do. The time demands immediate action to stop this plunder forthwith.'

But Narayan Joo, unmoved by Malla Khaliq's reaction, said with a smile, 'Are you out of control again? Let us move now. I was planning to see you at your home. We have to finalize the return tickets of Rathinder Singh. We shall also see my advocate.'

Saying this, Narayan Joo stood up and paid his respects to the Devi. Malla Khaliq bowed as did his friend. Then the two left for home through Kathi Darvaza, the big gate in the rampart built by the Mughal emperor Akbar.

There on the Dal, Malla Khaliq's family was already engaged in the routine morning chores. His second son Ghulam Ahmed had returned from the mosque and was greedily puffing the hookah in his room. His wife heated up his salt tea again in the pot. While pouring the hot tea in the cup, she teased her husband saying, 'The plane from Delhi arrives at one o'clock; why are you flying in the air much before that? You are reducing even the inner lining of the chilam to ashes.'

Ghulam Ahmed pushed the pipe of the hookah to one side and said, 'You should have been working for the CID. I fail to understand why you continue to have a vigil on me from dawn to dusk in these times of freedom.' Saying this, he turned the pipe of the hookah towards himself again, but Zoon snatched it away from his lips and said, 'You have this omelette first. I have warmed it up twice. Then I shall fill the chilam with fresh tobacco for you.'

'You know I'm not used to smoking early in the morning. It is your persistent poking that makes my mouth bitter, and then I prefer to fill my lungs with soot.'

'If that is the case, I will try not to be an impediment in your ways. Do whatever you deem good for yourself. I am least bothered.'

Ghulam Ahmed was a shrewd person. He had the knack of making people turn in his favour even if he had to hold their feet. He moved close to Zoon. 'Look, my darling. Try to understand that I have many complex issues to attend to, and you are diverting my attention. You ask me to give you an account of every moment of my life … where I had gone and what I did.'

'If I do not stay alert, you may go out of my control and I, like poor Zeb, will end up wailing over my destiny.'

Ghulam Ahmed laughed boisterously, but Zoon did not stop there. 'I am serious. These hippies are not to be trusted. They start feeling hot as soon as they find a man.'

Ghulam Ahmed guffawed even more loudly, but Zoon continued, 'Do you think I am so stupid that I cannot understand why this Mem reached here at the advent of spring? She has taken this houseboat on rent along with Qadir!'

'Now for God's sake, stop this nonsense. You have scissors for a tongue in your mouth! You never think before you speak.'

'All right, you please have your meal and leave. Tourists might be waiting for you.' Saying this, she went away.

Malla Khaliq and Narayan Joo had left Kathi Darvaza and were walking towards Rainawari to reach the houseboats. But as soon as they neared the gurudwara outside the gate, they noticed several police jeeps and police personnel standing there. Narayan Joo said, 'Oh no, I think there is some disturbance again somewhere. Let us walk towards our right and pass through Malakhah.'

Malla Khaliq had the same apprehension, but when he saw the number on the deputy inspector's jeep and the flag over it, he said. 'No, let us go straight; it is DIG Prahlad Singh's jeep. He might have come to visit the gurudwara and this police contingent has come with him.'

Narayan Joo also observed the flag over the jeep and felt confident. Holding each other's hands, the two friends walked towards the gurudwara. They moved cautiously as they thought Prahlad Singh was prostrating before the Granth Sahib. But when they reached near the gurudwara, Prahlad Singh came out in his full uniform. Seeing Malla Khaliq and Narayan Joo, he approached them for greetings. 'Hello, Haji Sahib, all well? How is your business running?' Then turning to Narayan Joo, he said, 'And you Pandit Sahib?'

'It is all because of your good wishes that this year's season has a good start,' said Malla Khaliq. 'Let us hope that the conditions remain stable and peace be restored.'

'Yes, with the grace of Wahi Guru, there will be further improvement in the conditions here.' Looking all around, Prahlad Singh said, 'What solace this place has to offer!'

It was for seeking solace that Malla Khaliq and Narayan Joo visited this place so early in the morning. 'It is the power of this sacred land that gives spiritual solace. The whole of Kashmir is like that, it is the valley of the rishis after all,' said Narayan Joo, in consonance with Prahlad Singh.

While they talked, a DSP and two inspectors came hastily towards the DIG. After they saluted him, Prahlad Singh inquired, 'Any success? Could you nab any of them?' Bowing his head, the DSP said, 'Sir, all of them escaped during the night.'

'Damn it! I want them all. All those hippies as well as their supporters – I want them. Some of our officers are certainly in league with these drug smugglers. Do you understand? If it were not so, how could they know when we were going to raid them?'

Malla Khaliq and Narayan Joo were listening very intently.

Before he sat in his jeep, Prahlad Singh said to Malla Khaliq, 'Come in, Haji Sahib. I will drop you to your residence.'

'No, sir. Narayan Joo's vehicle is waiting for us.'

Prahlad Singh left in his jeep. The DSP and his contingent also followed him in their jeep.

'Could you make out what they were talking about?' Narayan Joo said to Malla Khaliq.

'Yes, I did. A strange fear is gripping my mind. To be absolutely honest with you, I am on pinpricks because of Qadir.'

'But he is not indulging in drug smuggling. You are housing baseless forebodings in your mind that will just upset you. Come on. Let us move faster, it will be late otherwise.'

In the houseboat, Qadir and Jane were very agitated. They had concealed the consignment in the deserted hut at the rear end of the Dal Lake. Extremely nervous, Jane insisted that Qadir take the hidden consignment to the hideaway of the hippies. She told him that if they did not do so, that aged hippie was sure to reach there. Qadir tried to assuage Jane's fears. 'We will take a secret route to the ruined hut.' Having pacified Jane, he went to his own room. He had to pass Ghulam Ahmed's room, and as he did, he could hear Zoon's laughter. He halted to eavesdrop so he could know whether she told her husband something about him. This thorn of suspicion was constantly pricking him since that dreadful night when Zeb had lamented on her bad luck. After halting a little, he sneaked towards his room.

Zoon stopped laughing and told her husband, 'Come on, you too might be running after other women and here you try to make me trust your saying that you never hide anything from me.'

Ghulam Ahmed said to cajole her, 'Look, I swear by God that I reveal every secret to you.'

'Then tell me where you are planning to go today, and do not fib.'

Ghulam Ahmed knew he had run out of excuses. He said, 'I'm not going to the airport, I am in fact going to Pattan. There is a large apple orchard available to me on contract. In case I succeed in this deal, we will be relieved of this penury. But, please do not divulge this information to anyone, not even Abba. He is already irked over last year's contract.'

'All right, you are free to do whatever you deem feasible. But please do not ask me to seek money from my father.'

Holding her chin in his fingers, Ghulam Ahmed turned her face towards him and said, 'You always say so, but later on you do what I request you. You know I do not need his money for myself alone. I am not striving for any selfish ends. And this time, I do not need a huge amount.' In order to reassure Zoon, he told her that a broker in the apple trade would help him out financially. All this persuasion could not convince Zoon, but Ghulam Ahmed was stubborn. After a short pause, he said to Zoon, 'You know, there are people who run several jobs simultaneously. That is the only secret of their being millionaires. I request you to plead my case to your father, just for once, and then see how I make you rich.' He bent forward to hug her.

'Do not pester me. Leave my hand! Oh God! See, Abba is coming this way.'

Ghulam Ahmed let her go. On reaching the inner room, Zoon giggled and said, 'Abba is yet to return from Makhdoom Sahib's shrine.' Ghulam Ahmed felt assured that she would certainly plead his case to her father.

Reclining on an armchair on the deck of the houseboat, Rani Ranthambore was engrossed in a book. She heard some conversation going on out on the isle below. She could also hear the chatter of the children. She stood up and looking down saw Narayan Joo welcoming another tourist. He was a tall and handsome young man. His wife seemed to be in her early thirties. He had two sons, one Narpaul's age and the other one younger than him. Narayan Joo shook hands with them and said, 'All right, Bhonsley Sahib, I shall now go and see Raja Sahib. You are now in the safe hands of Haji Sahib.'

'Say that we are in safe custody,' said Bhonsley, with a smile at Malla Khaliq.

Placing his right hand on his chest, Malla Khaliq bowed his head and said, 'Yes, on my head and in my eyes!' He escorted the family to his houseboat Gulfam, asking Razaq to carry their baggage.

Rani Ranthambore returned to her armchair and thought, so this is Sudesh Bhonsley, the narcotic controller of Bombay whom Malla Khaliq had been talking about.

Narpaul came walking with loud steps up the wooden stairs of the houseboat. He held his grandmother's hand. 'Please ask Haji Sahib to take us on a trip.' He compelled her to leave her chair and climb down the stairs. In the drawing room, Narayan Joo was standing and talking to Rathinder Singh. Rathinder was telling him that he had to stay in Delhi for about two weeks and there would be no trouble getting a connecting flight. Narayan Joo collected the tickets. While he was checking the tickets, the rani entered with her grandson. With his hands folded, Narayan Joo greeted to the rani and sought leave of Raja Rathinder Singh who accompanied him to the exit. 'Please keep sitting – this embarrasses me,' said Narayan Joo. He came down and stepped into the trip-boat waiting for him.

Malla Khaliq asked him, 'So you are leaving—?'

'Yes. I have to go to the airport again.'

The trip-boat was leaving and Narayan Joo said to Malla Khaliq, rather loudly, 'Be careful, all right?'

'Yes, I have to be,' said Malla Khaliq in reply.

In the meantime, Narpaul had brought his grandmother to the doorstep. 'Look, my child, there is your Haji Uncle. Why don't you just call him?' Then turning to Malla Khaliq, Rani Ranthambore said, 'Haji Sahib, you have pampered him. Haji Uncle's name is always on the tip of his tongue.'

Malla Khaliq laid a compassionate hand on the boy's head and said, 'I did not know that I had grown so popular.'

Narpaul released his grandma's hand and held Malla Khaliq's hand instead. 'Haji Uncle, I can't wait any longer. You take out the little boat now and take us for a boat trip.'

Malla Khaliq somehow succeeded in convincing the child that he would surely take them on a trip after lunch.

Raja Rathinder was enjoying watching their argument. Narpaul ran off to convey this good news to his sister. Raja Rathinder congratulated Malla Khaliq on his third houseboat being also occupied now. 'It is all because of your prayers, and God's grace,' Malla Khaliq said and then told Raja Rathinder that Sudesh Bhonsley was a close friend of Narayan Joo's son and an upright officer. He further told him that he was to stay there just for a week.

'I will be glad to meet Mr Bhonsley.'

'But sir, they have already scheduled a trip to Gulmarg tomorrow and Pahalgam the day after.'

'Then it will not be possible to see him because I am leaving for Delhi the day after tomorrow.'

'Sir, Mr Bhonsley also desires to see you, and has already arranged for a joint dinner.'

'That will be great.'

Qadir had called for his boatman and had asked him to get his trip-boat there in the afternoon. Jane and Qadir knew that everyone would have a snooze after lunch and it would be easy for them to go to the ruined hut to retrieve their hidden consignment and take it to the hippies.

When there was complete silence, Qadir calmly came out of his room, closed the door quietly behind him, and moved to his houseboat by the rear side of the isle. Holding Bilal to her chest, Zeb was fast asleep in the room.

Razaq too was in his shed. He was not accustomed to sleeping during the daytime as he used his leisure time to study. He had left school when he was in the tenth standard, but wanted to complete his matriculation, continue with his studies and become an executive officer. Through the crevices of his shed, he noticed a shadow moving. Book in hand, he stood up and peeped through a crevice. Qadir was moving like a thief towards the rear prow of the houseboat. Had it been someone other than Qadir, he would have certainly gone out and stopped him. But it was Qadir and he was scared of him. Qadir managed to get Jane out from the hind window of the pantry. The boatman was waiting there. Both sat in the boat. He saw Jane bearing a brown bag. The boatman pushed the side of the houseboat with his oar and the boat glided in the water like a dart. Razaq continued watching them till they were out of sight. Then he returned to his place and started reading the book again. The words on the page, however, seemed to be running after each other. He placed the book aside and lay down to relax. He tried to make out why they had left the scene like thieves.

When it was four o'clock, Narpaul woke his sister up. The two hastily readied themselves and went to their grandparents' room. After seeking their permission, the two kids jumped from the prow of the houseboat to the isle. 'You just stay here,' said Narpaul. 'I will go get Haji Uncle.'

'I am already here!' Malla Khaliq called out.

'Oh Haji Uncle, you're great!' Narpaul ran towards him.

Malla Khaliq was accompanied by Qadir's son Bilal. The raja's granddaughter, Maya, went and held his hand in friendship. 'Let's take him along.'

'Sure!' said Malla Khaliq. He took Bilal in his arms and started going to the ghat. 'Come on. Let's go.' Malla Khaliq was not quite comfortable in Hindi or Urdu. Having had a regular association with European tourists right from his childhood, he had a workable knowledge of written and spoken English. He could use this little knowledge of the language for managing his business. He made the three children sit in the boat and rowed it towards Gagribal. Sitting at the deck of the houseboat, Rani Ranthambore fondly watched her grandchildren. The two children, with their hands raised, waved to her till she was out of their sight.

The boat passed behind the houseboats and reached the point of the rear Dal, where the vegetable growers had had an altercation with Malla Khaliq a few days ago. There was a mob at that place again. All of them were busy unloading clay from their boats and were in such haste filling the lake as if their life depended on it. Malla Khaliq slowed his boat and when Rahim Wangun saw him, he greeted him, '*As-salaam-alaikum*, Haji Sahib! You got angry with us for nothing.'

'You were taking the recourse of calling a full punchaath! Did you resolve your dispute?'

'Now please forget about the punchaath and the court. We finally reached an agreement that we shall fill up this available stretch of the lake, make it a piece of land and then distribute the land among ourselves.'

On hearing this, Malla Khaliq was aflame with rage. He thrust his oar into the water and said to them, 'Yes, go on filling up the womb of our mother with clay. Go on and then watch how she shall become sterile, and we all shall die of hunger.'

Ghana Batukh gave him a sarcastic reply. 'What fears you harbour in your brain, Haji Sahib! This lake can last for at least ten generations, I am sure. Your apprehension is baseless!' All of them burst into laughter. 'Now move your hands faster,' he said to his men.

Speeding up his rowing, Malla Khaliq left the spot, but told Ghana Batukh, 'Go on filling up. A stay order from the court will put an end to your nefarious activities.'

Malla Khaliq took out his wrath on the waters of the Dal by striking his oar harder. The children in the boat were a little frightened. He looked towards them, produced a smile on his face, and said, 'Now we are about to enter the larger lake.' He tried to divert their attention from those rude vegetable growers to the plentiful flowers that had bloomed all around the mansion on the

Kotarkhana isle. Narpaul asked Malla Khaliq, 'Are these guys going to fill up the whole of this lake?'

Malla Khaliq looked around and with a deep sigh said to him, 'Yes, my son. It seems so.' Maya was fascinated by the ripples in the lake. She saw how tiny fish frolicked through the weeds. Their bodies shimmered in the rays of the sun. All this seemed to be a dream to her. She turned to her brother when he posed another question to Malla Khaliq: 'Then shall this lake grow dry?' Without giving him a reply, Malla Khaliq turned his head away. Maya trembled with fear and said, 'Then all the little fish living in its waters will die!' On hearing these innocent words from the little girl, Malla Khaliq's eyes watered.

Malla Khaliq's boat was now passing through the larger Dal. Narpaul was keenly watching the bottom of the lake. After a while, he raised his head and asked Malla Khaliq, 'Haji Uncle, is this lake yours?'

Malla Khaliq was back in the world of the little children. 'Of course!'

In the meantime, the boy was lost in his own world. He had learnt from his grandfather that there were several springs in the bottom of the lake which always kept it replete with water. He had also learnt from him that there were numerous springs in Kashmir, and many fairy tales were associated with each of these springs. Narpaul was curious and asked him, 'Who is the owner of the springs that are in the bottom of the Dal?'

'The springs too are mine!' said Malla Khaliq.

'And the fairies which live in those springs?'

'They belong to you.'

'No, not all of them are mine. Only the princess of those fairies belongs to me.'

Malla Khaliq burst into laughter. The feuds of the vegetable growers, the sickness of the Dal, the loan from the bank, Qadir's recklessness – all these worries vanished from his mind. He moved his hand softly over Bilal's golden hair as he lay quietly in his lap. He looked up at the sky. It seemed as if the sun was playing hide-

and-seek in the trailing clouds. He was thankful to God that man's hands could not reach the sky or it too would have been ravaged.

Maya was engrossed in the waning and waxing of the reflection of the Zabarwan mountains in the waters of the lake. Narpaul, however, was expecting some sudden miracle to happen. He was rather bored with water all around him. Malla Khaliq had promised he would show them the spot where the milkman and the rush-mat maker lay. When he felt they had been on the lake for a long time, he said to Malla Khaliq, 'We have traversed so much of the lake, but the milkman and the rush-mat maker are nowhere to be seen.'

Malla Khaliq had in fact forgotten his promise. 'Sorry,' he said and turned the boat round.

Qadir knew that the police had intensified the campaign against the drug smugglers and hashish suppliers. He did not go directly to the deserted hut where the consignment of drugs was hidden. He took a long diversion by going to Navapore through the route of Rainawari. For the first time, Jane was feeling quite jittery. On reaching the destination, Qadir helped her out of the boat.

In the meantime, Malla Khaliq turned his boat into the very same swamp to show the kids the corner where the milkman and the rush-mat maker had changed into stone. While entering the ruined hut, Qadir noticed the distant boat moving closer. He pushed Jane towards the ruined hut. Jane, completely flabbergasted, asked Qadir, 'What happened?' But Qadir stood dumb, the only thing he could utter was 'Haji Sahib!' and with this, he pointed towards the boat that was advancing towards the swamp.

Narpaul, who was looking at the nests of birds in the thick rushes and bushes, suddenly exclaimed, 'Haji Uncle, Haji Uncle! Look there. The Mem living in your houseboat is there!'

Malla Khaliq could not discern anything except a vague figure that disappeared within a second into the ruined hut. All the purlieus of the Dal were enveloped in silence, and the sun was about to set. The din of croaking frogs gradually increased. Narpaul and Maya shrank in fear. Malla Khaliq started rowing faster, but the children said, 'No, Uncle, no. We won't go there. It looks like a place haunted by ghosts.' Malla Khaliq stopped rowing ahead.

Qadir was trembling with fear. He had hidden his boat on the other side of the swamp. There was no chance of coming out of the hut to go to the boat. The door of the ruined hut was distinctly visible from the spot where Malla Khaliq had stopped his boat. Jane had fished her binoculars out of her bag, and through a crevice, kept a watch on Malla Khaliq. Qadir came panting near her, snatched the binoculars from her hands and looked out. He saw Malla Khaliq in the stationary boat, looking towards the swamp.

On the boat, meanwhile, Narpaul crept silently near Malla Khaliq, and said, 'Haji Uncle, why don't you move the boat? We are very scared.' Maya started sobbing.

Malla Khaliq consoled the children and started rowing in the watercourse that was to his left.

When Qadir noticed his father's boat moving in the opposite direction, he and Jane ran and retrieved their precious drugs and put them into a large bag. As soon as they sat in the boat, a boat loaded with vegetables appeared amidst the thicket of rushes. The vegetable vendor looked at the Mem and greeted her loudly. Qadir was flummoxed when the boatman asked him, 'What made you come this way?' He could hardly maintain his composure and said in reply, 'I don't know what this brainless Mem found so charming in this deserted place that she wants to take photos of.'

Jane understood the word 'photo' and at once revealed her camera and said to the vegetable vendor, 'Just wait, man!'

Qadir said to the vegetable vendor, 'She requests you to stay in the same posture so that she may take your photo.'

This annoyed the vendor a little and he said, 'Lo, I know that much English.' Then he stared at Jane and in order to prove that he understood English, said to Qadir, 'Wait.' He combed his dishevelled hair and looked at her. 'Yes – now.'

When Jane focused her camera at him, the vegetable vendor stopped her again and said, 'How much will you pay me for the photo?'

Qadir angrily said to him, 'Listen, she is not here for shooting any film. I don't know what charm she sees in your face anyway.'

Jane wanted to get rid of the boring rascal and having clicked a photograph, she said to Qadir, 'Let's go!'

But the vegetable vendor moved his boat nearer, 'First my bakhshish! Me Ramzana understand! Film people give me bakhshish then leave.'

Jane took out a fifty-rupee note from her pocket and handed it over to Qadir. 'Give it to him.' Qadir stretched out his hand and gave it to the vegetable vendor. He tried to bargain, but Qadir lost his temper. He raised his hand to slap him. 'Will you move or should I bury you here along with your boat?'

'I'm leaving now! Don't lose your temper!' the boatman said and rowed his boat away. He knew that this son of Malla Khaliq was very hot-headed. But while leaving, he looked back saying, 'Memsahib, send me a copy of the photograph to his address.'

Qadir said in return, 'She will surely send you a copy of the photo, and that too in a frame.'

Their boatman asked Qadir, 'Which way should I row now?'

'First you go straight to Gagribal, and then to the houseboat Gulshan.'

Jane understood Qadir's plan, but after a while told him that George might be waiting for them. But Qadir convinced her that it would be better for them to reach home before it was dark. It was possible that Malla Khaliq had noticed them there, or he might suspect them. If they were too late, he would certainly make a thorough inquiry.

The sun was about to set. The horizon over the westerly Apharwat mountain revealed a strange colour. Thick dark clouds were trailing down into the depths. The margins of these clouds looked thin at several places and the setting sun produced a crimson hue that shone bright through those rents in the clouds. While Malla Khaliq was watching the sky, Aziz Dyad came near him and said, 'What are you gazing at in the sky? Come in and have your tea.'

'I don't know what God has apportioned to us,' said Malla Khaliq, turning his tearful eyes to her. 'Do you see how blood red the sun looks? And then those dark clouds!'

Aziz Dyad cast a glance at the sky and said to her husband, 'Clouds of this kind are not new to us. I fail to understand what ails you. You start even when a cat goes past you. Now leave these forebodings, and come in. I have yet to think of dinner.' Saying this, she walked towards the pantry and Malla Khaliq followed her.

Bhonsley had finished getting ready and was now waiting for his wife. Meanwhile his elder son came running into the room, clasped his hand and said, 'Daddy, Daddy, come out and see the sky!'

Bhonsley asked him to free his hand so that he could take his camera from the table. His wife and his other son were already standing on the prow of the houseboat. The moment he had a glimpse of the sky, he could not stop uttering, 'Amazing!' He focused his camera and started taking photographs. He said to his wife and children, 'See? This is Kashmir!'

The children stretched out their hands for the camera so that they could also take some photographs. 'First let me take some pictures of you and your mother, and then you can use the camera,' Bhonsley said to them. He made his wife and two children face the Zabarwan hills, so that he could catch the spectacle of the clouds in the west over the Apharwat summits in the background.

'But the sunlight is on our backs, it will make us look like ghosts,' his wife said. 'Let us have at least one snap like this as a souvenir. I have never seen such clouds in my life.'

'But be quick. Don't you see the light cast on the houseboats and the waters? See how those distant shikaarahs look ... it appears as though they are moving over molten gold.'

Bhonsley was quick in getting the photographs of his choice and then, turning towards the Zabarwan hills, asked his family to stand with Zabarwan as their backdrop.

While using the viewfinder of his camera, he detected Qadir in his boat and Jane coming out of it. He zoomed in on Jane and took a volley of photos of her. His wife was getting bored, and said, 'Enough now.'

Jane stood on the stairs of the houseboat Gulshan, waiting for Qadir. When she saw Bhonsley there, she looked petrified and ran into the houseboat. She was so terrified that she left her brown bag on the steps of the stairs. Qadir followed, picked up the bag and went in.

Bhonsley folded his camera and hurried to his own room in the houseboat. His wife and children continued standing on the prow watching the sunset. Bhonsley hastily took out his diary from the camera bag and turned its pages.

Jane was restless in the room. When Qadir stepped in, he rebuked her for being so careless and leaving the bag on the stairs. 'Imagine what would have happened if Razaq or Abba found the bag there?'

'But if I stayed there for one more second, Mr Bhonsley would have certainly seen me.'

'Is he a brute who will devour you?' asked Qadir, fuming.

'This Bhonsley is the same narcotic controller whom I wanted to avoid in Bombay and he is the reason I came to Kashmir.'

Qadir felt his heart sink to his ankles.

After rummaging through his diary, Mr Bhonsley called up the local police commissioner and conveyed the information to him.

'Please ensure that Jane does not suspect in any way that you have spotted her there,' the police commissioner said in reply.

'I don't think she has any inkling. But if a police contingent does not arrive immediately, she will disappear without leaving a trace behind. She fell into our snare not once but twice in Bombay, but slipped through our clasp like a slimy fish.'

'Please be sure that she does not escape again. I shall assign the DIG Vigilance to lead the raid,' the police commissioner assured Mr Bhonsley.

Having resolved that he would manage to take Jane out of the houseboat, as he had done before, Qadir came out. But he faced a hitch in the lack of a boat. He took cautious steps alongside Gulfam towards his own room. He came across Ghulam Ahmed near the houseboat. He managed to maintain his composure while speaking with him.

Zeb was assisting Aziz Dyad in the kitchen and Zoon and Mukhta were also there. Having reached his room, he jumped out through the rear window of his room. Near the swamp of rushes, he found a small trip-boat belonging to the neighbouring vegetable vendors. He quietly stepped into the trip-boat, and, rowing it through the backwaters, reached his houseboat.

Razaq, dressed up in his uniform, was in his room combing his hair before a mirror in the wall. Hearing noise from outside, he peeped through the rents of his shed and saw Jane. He saw that Jane was trembling. In one swoop, Qadir got her into the boat and manoeuvred the boat towards the willow copses in the rear end of the Dal. He rowed through the Mar Canal and got Jane to the road at Navapore area some two miles away.

In the houseboat, Bhonsley called up the Kashmir police commissioner who promised to deploy police personnel in plain clothes to apprehend Jane.

A boat race of schoolchildren which had started from Gagribal was vividly visible from the deck of the houseboat. The kids, along with Mrs Bhonsley and Malla Khaliq's son Noor Mohammad, sat there, watching the race.

Bhonsley moved the curtain to one side of the frame and continued staring at Gulshan. 'Now it is not possible for Jane Lockwood to escape,' he said to himself.

Noor Mohammad sighted a shikaarah approaching their houseboats. He recognized the DIG who had visited their houseboats several times to house his official guests. He wondered if his father had woken up from his siesta yet and turning to Mrs Bhonsley said, 'I am heading downstairs, there are some guests coming.'

When he reached downstairs, he was shocked to see the DIG and his people barging forcibly into Qadir's houseboat. The DIG whispered something earnestly to Mr Bhonsley. Malla Khaliq and Ghulam Ahmed were standing there, perplexed. Instead of reciprocating Malla Khaliq's greetings, the DIG said to him, 'You will forgive me, please.' Saying this, he too rushed to Gulshan. Neither Malla Khaliq nor Noor Mohammad could understand what was going on. When Bhonsley saw Malla Khaliq, he said to him, 'Please do not panic, Haji Sahib, all will be well.'

Inside the houseboat, the DIG found that the police personnel in plain clothes were moving about frantically. 'Did you find anything? It looks like she has escaped.'

Bhonsley cursed himself for not having caught Jane in the houseboat and for waiting for the police. Embarrassed, he said, 'Sorry, DIG, it is all my fault.'

'Do not worry, we will find her even if she is hiding in a rat-hole.'

He looked at Malla Khaliq who stood shamefacedly in a corner, rubbing his hands. His family had assembled at the isle. All of them looked pale. The DIG went near Malla Khaliq and expressed his apology. 'Haji Sahib, I hope you will forgive me for having searched your houseboats. The young English woman residing in your houseboat is a big smuggler. She has already kept the police of Delhi and Bombay on tenterhooks.'

But Malla Khaliq could not even raise his eyes to the DIG and said to him, 'Sir, I must beg for your forgiveness for housing such a notorious smuggler in my houseboat. Had I had even a slight inkling of her true intentions, I myself would have dragged her to your office by her hair. '

'There is nothing to be worried about. We will find her even if she is hiding in a crow's nest. But I request you to be a little vigilant in the future.'

When the DIG's boat left, Malla Khaliq returned to his barge. Parveen, who had been watching the scene, dashed to Zeb's room. She saw Razaq standing outside. She stopped and cast a bewildered look at his face. Razaq stood brooding, and though he had an urge to narrate everything that had seen to Parveen, he didn't dare utter a word. On seeing him so dumbfounded, Parveen was irate and said to him, 'Why are you staring at me like a mute deer? Why don't you say something?' But Razaq could not say anything in reply. With an impatient turn, she moved on towards Zeb's room. Zeb was busy ironing Bilal's clothes.

Parveen was jubilant and looked like she had found a treasure chest. The moment she entered the room, she gave Zeb a tight hug. 'Bhabhi, be happy and sacrifice a lamb. You need to make an offering of *tahar* to God.'

'What is the matter?'

'Jane has fled like a snake smoked out of its hole.'

'Who made her flee? Abba?'

'Oh no, not Abba. It was the police.'

'What do you mean? Tell me what happened.'

'She is a smuggler of hashish. She fled before the police could catch her in your houseboat. It was the DIG himself who was leading the raid. But she had already escaped somehow.'

Knowing that Jane had escaped before the police could catch hold of her, Zeb's heart began to sink. She asked Parveen, 'And where is your brother Qadir?'

'Who knows? I did not see him there. We had assembled in the open – Abba, Noor Lala, Ama Sahib, grandma – everyone, but he was not there.'

On hearing this, Zeb sank down. Parveen sat down to console her. 'You need not worry. Qadir Bhaijaan is not such a fool to be seduced by her.'

Zeb could not speak. She had forgotten to switch off the iron and smoke started to billow from it. Seeing the smoke, Parveen stood up and switched off the iron. There was a burnt patch on Bilal's shirt.

In the pantry, everyone was stunned and grief-stricken. Aziz Dyad, Mukhta, Zoon, Noor Mohammad and Malla Khaliq – stood in absolute brooding silence. Malla Khaliq somehow raised his head to look at Aziz Dyad and saw tears surging from her eyes. In a feeble voice, he flung sarcastic words at her. 'Do you see what sort of European visitor this darling of yours has brought to our house? He has tainted my face with shame. He has not left me fit to face anyone outside. The only favour he did me was that I was not handcuffed by the police.'

Observing his father's rage, Noor Mohammad tried to douse the fire and said, 'Abba, didn't you see that even the DIG had come in a civil dress? I don't think anybody will know what they had come for.'

'Whether anybody knows or not, I'm sure your father will spread the word to the whole world with his laments,' Aziz Dyad said.

Malla Khaliq was about to burst forth with more rage, but he was struck dumb when his second son entered in panic to announce that Qadir was also missing. 'I sought him everywhere that he could possibly be. Now it's clear that it was he who led Jane away.'

Malla Khaliq, as if struck by a thunderbolt, said, 'I do not know what sins I have committed that a son of this sort was born to me!'

Ghulam Ahmed stoked the fire. 'I am afraid the police might arrest Qadir along with her.'

Hearing the word police, Aziz Dyad started quivering with fear. 'All of you waste no time in wishing misfortune upon him. No one is serious about even looking for him! Who knows if my poor child is in trouble!'

'He has put us in trouble! He will be enjoying himself with that harlot. He has brought me disgrace and shame. Not me alone but all of you. How can you be blind to that?'

Having reached Navapore, Qadir hired an auto and was moving fast towards Zakoor where the orchards of his friend Gul Beg lay.

Jane was silent in her seat. She crouched as low as she could so that no policeman could see her. The driver of the auto stopped and said to him, 'Where would you like me to go? To Zakoor village? You are already there.'

Hearing the driver, Qadir started as if he had been awakened from a deep sleep. 'Yes, do you see that signboard there?' he said. 'You stop there.'

'Why didn't you just tell me that you have to go to Gul Beg Sahib's?' Saying this, the driver started his auto again and drove towards the right and stopped near the signboard. The board bore a picture of American apples in the upper corner, and a jumble of pears at the bottom. The centre bore writing in bold English letters in green which read, 'GUL BEG FARMS'.

Qadir took out a hundred-rupee note and held it out to the driver. 'But I do not have change,' said the driver.

'Who asked you to return the change?' asked Qadir, as he helped Jane alight. The auto-driver cast a cursory look at them and saying '*Salaam-alaikum*', he restarted his auto. But before leaving the spot, he cast another glance at the two.

Qadir carried the heavier bag, and Jane held the brown bag. Qadir opened the gate and entered the farm while assuring Jane, 'Come on. This is like our own house.' Jane hastened to enter the orchard and Qadir closed the gate again. In the meantime, a dog started barking inside the farm. Jane was about to run out in fear, but Qadir caught hold of her wrist. 'This dog is always tethered there. And then when it sees me, it stops barking. It knows me quite well.'

The orchard belonged to Gul Beg, a person who was given to having friends around him. However, his wicked deeds had made his father, a gentle farmer, disown him. He was too naive to understand how his son had earned so much wealth in such a short period. But those who were acquainted with Gul Beg knew well that he had amassed such a huge fortune purely through drug trafficking. It was his money that gave him the wisdom to procure Nand Lal Dhar's large orchard which had become an unkempt barren land after his death since his two sons were settled in the States. After obtaining the possession of the orchard, Gul Beg worked endlessly to manage the orchard and make it profitable again. His hard work was rewarded by God, and within a couple of years, he was a rich man. The first thing he did after becoming rich was to divorce his wife, whom his father had arranged for him. He then married a pretty girl from the city. Despite having a good-natured and pretty wife at home, he did not give up the habit of enjoying extramarital affairs. His wife realized that she could not redeem her husband, and finally ran away along with her ornaments to her parents' house, never to return to him. His third marriage had a perverse foundation and did not last for more than two months. Now he resided like a ghost, all alone in his huge bungalow amidst the vast orchard.

Qadir was Gul Beg's friend and was sure that he was the only one who could provide Jane with a safe hiding place. Gul Beg's contacts with the police would also help her escape their grip. He was adept at bribing the police of the other regions as well. While Qadir was reassuring Jane, the dog's bark made Gul Beg come out of his house. On seeing the two, he came running near them. He recognized Qadir and gave him a warm hug.

'Is it you, my prince? I thought it was a thief intending to walk off with my apples.'

'Which brother-in-law of yours has the guts to enter the estate of Gul Beg!' Qadir said in a warm tone.

Seeing Jane standing behind an apple tree, Qadir freed himself from his friend's clasp and said, 'Jane, come here.'

When Gul Beg had a glimpse of Jane, he yelled in his vernacular, 'My gosh! What a fairy from the Quaf have you brought along?'

'I shall tell you all,' Qadir replied with a smile.

Gul Beg felt as if a swan had come willingly into his snare. But being an experienced huntsman, he did not display any urgency and won her confidence by inviting her inside the bungalow in his smart, crisp English. He ordered his servant to get the guests fresh apple juice. 'I hope you'll like the juice of our apples,' he said to Jane.

Jane felt relaxed and began to assess the fortune of Gul Beg. Having understood Gul Beg's demeanour, she was sure that she could easily seduce him. Thus she sat quite calmly on the sofa. The servant brought tumblers of sparkling apple juice, placed them on the table and left.

Gul Beg and Qadir returned. Sitting beside Jane, Gul Beg said to her, 'Qadir has just told me everything. You need not worry. You are safe here.' He then looked at Qadir and said, 'My dear prince, it is already late. Let me open my bar. Let us drown ourselves in the waters of truth. Sitting innocently like children in the presence of this beauty is a sin in Gul Beg's religion. Do you hear, my prince?' Having said this, he stood up and unlocked a cupboard full with all kinds of wines and spirits. Qadir understood Gul Beg's intentions. He moved near Jane and, holding her hand in his own, he said to her, 'Be careful.'

Gul Beg put three glasses and a bottle on a tray. He got soda from the fridge and then squatted in front of Jane.

'Water or soda?' he asked Jane.

'No thanks, I don't drink,' said Jane in reply.

Gul Beg looked at Qadir in amazement and said, 'What does she say, my prince?'

'Yes, she tells you the truth. She does not drink.'

'Then what does she relish, the blood of hashish addicts?' Gul Beg said in Kashmiri.

'No, no hashish!' Jane hastened to say.

'How about some more juice?'

'No thank you.'

Gul Beg realized that it was not wise to tighten his grip in such haste. So he turned to Qadir and said, 'And now tell me, my prince, should I pour out some for you, or are you also observing a fast today?'

Qadir looked at Jane and found her lost in thought. He heaved a deep sigh and said with disinterest, 'It will not be polite of me not to give you company. But a small one, please.'

'Are you making a show of your virtues to this fairy? I know your ways, my prince,' he said as he first poured whisky into Qadir's glass, and then into his own.

'To this fairy's health!' Gul Beg said, extending his glass towards Jane, and had his first sip. Qadir had his glass in hand, but was yet to drink it. This annoyed Gul Beg. 'Why don't you drink? It is Scotch.'

Qadir cast another glance at Jane. Jane smiled and, holding his glass in her hands, moved it to his lips.

'Now go ahead, she has finally granted you permission,' Gul Beg said.

After heaving a long and cold sigh, Qadir started explaining his worries. 'I am really scared for I have to be home again. If Abba comes to know that I tasted alcohol, he will send me to hell.'

'But you cannot get any bus or auto at this time. You have no option but to spend the night here.'

'Then let me give them a call.'

'I wish there were a telephone connection. They are constructing a new exchange, and all the lines are temporarily disconnected … so, in the name of Gul Beg, go ahead and guzzle!'

Qadir knew that if he did not drink, Gul Beg would get enraged and then he knew no limits. So he began to sip.

Jane took out a pack of cigarettes, offered one to Gul Beg and sat with ease as if it was her own house. Qadir was engulfed in his many worries. On the one hand, he dreaded the situation at home as he did not know what happened after they left, and on the other, he did not want to be deprived of the opportunity to spend the night with Jane. Who knew what tomorrow would bring! He finished his glass in one long gulp and handed it to Gul Beg. Jane lifted the brown bag that had fallen down from the corner of the sofa and placed it on her lap.

Malla Khaliq's house was sunk in gloom. Worried to the core and in need of some solace, he took a canoe, tossed it into the lake and began rowing towards Gagribal in the dark. Many taxis were always there for the convenience of tourists. He hired a taxi and reached Narayan Joo's house at Gogji Bagh.

Narayan Joo was surprised to see Malla Khaliq clad in his phiran and asked him nervously, 'What brings you here at this time of the night? Is everything all right?'

'Narayan Joo, I have been struck by lightning! What happened today has never happened before. The police raided our houseboats. It was the DIG himself who led the search. The whole contingent was there to apprehend that dirty young woman, Jane.'

'So she has finally been arrested, is it?'

'No, she had already escaped by the time the police arrived.'

'She is an important link in the chain of smugglers in Bombay, they say.'

'That she has been identified is good, but what vexes me more is that Qadir is also missing.'

A sudden pallor appeared on Narayan Joo's face as he added up the disappearance of Jane to that of Qadir. Ominous premonitions popped up in his mind. If the police apprehended Qadir along with Jane, his friend would really be in great trouble. His reputation would get besmeared. The name that he had earned not only in his dynasty and the community, but also among people of clout, would get covered with dirt. He started reflecting on some possible ways out so that Malla Khaliq's honour would be safe and Qadir could also be saved from the police.

Malla Khaliq, already sinking with fear, felt heavier when he saw Narayan Joo silent. 'Why don't you say something?'

'I think … we must call DIG Prahlad Singh and tell him everything.'

'No, no. If we go directly to DIG Prahlad Singh and tell him about Qadir, that would further complicate the issue. He is the kind of officer who would not excuse his own father if he were caught committing a crime.'

'If not him, then you know SHO Rahim Khan. He respects you and can easily help Qadir to escape this situation … and we could thank him with some bottles and some smokes.'

'But it is already midnight. Is it okay to call on him at this hour?'

'Let us wait until dawn. It is also possible that Qadir might be hiding with some friend of his, and will come home before sunrise.'

'Oh, may your words come true!'

'You better send the taxi back and spend the night here.'

'No, no. My wife will simply breathe her last then. Let me go now.'

'Do not be so nervous. Let us see what God decides. I will ring you up early tomorrow.'

Gul Beg emptied his plate and guzzled the remaining whisky as if it were water. Jane was already heavy with sleep and he cast a piercing glance at her. He said to Qadir, 'So let me show this memsahib her room.'

Qadir started. 'Aren't we to sleep in the bedroom upstairs?'

'Of course, where else?'

Qadir lifted the bag and said to Gul Beg, 'You need not bother, I know where it is.'

Gul Beg chuckled and said, 'You have no faith in me, my dear prince. Yet I forgive you. Go and enjoy. It is your night.'

Qadir said to Jane, 'Come on.'

Gul Beg was already tipsy. He stood up unsteadily to say goodnight to Jane, then sat down on the sofa and wistfully watched Qadir climbing up the stairs with Jane.

Malla Khaliq returned to his houseboats. It was one-thirty in the morning and Noor Mohammad alone stood waiting for his father to return. The moment he had helped his father come over to the isle, he burst out, 'Did you think I was dead that you left all alone in search of Qadir?'

'I had not left in search of him. How will I know where he has buried himself? I went to call on Narayan Joo for his counsel.'

'And? What did he say?' Noor Mohammad asked impatiently.

Malla Khaliq responded bitterly. 'I shall tell you all, but let me
go in. Or are you planning to interrogate me here and now?'

Noor Mohammad dropped his head and followed his father to
his room. Aziz Dyad was also awake, waiting for her husband. When
she glanced at her husband's face, she felt as though her heart was
being chopped into pieces. It looked like he had grown very old
and feeble in one day – his back was bent and his shoulders sagged.
She asked Noor Mohammad, 'Tell me, could you not locate him
anywhere?'

Malla Khaliq said, smouldering in anger, 'It is now up to the
police to get him back. You just prepare to arrange for a sumptuous
sacrifice.'

Aziz Dyad was flabbergasted.

Noor Mohammad knew that even a slight digression could
escalate the issue. He told his mother that his father had gone to
Narayan Joo for his advice. In the meantime, Malla Khaliq looked
at Aziz Dyad who stood shrunk in a corner. His heart suddenly
melted with pity for her. What was her fault after all? He moved
near her and said, 'Everything will be fine. I was not in search of
Qadir. I was with Narayan Joo to seek his counsel. He assured me
that with the rise of the sun we will find some way so that Qadir
will come home and our name shall remain unharmed.'

They lay down to sleep and Noor Mohammad went back to
his room.

Qadir woke up with the first ray of the sun. He stretched himself
and turned towards Jane who lay sleeping beside him. He felt the
force of desire again, but reminded himself that he had to be home
well before his Abba returned from Makhdoom Sahib's shrine. If
he failed, there could be a calamity. He woke Jane up and told her
that if he did not hasten to reach home, the whole issue could get
so knotty that he would not be able to assist her in fleeing Kashmir.
Jane hurried out of bed and put on her clothes. Qadir opened
the door and she followed him downstairs. He went to Gul Beg's

bedroom and knocked on the door. There was no response. But when Qadir continued knocking, Gul Beg yelled, 'Who is it who has sprung from some swamp when it is still dark?'

Qadir replied, 'This is Qadir.' The door was not locked and Qadir opened it cautiously and went in. Gul Beg turned over and looked at Qadir with sleepy eyes. With a long yawn, he asked him, 'Tell me what you want.'

'Nothing. I am leaving now.'

'Have I kept you shackled here? You may leave and may God keep you safe.'

'I want Jane to stay here with you.'

Hearing Jane's name, Gul Beg's eyes widened. 'Good morning. I had forgotten her, really. Slept well? But you rascal wouldn't have let her sleep.'

'Yes, very well,' Jane said and looked at Qadir. 'When will you be back, Qadir?'

Qadir convinced her that he would make all arrangements for her safe exit from Kashmir and be back soon. And then he said to Gul Beg, 'Will you let her stay here with you for a couple of days?'

'Oh surely, my prince, she may stay here if she wants to.'

'I am leaving my friend in your care. I hope you will not do anything to harm the bonds of our trust and friendship.'

'If you have no faith in me, you may take her along.'

This reply made Qadir uneasy and he hastened to say, 'If I did not have faith in you, I would not have brought her here in the first place.'

Gul Beg got out of his bed, stood beside Qadir and laid his hands on his shoulders and said to him, 'You may leave with Gul Beg's name on your tongue, and see what he does for you.' Qadir took leave of Jane and hurried towards the gate of the orchard.

Gul Beg cast a warm glance at Jane and said, 'Relax. You're safe here.'

'Thank you,' she said and went back to the room in which she had spent the night with Qadir.

The morning light was still dim when Qadir reached the general road. He saw a vehicle, with its headlights on, coming towards him. He stood in the middle of the road to flag it down. The truck stopped and the conductor asked him, 'Where do you want to go?'

'Just near the Navapore Bridge.'

The conductor took pity on him and made room for him beside the driver.

At the quay of Navapore, Qadir had left his canoe in the custody of a barge owner. Having reached Navapore, he hurriedly sat in his canoe and rowed it towards the Dal Lake.

The cliffs of the Zabarwan were now bright with morning light and a golden hue shimmered across the waters of the lake. Qadir rowed with all the force in his arms. On his way, he thought of rowing his canoe behind the houseboat of Kaw's so he could see if the hippies who were in league with Jane were still there or had been apprehended by the police. But he decided against it and continued rowing through the swamps covered with rushes to reach home. By then the sun was well above the summits, shining like a crown.

Malla Khaliq had left for Makhdoom Sahib's shrine. He shed tears there and prayed for absolution. He had left the shrine with the hope that the Lord would soon dispel all his worries and was back home before anyone in his family had woken up. Aziz Dyad felt reassured to see her husband's face bright with hope. She was waiting with a hot samovar of tea. Placing his hand on her shoulder, Malla Khaliq said, 'You should not worry. The Lord shall dispel all our dread, I am sure. Come and pour me some tea now.'

Aziz Dyad was quick in pouring tea into the cup for him. Taking the cup from her hands, Malla Khaliq asked her, 'Has Parveen woken up? Isn't she usually in the kitchen well before you?'

'Even today she was here before I came in, but Bilal had woken up even before her. You know he had been wearing muddy clothes since yesterday evening. So she took him to the washroom to clean him up.'

'This one person has caused so much trouble to the entire family,' Malla Khaliq said with a long sigh and began to sip his tea.

Qadir anchored the boat and reached the hind prow of Gulshan. Parveen, who was towelling Bilal, saw Qadir from a distance. She hastened to help Bilal wear his clothes, took him in her arms and ran towards the kitchen and shouted to break the news, 'Abba, Abba, Qadir Bhaijaan has returned!'

Malla Khaliq closed his eyes and raised his head to express his thanks to his Lord. Hearing about Qadir's return, Ghulam Ahmed left the kitchen without saying a word to anyone.

Feigning nonchalance, Qadir ambled towards the kitchen, but Ghulam Ahmed stopped him there. 'Where the hell have you been?' He dragged him to the kitchen.

As soon as Qadir entered the pantry, Aziz Dyad stood up and roared like a lioness, 'Where were you the whole night? Speak up!'

Qadir also feigned anger and said, 'Tell me what has happened to all of you, Amma? Is it for the first time that I was away from home?'

Aziz Dyad shook with anger. Ghulam Ahmed helped her sit down and then said to Qadir, 'Sit down. Do you want all the neighbours to know what has happened?'

Suppressing his anger, Qadir sat down. Malla Khaliq, who felt like his blood could be bursting out of his veins, raised his head, cast a piercing look at Qadir's face and said, 'Now tell me, where did you hide her?'

'Whom?'

'You say "whom" as though you know nothing! I mean Jane!'

'Jane? Is she not there in the houseboat?'

Malla Khaliq could no longer control himself. 'Look at me, you shameless rascal. I will not digest this false innocence of yours. You have taken her away, I know it for certain.'

'What is all this about, Abba?'

'Let your Abba be struck by a thunderbolt! You have already shamed him. The DIG, who once used to swear by my honesty, came here to search my house.'

Qadir did not know that things had taken such a frightening turn. Just then, Razaq entered carrying the cups and trays. The moment Qadir saw him there, he was struck dumb. Razaq blushed deeply. Having kept all the things in the kitchen, he left with his head bowed. Malla Khaliq started interrogating Qadir again. 'Yes, all of us here are your enemies. We are always eager to find faults in you.' Qadir was about to say something in his defence, but Malla Khaliq gave him a heavy pat. 'Will you shut up? Go to your room where your wife is wailing over that she-monkey.'

As soon as Zeb saw Qadir, she said, 'Do not enter the room carrying traces of that harlot.'

Qadir raised his hand to slap Zeb, but for some reason held himself back. Zeb held his raised hand in both her hands and placed it over her throat. 'Go on, throttle me to death. Why don't you? Kill me so that you can add a feather to your father's cap—'

Qadir released himself from her grip and stormed out of the room in a blinding fury. While Razaq was returning to the pantry after serving breakfast to Raja Rathinder Singh, he bumped into Qadir. The tray fell from his hand and some of the crockery broke. Qadir raised his hand to vent his repressed anger on Razaq, but Razaq caught hold of his raised hand and said through gritted teeth, 'You can take your hooliganism to some other person. If I open my mouth, you will be handcuffed in no time.'

Qadir realized that this was not the time to have a scuffle with Razaq, so he scurried out of the scene like a rat.

Seeing Razaq collecting the broken utensils, Malla Khaliq walked over to him. Narayan Joo, who had come to visit his friend, followed. Malla Khaliq asked him, 'What happened, Razaq?'

'I just stumbled here.'

'My son, you must be careful.'

'That is what I am trying to do.'

Malla Khaliq moved ahead. Narayan Joo placed a hand on his shoulder and said, 'You see, all is well again. I think you have grown old and so you overreact to small things.'

'Was it really a small thing?' asked Malla Khaliq.

'Well, I agree that it was no ordinary matter, but it was small. I want to say something serious to you—'

'What?'

'The ardour of youth does not abate so easily. I advise you to keep a constant vigil on Qadir and tighten your ropes on him.'

'Yes, my friend, you are right. I hope this jolt will teach him a lesson.'

Narayan Joo was about to say something, but hearing the sound of hammering, he stopped. He saw Noor Mohammad fixing a 'TO LET' board on the rails of Gulshan. He called out to him, 'No, no. Noor Mohammad, what are you doing? This is a bad omen. Bring the board down. A big party is coming within two days.'

Malla Khaliq also advised Noor Mohammad. 'Yes, get that board down. Pray that this type of board may never be fixed to our houseboats again.'

Narayan Joo said to him, 'I have such strong misgivings when I see a board bearing the words "TO LET" fixed to any houseboat.'

But Malla Khaliq said, 'This board on Qadir's houseboat might lead to gossip among the neighbours.'

'How is that? It is quite normal to put a houseboat up for rent in an off season.'

Having seen them from a distance, Qadir retracted. Meanwhile Ghulam Ahmed came to seek his father's permission to leave. His father prayed for him, 'You may go. May God bless you! But come back early.' Ghulam Ahmed was in a hurry and left without saying anything further. Malla Khaliq said to Narayan Joo, 'I do not know what is on his mind.'

'But Haji Sahib, he is not a prisoner after all. If you watch every movement of theirs like this, you will lose them one by one. Now let us go, it will be late otherwise. The SHO will not be available if we are late.'

A new ambassador car sped on to Zakoor road and came to a sharp halt near Gul Beg's gate. The screech of the breaks made the dog lying there whine and run away. The door of the car opened and Ghulam Ahmed alighted. After surveying the area, he said to the rich man who was still sitting in the car, 'Why don't you come down? This is the orchard of Gul Beg. You can peep through the gaps in the gate and see how rich the orchard is with apples.' The man in the car was the contractor with whom Ghulam Ahmed was to enter into a partnership and purchase an apple orchard at Pattan. Khwaja Amir Din came out of the car and looked at the orchard through the gaps in the gate and exclaimed with delight, 'Oh my God! This type of crop is hardly seen anywhere else.'

'Yes. I told you that if anybody wants to learn how to maintain their orchards, he should learn it from Gul Beg. Please wait here while I go and see if he is in.'

Ghulam Ahmed opened the gate and entered the orchard. He pressed the doorbell, but it did not ring. Then he called out to Gul Beg, but there was no response. He walked all around the bungalow, and finding the back door unlatched, slipped indoors and climbed up the stairs. He heard a woman chuckle inside a room. Ghulam Ahmed silently moved closer to the door, knocked on it and called, 'Beg Sahib!' Finally, Gul Beg appeared, wrapping his naked body with a gown and said, 'Who the devil is there to die so soon at this hour?'

'It's me, Ghulam Ahmed.'

'Yes. But is this the way to enter the house of a man of respect, that too without permission?' Gul Beg staggered unsteadily on his feet. He held the door to balance himself and that threw it wide open. The room was filled with smoke and Ghulam Ahmed had to cover his nose with his handkerchief. Gul Beg roared at him, 'Why are you still standing here? Get out! Should I call the police?'

Inside the room was Jane, trying to cover her nakedness with a sheet. 'So this whore is here with you,' Ghulam Ahmed said.

Gul Beg closed the door with his foot and jostled Ghulam Ahmed towards the stairs. 'Get out! I say get lost!' he said.

Ghulam Ahmed hurried down the stairs, and ran towards the outer gate of the orchard, ignoring the dog that had started barking again. There he tried to calm himself and rubbed his face with his handkerchief. Amir Din was waiting near the car. Seeing Ghulam Ahmed back, he asked, 'Is he not in?'

'No. His servant told me that he left for Delhi yesterday. He runs many businesses. Let us get going, we have to reach Pattan.'

Amir started his car and began to drive to Srinagar city. Ghulam Ahmed wished to go straight to DIG Prahlad Singh and tell him of Jane's hideout, but first, he wanted to discuss matters with his father and Noor Mohammad.

Malla Khaliq was puffing at his hookah in a frenzy. Aziz Dyad was busy peeling potatoes, but her attention was fixed on her husband. She said to him, 'You have burnt even the cinder-stopper of the chilam.'

Malla Khaliq felt like he himself was getting reduced to ashes. He said in a fiery tone, 'Why are you concerned? It is I who has to go outdoors. I have to face the public. The scandal about Jane must have spread in the locality. Nobody will say anything to us outright, but they must be gossiping about the incident. I heard a son of Kaw's saying that he did not find Qadir in the houseboat. I turned a deaf ear and walked away.'

'Do you really think I don't share your pains? My heart aches too, but this disquiet will not help you or anyone. No one has any information about the police raid, otherwise that nosy Nabir Tancha would have started inquiring.'

'How can one say anything for certain?'

'Why should it matter to them? Tourists from so many distant places come and lodge in our houseboats, no one is interested and besides, how can anyone tell what secrets tourists carry with them?'

Ghulam Ahmed stepped in and after greeting his parents, sat in a corner, absorbed in his thoughts. Malla Khaliq asked him why he returned so soon.

'It does not take much time when you have a car,' Ghulam Ahmed replied, trying to put a stop to the conversation there.

Meanwhile, Noor Mohammad and Qadir also came to see their father. Malla Khaliq kept the hookah aside and said to Aziz Dyad with a jeering smile, 'You must have offered some sacrifice today. All three of your sons stand before you!'

'I wish God bestows my life too to them,' Aziz Dyad said, looking fondly at her sons.

Looking at the glum faces of his sons, Malla Khaliq said, 'What is wrong with you lot? More bad news? Tell me.'

It was Noor Mohammad who opened his mouth first. 'Abba, I came here only to tell you that Mr Bhonsley plans to visit Pahalgam tomorrow. He told me that he would stay there for about ten days and then—'

Malla Khaliq did not let him complete the sentence. 'That means the second boat will also be left empty.'

This gave Ghulam Ahmed a chance to suggest to his father that they should start some other business. 'It is nothing new to us. This is why I keep suggesting that we try our luck in some other business.'

Noor Mohammad did not want the can of worms to open again and tried to divert the conversation. He said, 'Abba, Raja Rathinder Singh was—'

This made Malla Khaliq tremble. He interrupted Noor Mohammad and asked, 'Has he also planned to go to some other place?'

'No, Abba. He is not leaving any time soon. He asked me why Jane's photograph has appeared in the local newspapers.'

A sudden pallor came over Malla Khaliq's face. He asked Noor Mohammad, 'What else was written in the newspapers?'

'Nothing much except that the Mem is missing.'

'And what did you say to Raja Rathinder Singh?'

'I had nothing to say, so I lied. I told him that her booking with us had expired. She had wanted to go to Ladakh and she might have gone there.'

'If her photograph has appeared in the newspaper, she will be apprehended soon. Jane has brought such shame to us!' He heaved a long sigh.

Qadir hung his head and helped his mother chop onions. Ghulam Ahmed, who had thus far been silent about Gul Beg and Jane's story, gave a new twist to their conversation. 'Abba, I saw Jane.'

Qadir dropped the knife.

'Where did you see her?' Malla Khaliq asked.

'I was going through Zakoor when I passed Gul Beg's farm. I thought it proper to see him at his house and inquire about the condition of this year's apple crop. When I entered the bungalow, I found that harlot drunk in Gul Beg's room.'

Hearing this, Malla Khaliq turned to Qadir and roared, 'That means you had gone to leave that whore with that rogue friend of yours!'

Qadir brazenly replied, 'May a thunderbolt strike the one who went to Zakoor. I was at Barzul with Ghulam Hassan.'

Malla Khaliq stood up and pounced on Qadir. 'You are a tramp, a vagabond and a mean rascal!' He lifted a big log of wood lying there, intending to smash Qadir's head, but Noor Mohammad and Ghulam Ahmed stopped him.

Aziz Dyad shouted, 'Are you mad? Do you want to kill your married son? This will surely take us to hell.'

Malla Khaliq's rage abated a little and he flung the log of wood aside. Walking towards the door, he said, 'I will go to the DIG and tell him where this Mem is hiding.'

Ghulam Ahmed blocked his way. 'What are you going to do, Abba? If she is apprehended there and she mentions Qadir's support, we will all get into a big mess.'

Malla Khaliq sat down. Aziz Dyad said to her sons, 'Are we now to mourn the death of that wicked woman, or attend to our daily chores? It is time to arrange for the meals of the guests. Let us all go and start working.'

Parveen placed a handful of clothes for washing near the water tap. Razaq rolled up his sleeves, filled a tub with water and churned it to make the soap lather until the tub overflowed. Seeing the suds brimming over, Parveen asked him, 'Why are you so lost today?'

'Nothing very serious. I was thinking about Sir. My heart rips seeing him in this condition.'

Parveen cast a fond look at Razaq and said, 'Do you know what Abba said to Amma the day before yesterday? He told her that he has trust only in you.'

'No, I am not worth his trust. I have deceived him.'

'What do you mean?'

Razaq, bent forward to soak the clothes in the soap water, sat down with his head hung and said, 'I cannot keep any secret from you. The day the police raided the houseboats, I saw Qadir escape through the swamps with Jane.'

'What? You saw them fleeing together and yet you did not inform Abba? You could have stopped them!'

'I thought that might complicate matters and harm the name of your family.'

'What do you mean the name of *your* family? Say name of *our* family. Abba loves you like his own son. I am always here to spare a piece of candy for you, and yet you say *your family*! You may leave! I will wash all the clothes myself.'

Razaq felt mortified, but at the same time a strange feeling of tenderness pervaded his whole being. He sought Parveen's pardon and began washing the clothes. Parveen's mother called out to her. Smiling at Razaq, she said to him, 'Never again should you consider yourself separate from this family. Do you understand?' Then, she dashed to the pantry.

Narayan Joo came back from Pahalgam after arranging a hotel for Mr Bhonsley. Malla Khaliq saw him alighting from the shikaarah and hurried to receive him. Narayan Joo said to him, 'What makes you so perturbed? Is all well?'

'I'm afraid not – Ghulam Ahmed saw Jane in Gul Beg's bungalow!'

Narayan Joo smiled and said, 'So this trivial piece of information disturbs you? It is good. Gul Beg has a clout in the men of rank. Who knows whom he might be pleasing by using Jane!'

'But what if she mentions her connection with Qadir?'

'You stay calm. People like Jane are not so pig-headed. Even if she is apprehended, there will be no mention of him. Besides, with her wiles, she can go to any extent to save herself.'

In the meantime, Bhonsley came out and stood at the prow of the houseboat, waiting for Narayan Joo. Seeing him, Narayan Joo moved to the prow. He handed over all the papers to Bhonsley after which Bhonsley thanked him and went back inside. Narayan Joo turned to Malla Khaliq and advised him not to remain vexed for nothing. 'But the issue is such,' said Malla Khaliq. 'I think I must inform the police.'

'Bravo! You inform the police and invite trouble for yourself.'

'I am just lost – my brain has ceased to work.'

'First, you need to be calm. Jane has left your houseboat. Qadir is home again. You should thank God.' He then turned to the quay where his shikaarah was waiting. 'So I am leaving. Yesterday I received a call from Vijay Kumar in Bombay. There is another party coming very soon.'

Qadir was consumed with jealousy every time he thought of Gul Beg and Jane. He was also worried that she might have divulged secrets to Gul Beg. He took out a cigarette. How could that imp Gul Beg seduce Jane! But this did not give him as much pain as the thought that the hen that laid golden eggs had escaped from his hands. His dream of becoming a millionaire had been reduced to dust.

The consignment of drugs that was stashed in Jane's brown bag cost approximately three lakh rupees. He was sure that Gul Beg would devour that money. While smoking cigarette after cigarette, Qadir did not even realize that it was quarter to four in the morning. He glanced at Zeb, who was snoring slightly in her sleep. He quickly snuffed out the cigarette and stood up silently. He thought that if he could not make it to Gul Beg's farm before dawn, all his labour would go to waste. He calmly took his bag from the inner room, stuffed it with a few clothes, softly opened the door and left.

He reached Zakoor well before dawn. The muezzin of the dargah recited the prayer call, and some people were out on the streets. Hiding his face from passers-by, Qadir managed to reach Gul Beg's outer gate. It was latched from inside. He jumped over the fence. The dog began to bark fiercely. There was a light on and Qadir moved towards it. It turned out to be the headlights of Gul Beg's car. Suddenly, the engine started and the car sped towards Qadir. He stood frozen at the centre of the road and spread out his arms. The car stopped near him. Gul Beg came out and ran towards Qadir. He held Qadir's collar and said, 'You? At this hour! Did you jump over the fence? If the dog were not tethered, it might have dismembered your body.'

Qadir said, 'Where is Jane?'

'In the car.'

'And where is she going? People have come to know that she is with you here.'

'I know. Your dimwitted and indiscreet brother had come to pry into my business.'

'Her photograph has appeared in the local newspapers. If anyone traces her here—'

Gul Beg cut him off, saying, 'You need not worry about that. I will take her to Delhi safely.' By now, Jane had also come out of the car. Gul Beg jostled her arm and said, 'Get in, we're running late.'

Qadir blocked their way and told Jane, 'I will accompany you to Delhi.'

Gul Beg pushed him aside and said, 'You need not come when I am with her.' He then got into the car with Jane, pressed the accelerator and dashed out.

Qadir ran after the car but then stopped. He kicked Gul Beg's gate with all his strength. The dog inside the farm barked and scratched the ground with its paws.

Malla Khaliq was home from Makhdoom Sahib's shrine well before it was morning. Bhonsley was leaving for Pahalgam soon after breakfast. Aziz Dyad was already in the pantry. Qadir was in luck to be home by the time it was light. He was not as angry with Gul Beg as he was with Jane. Walking from behind the prow of Gulshan, he entered his room. He kept his bag in the almirah and came out onto the porch of the houseboat and stretched, pretending to have just gotten out of bed.

Meanwhile, Bhonsley's son came running to his father and said, 'Let us hurry now, Papa. If we are late, there will be no horses left for us.'

'No, my child, all the horses shall wait for you,' Malla Khaliq said, trying to console the boy.

'I'm not a child,' the boy said.

Keeping an affectionate hand on his head, Malla Khaliq sought his pardon, saying, 'I am sorry. I did not even remember that you are already a young man.'

Bhonsley told Malla Khaliq that he had lived in many a grand hotel, but nowhere did he find the comfort of this houseboat. 'It is no less than my own home here.'

Mrs Bhonsley added, 'And all this affection of yours and tender care can never be matched anywhere.'

'Your praise embarrasses me,' said Malla Khaliq.

'No, I'm only telling you the truth.'

Bhonsley laid his hand on Malla Khaliq's shoulder. Malla Khaliq bowed to him with his hand placed on his chest, saying, 'Always at your service. In fact the houseboats belong to you – we are just the caretakers.'

At this point, Noor Mohammad came to tell Bhonsley that the DIG was on the line and wanted to talk to him. Bhonsley followed Noor Mohammad, and taking the receiver from him and, said, 'Good morning, DIG Sahib. Really? So she has finally been caught! Thank you for this good news, that too early in the morning. Where? … Good … Hmm … Yes, the rest of the action is up to the Bombay police. It is their job now … yes, we are about to leave. Thank you very much.'

Malla Khaliq, Noor Mohammad and Razaq were listening with ashen faces. Keeping the receiver down, Bhonsley said to his wife, 'Thank God! Jane Lockwood has finally been arrested.'

'Where?' his wife asked him.

'Near the Banihal tunnel. She was trying to flee in a car.'

Qadir was at the isle, waiting for his father. Razaq descended from Gul and broke the news to Qadir. 'Jane has been arrested by the police.'

Qadir's heart sank to his toes. He ran to his room and entered the bathroom and put his head under the running tap but the cold water could not calm his nerves. While rubbing his head with a towel afterwards, his gaze fell upon his reflection in the mirror. There were black circles around his eyes. He sat in a corner and reflected on what seemed like his only two options – either commit suicide by jumping into the lake or flee from home to some far-off place and start anew. No, no. I am not a coward to commit suicide, I must somehow get away from this hell.

Malla Khaliq phoned Narayan Joo to inform him that Jane had been apprehended near the Banihal tunnel. Narayan Joo told him that the news had already appeared in the local daily.

'What should we do now?' Malla Khaliq asked Narayan Joo.

'What should we do except watch what is to unfold? Let us wait for a day or so, and in case of any emergency, we can see the DIG. Oh yes, please ask Qadir to stay home for a few days.'

Malla Khaliq went straight to Qadir's room. Qadir stood up in horror as if the angel of death had appeared in front of him. Malla Khaliq said to him, 'You know, I saw you coming back from some escapade again this morning. I tell you this now. If you have any regard for the honour of the family, do not leave the house again unless I grant you permission.'

After his father left the room, Qadir sat down again, lit another cigarette and started pondering over the way out of this misfortune. In the meantime, Zeb entered the room. 'What are you doing here? Go, your mother is waiting for you.' Qadir maintained his silence as if he had heard nothing. 'Why don't you go? You have pushed the whole family in this vortex, what are you mourning now? See, that fairy of yours is now in police custody. Just wait and watch how the police will torture her now.' Qadir stood up, shoved her aside and stormed out of the room. Zeb followed him.

On the isle, Zeb passed Parveen who was holding two dolls – a groom and a bride – in her hands. Seeing the dolls, Zeb stopped and asked her, 'Where did you get these from?'

'Rani Sahiba gave them to me.'

'Did you ask for them?'

'No, she just gave these to me when I had gone to give her the phiran and ornaments she had asked for. You should have seen how beautiful she looked in that outfit.'

'So you were there with her all this time? If your Abba comes to know about this—?'

'But it was Abba who sent me there. These dolls were lying there on a tea-table. I gazed at them while Rani Sahiba was dressing up. She saw me staring at the dolls and asked me if I liked them. I nodded and she gave me both the dolls. I would not have accepted them, but she insisted. Aren't they pretty?'

Then seeing Malla Khaliq walking that way, Parveen hid the dolls behind her. He called her, 'Parveen, go and see what Razaq is doing there.'

'All right, Abba.' She capered towards Razaq's shed.

'Razaq, Razaq!' she called out to him.

Razaq was putting on his shoes. When he heard Parveen calling out for him, the shoe fell from his hand. Parveen stood at the door, taunting him, saying, 'Oh, so his highness is here, not knowing that he is being sought there. He is still tidying himself.'

Razaq hastened to put on his shoes. While coming out, he stopped and asked her, 'Will you show me what you are hiding there behind you?'

'No, don't touch them. Rani Sahiba has given these to me.'

'Will you at least give me some space to come out?'

Parveen extended both her hands bearing the dolls towards him. She said, 'How do you like them?'

'Very beautiful, especially the bride.'

'So you like her more. You can have her. Take it. I give it to you.'

Razaq blushed and his heart pounded heavily. Parveen stammered and said coyly, 'Don't you like the doll?' Razaq nodded. Parveen felt her earlobes turning hot. She said, almost in a whisper, 'And I like this groom.'

'You please keep both the dolls. Why should I play with them?'

'Idiot!'

Having said this, she ran away, leaving the bride there. Dazed, Razaq took the doll and kept it on his pillow and went out of his shed.

Malla Khaliq held the pipe of his hookah in his motionless lips. He gazed blankly at the floor. Aziz Dyad, too, with her head hung down, remained silent. Ghulam Ahmed was desperate to hear a word from his father. 'Abba, if you continue to remain quiet like this, I am afraid my heart will surely burst out. Say something, please.'

Malla Khaliq sighed. 'I am a foolish old man. Why should anyone consult me?'

Ghulam Ahmed moved near his father and said, 'Abba, do not talk like that. We need your advice and support. Last year's losses in the business held me back from sharing my worries with you. That is why I did not tell you anything. But this year, I have got a good orchard. Give me another chance.'

Malla Khaliq sighed again and glanced at his wife. Then he said to Ghulam Ahmed, 'It is good that you have finalized the deal, but how did you manage the money?'

'I got some money from Zoon's father, and the rest of the money was invested by the dealer.'

'So you once again went with a begging bowl to your father-in-law. Is your own father dead?'

'How could we arrange such a huge amount? We are not even able to repay the bank loan.'

'Narayan Joo is still alive, we could have borrowed from him.'

'But is it not better to seek help from those who are your own rather than from strangers?'

'Narayan Joo is no stranger! My blood brother would not do what all he has done for me. He has always helped us – even after the raid of the tribesmen, when we were reduced to paupers. We were forced to put up our utensils for sale. Those difficult times, which were worse than doomsday, did not break our relationship. Yet you consider Narayan Joo an outsider? Do you have any inkling how big his business is in Bombay? Yet, there is hardly any shrinking in his love for me and my family. Tell me, is it not true?'

'I did not mean that. I respect Lala Sahib as much as I respect you. I strive so hard only to see some increase in our income. Be honest and tell me if our business is stable. Even if there is a good tourist season, our business does not last for more than three months and for the rest of the year, we remain idle. Besides, our family has expanded, and the children of yesterday are adults now.'

Malla Khaliq raised his eyes towards his wife.

'Perhaps he is right,' she said.

'Hmm – perhaps he is right.' Saying this, he stood up as if he had lost the case. He went and sat near the window, gazing at his houseboats with tears in his eyes.

Ghulam Ahmed sensed that his father was in distress and he went near him saying, 'Do not be so nervous, Abba. I will not let any harm come to this old business of ours. I promise you.'

'But the harm is already done. Look at Qadir, how he has stopped working since he got involved with Jane. If Razaq were not here, I think our guests would not be served even a cup of tea.'

'Let us thank God that Jane was caught in Gul Beg's car. Qadir is still lost in this fright. He will be well again when this story turns stale.'

'I do not think so. Once you develop a taste for crime, it is very difficult to get rid of it.' Saying this, Malla Khaliq stood up again and said to Ghulam Ahmed, 'Let's see how our Dastagir Sahib helps us out. You have an appointment with the broker, but take care that you are free soon. You have to reach the airport after that.'

Malla Khaliq told Aziz Dyad while going out to the isle, 'You keep breakfast ready for Raja Rathinder. I shall go and see what keeps Razaq busy.'

Aziz Dyad collected all the cups and the samovar, and said to Ghulam Ahmed, 'You may leave, my dear son. May my Dastagir help you in your endeavours.'

Parveen was experiencing a strange sensation, as if every particle of her being was simmering, since she had talked about those dolls to Razaq. Razaq, too, felt his heart sinking and rising whenever he saw her. Seeing her, Aziz Dyad said, 'What is this frolicking about like a wild goat with your dishevelled hair? Come here, I will do your hair.'

Parveen squatted in front of her mother and said, 'Come on now, you pull my hair apart as you wish.'

Aziz Dyad pushed her back, but said fondly, 'Go away. Why should I do your hair? Go and do it yourself. You have grown like a shepherdess of the jungle, and yet you have not learnt to tie your hair.'

'But I love it when you comb my hair with your hands!'

'You can enjoy this love from your mother for some more days, but who will pamper you like this when you are at your in-laws' house?'

Hearing these words, Parveen gave a slight push to her mother and stood up. 'I am not the one to go to any in-laws' house. Do you hear me?' she said and left the room. Her mother called out to her again, but she did not return.

Having placed all Mrs Mundra's belongings in the bedroom, Razaq asked Malla Khaliq, 'What would they like to have, tea or coffee?'

'No tea, nor coffee,' said Mrs Mundra. 'Mr Narayan, you were talking of some qahva. You said it is better than Chinese tea.'

'Yes, it is called qahva,' Narayan Joo said.

'Let's try it.'

Malla Khaliq said to Razaq, 'You stay here, I will have it sent.'

'I take your leave, madam,' Narayan Joo said as he followed Malla Khaliq to the isle.

The two friends had decided to visit the DIG's office to assess the developments in Jane's case. Before leaving, Malla Khaliq advised Noor Mohammad, 'You should keep a watch on Qadir.'

As soon as Malla Khaliq and Ghulam Ahmed walked out of sight, Qadir came out and went to the ghat. But Noor Mohammad accosted him, 'Where are you going?'

'To perdition,' replied Qadir. 'I am not a jailbird after all. You do not even let me breathe freely.'

Noor Mohammad did not think it proper to have an argument with him and went to the pantry. Qadir sat on a step of the ghat. Seeing him there, his little son came running to him. Qadir cast a fierce look at him. 'What do you want from me?' These sharp words from his father frightened the little boy and he retracted. As he backtracked, he slipped and was about to fall in the water, but Ghulam Qadir swooped and saved him. Zeb came running. Qadir angrily handed over the child to her and said, 'Better appoint a babysitter if you do not know how to take care of your child. He was about to drown in the lake.'

Zeb replied, 'Yes, why not? My child's father earns millions!'

Noor Mohammad noticed the brawl and walked up to them and said, 'What is wrong with you two? There are guests in the houseboats. Do you want them to flee?'

Zeb took her child in her arms and ran to her room. Qadir said to Noor Mohammad, 'You may attend to your work peacefully. I'm not going to run away.'

There was a huge crowd at DIG Prahlad Singh's office. He had an appointment with Narayan Joo and Malla Khaliq and had enough experience to know what the two friends had come for. He apologized to Malla Khaliq for having ordered a raid on his houseboats. He explained further, 'We were free from this menace so far, but for the last few years, the smugglers have spread this addiction among the youth. You know, young men and women in many foreign countries can hardly live without drugs.'

'You refer to foreign countries,' said Narayan Joo. 'I'll tell you what happens in our own Bombay. In front of my son's house, there is a big diamond merchant, with a business in billions. But both his sons got so addicted to drugs that he has to keep them under lock and key before leaving his house. They wail in agony without their daily dose and then, recently one of them died a miserable death.'

'No, sir, we shall not allow things to worsen to that extent. We must thank God that Jane had left Haji Sahib's houseboat. Her arrest has provided us clues about the gang of hippies who run their illicit business from the rear side of the lake. If she had continued to lodge in your houseboat, that would have certainly had an adverse impact on your family. Now we have dispatched her to Bombay.'

Malla Khaliq was frightened to hear all this. 'But Ghulam Qadir did not know what a dangerous woman that young Mem was.'

'She named Qadir as one of her accomplices.'

Narayan Joo was quick to plead for Ghulam Qadir. 'Yes, she could name anybody in order to save herself.'

Prahlad Singh looked up at Narayan Joo, and said with a smile, 'You are right. We do not implicate anybody with crime unless we have some solid proof. That is why we let Gul Beg go even though she was found in his car.' Then turning to Malla Khaliq he said, 'It is my suggestion that you ask your sons to have a thorough knowledge of your tenants' background.'

'Sir, you have been considerate in saving my honour. I will remember your kindness till I breathe my last.' Saying this, Malla Khaliq took leave of Prahlad Singh. Narayan Joo also thanked Prahlad Singh. The two friends came out and sat in Narayan Joo's car. 'Leave me at my office and drop Haji Sahib at Gagribal,' Narayan Joo directed his driver. The car started and Narayan Joo turned to Malla Khaliq. 'Haji Sahib, now you must offer a niyaz. We have had a narrow escape.'

'Yes, we must offer a niyaz. This rogue of a son of mine had placed the whole family at such a great risk.'

'Be careful when you are home. You should not torment Ghulam Qadir. It is wise to be polite with him, otherwise I am afraid you may lose him forever.'

'Don't worry. I will digest the whole venom myself.'

Aziz Dyad was in the kitchen, making arrangements for dinner. Zeb sat beside her, chopping vegetables. Aziz Dyad lit the gas burner, placed a vessel over it to boil water for tea and then she said to Zeb, 'Do you know where your Abba has gone? He should have told us what to cook for this new lady guest.'

Just then, Malla Khaliq entered the kitchen and asked Zeb, 'Where is Ghulam Qadir?'

'He may be sleeping in his room. I do not know if he is well. He does not say anything and remains melancholic all the time,' Zeb said.

'He is probably still frightened of the police. Go and tell him that all is well now. I have returned from the DIG's office. Please do this at the earliest, my daughter. We must all encourage him so that he busies himself with his work.'

Aziz Dyad was very happy to hear all this. She said to Zeb, 'Yes, your Abba is right. I will take care of dinner, please go and convey this happy news to him.'

Zeb left at once. Noor Mohammad cast a glance at her happy face and then went into the kitchen. He asked his mother, 'Where have you sent Zeb to? I saw her so happy after a long time.'

'Your father has brought some happy news,' Aziz Dyad told him.

Malla Khaliq gave the details of his meeting with DIG Prahlad Singh. 'I sent her to her room so that she communicates this good news to Ghulam Qadir.'

Heaving a long sigh, Aziz Dyad said, 'Poor Zeb! She was always like a full blossomed rose, but see what a pallor has seized her in these few days.'

The room was filled with smoke, and Qadir was puffing a cigarette when Zeb entered. She snatched away the cigarette from his hand and threw it out of the window. 'Have some pity on your lungs at least.' Qadir cast a ferocious look at her face.

'Why are you looking at me like this? Do you want to devour me?' she asked.

'Why are you worried? I am not enjoying these cigarettes from your father's income.'

'Not my father's income, but your own father's money is being reduced to ashes. Now cheer up, Abba has freed you from the trap of the police. You must go prostrate at his feet and beg for his pardon. Then you can engage in some meaningful work. Your houseboat is still empty. Go and get new guests.'

Qadir was as angry as ever and said, 'Am I scared of the police? I have not committed any crime.'

Zeb sensed it would be safer not to irk him further. 'All right, why should we debate? Now get up. This is the time when the buses from Jammu arrive. Take a trip to the Tourist Reception Centre.'

Qadir defiantly pulled out a pack of cigarettes from his pocket and was about to light another when Zeb swooped and snatched the lighter from his hand. But Qadir pounced at her and got his lighter back. 'If you stretch your hand again, I shall surely rip it apart.'

But Zeb dared him. 'Even if you slash my entire body, I will not let you follow any wrong path. Who knows what these cigarettes contain?'

'Even if they contain poison, how the hell is it your concern? I am not to going to the tourist centre or the airport. I simply abhor this trade. If you continue bugging me like this, I will flee from home.'

'Where will you go? "She" has been taken away by the police, and sent to Bombay.'

Hearing Zeb's jibe, Qadir stood up, and Zeb shrank in a corner. His eyes were red with ire. 'Do not get scared, I am not here to slay you. Listen, I have taken a decision. I shall leave this houseboat work and start some business. Now, I have the knack and the skills to pursue business.'

Zeb giggled. 'Oh, why not! You and business! You cannot run this one houseboat. I know what knack in business you have. If my Dastagir Sahib was not merciful to you, you would have been behind bars by now.'

'You shut up, or I shall pluck your tongue out!'

Zeb started wailing over her destiny. 'Oh my God, this son of such a good Haji Sahib is possessed! Where are those promises of yours? Oh Qadir, you used to be so good!'

'When everyone is busy making their destiny and fortune, why should I alone be blamed for the crime?'

'All right, if you are really serious about pursuing your own trade, you should consult Abba. Or is it that the business you wish to pursue is not worth mentioning? Why don't you understand that this dubious business ends in disgrace?'

'So I have to take advice from you now! And Abba senses poison in every new thing. How can I seek his counsel? But let me tell you one thing: if I do not return to this house as a millionaire, I am not worthy of my name Qadir.'

'But if you are going away, at least tell me where to.'

'I am going to Delhi. Gul Beg told me that if one is interested in setting up a rich trade, one must go to Delhi or Bombay.'

'So you have decided to leave us and go to Delhi? Are you going there in search of Jane?'

'Do you think I will stay here with you to hear all your taunts?'

'I will poison myself to death.'

'Why don't you do that? Oh my God, what a menace she is!'

'I am going to tell Abba all this.'

Qadir gripped her throat and said, 'If you do so, I will throttle you to death.'

There was a sudden clap of thunder. At the same time a hawk seized a bird, and the resulting screech startled Bilal who was sleeping under a blanket. Qadir withdrew his hands. Zeb held Bilal in an embrace. The child raised his eyes to his father, but Qadir turned his head towards the window. Then he stood up suddenly and went out.

He went straight away to Gulshan where he had hidden the portion of Jane's income in the floor under some wooden planks. He heaved a sigh of relief when he found the bag containing the money safe in the spot where he had kept it. He lifted the bag to take it, but then thought it would be safer to keep it there as it was. He said to himself, 'Now there is no hindrance. I shall show them how Qadir's dream of becoming a millionaire comes true.'

Meanwhile Noor Mohammad, who was in search of Qadir, entered the houseboat. Hearing his call, Qadir quickly came out to meet him. Noor Mohammad made him sit beside him and tried to advise him. 'Why are you still trying to play this hide-and-seek? Let us forget whatever has happened. You should start your life afresh. Come on, I shall take you to Abba.'

'No, no. Not now. I cannot face him yet.'

'But he is not blaming you for anything.'

'No, not this time, please. I will soon see him myself. Do not force me now.'

'All right. But take my advice. Please do not be friends with Gul Beg. He is not a good man. You know wealth alone is not all. We cannot do what he does. People respect our Abba. People swear by his honesty.'

'I have nothing to do with Gul Beg. Besides, he might have been arrested along with Jane.'

'No. Abba said that the police could not prove his complicity in Jane's crimes, and so they let him off. Or it might be that he bribed the police. But why should we bother about him? I will go and see if Raja Rathinder Singh wants anything. And Lala Sahib is also here. He has to accompany Abba to the shawl-maker. Razaq is busy in Gulfam.' Having said all this to Qadir, he left the houseboat Gulshan.

Ghulam Qadir sat down relaxed on the sofa. He felt as if he had found a treasure. 'So Gul Beg is at large. And I was worrying that he might be with Jane in Delhi. Now I will settle all my old scores with him,' he muttered to himself.

Amir Joo dwelt in a shanty in the rear Dal. There was no embroiderer as skilled as him in all of Kashmir. His eyesight was about to die out soon, yet he was not free from the debts of the big shawl merchant of Kothibagh. Malla Khaliq's shikaarah passed through the water avenues shaded by the thickets of willows and reached the little isle where Amir Joo resided. He found him sitting on a rush-mat in the compound, busy at work on a pashmina shawl. His daughter, scrubbing utensils, called him, 'Father, Haji Sahib is coming here.' Amir Joo hurried and went to receive him. He held the prow of the shikaarah in his hands and fastened it to the bank. Malla Khaliq and Narayan Joo came out of the shikaarah.

Malla Khaliq explained the purpose of his visit. But Amir Joo said hesitantly, 'But I am not a better artisan than the shawl merchant Abdullah Shah.'

'He has gone to Delhi, and we do not know when he will return. We have very little time because Raja Sahib has to fly back.'

'I am already under his debt, you know.'

Amir Joo never dared have any transaction with any customer without Abdullah Shah's permission. Narayan Joo assured him that even if Abdullah Shah came to know about this deal, Malla Khaliq would defend him. Amir Joo said to Malla Khaliq in a confiding manner, 'You know, I have a marriageable daughter for whom I have painstakingly made a few shawls. By quietly selling them, I would be able to meet all the expenses. Abdullah

Shah does not know about this. I will bring those shawls to your houseboat tomorrow.'

'You need not worry. You show your shawls to Raja Sahib. He will pay you as much as you like.' Malla Khaliq gave him confidence. The two friends took his leave and sat in the shikaarah.

'My son, turn the boat towards Dalgate,' Narayan Joo said to the boatman.

'Why? What do you have to do there?' asked Malla Khaliq.

Narayan Joo smiled and said, 'When your Nisar Ahmed returns after completing his medical training, you should first get him to cure you of your forgetfulness. Don't you remember that today is Makhan Lal's daughter's wedding?'

'Oh yes. I am really out of sorts.'

Makhan Lal was a big fruit merchant. He paid thousands of rupees to the ruling party as donation for which many rulers often visited him. When Narayan Joo and Malla Khaliq reached his bungalow, there was great hustle and bustle there. Very little time was left for the reception. The two friends managed to congratulate Makhan Lal who was busy chatting with ministers. Then he came to Narayan Joo and Malla Khaliq and embraced both of them. He escorted them to the reception hall. Malla Khaliq glanced all around. He saw a few girls busy preparing the rangoli on which the groom would stand awaiting the bride. He was lost in ruminations when someone placed a hand on his shoulder. '*As-salaam-alaikum,* Haji Sahib!'

Malla Khaliq lost his train of thought and looked behind him to see Haji Ramzan standing there. He had received a marriage proposal of his son for Parveen. Haji Ramzan embraced him.

Malla Khaliq asked him, 'When did you return from Delhi?'

'Just yesterday. Parvez Ahmed, too, has arrived here.' Haji Ramzan looked towards his right and called out to a handsome youth standing there, 'Parvez, come here. Here is Haji Sahib, proprietor of Gul, Gulshan and Gulfam.'

With much courteousness, Parvez greeted Malla Khaliq. Malla Khaliq was quite pleased with what met the eye and his heart felt the pleasant warmth of trust and confidence. Seeing Haji Ramzan there, Narayan Joo stood up and said to him, '*As-salaam-alaikum,* Haji Sahib! When did you come?'

'Just yesterday.' Then he introduced his son Parvez to Narayan Joo. It took Narayan Joo no time to like the young man.

While they were enjoying this warm tête-à-tête, the sound of the conch resounded in the air. The groom had arrived. All the friends and relatives came out to receive the guests. The women came out in the porch of the house and started their wedding lays. The little girls ran barefoot to have the first look at the bridegroom. All the aunts of the bride sang full-throated:

> *Yindiraazi brwanh brwanh ratha sawaaryey*
> *Haaryi aav varnnyey dyivaa dyev*

(The groom, like the God Inder, riding his chariot,
Comes to marry our darling, our pretty mynah)

All the kith and kin and friends of Makhan Lal offered the groom their flower garlands. Then the groom was led to the vyoog.

Malla Khaliq cast affectionate glances at them and then at Parvez, who was standing just near the vyoog. He was thinking about the wedding of his own daughter. He continued staring at the face of the bride till he discerned the face of Parveen in the face of the pretty daughter of Makhan Lal. He snapped out of his dream when the bride and bridegroom were being escorted to worship the family deities.

All the guests left one by one. Narayan Joo and Malla Khaliq drove towards Gagribal. Having passed Dalgate, Narayan Joo placed his hand on Malla Khaliq's hand and said, 'Haji Sahib, what keeps you preoccupied?'

'Nothing in particular.' Malla Khaliq tried to evade details, but his friend knew well what Malla Khaliq was absorbed in. 'The boy is really charming,' said Narayan Joo. 'You should not dither but send your consent without delay.'

'You read my mind. But Haji Ramzan did not even utter a word about this issue.'

Malla Khaliq worried that Haji Ramzan might have heard about the trouble with Jane.

Narayan Joo laughed and said, 'Haji Sahib, why are you being so naive? You go and start preparations for the marriage. Didn't you see how fervently Haji Ramzan introduced his son to us?'

The car stopped near Nehru Park. Narayan Joo said to Malla Khaliq, 'Be happy. You should seek counsel of your wife and take this alliance forward.'

Malla Khaliq alighted from the car. He caught sight of fresh pomegranates on a vendor's pushcart. Without haggling, he bought two kilograms of the fruit and sat in his shikaarah to go home.

Noor Mohammad was sitting alone in a corner and puffing on his hookah. His wife, having washed all the clothes, came in while drying her hands with the bottom of her headcloth. 'Why are you still here? Is all well?'

'I am just worried about Nisar Ahmed. I hope he qualifies in the test. His result is expected this month.'

'Judging by the look on your face, I thought something serious had happened. Has he ever failed in any examination that you are worried this time? Take it from me he will do very well. Get up now, please. You know you have to go to the market.'

Noor Mohammad was also anxious about his father. 'I do not know why Abba is so late.'

'He has been here for over half an hour! Now get up and change.'

Noor Mohammad stood up and started changing his clothes.

Parveen brought pomegranate in a bowl and kept it before her father. Malla Khaliq, placing his hand on her head, looked at her face and said, 'If you were not here, who would take care of me?'

Parveen looked at her mother and said, 'Do you hear what he says?'

Aziz Dyad smiled. 'Yes, yes. This is what I have earned after serving him for all these forty years.'

'But I know Abba quite thoroughly. Nobody can equal him in flattering people.'

'Yes, particularly when he flatters his daughter and daughters-in law,' said Aziz Dyad.

Malla Khaliq selected a big pomegranate and offered it to Parveen. 'Take it, my darling. This is your share, the biggest one.'

'But how can just one pomegranate suffice for me?' She stretched out her hand for another one. 'Take this one too, darling.' Parveen took both the pomegranates and walked to the isle. Then in one dash, she went to the rear swamp.

Aziz Dyad could make out that something good had happened that made her husband so happy. She asked him, 'What is so special today that you shower so much affection on Parveen?'

'Today I saw Ramzan Joo's son, Parvez Ahmed. I can't describe in words how handsome and courteous he is.'

'Where did you see him?'

'At the wedding of the daughter of Makhan Lal of Gulab Bagh. He had come along with his father. Narayan Joo also liked the boy. He told me that I should not miss the alliance.'

'Were you able to talk about this with Ramzan Sahib?'

'How could I talk about this over there? But the way he introduced his son to me clearly showed that he was interested. What is your opinion? Should I send them our consent?'

'Yes, but wait until they send a message one more time.'

Malla Khaliq sat leaning against the pillow, and brought his hookah nearer. 'Thank God. Perhaps happy days are coming back to us.'

'All will be well. You should just take care of yourself now. You should not get upset over every trivial thing.'

Razaq was washing some crockery near the water tap behind the houseboats. He saw a big round pomegranate roll towards him like a cricket ball. Razaq was so startled he could hardly hold the cup in his hands. Parveen stood at a distance, chuckling. She came near him and said, 'Why don't you pick it up? It is a pomegranate after all, not a hand grenade.'

He picked up the pomegranate and tried to return it to Parveen. She took out another pomegranate from her pocket. 'See, I have one for myself. That one is for you.'

Razaq cast one glance at the fruit in his hand and then looked at Parveen's face.

Parveen said, 'Stupid. He never understands anything.' Saying this, she laughed and went away, romping like a gazelle. Razaq stood transfixed, gazing at her retreating figure.

Noor Mohammad looked through the window of his room and saw his father ambling near the ghat and looking towards the lake. He grew nervous and ran to meet him. Malla Khaliq was now on the steps of the ghat. Noor Mohammad asked him, 'What are you doing here, Abba? Is all well?'

'I am anxious because Amir Joo is late. Raja Sahib's spouse has asked me thrice about the shawls since morning.'

'He might be afraid of Abdullah Shah.'

'There he comes. Go and tell Rani Sahiba that the shawl vendor is here.'

Amir Joo's boat touched the ghat. '*As-salaam-alaikum!* Haji Sahib. Am I too late?'

'Come on now without further delay.'

Malla Khaliq had spoken highly of Amir Joo's art, so Rathinder Singh and his wife were eager to see the shawls. 'Let us see what you have brought for us.' Amir Joo spread out his shawls. Meanwhile, Noor Mohammad came in and whispered something to Malla Khaliq.

Abdullah Shah's shikaarah had touched the ghat. He seemed to be in a mood to quarrel. On coming nearer, without a *salaam*, he said to Malla Khaliq, 'So nice of you! You decided to sever our lifelong relations. Could you not wait for a day or two?'

'If I could wait, why would I have ever asked Amir Joo to come urgently?' Malla Khaliq explained his position.

'That means Sul Joo was right. How did this pauper dare take over from Abdullah Shah who has always saved him?' Saying this, he dashed into the drawing room of Gul. On stepping in, he bowed before Raja Rathinder and his rani, saying, 'Good morning, Your Highness!'

Seeing Abdullah Shah there, Amir Joo felt as if he had been struck by a thunderbolt. Raja Rathinder Singh looked at him in surprise.

'Haji Abdullah Shah, the renowned shawl merchant at your service. I arrived from New Delhi just today. Haji Sahib had sent me a message.' Saying thus, Abdullah Shah snatched away the shawl from Amir Joo's hands. Shoving him aside, he threatened him in their vernacular, 'Now you will see how I am going to ruin you.' Then like a typical unreliable salesman, he exaggerated the qualities of the same shawl. Amir Joo, with his head hung low, stood up, came out to the isle and walked up to Malla Khaliq. 'This is what I feared. Haji Sahib, you have ruined me. I had kept these shawls hidden for a purpose.' He went to his small boat and rowed sorrowfully towards his house.

Noor Mohammad said to his father, 'What will this hapless person do now?'

'It is God's will. The poor chap tried to convince me, but how would I know that this Abdullah Shah would resurface so suddenly.'

Inside the guest room, Raja Rathinder Singh and his rani were already spellbound by Abdullah Shah's art of persuasion.

Noor Mohammad came near his father and murmured to him, 'He has already swayed them. Who knows how much he will swindle from them!'

'Amir Joo had prepared these shawls painstakingly and kept them hidden for his own daughter's wedding. He wanted to sell them without letting anyone know.'

Abdullah Shah came out cheerfully and walked up to Malla Khaliq. 'Thank God. The people of royal dynasties always appreciated good shawls. Look at other nobles of today, they cannot even recognize a donkey from a horse.' Casting his glance around, he said, 'Where did that beggar Amir run off to?'

Neither Malla Khaliq nor Noor Mohammad gave him any reply.

'So, should I take leave of you? I have yet to go home.' Saying this, he tried to keep the bundles of currency notes in his pocket, but Malla Khaliq caught hold of his hand and took him behind the houseboat.

'What do you want?' Abdullah Shah asked Malla Khaliq.

'Our commission,' said Malla Khaliq, with his hands extended.

'Since when have you started asking for commission, Haji Sahib?'

'Just from today. You know we too have to run our house.'

Feeling constrained, Abdullah Shah took out six hundred rupees from the bundle and handed over the money to Malla Khaliq. Malla Khaliq kept the money in his left hand and extended his right hand again to Abdullah Shah, saying, 'I mean commission. I am not asking for alms. You have been earning at our houseboats for the last forty years. Today is my turn to get the total commission of all these years from you.'

Abdullah Shah separated eight thousand rupees from the bundle of notes and handing them over to Malla Khaliq said, 'You are looting a poor fellow.'

Putting the money into his pocket, Malla Khaliq said, 'I will ask Raja Sahib, how much he has paid you. In case you have to pay some more, I shall certainly get that from you.'

Abdullah Shah cast a fierce glance at him and hurried out of the scene, saying, 'Yes, yes. My father has left behind a fortune for me.' He sat in his boat, and called out to Malla Khaliq, 'Haji Sahib, you have not been fair to me.' When his boat moved away, Noor Mohammad came near his father, and asked him in a broken voice, 'What is this, Abba? You have violated your lifelong principle of not taking commission from anyone.'

Malla Khaliq took out all the money that he had extorted from

Abdullah Shah and gave it to Noor Mohammad. 'Please go and give this money to Amir Joo.'

When the sun rose, the Dal Lake was enveloped by clouds. It looked like it would rain soon. But after noon, the clouds dispersed and the sun shone again. Malla Khaliq said to his wife, 'All of us are here together today – is it not a good idea to spread a sheet outside in the open and have our meal?'

Aziz Dyad could hardly believe her ears. It had been a long time since her husband had suggested something like this. He called her daughter and all her daughters-in-law and within no time, all the arrangements had been made out in the sun. Aziz Dyad deputed Parveen to summon everyone. Qadir was the first to appear. Seeing him, Malla Khaliq was very happy and asked him to sit beside him.

While handling out the rice bowls to her daughters-in-law, Aziz Dyad said to Zoon, 'Will you please see where Razaq is?'

'He might still be serving lunch to the guests in the boats,' said Noor Mohammad. 'Sit down, he will come by himself.'

Razaq had finished serving Rathinder Singh and his family. He poured coffee for Mrs Mundra, cleaned the table and came out.

Naina Mundra took her coffee and sat down on the sofa. She heard the laughter of Malla Khaliq and the chatter of women outside. She drew aside the curtain and saw Malla Khaliq's family relishing their lunch together. She heaved a cold sigh. In the meantime, her maid entered the room and said, 'Baba has had lunch and is having a siesta.' Mrs Mundra looked at her and asked her to sit. The maid squatted on the carpet near her feet. Mrs Mundra drew the curtain aside again. 'How happy they are together, Tulsi Bai! How fortunate they are. Do you remember the last time Mr Mundra had the time to sit with us for lunch?'

'Sahib is too busy with his work. He has such a big business, how can he afford such leisures? He is shouldering such a huge responsibility. And this family has hardly anything to do. They sit all the day at their home,' Tulsi Bai said.

Mrs Mundra sighed again and said, 'Yes, you are right. How can he find respite from his work?'

She handed over the cup to Tulsi Bai and then reclined, resting her head against the sofa.

Malla Khaliq's family finished their meal, except Razaq who was sitting aside and was still eating. He intermittently, but very warily, kept eyeing Parveen. She, too, seeking one excuse or another, kept looking at him, making sure she was not being watched. Noor Mohammad washed his hands, and stood up to get the hookah when someone called him. 'Noor Mohammad, I have a letter for you.' It was the postman who handed over the letter to him and sat in his boat to count the letters.

Noor Mohammad checked the envelope. It was a letter from his son Nisar Ahmed from Jaipur.

'Abba, it is from Nisar Ahmed. Congratulations, Abba. Nisar Ahmed has passed the examination with a first division.' Malla Khaliq could not contain his joy and stood up. He held Noor Mohammad in a tight hug. The he turned to his wife, 'Are you still sitting there? Go and make preparations for a *niyaz*. Our Nisar Ahmed is now a doctor.'

All the family members came one by one and greeted Noor Mohammad. Mukhta was surrounded by her sisters-in-law. Ghulam Ahmed embraced Noor Mohammad, and Ghulam Qadir also kissed his forehead. The whole family rejoiced. Parveen lifted Aziz Dyad in her arms and gave her a swing. Aziz Dyad screamed, 'Parveen, you will drop me and powder my bones.'

'I will not leave you unless you tell me what gift you have for me on this occasion.'

'I will make you a dress of brocade on your wedding.'

On hearing the word 'wedding', she let her mother go and moved aside in a huff. Everyone else burst into laughter.

On hearing this cheerful din, Mrs Mundra craned her head out of the window of the houseboat. Rani Ranthambore also watched the spectacle inquisitively. Malla Khaliq caught sight of Mrs Mundra and came running near her. He broke the good news to her. 'My grandson Nisar Ahmed is coming home after graduating from medical school!'

Rani Ranthambore heard the news and congratulated him. Malla Khaliq then ran to her and said, 'Thank you, Your Highness. I can hardly believe that our Nisar Ahmed is now a doctor. He is the first doctor in our clan.' In the meantime, Raja Rathinder Singh had also come to the veranda. He also congratulated Malla Khaliq, saying, 'It is really a matter of pride for all of you.'

'I can hardly believe that the little child who used to play here in our compound is now a doctor. Doctor Nisar Ahmed!'

Watching him from a distance, Aziz Dyad said to Noor Mohammad, 'Go get your father here. I am afraid he might go mad with joy.'

Noor Mohammad went near his father. Malla Khaliq said to him, 'Come here, Noor Mohammad.' He then said to Rathinder Singh, 'Nisar Ahmed is his son.' Rathinder Singh congratulated him.

'It is all because of Abba,' Noor Mohammad said to him. Then he said to his father, 'Amma is calling you there.'

'Excuse me, Your Highness!' said Malla Khaliq.

His wife said harshly to him, 'How crazily you were behaving with them! This shows your shallowness.'

'This miracle has happened because of their fortunate arrival,' said Malla Khaliq.

'This is no miracle, Abba,' said Mukhta. 'It happened as a result of your prayers and Nisar's hard work.'

'Yes. She is right,' Aziz Dyad agreed. 'Now sit for a while and calm down. Your knees must be aching. No more of this boyish merrymaking.'

'Believe me I can hardly believe the news! Ghulam Ahmed, please go to Dalgate and ask Lasa the baker to keep twenty dozen ghee-bread ready for us by evening. We shall visit the dargah in the morning with the oblation.'

In the evening, the family prepared some additional dishes and celebrated Nisar Ahmed's success.

While having dinner, Malla Khaliq asked Noor Mohammad, 'What else has he written in the letter? When is he to come here?'

'On the fourth of next month is what his letter says.' Noor Mohammad preferred to be brief. 'He has booked his ticket.'

'Only a few days are left till then.' When dinner was over, Malla Khaliq said, 'Now go to your beds. We have to get up early in the morning. We must reach the dargah well before sunrise.'

Once they were inside their room, Mukhta asked Noor Mohammad, 'Why do you seem to be lost? You did not express much joy after reading the letter.'

'Do you know what Nisar Ahmed has written in his letter?' Taking out the letter from his pocket, Noor Mohammad said, 'Now, take this and see for yourself.'

'How can I see? I am not literate. Tell me frankly what else he has written.'

'He has written that he is not going to stay here to seek a government job. He is going to open his own clinic and his own medical shop. And for this, a boat will not do, so he will have to hire a house. If God wishes, he will purchase a house of his own.'

'Well, he is not wrong. Who will come to seek medical care in a houseboat? You have to seek Abba's counsel. Let us see what he thinks about this.'

'How can I tell Abba that Nisar Ahmed intends to give up living in the boats and start his business in a house on land? Are you crazy? How can I muster the courage to talk like that to Abba? And if Nisar Ahmed really rents a house, we will have to shift there sooner or later. That means we will have to live in a rented house.'

'What else should we do then? Can you consult your mother?'

'That is what I was thinking as well. Let us see what she thinks about this issue.'

'All right.'

'But be careful. Do not divulge this to anyone else in the family, particularly to Abba.'

Having decided thus, they went to bed.

Parveen handed over a basket of vegetables to Zeb, and went out of the kitchen, saying, 'Let me see if this Razaq has given the ironed clothes to Rani Sahiba.'

She could not find Razaq outside. Then it struck her that he must be studying in his shed as he usually did every day during the interval between serving bed tea and breakfast to the guests. Razaq had resolved to pass his matriculation as a private candidate. Parveen knocked on the door of the shed. As soon as Razaq opened the door, Parveen assumed an irate tone and said, 'So you are sitting here! Raja Sahib wants you at once!' Hearing this, he sprang up. Parveen laughed and stared at him affectionately. She asked him tenderly, 'Why are you bent upon tiring yourself by reading so much? What officer's position is lying vacant for you?'

Razaq closed the book, moved near her and said, 'Not just "officer", but "a big officer". You just wait and watch.'

Parveen laughed again.

'Yes. You can jeer at me as much as you like. I have nothing to say now.'

Parveen said nothing in reply. She eyed the pomegranate on the desk. 'Why didn't you eat that?'

'It is a gift from you. I will keep it as a souvenir.'

Suddenly, Noor Mohammad was heard calling, 'Razaq!' Hearing this, Parveen's face paled. 'Oh, they are back from the dargah.' Saying this she dashed towards the rear swamp.

After having his morning tea, Malla Khaliq came out of the pantry. Noor Mohammad asked him, 'Where are you going so early?'

'Yesterday, in all that hurry, I forgot to convey the good news to Narayan Joo,' said Malla Khaliq.

'I phoned him, but he was not at home.'

Noor Mohammad's head felt heavy from lack of sleep the previous night. He decided to tell his mother. He saw Aziz Dyad through the window, hanging out washed clothes. When she walked towards him after finishing her job, his heart pounded in his chest. Aziz Dyad sat beside him and said, 'Why do you sit brooding like this?'

Noor Mohammad mustered all his courage and said, 'Amma, I have not had even a wink of sleep.'

'Yes, it is difficult to sleep when one is overjoyed.'

Noor Mohammad's eyes brimmed with tears. Aziz Dyad felt her heart sink. 'What is wrong?'

Noor Mohammad told her what Nisar Ahmed had written in his letter.

'Have you told your father?'

'No, he was so happy that I couldn't.'

Aziz Dyad heaved a long cold sigh and said, 'You have been wise. He pretends he is calm, but I alone know how this worry gnaws him inwardly that sooner or later, his family will break into fragments.'

Noor Mohammad said, 'Nobody knows Abba's forbearance better than I do. Ghulam Ahmed strives to come out of the rut by purchasing apple orchards, but all is in vain. Yet Abba is silent. And who knows Ghulam Qadir better than I? Abba endures all this because he does not want his children to stray in different directions. How will he bear Nisar Ahmed's decision to live separately?'

'I know it well, but what can we do? Today you, our children, are with us, then you have your children, and they will have their own children. Who can possibly dream of keeping his brood tethered to himself? Nisar Ahmed is right. How can he establish his clinic here? You need not worry too much. I will talk to your Abba. You go ahead and pick a good house for our Doctor Sahib. But keep in mind that the house should be located in the Boulevard just across. Now, my son, please see to Raja Sahib's preparations for going to Pahalgam.'

At Narayan Joo's bungalow, a friendly squabble was going on between the two friends. When Narayan Joo saw Malla Khaliq carrying a box of sweets in his hand, he speedily settled everything with his new customer and greeted his friend. 'First tell me what took you so long to give me this good news? Did you fear any evil eye? I phoned Noor Mohammad just a while ago to inquire about Rathinder Singh's programme and came to know that Nisar Ahmed has passed his examinations.'

Malla Khaliq explained, 'Your grudge is quite justified and I beg your pardon. I was not within my bounds. You know how keenly we desired that Nisar Ahmed should do something that my children could not do. Noor Mohammad had no alternative but to give up his education after his matriculation so that he could help me. Ghulam Ahmed was always averse to studies. And though I had managed to convince Ghulam Qadir to enter college level, he lost his direction. Then there was only one hope left, and Nisar Ahmed has fulfilled my yearning. Believe me, yesterday I lost my wits because of the ecstasy. My brother, please forgive me.' Saying this, he bent forward to touch Narayan Joo's feet, but the latter stood up and held Malla Khaliq in a big hug.

Malla Khaliq unwrapped the box of sweets, took out a piece of barfi. 'Savour this little piece of sweet, it might assuage your anger.'

'You know the doctor has advised me not to eat sweets,' Narayan Joo said, 'but today is a day of utmost joy, and we cannot observe any abstinence. Cheers, old man!' turning to Malla Khaliq, he put the piece of barfi into his mouth. Then he picked up a sweet and offered it to Malla Khaliq. 'To Doctor Nisar's health!'

Tears rolled down Malla Khaliq's cheeks, but there was a warm smile playing on his face. The two friends started conversing about their joys and sorrows. During this heart-to-heart, Malla Khaliq grew serious, and Narayan Joo asked him, 'What worries you now?'

'I wish that Parveen's boat too should find its wharf.'

'Did you receive another message from Haji Ramzan?'

'Yes, in fact the mediator came to our house. But I told him that I would prefer to talk to Haji Sahib myself.'

'If you agree, I can go and settle everything with him.'

'Let us wait for a couple of days.'

'I think his son is really gentle and well behaved.'

'Yes, I think so too. Then again, everyone comes to this world with his or her preordained destiny.'

'It is better to leave all to God.'

Many days slipped away, but Noor Mohammad could not muster the guts to disclose the secret about Nisar's letter to Malla Khaliq, and neither could his mother. Malla Khaliq's happiness remained unabated. Their neighbours thronged in to greet them. Malla Khaliq was unmindful of his earlier worry that two of his houseboats were still lying empty. Raja Rathinder had gone to Pahalgam along with his family. Qadir's houseboat was under a jinx. Malla Khaliq did not pay attention to what progress Ghulam Ahmed had made in his apple trade either, or when Qadir came and left.

He had consulted Narayan Joo and decided that as soon as Nisar Ahmed arrived, he would take him to the health minister for a job. He had helped the minister during his election campaign amongst the boatmen. He was dreaming of the day when Nisar Ahmed would join the big hospital. Cherishing these dreams, he visited Makhdoom Sahib's shrine early in the morning. One day, he met Ramzan Haji at the shrine. While they were putting on their shoes after offering their morning prayers, Ramzan Haji held his arm and led him aside. The two sat under a plane tree and Ramzan Haji began. 'You must please forgive me for not giving you a call or coming personally to your house. Our record-keeper is newly appointed and he had made a lot of mess in the records because of his inexperience.' And then he began to talk about the marriage. 'Your daughter Parveen has won my wife's heart. I wanted to visit your house so that I could ask for your consent. But see how God has willed that we meet at the feet of Makhdoom Sahib. I am sure this marriage has the blessings of the saint.'

Malla Khaliq remained silent for a while, and then said, 'I too am sure that Parvez Sahib is a very refined young man. But I think it is better that we seek his approval before going any further. If he agrees, I have no objection. So far as our wives are concerned, they have perhaps already consulted each other on this issue. It is better that we seek their approval too.'

'That is in keeping with propriety. You go and seek Aziz Dyad's consent. So far as I am concerned, I have already got my wife's consent. In fact, it was at her behest that I entered into this discussion with you.'

Aziz Dyad was waiting for her husband with his morning tea. As Zeb walked into the kitchen looking pale and weary, she asked her, 'Did Ghulam Qadir have his tea?'

'Yes, he did, he poured it directly into his throat and left. God alone knows where he goes so early in the morning!' said Zeb.

Qadir was yet to realize the need for correcting his behaviour. In the small hours of the morning, he stealthily visited Gul Beg who beguiled him by many a charming dream. He had convinced Qadir that if he succeeded in carrying a few consignments of hashish to Bombay, he would roll in millions.

Aziz Dyad was lost in her own musings and did not say a word in reply to Zeb. She had come to the decision that she would have a talk about Nisar Ahmed with her husband. She called Parveen. 'Parveen! Bring me the basket of bread. Your father will be coming soon.'

Zeb stood up. 'I will get it, Amma.'

'No, you sit here. She is not a bride with henna-wet hands.'

In no time, Parveen appeared with the basket. She said, 'You have unnecessarily pampered Razaq. See, he does not bother to bring you this basket of bread. He is a big businessman after all!'

Meanwhile, Malla Khaliq walked into the kitchen, coughing to announce his presence, with Noor Mohammad in tow.

'Why are you so late?' Aziz Dyad asked, looking intently into his face.

'When there is something good to be done, it always takes some time,' Malla Khaliq said, casting an affectionate glance at Parveen and then sitting down close to his wife.

Noor Mohammad said to him, 'Abba, I will go see what Mrs Mundra needs.'

'Sit for a while, you can ask her later,' said Malla Khaliq. Noor Mohammad felt that his mother might have had a talk about Nisar Ahmed with him.

Malla Khaliq glanced at Parveen and then turned to his wife. 'It is rightly said that when God wishes it, He opens all the doors of His mercy. We received the good news from Nisar Ahmed just a couple of days ago, and today Haji Ramzan approached me in person with the marriage proposal for Parveen.'

'Where did he meet you?' Aziz Dyad asked.

'At Makhdoom Sahib's. I have not seen him attending that shrine often. But I think today it was his intention to ask for our daughter's hand.'

Noor Mohammad forgot his own worries, and asked his father in great relief, 'And what was your reply?'

'I waited for him to start. How could I feign to have baseless aplomb, that too at the door of the patron saint? I accepted his proposal, nevertheless, and asked him to let me have a day or so to consult my family.'

Parveen sat with her head lowered.

Aziz Dyad said, 'Why? What do we have to wait for? I shall send them the message that they may fix an auspicious date and come here to see Parveen Lala.'

Noor Mohammad supported his mother's decision. 'Amma is right. Where will we find a nicer family and that too with such a big business?'

Hearing this, Parveen stood up on her toes and dashed out of the pantry.

Malla Khaliq said, 'I do not understand why a daughter scurries when she hears about her marriage.'

'What else would she do?' Aziz Dyad said. 'Should she have continued sitting here and argued about it?'

After congratulating his parents, Noor Mohammad left to see if Mrs Mundra needed anything. Zeb embraced Aziz Dyad and said, 'What a good proposal for Parveen! You were worrying for no reason.'

Parveen sat in her canoe and glided towards the swamps. Noor Mohammad saw her and called out, 'Where are you going?'

Parveen replied, 'Nisar is coming tomorrow. He relishes lotus seeds. I'll go and collect a heap of them.'

Noor Mohammad smiled while entering Gulfam. 'Crazy girl!'

Rowing her boat in full speed, Parveen reached a small swamp. There she turned the prow and glided calmly through the willow thicket towards the rear swamps. She knew well that Razaq, when free from his daily errands, sat there with his books. She tied the boat to a peg and in one jump stepped up to the bank. Razaq was surprised to see her there. Parveen, panting slightly, told him, 'Here you are! Always studying! You know nothing about the world around you! Now get up. We have to collect a lot of lotus pods. Quickly, you know our Doctor Sahib is coming tomorrow.'

Razaq took the oar from her hand and started rowing the boat towards the lotus fields in the lake. Having reached the lotus plants, Razaq started collecting pods. He gathered all the lotus pods around him, and said to Parveen, 'Only these few seed heads are available here. And then there is a barbed wire ahead.'

Parveen looked at him. Razaq was unable to make out what it meant. 'Should I turn the boat round?' Parveen remained silent, but continued staring at him. Razaq was scared. 'Why don't you say something? Should I row back?' he muttered.

A surge of tears burst forth from Parveen's eyes, and she said, 'They are arranging my wedding. Abba, Amma, Noor Sahib, all of them.'

'And when you are wedded off, you will leave this house.' Razaq said naively.

This infuriated Parveen. 'And you will remain here, looking for my shadows.'

Hearing this, a stark pallor seized Razaq's face, but he was unable to find the proper words to say. Parveen was annoyed beyond her limits and asked in an aggressive tone, 'Why don't you do something?'

'But what could I do? Can't they stall this marriage until I pass my matriculation?'

'Why don't you understand? They will take me away and you will be left behind wailing for me. There is still time for you to do something. Abba holds you dear, he is sure to listen to you.'

Razaq grew conscious of his helplessness and said, 'Who am I, and what? I survive on the crumbs that Abba throws away. I am his servant, what can I do?'

Parveen snatched the oar from Razaq's hand and turned the boat. 'Then sit still and curse your life,' she said, and without looking around, rowed the boat fast through the lotuses, mangled many of them and stopped abruptly near the swamp where she had picked up Razaq. The boat was tethered to the bank, yet Razaq remained sitting in the boat. Parveen was angry with herself, and all the things around. Burning with anger, she said to Razaq, 'Why don't you get up now, your books are waiting for you.'

Razaq stood up on his feeble knees and climbed up the bank. He did not dare look back.

Parveen untied the boat and left.

Aziz Dyad finally mustered the courage to reveal the contents of Nisar's letter to her husband. Malla Khaliq was too stunned to utter a word. He remained mute with his eyes shut tight. For a long time, Aziz Dyad did not dare say a word to him. Then when Malla Khaliq opened his eyes, a torrent of tears rolled down his face. 'Well, this was bound to happen sooner or later. Do you know what Mrs Mundra told me? She said, "Haji Sahib, how lucky you are! Your whole family lives together. No differences, nor any squabbles. How refreshing is your cheerful laughter when you sit and dine together." But she does not know that all this is just the facade of our life. I alone know how many cracks have appeared in my family. The day is not far when this family shall disintegrate.'

Aziz Dyad was on the verge of bursting into tears herself, yet she said to console her husband, 'I can well understand. More than me, Noor Mohammad is restless like a fish on a hot pale. He could not muster the courage to talk to you about this.'

'The poor fellow is not to blame. It is the fruit of all that I desired. Nisar was so sharp that I did not want to be an impediment in his career. Whenever I saw the sons of others prospering through education, I longed that my grandchildren should get education, even though my own children could not.'

'Then you need not be so worried. Look at me. Our world is our children and then this world belongs to their children.'

'What you say is true, but you know our own brood is drifting away from us. Nisar Ahmed prefers to live on land. He is not married yet. His mother Mukhta has to live with him so that he is not left alone. Then why should we keep her husband tethered here? I am not so selfish.'

The night passed and the morning sprinkled dew on the velvety grass. Zeb carried the samovar of tea to her room; she looked very happy. Qadir had returned early in the evening after staying away for a week. After a long time, he had showered his love on her as he used to earlier. She went into the room and sat before Qadir. He glanced at her and said, 'How do you show so much kindness towards a useless person like me?'

Zeb smiled and replied, 'Our boat is empty nowadays. I thought I should not forget my habit of getting bed tea for our guests. Now have your tea.' She handed him the cup and then squatted and said, 'The boats of Ghulam Ahmed and Noor Mohammad are occupied. Our boat alone stands empty. This is the season to earn some money. How long will we rely on Abba?'

Qadir thrust his hand into the pocket of his jacket, took out a bundle of notes and placed it before Zeb.

'No more, we shall henceforth have our own food, and that too with a variety of dishes. Just watch how this worthless fellow of yours turns into a millionaire. Here, keep this money.'

Zeb gazed at the money with amazement. 'Where did you get so much money from?'

'I robbed a bank! I looted someone! This money is of my own hard work, take it. It is the share I got in the export business which I have started in collaboration with Gul Beg.'

'I don't know why my heart starts sinking when I hear Gul Beg's name,' Zeb said.

'You don't know what a wonderful man Gul Beg is. Have you ever seen him? He doesn't pay any attention to Ghulam Ahmed or Noor Mohammad. That is why they are jealous of him. He is my bosom friend and also my well-wisher. But please do not mention his name to anyone yet. Now take this money and keep it safely.'

'You better give this money to Abba; it is your first earning after all. He will be really very happy to know that you have started a business of your own. They have started making preparations for Parveen's wedding. Abba must be in dire need.'

'Yes, I will give it all to Abba, but not yet. I will invest this money in expanding my business. And then I know if I give this money to Abba, he will give it to Ghulam Ahmed who will fritter it away in his futile apple business. Now take it before somebody comes in.'

Noor Mohammad cast a distressed look at his father as if he had committed some crime. Malla Khaliq asked him, 'Why do you look so wretched? I have been dreaming of this auspicious day for the last six years. Today is the happiest day of my life. My Nisar Ahmed is coming here as a doctor. Do you remember what he said when he came for vacations? He used to tell me, "Abba, once I am a doctor, I'll get you and my grandmother such a tonic that will give you a fresh lease of youth." First you tell me if you have furnished the house well. Did you change the sofa set and the dining table?'

Noor Mohammad held his father's hand, his eyes surging with tears; yet he could not utter a word. Malla Khaliq held Noor Mohammad close and said, 'Today is a day of celebration. You have to confront the ordeals of life with full vigour. We will make Nisar Ahmed stay here for a couple of weeks and then you will take Mukhta and live in Nisar Ahmed's new house.'

'Abba, we won't go there.'

'Why? Is he to live all alone there? Should he have his meals at hotels? What childish talk!'

'But Abba, how can we leave you and Amma alone here?'

'But you are not going to England. You will continue coming here to work.'

'Abba, you tell all this to Mukhta yourself. I am sure she will never agree with this arrangement.'

'What? It is still my order that works here. You go and tell her.'

Wiping his tears, Noor Mohammad left the room.

Malla Khaliq said to Zeb, 'My daughter, you go and tell Ghulam Qadir to accompany Noor Mohammad to the airport.'

Malla Khaliq took out his coat and qaraquli cap from the almirah.

'Where are you going now? You have already asked Noor Mohammad to go to the airport. What are you stepping out for?' Aziz Dyad asked him.

'I am going to Narayan Joo's house. Ghulam Ahmed is in need of some money. And then I will see how much I owe him. After all, we have to marry our daughter off. I will be back soon.'

In the afternoon, Mrs Mundra returned with her husband Gautam Mundra and they were escorted to their houseboat by Ghulam Qadir.

Mr Mundra stood on the porch of Gulfam and exclaimed, 'What a peaceful place! It was so hectic in the States this time.' Holding Mrs Mundra by the waist, he entered the houseboat. Ghulam Qadir arranged to send the belongings to their bedroom, and while leaving, he said to Mr Mundra, 'Kindly ring the bell if you need anything.'

As soon as Ghulam Qadir bowed out and went into his room, the phone rang. He lifted the receiver. 'Hello! So you are there. I had gone to the airport, just got back home. At this hour? Where?

At Zakoor farm? No, please, no meeting today. Nisar Ahmed is coming home. I will be there early in the morning. What? You have received some new consignment? All right. I'll be there at eleven o'clock sharp. Don't worry. I am Qadir, after all. How can he dodge me? I must hang up now. Abba is home.'

It was Gul Beg on the phone. He had completely ensnared Qadir. Gul Beg's lust for money was insatiable. It was hashish trafficking that helped him prosper. But he kept himself away from this business for he had engaged many others like Ghulam Qadir in this trade. Qadir was a literate fellow and as such Gul Beg had made him a partner to the extent of a quarter in the profit. He had acquired the tricks of the trade from Jane. He had resolved to pursue it for a couple of years, until he had gathered sufficient money to start his own hotel business.

Qadir looked out of the window. Malla Khaliq's boat had touched the ghat. He went out to help him come up the isle. Seeing this warm behaviour, Malla Khaliq felt affectionate towards Qadir. He said, 'Has Mr Mundra reached here? Was his plane on time?'

'The flight landed fifteen minutes ahead of schedule.'

'What is he like?'

'He seems to be a good person. Of course, a little reserved.'

'I will go and greet him. Come with me – no, you better stay here. Noor Mohammad might be coming shortly with Nisar Ahmed.'

He went into Gulfam. Razaq, too, was there with coffee for the guests. Mrs Mundra introduced Malla Khaliq to her husband. He stood up and shook hands with Malla Khaliq. 'You have an excellent houseboat.'

Mrs Mundra, casting a smile at Malla Khaliq, said, 'He is such an excellent person himself – a great patriarch.'

Bowing forward with humility, Malla Khaliq said, 'All your kindness, madam.'

Aziz Dyad was impatiently waiting for her husband. As soon as he entered the room, she said, 'Where have you been so long? Ramzan Sahib was on the phone for you. When I told him that you were out, he gave the phone to his wife. In fact, it was she who wished to have a talk. They are coming here the day after tomorrow to meet Parveen.'

'And what did you tell them?'

'I told them, it is all right.'

'But so early?'

'The sooner the engagement is done, the better it is. You need not worry. I have already made preparations.'

In the meantime, Qadir came in running. 'Abba, Noor Mohammad is coming.'

Malla Khaliq sprang up. 'Please call everyone – Mukhta, Zoon, Zeb, and Parveen, all.'

'They might already be there at the ghat.'

They went out. Aziz Dyad hurried after them. She was about to fall, and Parveen came running to hold her.

Nisar jumped out of the boat to the isle and hugged each of his family members. His grandfather watched this beautiful scene from a little distance, his eyes brimming with tears. Nisar caught sight of him and capered to give him a tight hug. Malla Khaliq kissed him on the forehead and held him close.

Nisar Ahmed muttered, 'It was, in fact, your dream, wasn't it?'

'Of course, it was. Now, it is time that you dedicate yourself to serving the poor and the helpless,' Malla Khaliq said, wiping his tears.

Mrs Mundra, who was watching the scene unfurl from her houseboat, lost no time in congratulating Malla Khaliq. She called out, 'Haji Sahib, I wish you many happy returns! Your scion is home as a doctor. There has to be a feast on this occasion.'

'Surely. A grand feast.'

Ghulam Qadir carried Nisar Ahmed's luggage to his houseboat. 'Abba, let the doctor stay in my houseboat.'

'Yes, I too think so,' said Malla Khaliq.

Nisar Ahmed did not approve of this plan. He said, 'Do you intend on separating me from my family. I will stay with you. I am no lord to stay in the houseboat.'

Placing his hand on Nisar's shoulder, Malla Khaliq said, 'There is little room inside the house.'

Noor Mohammad was also of the opinion that Nisar should stay in the houseboat. He said to his father, 'Let's sit together for a while and then decide.'

When all of them thronged into the kitchen to have their dinner, Malla Khaliq looked fondly over his brood. Ghulam Ahmed's in-laws had come over in the afternoon and had brought along seven-year-old Mukhtar Ahmed, Ghulam Ahmed's son.

Everyone looked happy, except Noor Mohammad. Ghulam Ahmed asked him, 'Are you well, dear brother? Why are you so silent?'

'It is a little fatigue, nothing else. I had to keep waiting for a long time at the airport.'

Malla Khaliq moved the bowl of mutton closer to Nisar Ahmed and picked up his choicest breast-piece and placed it on his plate. Nisar Ahmed noticed this and said in an angry tone, 'Are you still having fatty meat? You should know fats are very harmful to health, bad for the heart, and especially at your age.'

Everyone laughed out boisterously.

'You see, my Doctor Sahib, I will never touch fatty meat again. I henceforth dedicate the rest of my life to you,' Malla Khaliq said, while putting the mutton away.

Aziz Dyad, however, did not appreciate this prescription from Nisar. 'You may practise all your medical knowledge on your Abba, but not on us. If you prescribe stewed vegetables to us, I will surely lie crestfallen.'

Parveen too jeered at him. 'And if you have a doctor as your bride, all of us will be at a loss. If she ever invites us to your house, we will have to savour stewed vegetables, and that too without salt and pepper.'

Nisar Ahmed looked upwards and said, 'Oh God, help me now! I have been singled out by all my kin.'

Zeb said, 'That is why we advise you to get married. Then you will not be alone in your combats with Parveen.'

'Let me arrange life here first. It is my dear aunt's turn to be married off to a good guy. Then you can think of me.'

The mention of marriage jarred Parveen and she said to her mother, 'You see how he taunts me by calling me "dear aunt"? And you watch all this without scolding him.'

'What can they say? Tell me, are you not my aunt?' Nisar continued to tease her.

'But I am younger than you by two years!'

'How does that matter? I am serious, you are still technically my aunt. We have to think of marrying you off. You gave up your studies after the eighth standard. What are you still idling here for then?'

Parveen was not one to accept defeat so easily. She said with aplomb, 'What was there for me to do after studying further? The same cooking and scrubbing—'

Emboldened by this comment from Parveen, Zeb said, 'Yes, there she is right. I also did my matriculation, but what was my gain?'

Malla Khaliq put an end to the argument. He told Nisar Ahmed that Parveen's marriage had been fixed and that Ramzan Haji's wife was to come after two days to confirm the date.

Nisar was happy to know that, for Parvez had been his classmate. He extended his hand to Parveen for a handshake, saying, 'Congratulations, dear aunty!'

Parveen suddenly stood up and left the room without washing her hands.

Feigning anger, Aziz Dyad said, 'See, you made her run away!'

Malla Khaliq supported Nisar. 'He did not say anything wrong. If they are not to cajole each other, who else will?' Then he diverted from the issue and talked about establishing a clinic for Nisar Ahmed. Noor Mohammad felt calmer now. It was decided that Nisar would stay on with the family until Parveen's marriage.

Finally the day came when Parveen's future mother-in-law was to visit to meet her future daughter-in-law formally. Hectic preparations were carried out since morning. Razaq, who felt weary, was busy running kinds of errands. He had already straightened up the drawing room of Gulshan. Meanwhile, Malla Khaliq suddenly realized Nisar Ahmed was missing from the scene. He asked Noor Mohammad, but he didn't know either. Razaq had seen him passing Gul, but he did not dare tell this to Malla Khaliq. He felt restless and utterly disinterested in his work today. He wanted to meet Parveen. He felt like every second was as heavy as a mountain upon his back. Without saying a word to anyone, he went about finishing the tasks allotted to him. Ghulam Qadir mocked him at some point, saying, 'Razaq, who will change the stinking flowers in this flower vase? Is your father going to do this?' But he did not feel any sting and just quietly took the flower vase, cleaned it and decked it with fresh flowers.

When he went outdoors, he glanced at Nisar Ahmed's boat, which was gliding towards the isle. He did not even feel like running to inform Malla Khaliq that the Doctor Sahib had returned. With his head hung low, he went back into the houseboat and placed the flower vase on the table. He peeped through the window and saw Nisar talking to his father while drying his wet hair with a towel. Malla Khaliq soon joined them and asked Nisar, 'Where were you, Doctor Sahib?'

Casting a warm glance at his grandfather, he said, 'Who can resist the temptation of seeing the crystal clear waters of the Dal Lake, particularly someone who has lived in scorching deserts for six years? I just went to Gagribal to soothe my burning body in the waters.'

'That is all right, but you should have informed us before you left. We searched for you everywhere here.'

'I am sorry, Abba.'

While they were engaged in this chat, Razaq came out from Gulfam with a breakfast tray in his hand. Nisar glanced at him and Razaq greeted him with his salaam. When he moved towards the kitchen, Nisar asked his grandfather, 'How long has this Razaq been here?'

'Eight months, more or less. Why?'

'I think he is an honest and hard-working person. He also seems to be educated.'

'It is very difficult to find such boys nowadays. He has no mother and his father has remarried. His stepmother tormented him so much that he had no option but to run away from home. He was in tenth standard then, but had to drop out of school. He had been loitering for two years when I brought him here. But how did you guess he is educated?'

'I was woken up by the sound of a door creaking,' Nisar replied. 'I felt that someone was walking behind the room. I went out and saw him going into his shed. The light was on there. When the light was not put out for a long time, I went near his shed and peeped through a rent. I saw him engrossed in his studies, with books and notebooks in front of him.'

'He yearns to pass his matriculation examination. That is why he studies till late night when he is free from running all the errands in the house.' Malla Khaliq then praised Razaq's work. 'To be honest, he has shouldered the burden of all my work here.'

Everyone engaged themselves in finalizing the arrangements for catering to the guests. Cakes and pastries were beautifully placed in trays, a huge platter of almond kernels and other dry fruits were also kept ready. Ghulam Ahmed got crisp bread baked with fresh ghee from the market. Then he left for Ahdoo's hotel to fetch the best of kebabs and cooked lamb shanks.

When he returned with all these items from the market and reached the wharf at Nehru Park, he caught sight of Raja Rathinder Singh who was assisting his wife in climbing down the stairs; his children were already seated in the shikaarah. Ghulam Ahmed stopped the taxi and hurried to the boatman. 'Ramzana, I too have to go across, wait a minute.' He then unloaded the tiffins from the taxi and carried his entire load into the boat. He first greeted Raja Rathinder Singh and then said to Ramzana, 'Come and help me, please. Keep all these things in the hind prow, and I will sit there.' Then he said to Rathinder Singh, 'You will excuse me for this annoyance. I am in a hurry to get all these goods home and that is why I stopped your boat. You know, some guests are expected today to meet Parveen. It is her mother-in-law-to-be who is coming.'

The rani looked curious. She said, 'But why? She must have seen Parveen on some occasion and then sent the proposal.'

'Yes, that is true. But it is our custom here.' Then turning to the boatman, he said, 'Now, Ramzana, please be a little faster.'

Malla Khaliq sighted his boat from a distance and recognized Rathinder Singh and his family. Noor Mohammad, who was sitting beside his father in the veranda, said to him, 'I wonder they have returned so soon!'

'Why should they stay there longer? Rathinder Singh had no interest in going to Pahalgam. He had, in fact, come here to get some rest.'

Parveen sat petrified in Zeb's room while Zeb, like a trained costume designer, was busy adorning her. In her bridal attire which was intricately embroidered with silver thread, Parveen looked very beautiful. When Zeb put the headcloth with crystals on her head, it seemed as if the constellations had come along with all their starry legions to bless her beauty. Zeb whispered, 'Look into the mirror. Oh God! Save her from the evil eye!' Parveen raised her eyes towards the mirror. She heaved a deep sigh and her eyes watered. Laying an affectionate hand on her shoulder, Zeb said, 'What one desires is not always fulfilled. So I advise that you forget all that has happened. Have courage and go ahead. Therein lies the honour of this family.' Parveen cast a piteous glance towards her. Before Zeb could say anything more, the door opened and Aziz Dyad hurried in. 'Have you finished, Zeb? Haji Sahib's car has already reached the wharf. Now stand up, my darling. It will not take them much time to row across. Come with me.'

Aziz Dyad held Haji Ramzan's wife in a tight hug.

Mukhta came out with a kangri and isband. Close behind her walked Zeb, escorting Parveen. Razaq came out of the houseboat with a tray. When he saw Parveen advancing towards the houseboat, he moved aside to make way. Parveen was walking listlessly towards the houseboat with her head bowed in resignation. She did not, therefore, notice Razaq there. But when she placed her first step on the stairs, she heard Malla Khaliq calling Razaq.

Parveen stopped in her tracks. She felt as if she were a sacrificial lamb being led to the slaughterhouse. She could not control herself and looked behind towards her father and Razaq. Zeb caught hold of her hand and firmly led her on.

In the drawing room, the two chief ladies were busy talking. Ramzan Haji's wife was not only a well-off woman, but also a large-hearted, warm lady. She was four times the bulk of Aziz Dyad, and had a pretty round face. She also bore a happy temperament and giggled at everything. The two other ladies with her were her stepdaughters. Both the daughters were already married. Parvez was the only son of Haji Ramzan who would carry on the family business.

When Parveen stepped into the drawing room, both the daughters stood up and made her sit between them. Ramzan Haji's wife kissed her forehead. Aziz Dyad put a handful of the isband into the embers in the kangri. Qadir spread the dining sheet, and then Razaq came in with a tray of dry fruits and placed it very slowly before Haji Ramzan's wife. For a fleeting moment, his eyes met Parveen's. He started and left the room, with Ghulam Qadir following him. Ramzan Haji's elder daughter took some almonds and pieces of mishri and fed Parveen. Her eyes were brimming with tears. The other daughter noticed it. She removed the smoking kangri and said to Aziz Dyad, 'The smoke from the isband is watering Parveen's eyes.' Mukhta called 'Razaq, Razaq!' Hearing the call, Razaq re-entered. 'Keep this kangri outside.' With his head hung, he bent forward to lift the kangri. He yearned to exchange one more glance with Parveen, but he couldn't do it. He took the kangri and left.

Noor Mohammad escorted Rani Ranthambore to the drawing room. He said to Zeb, 'Let her sit beside Parveen. You should explain every custom to her.' Aziz Dyad whispered to Haji Ramzan's wife and the two daughters who this rich lady was.

Parveen shrank to leave enough room for the rani to sit comfortably. And then Haji Ramzan's daughters started adorning her with gold ornaments. Parveen was still shedding tears. The rani took out a handkerchief from her bag and wiped her tears. Then she looked into Parveen's face and her eyes moistened. Aziz Dyad could not stop her tears either. Ramzan Haji's wife raised her spirits, saying, 'I wish every mother of every daughter this happy occasion. Why do you shed tears? I will house her in my heart.' Aziz Dyad wiped her tears with her headcloth and smiled. With her eyes cast down, Parveen sat like a cold wall of stone.

When the women finished adorning Parveen with gold ornaments, Ramzan Haji's wife kissed her forehead and filled her lap with coins of gold. Her daughters also presented the bride-to-be with some gold coins.

The rani turned to Parveen. She touched her chin and looked intently at her face. Then she said, 'My friend looks like a fairy descended from the sky.' Looking around at everyone, the rani continued, 'Perhaps you are amazed that I called her my friend. You may ask her if she accepts to be my friend or not. You adorned her today the same way she adorned me once with a Kashmiri phiran and silver ornaments. From that very day, we decided to be friends, isn't it so, Parveen?' Parveen replied with a nod. The rani then looked towards Haji Ramzan's wife and said, 'Your son is really lucky to get such a princess as his bride.'

Haji Ramzan's wife smiled and said, 'And our Parvez Lala also is no less handsome than a prince.'

Zeb explained to the rani what had been said in the vernacular. 'So obviously all your grandsons and granddaughters, too, will be pretty.' Everyone laughed and Haji Ramzan's wife uttered '*insha-allah*'.

Razaq came in again with a tasht and naer. He helped all of them wash their hands one by one, but when he was near Parveen, Zeb got worried. She quickly took the ewer and the flask from Razaq's hands and said to him, 'You go help Qadir Sahib with the plates.' Razaq felt as though he had escaped from the gallows.

Malla Khaliq was strolling nervously on the isle. Noor Mohammad perceived his restlessness and went near him. 'Why are you so worried? We are not failing in any way in entertaining the guests.'

'I am not worried about that. You know we have brought up Parveen with so much of love and care, and see now she is going to be separated from us. This is the ache that I bear as a stone in my bosom.'

Noor Mohammad heaved a deep sigh. 'How can we help that? This is God's rule, and we all have been following it since time immemorial.'

Malla Khaliq sat in a chair and looked towards the sky muttered.

A full moon shone behind the summits of the Zabarwan mountains and gleamed through the clouds. Razaq had finished washing all the utensils and was keeping them in the basket when he caught sight of Malla Khaliq. Razaq quickly followed him. Hearing the rustle of dry leaves, Malla Khaliq stopped and turned to him.

'Razaq! I didn't see you there. Is all well?'

Razaq did not say a word. He had resolved to reveal the malaise of his heart to Malla Khaliq, but he felt bereft of all expression when he came face-to-face with him. Malla Khaliq repeated his question, 'Tell me, my dear son. Why are you so morose?'

Razaq still could not get the words out.

'What is it? Has anybody been rude to you?'

Razaq stammered, 'No … nothing.'

Malla Khaliq said, 'Go in, my son, and eat something. You have been so busy the whole day, and obviously must be quite tired. Then get some sleep.'

Razaq cast a glum look at him and then left for his shed. Having entered the shed, he opened the window, sat on the wooden box, and gazed at the Zabarwan mountain. The moon looked helpless in the snare of the quivering branches of the willows. He heaved a deep sigh and stood up. He squatted on the rush mat, opened the notebook that lay there with the pen in it as a mark, and began writing a letter to Malla Khaliq.

'My gracious master, you asked me what ailed me. In fact, I was eager to give voice to my hidden sickness, but in spite of all my attempts, I dithered as words failed me. Thus I am writing this letter to you. To be honest with you, Parveen Lala and I have been very close to each other and have been dreaming of creating a world of our own. She is not happy with the relation that you—' His pen stopped there abruptly. His heart shuddered. He felt as if some stranger had emerged from his soul and hurled him from a daunting height while reprimanding him saying, 'Why are you so crazy? Why do you aspire to capture the shining stars in the sky with your airy ropes? You are a pauper, surviving on the leftovers of Haji Sahib's house! If this letter reaches Malla Khaliq or his sons, they will chop you into pieces. Not only you, but also Parveen.' Razaq let out an involuntary yell, 'Oh my God! What should I do? If I do not express myself, Parveen will be but a living corpse.' His inner voice emerged again. 'Time will heal her. Did you not notice how Haji Ramzan's wife and daughters showered Parveen with love? Do you fail to understand what a prestigious, honourable family she is being wedded into? And what have you to offer her? You cannot even provide her with clothes to wear. She is about to have all her desires fulfilled and here you are, trying to dishonour her family and make her the scapegoat! Is this what you do to someone you love?' With an uncontrollable shudder, he ripped the leaf off the notebook, and tore it into pieces. Then he stretched himself on the bed.

The moon seemed to be drifting in and out of the criss-cross of willow branches. He continued gazing at it. The whole world was shrouded in darkness. Time seemed to be standing still. He heard a boatman singing an amorous song in the distance.

Mooh maetch wata myani zan maeshiravakh
Yaad pemai thari thawakh kyah.
Shahar treavith potvan te pravakh,
Yaad pemai thari thawakh kyah

(Oh my pleasure-seeking love,
You might forget the paths to me
Howsoever you try
You cannot help but remember me.
You might be in a city
Or dwelling in some hinterland but
You cannot help but remember me)

At the same hour, in her room, Parveen felt a restlessness seize her. She was seized by a mad desire to run to Razaq, rip away all her clothes and surrender her body to him before any other man could touch her. Every word of the boatman's song pierced her like an arrow.

The boatman was now very close to the houseboat. He continued singing. With every stroke of the oar, he called out to the separated lovers:

Yti bani tati kanh divtah samikhi,
Ta khoni lalanaavi sonzlove maenz,
Atha saet vache tani mutchrivi,
Yaad pemai thari thawakh kyah

(This too is likely that you meet some God
Who shall lull you through bright rainbows.
And when he starts unbuttoning you and
Suddenly you are reminded of my touch
Then what shall you do …)

Every particle of Parveen's body simmered. She stood up, opened the window and looked around. Razaq's shed was distinctly visible in the moonlight. The window of the shed was open. She imagined if Razaq was sitting at the sill, staring towards her window in the dark. She could not hold herself back any more. She opened the door and sneaked behind the house. The boatman's song had faded away. Razaq saw her coming towards him. He was perplexed, and opened the door to come out. But Parveen pushed him in, went in and slammed the door behind her. She wrapped him in a tight hug. Razaq's eyes were drowned in darkness. He could not decide what to do. Parveen was glued to his body, and he quivered like a helpless pigeon. Then Razaq's love also surged forth. It was a sweet feeling, a virgin sap that pervaded every bit of their bodies making them oblivious to the world outside. Razaq finally took her in his arms and held her close to his chest. Parveen raised her eyes to his face and then closed her eyes in prayer: 'Oh, that I could breathe my last in this blissful moment. Oh that I could attain freedom while remaining captive in your arms!'

Razaq woke with a start. He freed himself from Parveen's clasp and turned his back to her. He started cursing himself, 'What have I done! Oh, I should not have lost my senses!'

Parveen held his shoulders and made him turn towards her. She said to him, 'Look into my eyes.'

Razaq gave her a shove and said angrily, 'You please leave before doom befalls us. For God's sake, leave.'

Parveen nestled closer to him and said, 'Razaq, there is still time. You take me away from here to some other place. If you don't, you will repent it forever.' Razaq held her wrist and dragged her towards the door. Trying to free herself from his grip, Parveen said, 'Let me go.'

Razaq let go of her and, folding both his hands, implored, 'For God's sake, do not be crazy. Our love is as hallowed as the morning dew on the leaves of lotuses. This love shall stay in my heart. Do not desecrate it.'

Parveen was about to speak when they heard the sound of something falling down in the swamps. It was perhaps an owl that had swooped into some nest. Parveen got scared. She cast an angry look at Razaq and ran out. Before getting out of sight, she jeered Razaq for his cowardice. 'You are a spineless fellow, a coward!'

Razaq stood still, like a mound of clay. After a while, he moved towards the window and peeped out. Parveen had reached her room. Razaq remained gazing till she climbed over the sill and went into her room.

Malla Khaliq returned from Makhdoom Sahib's shrine earlier than usual. It was decided that soon after the engagement of Parveen, Noor Mohammad and his wife would go make arrangements at Nisar Ahmed's new house. He did not therefore have his second cup of tea, as he usually did. Aziz Dyad knew what saddened her husband, and she asked him, 'Why do you get up? You did not even empty your cup.' Malla Khaliq replied in a vexed tone, 'I do not feel the need to have more, why should I force myself?' Then he went out of the room. Aziz Dyad looked towards Zeb who was sorting kale leaves. She heaved a long sigh and said, 'Your Abba is not well, I guess. Our guardian saint should come to our rescue or I am afraid he is going to give up.'

'He is possessive of his dear Parveen, and thinks that she is here now only as a guest for a few days,' said Zeb, trying to console her.

But only Aziz Dyad knew what anxiety was gnawing away at his heart. 'My dear daughter,' she said, 'your Abba knows better than anybody else that a daughter is finally to be wedded off. What ails him now is that Noor Mohammad, his best support, is to leave home along with his son.'

Zeb tried to lift Aziz Dyad's spirits. 'But Noor Bhaijaan is not going to stay there forever. His son will get married and then he will return.'

'God only knows when all this is going to happen, if at all it does. Ghulam Qadir must have finished his morning bath; go serve him tea in his room.'

Zeb took the small samovar and went to her room. When she was going out, Aziz Dyad said to her, 'Wake up Parveen also. Tell her to get up and help you in removing the things strewn yesterday.'

The previous night had been a long painful night for Parveen. She remained sitting still near the windowsill. She shuddered when

Zeb opened the door. Zeb sensed something amiss and asked, 'Are you all right?'

Parveen heaved a deep sigh and said, 'What is there to say now? Everything has ended – everything.'

'Nothing has ended. You should thank God that no one in the family knows your secret. Think what muck would have besmeared Abba's cap if your secret were to be out. Such vain infatuations are nothing but dreams that like the will-o'-the-wisp which comes in your way to waylay you. Now accept what destiny offers you. Think of Abba's honour, if nothing else.'

Parveen's eyes spilled over with a gush of pained tears. Zeb too wiped her tears. 'Amma is waiting for you with tea. Then you must help me with some chores.'

Noor Mohammad sat in a corner of his room and gazed at Mukhta. She looked at her husband and said, 'Nothing can come out of this brooding. Now at least help me in folding your clothes so I can put them into the trunk.'

Noor Mohammad was angry with himself. He said, 'Am I to leave this house with all my clothes? I have already put one set of night clothes in the bag, and the rest of the clothes I will put on. Tomorrow I will come back and change. Now hurry up and do not plague me further.'

Hearing this, Mukhta banged the lid of the trunk shut. 'You behave as if we are being taken away to be put in a cell. If Nisar Sahib finds you in this huff, he will surely run back to Jaipur. Do you want that?'

Noor Mohammad felt helpless. He stood up, opened the almirah and started taking out his clothes.

Malla Khaliq finished the morning survey of Gul. From there he phoned Narayan Joo, but his manager informed him that he had left with tickets for Raja Rathinder Singh. He therefore went out and sat down on the ghat to wait for him. Aziz Dyad found him there. 'Why are you sitting all alone over here? Don't you want to eat something?'

'Didn't I tell you that I am not hungry?' Malla Khaliq replied, without even turning to look at her.

'All right. If you do not want to eat anything, don't, but tell me what this hide-and-seek is all about.'

'I am not playing hide-and-seek. I am waiting for Narayan Joo to come. You know Rathinder Singh is to leave tomorrow.'

'You could give him a ring; what will you gain by sitting here so sullenly?'

'That much intelligence I also have. He has left his house to bring the tickets here. That is why I am sitting here waiting for him. Do you understand?'

'Why do you get so irritated for nothing? Noor Mohammad was sincere in telling you that he wished to stay here. Why didn't you agree with him?'

'For God's sake, forgive me now. Go in. Narayan Joo is about to reach. I will have to listen to his lecture too.'

Not wanting to argue further, Aziz Dyad turned round and walked towards the pantry.

Narayan Joo's shikaarah was anchored, and he alighted on the bank in one jump. He said to his friend with an affable smile, 'Did you see my agility, Haji Sahib?' Malla Khaliq did not reply. Narayan Joo moved closer to him and said, 'Why is our Haji Sahib brooding?'

'How can I tell you? You know Nisar Ahmed is going to leave this house today and live on land.'

Laying his hand on Malla Khaliq's shoulder, Narayan Joo said with warm affection, 'Oh, this is the cause! You yourself were so keen to see Nisar Ahmed complete his education. Now when he has, he is not going to sit on your knees. Haji Sahib, why don't you understand the pace of the times? You see—'

Without letting him continue, Malla Khaliq shoved Narayan Joo's hand away from his shoulder and climbed up the steps to the isle. 'It is easy to lecture,' he said. 'But only the suffering person knows his pangs.'

'I do not mean to lecture you, I want to tell you the truth. Do you think that I do not feel your pain? But this idle pining will not benefit you. And Nisar Ahmed is not going to any foreign country. Moreover, Noor Mohammad will keep visiting you every morning. How does it matter whether he sleeps here or there?'

In order to end the issue there, Malla Khaliq said, 'Are the tickets confirmed, or are they still on the waiting list?'

'I got them confirmed in the special quota.'

'Please inform Raja Sahib. He was very anxious.'

Narayan Joo walked towards Gul and Malla Khaliq went to his own room.

On entering his room, he saw Nisar Ahmed waiting for him.

Nisar got up and waited for him to sit. Malla Khaliq then glanced at Nisar Ahmed who sat with his head hung down as if he had committed some crime. All of a sudden, compassion overwhelmed Malla Khaliq and he moved closer to him. He said to Nisar, 'Why are you brooding like this? Why don't you go and help your mother?'

Nisar Ahmed could not say a word, he embraced his old grandfather and began to sob.

'See what a crazy fellow he is! You are not going to migrate to London! Why are all of you so sullen? In fact, I myself asked Noor Mohammad to search for a good bungalow where our Doctor Sahib could establish his own dispensary. You were yet to reach here. Do you understand me? And we shall make it a rule that we sit for long hours together once or twice in a week. Now please start, my darling; it will get late otherwise.'

Nisar Ahmed said in a sad tone, 'You are really great, Abba.'

'And you will be greater. You alone shall bring me respect. Now go and be brave. You may ask Razaq to come here. He is not to be seen anywhere.'

Razaq had finished packing Raja Rathinder's belongings, but he seemed to be restless. Rani Ranthambore was keeping the keys in her purse after having locked her attaché cases. 'Razaq,' she said.

'Yes, Rani Sahiba.'

'Go and tell Parveen that Rani Sahiba wants to see her.'

Razaq felt his heart stop. He stood still.

'Did you not hear what I said?'

'Yes, yes, Rani Sahiba, I heard you. Do you need anything else?'

'No, nothing. Just send Parveen in. Now go.'

Razaq did not have the courage to face Parveen. He saw Malla Khaliq who had gone to the ghat to escort Narayan Joo. Malla Khaliq shook hands with his friend and then turned to Razaq. 'Where have you been since morning?'

Razaq hung his head. 'Raja Sahib is leaving today, as you know. I assisted them in packing up.'

Malla Khaliq said rather angrily, 'Do you think it below your dignity now to pay me morning greetings?'

'No, sir. I had come, but seeing you irate while leaving the pantry, I held back.'

Malla Khaliq felt as if he had been caught red-handed. 'It's all right. Has Rani Sahiba finished packing?'

Razaq felt relieved that he was free from further inquisition. Availing himself of this opportunity, he said to Malla Khaliq, 'Rani Sahiba says she wants to see Parveen in her room.'

'All right, I will ask her to go there. Why don't you see if Noor Mohammad needs any help?' Saying this, Malla Khaliq strode towards his room. Upon crossing the threshold, he asked, 'Is Parveen well? I have not seen her since morning.'

Without looking up at her husband, Aziz Dyad remarked, 'Thank God, he is now again in his usual mood. And finally, he remembers his family.'

Malla Khaliq sat down close to his wife. 'For all my life, I have been serving this queen of the house. I merit pardon for this little negligence.'

'If you lose your spirit like this, and that too at trivial things, how can we survive these last days of our lives?'

'I agree. I will be braver henceforth and face all storms.'

'Come, come! That you could do when you were young.'

'But I am no centenarian yet! I can row my boat without a halt and overtake all others.'

Aziz Dyad turned to him and said warmly, 'It is all right. Tell me why you inquired about Parveen.'

'Where is she? Rani Sahiba wants to see her.'

'Why?'

'How do I know? She asked Razaq to send her in.'

'She might be with Noor Mohammad. I sent her there to help him.'

'Will you please go and tell her that Rani Sahiba needs her?'

Aziz Dyad got up and walked out of the room.

Rani Sahiba had yet to finish packing some of her luggage. She was busy passing items to Razaq, who kept them neatly in the bag. Then she asked him, 'Didn't you convey my message to Parveen?'

Razaq told her that he had passed the message on to Haji Sahib. Rani cast a penetrating glance at his face and said, 'Why do you look so down? You should consult a doctor.'

Razaq sighed and said, 'My doctor is here in this very house.'

'Oh yes. I forgot that Haji Sahib's grandson is a doctor.'

Razaq had no words in reply.

'Didn't your doctor give you any medicine?'

Razaq sighed again and was about to say something when Parveen appeared at the door. As soon as she stepped in, she froze in her tracks. Razaq paid the rani his salaam and went out.

'Are you feeling shy to come in? Look around, none of your in-laws are here. Come in,' the rani said to her.

Parveen looked at the suitcases and said, 'So you are leaving?'

'Yes, my daughter. One has to leave after all.'

'Why can't you take me along as your daughter?'

The rani felt as if all her wounds had opened again. Holding Parveen's hands in hers, she said, 'Don't say that! You are your father Haji Sahib's soul. If I took you along with me, what would happen to him?' Then the rani set her hands free and heaved a long sigh. 'I also had a daughter, much like you, though perhaps not as pretty. But her eyes were bigger and more limpid than yours.' She continued, 'She was very fond of horse racing. One day while riding on rough grounds, her horse stumbled and she fell into a very deep gorge. We could not even recover her body.'

Then the rani got up and went to the dressing table. She pulled open the drawers and took out an old-fashioned box. She opened the box, took out a ring and, holding Parveen's hand in hers, put it on her finger. Parveen dithered and said, 'No, no. You have already given me so much.'

'I gave that to the would-be bride. This ring I am giving to my own daughter. Keep it safe; it is a diamond ring.'

'Diamond! In olden times, some queens used to keep a diamond hidden with them so that they could end their life by swallowing it.'

'Don't say such ominous words. It is not a diamond to be swallowed, but to be worn. God will keep your married life safe from all hazards. Your mother must be looking for you. You may go now.' She kissed Parveen's forehead.

Razaq stood in the corridor waiting for her, but Parveen ignored him. Trying to stop her, he said, 'Parveen, please talk to me.'

Parveen stopped, cast an angry look at him and said, 'Coward, gutless fool!' She shoved away the hand he had raised to block her path and stormed away.

The sun was trailing towards the distant cliffs of the Apharwat mountain when Malla Khaliq entered Noor Mohammad's room, where the whole family had assembled, and said, 'The sun is about to set. Now get up or it will be too late.'

The whole family came out to the isle. Seeing the luggage,

Malla Khaliq heaved a long sigh and called Razaq who was still standing near Gul. 'Are you still waiting to put all this stuff into the boat?'

Without giving him any reply, Razaq picked up the bigger suitcases and moved quickly to the ghat. Nisar Ahmed carried some odds and ends. Ghulam Ahmed and Ghulam Qadir also assisted him.

After keeping all the items in the boat, Nisar Ahmed was ashore again, embracing Zoon, Zeb and Parveen by turns, exchanging farewells. Then he went to Aziz Dyad, shook her by her shoulders to cheer her up and said goodbye.

'Curse this "goodbye"! Am I the only person in the family who deserves a stiff, English goodbye?'

'That's only because you are so special …'

'Now remember, if you do not come see us every day, I will come and settle myself in your new house. Do you hear me?' Nisar held her again in his arms, and she burst into tears.

When the boat was at quite a distance, Aziz Dyad wiped her tears and turned towards the isle. Her daughters-in-law and Parveen followed her. Malla Khaliq remained gazing at the boat until it went out of sight. Then he quickly went to Gulshan and climbed up the stairs to the deck. He could still watch the boat trailing away towards the light of the setting sun. He stood like a man who had lost a bet.

Malla Khaliq and Aziz Dyad were making plans for Parveen's wedding. Aziz Dyad had spread out her own jewellery before Malla Khaliq. 'You need not worry about the ornaments. We can get new ones by melting these. These were gifted to me by your mother.' Malla Khaliq held her hands and said, 'I don't know whether these ornaments were gifted to you by my mother or father. I am simply conscious of the fact that I could not get you even a single ring in all my life.'

'You have showered three daughters-in-law with gold. They

are as dear to me as my own daughter. You have given me so much that is invaluable and I cannot repay you for – my loyal sons, my beautiful daughter, and my dear grandchildren. I have this blossoming garden around me. What else do I need?'

'No, no. You keep these knick-knacks for yourself. You need not worry. God has always been kind to me. He will surely show me a way out.'

'I am giving all this to my own daughter. Is there anyone dearer to me in this world? Besides, I am not going to carry all this along with me to my grave.'

'I wonder why Haji Ramzan Sahib is in such a hurry. He could have waited a year or so for the wedding.'

Aziz Dyad was a seasoned lady. She said, 'We are after all the parents of a daughter. You also have a honourable name in the community. If we hesitated in any way, people might take offence. They will begin to say that Malla Khaliq isn't even able to marry off his only daughter, that's why he has put it off for next year.'

'You are right. In fact, I have already made most arrangements. The only worry I have is about the jewellery. You have eased that worry as well now. But remember, these ornaments are your debt on me.'

'Come, come! There are so many other debts you have already. How many debts can you repay me!' she teased.

'One and all, remember. You only pray that the tourist season be in full swing again.'

'I pray that God grants you all your prayers. Let us sleep now, it is already midnight.'

Aziz Dyad woke her husband up in the morning to remind him that Raja Rathinder Singh was going back. Malla Khaliq hastened to get up, had a bath, offered his prayers, and quickly had a cup of tea.

Raja Rathinder Singh and his wife had already readied themselves for the journey. Their flight was in two hours. Noor Mohammad had come in at dawn and had made Razaq carry their luggage to the ghat. Malla Khaliq said, 'You're up so early!'

'Abba I could not sleep peacefully there. Then the worry that Raja Sahib is leaving …'

Raja Rathinder Singh came out of the houseboat, and Malla Khaliq went near him. 'Good morning, Your Highness.'

'Good morning. How are you?'

'By God's grace and your kindness, all is well.'

'All set?' he asked Noor Mohammad.

'Yes, sir,' Noor Mohammad said. 'Your luggage is already in the shikaarah.'

In the meantime, the rani appeared holding her grandson's hand. 'We had a very good time here. We did not even feel like we were away from our own home.'

Raja Rathinder Singh held Malla Khaliq's hand and said, 'It was really wonderful. We will never forget your affection. If God wishes, we will spend next summer here with you again.'

'Most welcome, sir. The houseboats belong to you. If you come again, that will be our good fortune. We wish you could have stayed for one more week, we feel honoured by your presence.'

The rani said to him, 'I cannot express in words how sad we are to leave. But we are helpless. We have to visit many countries before going back to the USA. Besides, you know how difficult it was for Mr Narayan Joo to get our booking confirmed.'

Malla Khaliq stood on the shore and waved to them until they were out of sight. Then he returned to Gul and cast a piteous look at it. He said to Razaq, who stood gloomily at a distance, 'Razaq, now shut all the doors and windows there.'

Razaq silently moved towards the houseboat.

Malla Khaliq was not one to give up so easily. Nevertheless, he felt very helpless and lonely since Noor Mohammad had left the house. Lost in thoughts, he did not notice Ghulam Qadir while going into his room. Ghulam Qadir, who sat nestled near his mother, stood up and greeted his father. Malla Khaliq came out of his reverie and said to him, 'How is it that the sun is shining to brighten our gables? I thank God that you have remembered us and bothered to see us.'

Ghulam Qadir said, 'When didn't I care about you? But, Abba, being too busy with my work, I could not find time to see you. Now Noor Mohammad is not here in the house. If I do not care about you, who else will? As far as Ama Toth Ghulam Ahmed is concerned, he hardly has any respite from his business.'

Malla Khaliq knew Ghulam Qadir inside out. Keeping his cap aside, he explained, 'Noor Mohammad has not moved away from the house. He is here before it dawns, and he stays here the whole day. There is hardly any job for him to attend to. Two of our houseboats are lying vacant. Gul, my father's legacy, is also empty now. What could he do here? I advised him to stay there and look after Nisar Ahmed's dispensary, but that is not ready. You know our business is already shrinking.'

Ghulam Qadir grabbed this opportune time to vent his desire. He said, 'To be honest, this business of running houseboats is quite unreliable.'

Malla Khaliq turned angrily to him and said, 'Yes, yes. That is why you are so engrossed in new business ventures of your own. Do you even pause to think about the fact that in hardly a week's time your sister's wedding is to take place?'

'That is why I came so early to see you here. But you were busy with Raja Rathinder Singh.'

Saying this, Ghulam Qadir took out a big bundle of notes and held out the money to his father. Malla Khaliq pushed the notes away and said, 'I know very well what business you are pursuing. Can I accept this murky money for the auspicious occasion of my daughter's marriage?'

Ghulam Qadir said insolently, 'Have I committed any theft? Have I broken into anyone's house? Everyone one else is pursuing the trade of their taste, and you love them. See Ama Toth, he has been swindling your money for two years for his fruit business, but he is still the apple of your eye. I alone am a villain, a loafer!'

Aziz Dyad was about to intervene when Malla Khaliq stopped

her. 'You better shut up. Let me talk. He is always bent upon maligning his brothers. I went to Pattan to see the apple orchards Ghulam Ahmed purchased. God has been very gracious this year. Go see for yourself how plentiful the apples there are. If the season favours him this year, he will be laden with gold. He is following a legal trade.'

'And what illicit earnings am I trying to get? Business is after all just business.'

'Let me know what business you are setting up.'

'I export carpets. Nothing but carpets.'

Malla Khaliq was struck dumb. Aziz Dyad turned angrily to her husband. 'Now why are you suddenly so mute? This poor son of mine has been taken for granted! Of course he blundered once, but that is no excuse for you to always taunt him.'

Ghulam Qadir felt rather emboldened. He presented the money once again to Malla Khaliq and said, 'Abba, please keep this money. I know we need a lot of money for Parveen's marriage. You keep this much for now and let us see how God helps us further.'

Malla Khaliq turned to the window and did not touch the money. Ghulam Qadir turned to his mother. 'Then you keep it, Amma.' Then he said to his father, 'I am also your son. When everyone else is engaged in making their fortune, I too have the right to follow my path.' He went out fuming.

Aziz Dyad went near Malla Khaliq and said, 'He is after all our child. I do not know why you get so irritated at every word he has to say to you.'

Malla Khaliq, already incensed, said to her, 'Go and fling this money in his face. I know it has come from an illicit trade. How would you even know? You stay indoors from dawn to dusk. You know nothing about this world. Your son is sure to bring some calamity upon the whole family. You just wait and watch.'

'We are not dependent on his earnings. I thought that you are a little hard up. We can repay every paisa to him later.'

'Why are you always so adamant on defending him? I have already made all the arrangements. I have yet to settle my accounts with Narayan Joo. You need not worry. I will not go beyond my limits. I have never been tempted to compete with others. Why should I do that this time?'

'You are free to do whatever you like, but for now I am keeping this money in the trunk. You never know when we may need it. '

Saying this, she went into the inner room. An enraged Malla Khaliq stood up. 'I will not budge even if I have to sell my houseboats. I may even mortgage them, but I will not spend a paisa of this accursed money.'

Inside their room, Ghulam Qadir was screaming at Zeb. 'What did you say? "Go and give this money to your Abba! He will give up his grudge." Now you see how well he gives up his grudges. This house is a veritable hell for me.'

Zeb tried to douse the fire and said very timidly, 'But what did he say?'

'He did everything short of slaying me. He rebuked me so harshly – as if I had committed murder. Oh, I am fed up now!'

He put on his cap and rose to go out. Zeb tried to stop him, 'Where are you going? You have not had even water since morning.'

'My father made me eat and drink a lot.'

'Eat a little or you will remain hungry the whole day.'

'You need not worry. There is plenty of poison available in the market.' He reached the ghat, drew a rowboat and rowed towards the Boulevard.

Malla Khaliq, too, was walking towards the ghat. He decided to meet Narayan Joo immediately and settle the pending accounts. If he was still facing a deficit of some money, he would take it from him as an advance. In case he failed, he would borrow from any other acquaintance. He was almost at the ghat when he heard the sound of utensils falling down with a resounding crash. He turned back, ran and helped Parveen stand up. He was angry with his wife. 'Was there no one else in the house that she sent you to scrub these utensils? No one cares that this daughter of ours is now a guest here.'

On hearing this, Parveen put her arms round her father and said, 'Abba, am I now so much an unwanted burden that you consider me a guest?'

'Never, my darling child. You will always remain in my heart. Now go in and change. Nisar is probably waiting for you. He wanted to take you to the market and assist you with buying all the items for your trousseau.'

'I am not going to get married. At least not so soon.'

Malla Khaliq comforted her by saying that it was very difficult to get such a good boy and such a good family.

Razaq secretly watched the whole scene from the window of his shed. He felt helpless. He hit his forehead, saying, 'Oh my God! Why did you send me to this world? What sin have I committed? I see my world being ransacked like this and yet I am not able to do anything to stop it!' He moaned, 'Parveen! I really am a coward, a gutless fellow. I tried to clasp air in my arms. What a fool I am! Please forgive me.'

Gul Beg was haggling with the smugglers on his porch. His eyes were focused on the gates for he had phoned Ghulam Qadir to make sure he reached Zakoor before noon. Yet there was no trace of him. Satar Shah finally said to him, 'They have to be at the airport. Besides, they hardly have anything to do with Ghulam Qadir, all their dealings are with you.'

'No. I want them to meet him one more time. It is ultimately he who will carry the consignment to them.'

'What do you say, Gul Sahib?' one of the two smugglers asked. 'I told you that it would be better that you talk to Ghulam Qadir directly.'

'We have nothing to say to him. He will get us the consignment and we will send you the money.'

'Do you trust him?' Satar Shah asked in order to make things clear.

'If I did not have trust in him, why would I make him a partner?

Look here, my brother, he will be carrying the consignment for the first time and so will not arouse any suspicion. You need not worry.'

'He is a little irascible and that worries me.'

The smugglers bade farewell to Gul Beg saying, 'So, Gul Sahib, let us leave. You send us the freight and we will send you the cash through Ghulam Qadir.'

Gul Beg stood gazing at them until the taxi drove out of the gate. Then he climbed up the stairs and dialled Ghulam Qadir's number. But no one answered the call. Qadir had already left to see him. In the meantime an auto stopped outside the gate. The gate opened and the dog, tethered to its peg, started growling. Ghulam Qadir dashed to meet Gul Beg who was fuming with anger.

'What is the point of coming now? They waited for two hours to see you. I think you are not fit for this kind of business,' Gul Beg said to him.

'It is very difficult for me to leave the house. Parveen's wedding is next week. If I do not stay in my house, Abba is sure to interrogate me. Besides, there was hardly any serious reason for me to be here with the guests. Everything has already been decided,' Qadir explained.

'Look here, Ghulam Qadir, we cannot have complete trust in anyone in the trade that we have chosen. Nevertheless, I told them that once you are free from your sister's wedding, you will deliver the freight to them.'

'Did they agree to wait till then?'

'They agreed after much persuasion.'

Ghulam Qadir felt relieved and sat down. Gul Beg took out his golden cigarette case and passed a cigarette to him. He lit the cigarette, drew a long puff and said, 'How much did they pay in advance?'

'Fifty thousand. This was why I was so eager to see you in their presence so there was no scope for any doubt.'

'Do you think I don't trust you? Look here, this Ghulam Qadir has so much faith in you that he does not even have in himself.'

'Yes. If we don't trust each other, the whole trade will end after a single deal.'

'Now please get up and bring me a soothing glass of beer.'

'You ask for beer? I will let you swim in wine. But make sure that this first freight reaches its destination.'

'Consider it done, brother.'

With every passing day, Parveen's wedding drew nearer, and Razaq grew increasingly morose and aloof. He was seen busy tidying the houseboats earlier than usual and then remain confined in his shed.

He sat brooding in his room when he heard the splatter of water from the tap in the compound. He peeped through the window. It was Parveen cleaning fish. Hidden behind the windowpane, Razaq observed her.

After cleaning the fish, she started cutting them into pieces. Lost in thought, she was looking towards the lake, when she accidentally cut a finger. Razaq shuddered at this sight. Parveen put the fish in a pail and kept her bruised finger under running water. But this did not stop the flow of blood. Seeing this, Razaq dashed out. He took out a handkerchief from his pocket, tore it into two pieces, and held Parveen's hand in his own. Parveen drew her hand back. 'Leave my hand. Let all the blood flow out from my body. Why are you concerned? Leave me be.'

'Am I so wicked that you hate me so much?'

'I say, leave me!'

But Razaq did not leave her hand and started bandaging it. 'You tell me what I can do. Tell me, please.'

'They will take me away after three or four days. And then you can stay here all alone.'

Razaq stared at her face. Tears washed his face. But he controlled himself and put a knot on the bandage. He bent towards her, and she cast a loving glance at him. He took the knife from Parveen and started cutting the fish. Parveen moved closer. Razaq looked all around. Ghulam Qadir's window was ajar. Zeb was probably there. Parveen said, 'Why are you so frightened? Look at me.'

Razaq looked up at Parveen.

'If you really want me,' said Parveen, 'there is still time for you to stop me from going away.'

'Do you really mean that? Can I stop you? Can I?'

'Yes. If you can talk to Abba, the marriage can be stopped. You are so dear to him.'

'What will I talk about?'

'Whatever is pent up in your heart.'

'No, no. I cannot do that.'

Parveen took hold of the basket of fish and stood up. 'Then remain mourning over your destiny and that of mine like a loser!' With an angry yank, she strode towards the kitchen.

Zeb witnessed the scene from behind the windowpane. She heaved a deep sigh and sat down against the wall.

Parveen kept the basket of cleaned fish in the kitchen and nestled close to her mother. Aziz Dyad screamed when she saw the bandage on Parveen's hand. 'Oh my God! What have you done to your hand?

'It's nothing. Just a minor cut.'

'Who asked you to clean the fish?'

'You. Who else?' said Parveen with a laugh.

Aziz Dyad started cursing herself. 'I have really lost my wits. When a bride is getting ready for her wedding, she shouldn't handle even a blade of grass.'

'It's okay. I will not even wash my own plate henceforth. Happy? Now show me your right hand.'

'Why?' asked Aziz Dyad.

'Just do as I say!'

Aziz Dyad smiled and shot out her right hand from the sleeve of her phiran. Parveen held her hand. 'Now close your eyes.'

Aziz Dyad shut her eyes and laughed.

'Stay like this, I will show you a magic trick.'

She took out the diamond ring the rani had given her from her pocket and wore it on her middle finger. Aziz Dyad could not bear the suspense any longer and she opened her eyes.

'Where did you get this ring from? I remember seeing a similar one on Rani Sahiba. Did she drop it before leaving?'

'No. I stole it from her bag.'

Aziz Dyad screamed. 'What? No! Tell me the truth!'

Parveen narrated the whole event. Parveen slipped the ring on to Aziz Dyad's finger and said, 'See how beautiful it looks on your hand.'

'It has such a big stone!'

Parveen laughed at her mother's innocence. 'It is not a stone, it is a real diamond.'

Aziz Dyad could hardly believe her ears that Rani Sahiba had gifted such an expensive ring to her daughter. 'Who knows how much she might have spent on it.'

'What do you have to with that? You just see how it suits your hand.'

Heaving a long sigh, Aziz Dyad said, 'What hands can it suit? These hands have become stone-hard from scrubbing utensils for the last forty years. There was a time when these hands of mine were as fair as yours. Do you know when your Abba held my little delicate hand in his brawny and tough hands the first time, it almost disappeared in his fat fingers.'

While she was lost in reminiscence, Malla Khaliq came in. Aziz Dyad immediately hid her hand behind her. Malla Khaliq asked Parveen, 'Is all well? Why does she hide her hand from me? Has she hurt it?'

Parveen laughed and said to him, 'No, Abba. There is nothing to worry about. In fact, she is wearing a ring.' Then she said to her mother, 'Show your hand to Abba.' Saying this, she took her mother's hand in hers and said to her father, 'Look, Abba, how this ring suits her hand!'

Malla Khaliq began to laugh. 'What prompted you to wear your young daughter's precious ring?'

'I forced her to wear it,' Parveen defended her mother.

Aziz Dyad handed it over to Parveen. 'Keep it carefully.'

Malla Khaliq asked, 'Where did you get it from?'

'Rani Sahiba gifted the ring to her before leaving,' Aziz Dyad replied on Parveen's behalf.

Malla Khaliq assessed the ring.

'A real diamond is studded in it, Abba. I did my best to resist, but she was insistent. She considers me her daughter. She said that she had a daughter of her own, but—'

Malla Khaliq said, 'I know.'

'How affectionate Rani Sahiba is!'

Malla Khaliq returned the ring to Parveen, and Aziz Dyad said to her, 'This is how sometimes strangers become more supportive than your kith and kin, my daughter. I don't know which city she belongs to, and see how within no time she became a member of our family.'

Malla Khaliq found a chance to lighten the burden on his mind. 'This is the only thing my sons don't understand. All these relations originate from these houseboats of ours. Don't you see how many letters I receive? Letters come from far-off countries across the oceans, where I can never reach. Is there any corner of our own country where we don't have acquaintances? All this is possible because of these houseboats, which your brothers want to sell.'

Aziz Dyad's forehead wrinkled in displeasure. 'See how he drags on a trivial issue! He can't stop finding fault with his own sons.'

Malla Khaliq quickly changed the topic and said, 'How foolish of me! I came here to see my daughter with a purpose and here I get caught in this unnecessary tête-à-tête.'

Sounding angry, Aziz Dyad said, 'Now don't you dare put any blame on me.'

Malla Khaliq cast a loving glance at her. 'I am blaming myself only. I had come here to have a heart-to-heart with my darling Parveen.' He squatted beside Parveen. 'My daughter, I am to be blamed for the harm I have caused you. It was partly my ignorance and partly my inability that I could not provide you with better schooling. Yet I feel proud to have given you lessons in the Quran which is complete education in itself. You are going to enter a new phase in your life. You will be in a new house. Just one advice from me: never lend a ear to backbiting and never get hoodwinked by anyone. If you hear something evil, do not believe it unless you know it for certain. You should respect all the elders and serve them wholeheartedly. Be content with what God bestows on you. Be thankful to God through thick and thin. If you follow this advice, I am sure you will always find your path covered with flowers.'

Parveen held her father in a tight hug and started crying. Seeing this, Aziz Dyad reproached her husband, 'Do you see how you have made my daughter cry?'

'Let her shed some tears. Tears will wash away all her hidden fears and she will be ready to face her new life.'

Parveen held her father closer and a torrent of tears fell from her eyes. Malla Khaliq comforted his daughter by rubbing her back. Aziz Dyad finally rose and helped Parveen stand up. Wiping her tears with the corner of her headcloth, she said to her, 'Go now, my darling. Spend some time with Zeb, she might be feeling lonely. Ghulam Qadir had to visit some friend and is not coming back tonight. Now go. My Dastagir will give you strength and brighten your destiny. You may sleep with Zeb tonight.'

Parveen thought if she sought Zeb's company in this condition, she would have to face a volley of questions. She thought it better to go to her own room, wash her face, change her dress and then go to Zeb's room. On entering her room, her own image in the mirror terrified her. She saw that all that weeping had turned her eyes as red as two dried apricots. She hurriedly entered the bathroom and came out after washing her hands and face. Then she sat down to brush her hair. Razaq's face appeared and disappeared in the mirror. In her dejection and anger, she flung aside the comb and squatted still like a mud wall. She forgot about Zeb. She heard Ghulam Ahmed saying to the boatman, 'Remember, you have to come here quite early, it is very difficult to get the bus later.'

Parveen shuddered; she lifted the comb again and hurriedly tied her hair. She went out to the isle.

The sun had already set and it was getting dark. The electric lamps in the houseboats on the lake looked like dim candles in the mist.

A lamp was shining in Razaq's shed too. The door was ajar. She longed to be there, in Razaq's tight embrace, and ask him why he had come to her house to ensnare her in his love. But she hurried towards Zeb's room.

Razaq sat behind his windowpane. He had placed the doll that Parveen had given him on his trunk. He gazed at it, thinking about how within three days a grandly decked palanquin would come to carry Parveen away and all that would remain with him would be this doll. He felt as if the doll were laughing at his helplessness now. Even after shutting his eyes firmly, the doll danced behind his closed lids. It seemed to be growing in size to assume the form of Parveen. He remembered how she had snatched away the basket of fish from him, calling him a coward venomously. He was drenched in a cold sweat. Taking the doll in his hands, he asked it, 'What could I possibly do? Tell me, what should I do?' He felt that the doll was also jeering at him – 'You are nothing but a coward!' Razaq flung himself down and started moaning, 'Oh my God! What should I do?'

'Where have you been? Amma had asked you to be here a long time ago!' Zeb called out to her sister-in-law.

'I was in my room, changing,' Parveen told her indolently.

'Now come have dinner. It would have gone cold by now.' Zeb filled two bowls with rice. While eating, she noticed the bandage on Parveen's hand. 'Have you injured your hand?'

'It's a small bruise. I got it while cleaning the fish.'

'And who has put this bandage on your hand?' Zeb asked, casting a penetrating look at her. 'See it has come loose. I'll tighten it a little.'

Parveen tried to pull her hand away, saying, 'Let it be as it is, it is only a scratch.'

'No, I can tell that it is very deep and will take a long time to heal. This poor Razaq will not change; he is a yokel even after staying in the city. He doesn't even know how to cover a wound.'

Parveen's heart thumped fast in her chest. She tried to brush aside the mention of Razaq and said, 'When is Bhaijaan expected here tomorrow?'

Zeb held her gaze. 'You crazy girl, I was shocked to see you so sad even after having received such a good proposal. Only now do I see why. I saw how the knife ran through your hand and how Razaq came running to bandage your finger.'

Parveen could hardly look up.

'Look here, Parveen. I have never considered you my sister-in-law. I am your friend. Don't hide anything from me.'

Feeling a little comforted, Parveen replied, 'No, Bhabi, it's nothing serious.'

'It is serious. Okay, tell me this. Do you like Razaq?'

'If you approve of Razaq, then please help us. Please talk to Abba. I will die otherwise.'

'No one dies. All this is idle talk.'

'No, I am serious.'

'Even if destiny helps you marry the man of your choice, there is no guarantee that you will be happy. I liked your brother. Ignoring all norms of modesty, I told my parents that if at all I had to get married, I would marry no one other than Ghulam Qadir; I would otherwise remain celibate all my life. My parents gave in. But look what's become of me now.'

'No, Bhabi, Razaq is not of that sort. Please do me this favour. You tell Abba. I am ready to face whatever happens afterwards.'

'Are you crazy? Qadir belonged to our own fraternity, yet there was such a hue and cry. My father was shocked to hear that his daughter had decided to marry of her own will, so much so that he gave up food and water. Your case is more complex: Razaq neither belongs to our fraternity, nor is he an equal to us in any way.'

'But does he lack anything?'

'He is after all a servant in our house. If anyone comes to know about this, we will be excommunicated.'

'My Bhabi, I nursed only one hope, that you would come to my help.'

'Why are you behaving like a toddler? Why don't you understand that you are going to ruin your life? I saw you two together, and kept the secret, but imagine what would have happened if any of your brothers saw you with Razaq, think what a catastrophe would have befallen both Razaq and Abba.'

A shudder ran through Parveen's body. Zeb held her close and said, 'Don't cry. Nothing can come of it. Now you leave everything to God. He alone will show you the right path. I too have finally entrusted myself to Him.'

Aziz Dyad was very worried yet she did not want to add her worries to those of her husband. But when Malla Khaliq insisted, she had no option but to talk. 'What else could I be thinking except that all three of our houseboats are lying empty.' Malla Khaliq was worried too but he tried to calm his wife. 'As long as I am alive, you need not worry so much. Today I settled all the accounts with Narayan Joo and Raja Rathinder. We have the amount required for the wedding.'

'That is all right. But if we exhaust all the earning of the season, what will we do later? How will we run the house? Our business may remain stagnant for the rest of the season.'

'Have you lost faith in God's grace so soon? He alone is to apportion a livelihood to us all. For the present, our only concern is the wedding. We have to maintain our social standing. We do not have many daughters. Parveen alone is the apple of our eye. Let us realize all our desires on this event.'

'That is true, yet one has to think of so many other factors. Now if I make a suggestion, will you follow that?'

'Have I ever disagreed with you?' Malla Khaliq said.

'Qadir approached me again. He asked me to tell you that if you need more money, you should not get worried for he has already managed that.'

Hearing Qadir's name, he was ablaze with anger. 'He dared to come tell you this and you just listened to him? Is Malla Khaliq so helpless that he should touch that illicit money? Have you spent any of that money he left here?'

'I knew you would get enraged. I have kept the money in the trunk. How could I touch that money without your permission?'

'That is good, but keep it in mind that you shouldn't take even a single paisa from there. Do you hear me? And tell that pampered son of yours that he should be taking proper care of his wife and child. Tell him to avoid getting entangled in the illicit activities his friends are getting him involved in.'

Aziz Dyad defended Ghulam Qadir by saying that he had reformed, but this further stoked Malla Khaliq's rage. He slammed the half-ajar window with a bang, came close to Aziz Dyad, and told her about all Ghulam Qadir's clandestine activities. 'I never want to cause you any anxiety and preferred to remain silent about his nasty deeds. Now it is time that you should also know that he visits that hashish smuggler Gul Beg almost daily to lick his feet. When night falls, he secretly takes the boat of the vegetable vendors and returns before sunrise. He is a bad-tempered young man, and I cannot redeem him. And this is not the proper time to argue with him. An open confrontation might bring us a bad name in the community. This is the reason that I prefer to turn a blind eye to what he does. Please try your best to persuade him to remain at home at least until Parveen gets married.'

Aziz Dyad felt the earth slipping away underneath her feet. 'I wonder why even Zeb did not tell me about this.'

'The poor helpless girl is already bothered about her parents. How could she tell you? You alone can make Qadir realize his mistakes. If I dare advise him, he is sure to attack me like a mad dog.'

Having unburdened his heart, Malla Khaliq lay down in bed.

Aziz Dyad stood up, switched the light off, and both of them remained silently awake till late at night.

The days began to slip away fast. Malla Khaliq did not have even a moment's respite. Noor Mohammad kept telling him, 'Abba, the doctor has advised you to rest. We all are here to take care of the arrangements.' But Malla Khaliq was not one to listen to any advice. When Doctor Nisar watched him so frenziedly engaged in work, he exploded. 'If you don't rest, I will cancel all the arrangements. Do you hear, Abba?'

'All right, all right, I am sitting down. I can argue with all of the others here, but not you.' Malla Khaliq sat in an armchair placed under the willows. He heaved a long sigh and murmured to himself, 'How can I tell them about the agony gnawing at me inwardly? With every passing minute, Parveen's departure from this home arrives closer and closer. The very thought that after only seven hours Parveen is going away as a bride in a palanquin, makes me feel bereft of life. I remain engrossed in work only so that I may forget this. How can my sons understand what an ordeal it is for parents to see their daughter married off. Only Aziz and I know this. Even Narayan Joo, who has stayed by my side through all my trials and tribulations, will not understand this ache for he has no daughters of his own.'

'Listen, Sula, why are you trying to erect a bungalow on a mere inch of space? Even a slight gale will topple this tent.' Hearing Narayan Joo's voice, Malla Khaliq came out of his reverie.

The tent owner Sula Dar gave Narayan Joo a pat reply, 'Am I a novice in my job, Panditji? Even if, God forbid, there is a bad storm, this pavilion will not move an inch.'

Malla Khaliq thought he would go supervise the tent, but seeing Nisar Ahmed standing beside Narayan Joo, he sank back in his armchair, muttering to himself, 'Let them do whatever they like.'

The electrician in charge of lights, carrying a bundle of wire in his hand, came to him. 'All the three tents and the house are fitted with lights. Is there any other place left?' Malla Khaliq, trying to avoid him, said, 'Here is our Doctor Sahib, ask him.'

'What can he tell me? Even though he is a doctor now, he is still a child.'

Malla Khaliq lost his cool. 'For God's sake, ask him!' The lights man did not think it proper to argue any further and silently moved away.

Having finished his supervision, Narayan Joo came near Malla Khaliq. 'Now, Haji Sahib, stand up and have a look around to see if anything else is needed.'

'How can I find faults in your arrangements?'

'No more of this mocking, stand up and take a look.'

'No, no. I have been advised to keep sitting and do nothing else.'

Narayan Joo shouted to Nisar Ahmed, 'Doctor Nisar Ahmed, what have you done to Haji Sahib? Why is he sitting here so sullenly?'

Nisar Ahmed came running, sat before Malla Khaliq and said, 'Are you angry with me, Abba?'

Malla Khaliq grew compassionate. Touching Nisar's head, he said, 'My dear son, why should I be angry with anybody, especially with you?'

Nisar Ahmed cast an affectionate glance at his grandfather and said to him, 'Please try to understand, Abba, if you get indisposed on the occasion ...'

Touching his friend's shoulder, Narayan Joo said, 'Doctor Sahib is right.'

Malla Khaliq forgot his worries and smiled at Narayan Joo.

'Good. Now go and make the arrangements.' Having said this, Nisar Ahmed stood up. 'So I have your permission, now?' Malla Khaliq said to him. All three laughed loudly and walked towards the tent. Malla Khaliq stopped and said to Nisar Ahmed, 'Tell me, is anyone looking after the cooking?'

Narayan Joo laughed and said, 'Lo, he cannot stay without worrying about something or the other. Noor Mohammad's father-in-law is already holding charge of that. He has been there since the first call of the cockerel.' Saying this, Narayan Joo raised the door cloth of the pavilion and said, 'Now see for yourself if all is well. There in front of the entrance is the cushioned seat for the groom. To his right is Mufti Sahib's seat. Are there any more orders for us to carry out?'

Malla Khaliq spread his arms to hold Narayan Joo in a warm embrace, but the latter took a step back. 'It wasn't me. Your grandson made all the arrangements.'

Malla Khaliq turned to Nisar Ahmed. 'Lala Sahib himself carried each carpet and spread it at its proper place.' Narayan Joo diverted the topic and said, 'Now you sit at ease. I will go to the airport. It is almost time for Vijay Kumar's flight to land.'

'But why should you go? Let us send Ghulam Qadir.' Malla Khaliq tried to stop him.

'No, no. There are so many chores to attend to. I will change my clothes and leave.' Saying this, Narayan Joo went out. Nisar Ahmed said to Malla Khaliq, 'I think the guests are about to arrive. Why don't you go sit in the guest room?'

Time sped by and the sun seemed to have dashed across the sky and reached the summits of the western Apharwat mountains. Shikaarahs flocked to Malla Khaliq's houseboats, nearly jostling. They unloaded bevies of guests. Malla Khaliq and Noor Mohammad were standing ready to greet and and usher the men to the chairs placed in rows on the isle. For the women, there was a separate pavilion erected in the rear of the isle. Sweet strains of *wanwun*, the wedding songs, sung by them filled the air.

Parveen, surrounded by girls, was being adorned. She sat still, looking languidly at them. One of her friends got her a mirror, but she shoved the mirror angrily. Her friends chuckled loudly and started teasing her. One of them lifted the mirror and said, 'She might be scared of the evil eye.' Another girl snatched it away and said, 'Let it be kept aside, for she is waiting to see her face only in the eyes of her groom.' Everyone giggled again. In the meantime, a girl came panting into the room and said, 'Now make haste. They are saying that the boat meant for the groom and his guests has

already left for Gagribal to bring them here.' She was followed by
Zeb wriggling through the throng of girls with a box of ornaments
in her hands. 'Move aside. Give the girl some air to breathe.' She
started dressing her in gold jewellery.

Parveen cast a piteous look at Zeb and her eyes overflowed with
tears. Zeb wiped her tears and held her close to her chest. 'This
does not become you. I know what an ordeal this moment is in
a girl's life. If I don't understand the ache in your heart, who else
will? Be brave. Peer Dastagir will resolve all your problems.'

The setting sun spread its resplendence all around. An opulently
bedecked shikaarah touched the ghat. Narayan Joo, his son Vijay
Kumar and his wife Kamini stepped out of it. Malla Khaliq ran
and held Vijay Kumar in a hug; Vijay Kumar bent and touched his
feet. Then Malla Khaliq went near Narayan Joo's daughter-in-law,
saying, 'How are you, my child?' She too bowed to touch his feet
and then congratulated him. Malla Khaliq complained, 'You had
promised to be here before the henna ceremony!' Narayan Joo
pleaded on behalf of her, saying, 'What will Kamini say to you? I
will tell you—' Malla Khaliq interrupted him, 'I am talking to my
daughter-in-law, why do you intervene?'

'I could not get leave from my office. After much wrangling I
got one week's leave. I am sorry about not coming earlier.'

'It is okay. You still made it, that gives me immense joy. You
please go into see your mother. She has been restlessly waiting
for you!'

In the meantime, a police-patrol boat arrived. Narayan Joo
spotted it and was alarmed. 'Damn it! How come this police
contingent is here?'

'It could be the DIG,' said Malla Khaliq. 'You yourself went to
deliver the invitation card to him.'

The police-boat touched the shore. DIG Prahlad Singh
reached the shore in one long step, and the two friends hurried
to welcome the officer. They escorted him and his accompanying
officials to the pavilion.

Vijay Kumar and Kamini went into Aziz Dyad's room. She was

busy arranging Parveen's trousseau in suitcases. Leaving her job unfinished, she stood up and embraced Kamini.

Malla Khaliq was an esteemed citizen. He had associations with many influential and dignified people of the city. Besides being the president of the Houseboat Owners' Association, he was a reputed social worker and had been nominated as a member of the Municipality Council. It was because of his status that many men of rank were there to welcome the marriage party in addition to his relatives and neighbours. Malla Khaliq and Narayan Joo stood at the ghat to receive all the guests. Malla Khaliq was helping the manager of Grindley's Bank climb the steps of the ghat, when suddenly Narayan Joo exclaimed, 'Damn!' Pointing to the advancing boat, he said, 'It is Gul Beg, Ghulam Qadir's partner. Did you send him an invitation card?'

Malla Khaliq grew pale. 'Do you think I am insane to invite such a big scoundrel?'

'Then Qadir must have invited him. You should have—' Narayan Joo was mid-sentence when Gul Beg came ashore in one long step.

'Congratulations, Haji Sahib! You did not invite me, but how could Gul Beg hold any grudge? It is after all the marriage of a daughter, and that too my partner's sister.'

Malla Khaliq remained dumbfounded and could not say anything except, 'It is all right.'

'Are you well, Panditji? Why do you look pale?' Gul Beg turned to Narayan Joo. 'You need not worry. This time we will have a plentiful harvest of apples. I will get you a box of first-rate apples. All your doubts will be washed away.'

'Thank you!' said Narayan Joo in an angry tone.

Malla Khaliq was drenched in sweat. He was unable to think of a way to get rid of this scoundrel. Ghulam Qadir came running, shook hands with Gul Beg and led him away. Gul Beg freed his hand and said sarcastically, 'You have sent invitation cards to the whole city, but did not consider this Gul Beg worthy of one. Nevertheless, it is my friend's sister's wedding and I wanted to be here to congratulate you.'

Ghulam Qadir felt ashamed. 'The cards were distributed by Ghulam Ahmed, and—'

'And he abhors me,' Gul Beg completed his sentence.

'Now, please come in. All the guests are in the pavilion.'

'No. I don't have that much time.' He led Qadir behind the pavilion so that no one would notice them. But Razaq saw them there, and he hid, trying to overhear. But he could hardly understand what transpired between them. Noor Mohammad had already seen Gul Beg coming there. He said to Ghulam Ahmed, who was keeping the ewers and flasks aside, 'How did this Gul Beg turn up here? We did not send him a card.'

Ghulam Ahmed said angrily, 'Ghulam Qadir might have sent him a card. Just look at Abba. See how irritated he looks!'

'It is but natural. Who in this town does not know about Gul Beg's misdeeds?'

'Should I ask Qadir about this?'

'Let him go to hell. See how thick he is with that hashish smuggler!'

Gul Beg had his hand on Qadir's shoulder. 'I know well how important it is for you to be here now. But in the trade that we pursue, every second matters. In case you fail in delivering the consignment on time, you may have to bear a loss of millions. You will have to leave for Delhi soon after you get free from this ceremony.'

'All right, I will leave after the celebrations. Keep my ticket ready.'

'Do you remember the code word?'

'Press Patent.'

'Yes, Press Patent. Now I should leave.'

'Can't you wait until the groom arrives?'

'Sorry. They are waiting for me there. I came here only to check if you are ready to leave for Delhi.'

'You just get the ticket confirmed.'

'Bye, and good luck!' Saying this, Gul Beg strode towards his shikaarah.

Narayan Joo heaved a sigh of relief. 'Thank God! We are free from the dirt.' Ghulam Qadir had accompanied him to the ghat. When the boat left the shore, Ghulam Ahmed said sarcastically to him, 'Why did you let your dear well-wisher leave without serving him the feast?'

Qadir cast a furious look at him. 'Had anyone sent him the invitation card? Is there any guest from my circle?'

Malla Khaliq heard this and said to Ghulam Ahmed in a way that Qadir would also hear it. 'I think we may have sent an invitation card to him as well. It is so kind of him to have come.'

'Haji Sahib, it is good that he left. Had DIG Prahlad Singh seen him here, his suspicions could have been confirmed.'

Qadir scratched his ear and strode fast towards the pavilion. He saw Razaq who still stood behind the pavilion. 'Why are you standing idle there, you indolent fellow? Go and put away these ropes in your shed.'

Razaq lifted the bundle of rope lying on the ground and stood up to go to his shed.

Zeb and Parveen's friends were escorting her to Gulshan. He stood there, gazing at them with despondent eyes; he felt an arrow pierce his heart and trembled. He would have certainly fallen down, had he not taken the support of the door-frame of his shed. He looked up again, but Parveen had moved out of sight. He entered the shed and fell on his bed.

The pitch of the wedding song in the pavilion heightened.

> *Kamraan shaharke Kamai deevo,*
> *Aakho Shari Sheerazo,*
> *Tchaer kyazi loguth sani shahzado,*
> *Heemaal her ital praran tchai*

> (Oh, Kamdev of the city of Kamran,
> Come through the city of Sheeraz,
> Why are you getting late
> Come see how your Heemal is waiting near the stairs)

Razaq plugged his ears with his hands, but he could not block out the singing voices. Feeling stifled, he stood up and started gathering the clothes scattered around him and placed them on his bedding. He folded his uniform neatly and hung his turban on the peg in the wall. He opened the trunk and took out the bag that he had carried with him when he came to Malla Khaliq's house. He stuffed all his clothes in it. He caught sight of the doll which Parveen had gifted to him, lying on the ground. He lifted the doll, dusted it with his shirt and then placed it on the trunk. He stared at it for a moment. Then he collected all his books and put them into the bag. He started staring at the doll again, but he heard a call: 'Razaq! Razaq, where are you?'

Malla Khaliq stood outside his shed searching for him. He replied, 'Just a moment!' Before Malla Khaliq could peep in through the window, Razaq hurriedly came out.

'Yes, sir.'

'What are you doing here? The wedding party is here, waiting around our boats. Where have you kept those garlands?'

'I have kept them in Gul. I thought they would shrivel if kept outside.'

'Go, get them and pass them to Noor Sahib.'

Narayan Joo came just then. 'What are you doing here chatting with this darling of yours? The party has arrived.'

'I know, I know. I was asking Razaq to fetch the garlands.'

'Now make haste. Don't you hear the band approaching?'

Hearing the band, all the women had come out barefoot and assembled on the isle and on the decks of the houseboats. The front of Malla Khaliq's houseboats was bright and luminous. All the owners of the other houseboats had gathered at the ghats. All eyes were fixed upon the rowboats in front. Ramzan Haji had booked a couple of such open bathing boats and had decked them up with lights styled after the royal boats of the rajas. The boats were being driven by motorboats. The leading boat carried the band. The closer these boats came, the louder the women sang:

Shabad Doori ki Kamai Deevo,
Aakho boni Shehjarav maenz,
Sonasund taaj kyah chooey shoobano,
Zan pana Yendrazai aav

(You the cupid from Shahbad Dooru
You came by the avenue through the shade of the magnificent
Chinar trees
How graceful looks your golden crown,
Looks like King Indra has come himself)

And when the fireworks burst out and filled the sky with star-shaped lights, the women momentarily forgot the beats and stared at the sky. Aziz Dyad came near them and said, 'Are you tired or is it that you have never seen such fireworks before?' They giggled in response. Aziz Dyad also laughed and said, 'Now I entreat you, please continue with your singing.'

The men stood at the ghat, bearing garlands for the groom. The bedecked boats alongside the open boats rowed faster and stopped near the steps of the ghat. The band stopped playing and made way for the groom. Noor Mohammad and Vijay Kumar walked down the steps and held out their hands to the groom and helped him climb ashore. Haji Ramzan and other guests in the party followed. Malla Khaliq greeted Haji Ramzan with a garland and embraced him. He then garlanded the groom with tinsels and currency notes.

In the lounge of the houseboat Gulshan, Parveen sat still, with her chin on her knees; she looked petrified. The moment the groom went into the pavilion, all her friends came giggling and gathered excitedly around her. Each one of them was eager to tell her how her groom looked. Parveen's niece Shahnaz pushed everyone aside and made her way to Parveen. 'Come on, peep through that window, you can see him from there. How handsome he looks, no less than Dilip Kumar.'

'Why Dilip Kumar?' said another friend. 'He is much more handsome than him.'

Shahnaz pulled her by the hand, but Parveen shouted at her, 'Leave my hand! I don't want to see him.' But Shahnaz was obstinate, and she pulled her harder. Parveen was irate. 'I told you that I am not interested in seeing him!'

Another friend said, 'She has to see him for the rest of her life!' All the girls let out a loud guffaw.

The band had stopped playing; only the singing of the women in the tent was heard. After a little while, that too stopped. The priests were now solemnly reading the sacred verses to consummate the nikah. Complete silence prevailed all round.

Razaq sat brooding in a corner of the isle. Lost in hazy thoughts, he threw pebbles into the water and gazed at the ripples that spread and vanished in the water. He was oblivious of the time. He would have remained lost had the clatter of ewers and flasks not brought him back. He looked towards the pavilion, and saw the Mufti who, after getting Parveen's consent, had come out accompanied by Malla Khaliq, Noor Mohammad and Ramzan Haji. When he returned to the pavilion meant for the men, the women started singing again.

Razaq got up and moved towards the pavilion with unsteady steps. He peeped through the curtain and saw the groom sitting directly facing the entrance. He gazed intently at the man who was now Parveen's husband. The groom was far more handsome than him, a more worldly person and very rich. What could a waif like him give her?

He walked to the same corner of the isle where he sat before. He felt like his heart had turned to stone. He wanted to raze the whole world to ruins, and then drown himself in the lake. He snapped back into his senses only when he heard the women singing the heart-wrenching song saying goodbye to the bride:

Maalichi kunza kar dedi havalai,
Wothi voyen wairvuk chui sawalai

(Entrust the keys of the house to your mother,
Arise o bride, think of your in-laws' house now)

Razaq tried his best not to move from that solitary corner, but his heart did not let him. 'Stand up now, for you might not see her ever again. This last vision of Parveen will remain etched in your heart as a sweet ache that will always give you courage to win back the lost dice in your life.' Saying this to himself, he stood up and went near Gulshan from where Parveen was to be sent off. As soon as Noor Mohammad escorted Parveen out of the pavilion, the singing intensified.

> *Sadhan veryan ditmai keatchye,*
> *Aekher drayakh peachye bai.*

(We pampered you with gifts for seventeen years
But you proved to be only our guest in the long run)

Parveen neared her mother.

> *Vunikh taam kertham heri bona raechi*
> *Malinich taethi gara gatchkhai,*
> *Dle chane sathvai raza chai,*
> *Maayi heatch maej chai pata laran.*

(Till today you were the guardian of my home,
Darling of your parents! Leave for your own home.
The palanquin for you is tied with seven ropes,
Fondly your mother is following you)

She stood glued to her mother and her body was shivering. Aziz Dyad also felt bereft of all energy, yet she kissed her and consoled her. But eventually, she lost control of herself and uttered a loud moan. She would have fallen had Noor Mohammad not held her. Mukhta came and separated Parveen from her mother. Then Parveen hugged each of her sisters-in-law, her childhood friends, and finally the women relatives. Finally Malla Khaliq came near her, laid his hand on her shoulder and said, 'Come on now, my darling child, they are waiting for you.' Parveen turned to him and gave him a tight hug. The walls of Malla Khaliq's inner fortress broke down and a torrent of tears sprang from his eyes. He held his daughter in embrace. Narayan Joo, who stood watching all this patiently, said to Malla Khaliq, 'Haji Sahib, if you also give in, what will happen to others?' But Narayan Joo himself teared up. Seeing this, Haji Ramzan approached them. 'You need not worry, we will take care of Parveen and keep her happy.' Malla Khaliq stood with folded hands before him. He would have even fallen at his feet, but Haji Ramzan held him in his arms, saying, 'What is all this for? Do not drown me in sins. Be bold and bid her farewell.'

Razaq, standing at a distance, watched this painful sight. He quietly pleaded with the Almighty, 'Oh God! Why did you bring me here? What sin had I committed?' His eyes were fixed on Parveen. 'Oh merciful God! Show your mercy and take my soul back! I do not have the strength to bear this separation.'

Parveen was being led towards the ghat. Razaq walked a step forward, and Parveen caught sight of him. Zeb was quick to notice this exchange and held her. Parveen cast an angry look at Razaq and then quickly climbed down the steps. Parvez lent his hand and helped her sit in the shikaarah.

Then Haji Sahib and the other wedding guests said goodbye.

The boats departed.

The women stood at the lowest step of the ghat and continued singing the farewell songs. Malla Khaliq continued standing at the ghat until the boats moved out of sight. He then called Noor Mohammad. 'Take all the guests to their rooms to sleep. And you too need some rest.'

'And you?'

'Yes, I will also go and get some sleep.'

Noor Mohammad escorted the guests and Malla Khaliq walked ahead to see if all was okay in the pavilions. Razaq, who stood near the pavilion, started collecting the chairs and other items lying strewn there. Malla Khaliq went near him and said, 'Have you had some food?'

'Yes, sir,' Razaq lied. Malla Khaliq placed his hand on his

shoulder and turned him round. Razaq saw his eyes baggy and red from weeping. Seeing his master's miserable face, Razaq tried to fall at his feet, but Malla Khaliq stopped him and said, 'No, no. We must prostrate only before the Almighty.' Razaq could not hold himself back and started to cry.

'I know you will also miss Parveen. Now go get some rest.'

Malla Khaliq laid his hand on Razaq's shoulder. Razaq sensed that he was broken from having sent off his beloved daughter, and he held his hand saying, 'Let us go in, sir.' After escorting him to his room, Razaq took his leave saying, 'Abba Sahib, kindly forgive me for all my faults.'

'Crazy fellow! You single-handedly made all the arrangements for this wedding. Why then this entreaty for forgiveness? Go, get some rest.'

Razaq went to his shed. All around there was darkness. He quietly opened the door and switched the light on. He took off the newly sewed clothes that Malla Khalliq had ordered for him as he had done for other family members. Changing into his old clothes, he folded the new ones and kept them aside. He switched the light off. Then looked through the window. A slight wind was blowing, otherwise it was all still, and nothing could be seen moving about. He took the doll in his hand, kissed it, and came out of the shed. He walked to the dilapidated ghat behind his shed. The water was still and clean there. He gazed at the doll lovingly. He heard Parveen say to him, 'What do you look at it for? Look at me.' He felt as if her voice emerged from the still waters of the lake. Parveen appeared in the lake, holding the bride and groom dolls in her hands. He remembered that evening when she had said, 'All right, you keep this female doll and I will keep the male doll. Then we shall wait for the day when you and I become one, and the two dolls will also get reunited.'

Razaq was lost in memories, when there was a big splash in the water ahead of him. Startled, Razaq saw that an owl had swooped down upon a fish. It flew towards the poplars nearby with the fish in its claws. Razaq was filled with pity and his hands shivered. He felt as if the doll in his hands was a pot of live embers. He was about to throw the doll into the water, but something held him back; he kissed the doll gently and released it in the water. He looked at it float away for a while and finally returned to his shed. He swung his bag on his shoulder and moved towards the rear swamps where the boat that Qadir had used to smuggle Jane away in was kept. Razaq untied the boat and sat in it. Using his hands as oars, he calmly paddled the boat through the willow grove to the bank. Then with one strong shove of the oar, the boat glided like an arrow over the lake. The reflection of the moon in the clear waters was cleaved into two by the boat. Having come out of the premises of the houseboats, Razaq rowed the boat towards the quay of Nehru Park.

Behind him, the two silver fragments reunited, and the moon regained its original visage.

Malla Khaliq remained sleepless till the cockerel's first crow. He had sat all alone on the front deck of Gul. He had spent the night looking at the cliffs of the Zabarwan mountains which looked like meditating recluses in the dark. He remembered how he had told Parveen many fairy tales about the mountains. He used to enjoy sitting in the sun with his little Parveen in his lap. 'Now my pari spread her wings and went away.' Malla Khaliq heaved a long and cold sigh. He was lost in such musings and hardly realized when Aziz Dyad came and sat down beside him. She placed her hand on his shoulder and said, 'What are you thinking about sitting here all alone?'

'My life now feels hollow, absolutely empty,' he said.

'May God save us! Why, all of us are still with you.' Aziz Dyad comforted him.

'She was the soul of our small world. Now, see how she took flight and left us behind.'

'Of course she went away, but only to build a world of her own. Now pray to your Dastagir that her world be filled with blossoms of joy.'

'Believe me, I feel very lonely now.'

Aziz Dyad held his hand and said, 'How are you alone? Am I not with you? Get up, now. The mountains are beginning to shine in the morning light. All the guests are still here. Send someone to the baker's shop.' But Malla Khaliq did not let go of her hand. 'Please stay here with me for a while. Nobody will wake up before sunrise.'

'Tell me what can I do for you?'

'I need nothing, you just stay with me. I feel like my heart is sinking.'

'If you had rested for a little while, you would have felt better.'

'How can I feel better now? It will soon be light and Noor Mohammad will leave along with his family to look after their dispensary. Qadir will again busy himself in his usual misdeeds. Ghulam Ahmed has to go to Pattan along with Zoon. This old couple alone will be left here.'

'What does Zoon have to do in Pattan? There are so many workers appointed there already, any one of them could prepare meals for Ahmed.'

'I also thought that we should not let Zoon go to Pattan because you cannot manage everything single-handedly. Everything is a mess here. Poor Zeb has her hands full with the young kid. How can she lend you a hand?'

'All right.' Saying this Aziz Dyad got up.

'Let me see why Razaq is still asleep. He could get up and fetch bread from the market.'

'Where are you going?' she asked him.

'I will wake him up. You go and arrange for the morning tea.'

Saying this, Malla Khaliq went to the ghat. The door of Razaq's shed was closed. He knocked at the door. 'Razaq, Razaq! Get up now, my son. See, it is morning already.'

There was no reply from inside. Malla Khaliq got irritated and called to him, knocking the door violently. 'Razaq! Oh Razaq! Why don't you get up?' The door flew ajar from his forceful knocking. He found the bedding folded and kept aside. The set of clothes that

Malla Khaliq had given him for the wedding lay there. His uniform
was hanging from a peg. Malla Khaliq began to feel rather anxious.
'Where could he have gone?' He came out of the shed and went
to the rear ghat. He did not find him there. Then he went to the
isle and searched him in every corner. But he couldn't find him
anywhere. Calling his name all around, he reached the pantry. Aziz
Dyad heard him and looked through the window. 'Why are you
creating a ruckus? He might be sleeping in some corner of the
boat, like a corpse.'

'How can he be so careless? He must have gone somewhere.'

'But what is he to do for you at this hour?'

'He could go across the lake and fetch bread. Okay, give the
basket to me. I will go myself.'

'You go and offer your prayers first. I have already sent Noor
Mohammad to fetch bread. He had to check his new house and
told me that he would get the bread on his way back.'

Malla Khaliq went near the copse of willows, performed
his ablutions, and sat down to offer his nimaz. The peaks of the
Zabarwan hills were already enveloped by the golden morning
light. Vapours had started rising from the surface of the lake. The
vegetable vendors were seen rowing their boats towards Dalgate.

Malla Khaliq had just finished his prayers when Noor
Mohammad's boat touched the shore. He walked towards the
kitchen and handed over the basket to his mother and then went
near his father and said, 'Abba, have you sent Razaq on any errand?'

'No. Have you seen him anywhere?'

'No, Abba. I saw the small boat of our neighbourhood's
vegetable vendor's anchored across the lake at the Nehru Park
ghat. I thought someone from their family has crossed over to the
market. But then I saw Ghana of their clan roaring and asking the
shikaarah owners about the bastard who had taken their boat in the
middle of the night. He told them that if he found the mischief-
monger, he would surely chop him to death. Had Ramzana not
found the boat there, they would have still been searching for the
boat in the swamps.'

Hearing this Malla Khaliq's limbs started shivering. He went into the kitchen muttering to himself, 'God knows where he has gone!' Noor Mohammad followed him and said, 'The rascal must have fled in the same boat.'

'What nonsense!' Malla Khaliq was furious.

'The baker Ama Kandur saw him fleeing with his bag on his shoulder.'

Malla Khaliq sat down in shock. Aziz Dyad came near him, saying, 'See how the waif has finally fled, like all the others of his kind. None of your pampering worked. They are all alike. You just overfeed them with affection and treat them like your own sons, but finally they leave without letting anyone know.'

Noor Mohammad, too, was intrigued. He said, 'Abba, if he had to flee at all, why did he choose last night to do so? I am sure he must have stolen many things from us.'

'No, no. He is absolutely different from the others! I don't know what happened to him. Maybe someone in the family rebuked him, otherwise he is not the kind to run away in this manner. He was so keen on studying further. He used to stay up late into the night with his book in his hands. A boy of such demeanour and prudence cannot be a pilferer.'

Noor Mohammad could not swallow this defence of Razaq. He said, 'Let us check in the house to see if anything is missing. I suggest we report his absence to the police. We have his home address.'

Aziz Dyad agreed. 'Noor Mohammad is right.'

Malla Khaliq became angry and said, 'God, give them a little wisdom! The guests are still here. Just a few hours ago we sent our daughter away, and you suggest that I knock the doors of the police!'

'Abba, times are very bad. No one can be trusted. He is sure to have stolen something precious.'

'Did you know that his salary for the last six months is still with me? How could he run away? Go and attend to your chores. Leave this to me. I warn you not to divulge this to anyone, particularly Qadir.'

Aziz Dyad agreed with her husband. 'Your Abba is right. Let the guests leave and then we can decide what to do. You go and wake Mukhta and Zoon. They have to serve tea to the guests.'

Noor Mohammad left, suppressing his rage. Malla Khaliq said to his wife, 'He seemed very gloomy the last few days.'

'He must have been pondering over his plans to run away.'

'No, I don't think so. Certainly something bad has happened to him. How he would take care of me. Even my own sons have not loved me so much. I am sure that someone said something to him. Let me check his room again.'

'Please calm down. Let us wait until all the guests have left.'

All the guests and family members were now awake. Ghulam Ahmed, Doctor Nisar and Ghulam Qadir were busy clearing the mess. Malla Khaliq's elder daughters-in-law were carrying tea in the samovars to Gulshan. Zeb followed them with a basket of bread with Bilal in tow. Ghulam Ahmed alone seemed ready to leave.

After having his tea, Malla Khaliq came out to the isle. Ghulam Ahmed came near him and said, 'So, Abba, I am leaving now. I will be home in three or four days. Zoon will stay here. Let me make the necessary arrangements there and then I will be back.'

Malla Khaliq placed his hand on his shoulder and said, 'You may go. God will look after you. I know it is a good time to do some business there. You need not worry about us. We will manage. And there is hardly any work to attend to here now. The houseboats are vacant. Go now, my dear. Make haste or you might miss the bus.'

'I will come back within a couple of days. By then it will almost be time for Parveen to return from her in-laws'.'

Then, having looked all around, he said to his father, 'Abba, I have not seen Razaq since morning.'

'He hadn't visited his home for a long time. I sent him on leave,' Malla Khaliq calmly replied and immediately turned towards houseboat Gulshan so that his face wouldn't give him away.

Malla Khaliq was losing his temper over every trivial issue. He was anxious because the houseboats were empty. And then, he missed Parveen a lot. But Razaq's disappearing like a thief was what vexed him most. Two days had passed since Parveen's marriage. Everyone in the family had gotten busy with their usual work. He alone remained moving about restlessly.

Today he had resolved to come out of his misery. Sitting against the windowsill of the pantry, he glanced towards the flower bed in front of Gulfam, that Razaq had tended to and nurtured. The bed was replete with autumnal flowers. Razaq had got the tubers of dahlia flowers from the chief gardener at the Emporium Garden two years ago. Each dahlia was about one foot in diameter. A few plants were about to give way under the weight of the large flowers. He stood up, took out a ball of jute thread and went out on the isle.

Just then, Bilal came running and started tugging at Malla Khaliq's phiran. Then he ran and stood aside to see if his grandfather was going to pick him up in his arms. But Malla Khaliq was still lost in thought and did not look at the boy. Bilal ran and held his hand that was busy tying the largest dahlia plant to its supporting stick. Malla Khaliq angrily called out to Zeb as he shooed the child away. 'Zeb ! Zeb! Please take this imp away.'

Zeb came running and dragged the child away, but the child was being obstinate. Malla Khaliq got all the more agitated,

'Why don't you take him away? See what a mess he has made here in this flower bed. He is always running after me like a chimpanzee …'

Hearing this clamour, Aziz Dyad came out and shouted at her husband. 'That spoiled darling of yours has run away and you get angry with this innocent child, who is your life and soul! I wonder why you have been behaving like a ferocious dog since that damned Razaq disappeared.'

Malla Khaliq felt mortified. He went to Zeb.

'My daughter, forgive me. I have been telling all of you that I have sent Razaq on vacation. That is a lie for I don't know where he is, why he left, or when he is to return.'

Zeb, wiping Bilal's tears, said to her father-in-law, 'Abba, he will not come back here.'

'What do you mean?' Malla Khaliq turned pale.

Zeb replied, 'Razaq is not going to come back to this place. It's good he left unharmed.'

'This means that my fear was not unfounded. I know it is Qadir who made him run away. He despised him for Razaq was a hurdle in his nefarious activities.'

'Please don't blame poor Qadir for this. He doesn't even have an inkling that Razaq has run away.'

'Then? What happened to him? You are hiding something from me. Tell me honestly, why did Razaq run away?'

Zeb took Bilal in her arms and ran to her room. Malla Khaliq was flummoxed. He turned to his wife who also looked amazed. She went to Zeb's room. 'Why didn't you tell your Abba why Razaq ran away?'

Aziz Dyad asked her again, 'You know something that we don't. What is it?'

'Razaq and Parveen were dreaming of getting married. It is good that he has run away, else he would have certainly brought the family a bad name.'

Aziz Dyad could not believe what Zeb had just said. 'Why are you blaming my innocent daughter? Can you imagine what would happen if your Abba came to know about this?'

'You know well that I am not one to talk about people behind their backs. How can I blame anyone, particularly Parveen, who is dearer to me than my real sister?'

'How do you know all this?'

'Parveen herself told me. She implored me that I plead with Abba because he holds Razaq dear.'

'Oh, what a thunderbolt there was in the offing!'

'I would have taken the secret with me to my grave—'

'So we have been wearing a dirty shoe on our head in place of a cap! And your Abba was too gullible to realize this.'

Zeb fell at Aziz Dyad's feet and begged her not to tell Malla

Khaliq. But Aziz Dyad said to her, 'Why should I not let him know? Let him know the malintent of that pampered mongrel.'

'But, Amma, one behaves recklessly when young. Besides, I must tell you that Razaq wasn't evil in any way. He would sacrifice his life for this family, especially for Abba.'

'He pretended to be good.'

'No, Amma, I tested him in all possible ways. Do you remember how he kept the secret of Jane and Qadir to himself? He had seen everything, but he never uttered a word. He ran away after seeing to it that all the work for the wedding was done perfectly. He did not even take six months' salary.'

'That is true. Had our own daughter not displayed weakness, how could he, a stranger, dare cast his eye on her?'

Aziz Dyad could not keep herself from telling her husband. Malla Khaliq stood staring at her, dumbstruck.

'Why don't you say something?'

Malla Khaliq heaved a deep sigh. 'That is why Razaq looked so downcast for the last so many days.'

'No. A thunderbolt had struck him. If he had crossed the line, people would have stoned us to death. It was Zeb who kept them under the veil and held Parveen back. I too had sensed that she was disturbed. Then I thought that the idea of leaving us was upsetting her.'

Malla Khaliq took out a pack of cigarettes from his pocket and turned to his wife. 'If you had sensed it, why didn't you tell me? Oh, if only Parveen had told me!'

Aziz Dyad's eyes shone bright as if burning like hot embers. 'What would you have done then? Would you have gotten your daughter married to that worthless urchin?'

'He was not a worthless waif. He belonged to a good family. And he had had schooling up to tenth class. If he had continued his studies, he would surely have been worthy of our family one day.'

Aziz Dyad could hardly believe what she was hearing. 'Oh my

Dastagir! What foul ideas fill his brain! If you talk like that in the presence of our family, they will consider you insane.' She was furious. She stood up, brought a matchbox and flung it towards Malla Khaliq. 'Now smoke a cigarette, it may help you think properly. God knows what spell that waif cast on you!'

Malla Khaliq threw the cigarette aside and went out of the room saying, 'Do not subject poor Zeb to any inquisition, I warn you.'

Taking long and quick strides, Malla Khaliq reached Razaq's shed; the door was ajar. He went in and started rummaging through everything there. He emptied Razaq's trunk, but found nothing there.

Zeb was happy that Qadir had been returning home earlier than usual of late and had been helping Malla Khaliq with errands. Malla Khaliq also began to feel that Qadir had perhaps begun to repent. But what he did not know was that on some pretext or the other, Qadir used to phone all his friends from the inner bedroom in Gulshan, especially Gul Beg.

Even tonight Qadir was home early. Zeb, having put Bilal to sleep, nestled close to him. Qadir seemed to respond passionately to her advances. Finally she placed her head on his chest and fell asleep. Qadir looked intently at her face, then carefully placed her head on the pillow and wriggled out. He took out a cigarette and smoked near the window. Staring into the darkness all around, he remembered what Gul Beg had told him on the phone. He resolved to go to Delhi on the excuse of attending a friend's wedding at Pulwama.

The next morning he sought Malla Khaliq's permission. Then he went to Zeb and gave her some money for day-to-day expenses. He said to her, 'You need not worry. I don't know exactly how many days Jan Mohammad's wedding ceremony will take. I may stay there for a week or so.'

Six days went by, yet there was no sign of Qadir's return. The tourist season had once again disappointed, because of the landslides and the turmoil in Punjab. Malla Khaliq was depressed. He had spent all his savings on Parveen's marriage. Nisar Ahmed, to help him out, used to send him money through his father. Malla Khaliq felt small and pained by this. In all this, he didn't realize that Ghulam Qadir had not returned from Pulwama.

When Malla Khaliq came to know that there was no information about Qadir's whereabouts, he was very angry with Zeb. 'Your heart has really turned into stone. Why were you silent for so many days?'

'Abba, he had told me that if he was late by a couple of days, I should not get worried. So I kept mum.'

'This very silence of yours has made him reckless.'

Noor Mohammad, who never dared to talk loudly in his father's presence, said to his mother, 'You tell Abba that it is of no use to blame this poor girl.'

Malla Khaliq lost his cool. 'She alone is not to be blamed for this. Your mother's attempts to hide his misdeeds have also emboldened him.'

Aziz Dyad retorted, 'Have you decided to tell everyone in Gagribal about our family affairs? We have no news of him, but nobody is bothered about searching for Qadir!'

'You can go by yourself in search of your darling. Why don't you go?'

Noor Mohammad tried to douse the fire. 'Abba, I think he must be at Gul Beg's house. Qadir was talking to him behind the tent on the day of the wedding. I will go today and bring him back.'

Apple harvesting was in full swing. Gul Beg was personally supervising the grading of apples. The labourers were plucking the fruit from the trees and getting basketfuls to unload on the heap below.

A labourer called out, 'Rahman Kaka, watch it, the ladder is not placed firmly.' Gul Beg saw an old labourer, carrying a basket of apples, trying to climb down the ladder. The ladder shook and Rahman tumbled down along with the basketful of apples.

Gul Beg ran to the old man, gripped his throat and slapped him hard. 'You old haggard bull! Do you think the apples belong to your bloody father that you don't mind the loss?'

Rahman Kaka shivered with rage and freeing himself from Gul Beg's grip, said, 'Do not use such abusive language. You can deduct the cost of the spoiled apples from my wages.'

Gul Beg was incensed at the labourer's gall to shout back at him. He pounced upon Rahman Kaka and started kicking him. All the labourers stopped working, thronged around the two and tried to force them apart. The chief labourer came forward, took Gul Beg to one side and said, 'Let him be sacrificed for your well-being. His mind is not steady.'

'I will break his skull to batter out his brain. The bloody thief! How can he have the cheek to answer back?'

Rahman shouted louder, 'Hey you, owner of this orchard! Have you forgotten that your father also used to till the land of a landlord? He had neither clothes to wear nor food to eat. And now here you are with a tilted cap on your head, boasting of being rich. You go and ask your father; he is still alive.'

Gul Beg caught hold of a stick and was about to thrash the labourer, when a white Ambassador entered the gate of the farm. Gul Beg threw the stick aside. Rahman Kaka came near him saying, 'Why did you throw the stick aside? Come, kill me. Why did you stop?'

Gul Beg said to the chief of the labourers, 'You take him away, or I will kill him right now.'

When he saw Noor Mohammad alighting from the car, he said to the labourers, 'What are you standing here for? Go and do your work. The boxes have to be loaded in the truck today.'

Noor Mohammad, after greeting him, asked, 'Is Ghulam Qadir here?'

'Ghulam Qadir! Why would he be here?'

'He has been away from home for about a week. We saw you speaking to him at our house.'

'Look here, I respect your father Haji Sahib. Had you been someone else, I would certainly teach him how to talk to Gul Beg.'

'That can be decided later on. You tell me where you have sent our Ghulam Qadir.'

'I already told you that he has no business here. It's been a long time since I saw him.'

'Maybe others will believe your lies, but not this Noor Mohammad.'

'Is he a toddler that I would keep him hidden? What is he worth after all?'

Rahman Kaka, who was still ablaze with rage, came nearer and said to Noor Mohammad, 'He is a fraudster. Your Ghulam Qadir was here just a couple of days ago, enjoying along with his other henchmen.'

Gul Beg again caught hold of Rahman Kaka. 'You bloody old bullock! How dare you continue talking out of place?'

But Rahman Kaka was not one to be shouted down. 'He sent Ghulam Qadir somewhere in a taxi.'

Gul Beg grew rabid like a wild dog, but Noor Mohammad took him aside and said, 'Will you tell me where you have sent him, or should I report you to the police?'

'Why go to only the police? You may approach even the chief minister. Gul Beg is not one to get scared of anyone. You believe this bastard old man? He has lost his wits! You ask all these labourers how we were just settling scores with him.'

Noor Mohammad turned to the other workers. 'For God's sake, tell me if Ghulam Qadir was here or not.'

The workers remained silent.

Noor Mohammad confronted Gul Beg again. 'If Ghulam Qadir is not back home by evening, be ready to face the consequences.'

Having said this, he sat in the taxi and left. Gul Beg shouted after him, 'All the officers of your city bow before Gul Beg! How dare you come here and threaten me?'

Then he turned to Rahman Kaka and said, 'Just you watch, if I don't make you beg on the streets, my name is not Gul Beg!'

'You are not my God. You just pay me my wages and then I will not come even to spit at this orchard of yours.'

Gul Beg said to his clerk, 'Pay all we owe to this beggar and let him out of my sight!'

Noor Mohammad was bitter with the poison of anger. He went to Doctor Nisar's bungalow, sought his counsel, and both of them left together to see Malla Khaliq. Malla Khaliq sat with his head hung down. Narayan Joo was also looking downwards and pulling stalks of grass. Noor Mohammad did not have the nerve to utter a word. He cast a piteous look at his father who had a scrap of paper on his knees. Then he looked at his son. Doctor Nisar gathered courage to tell his grandfather, 'Qadir Uncle was not at Gul Beg's farm.'

Narayan Joo raised his head and said, 'How could he be there? He must be caught in the net of some big problem after having reached Delhi.'

'What?' Doctor Nisar was alarmed.

Malla Khaliq passed the chit of paper to Nisar Ahmed. Noor Mohammad mustered up some courage to ask his father, 'What is this paper about?'

Narayan Joo turned to him and said, 'Your brother has written this letter from the airport to inform you that he left for Delhi to do some business there.'

Malla Khaliq's eyes were red. 'Read out the note to your father,' he said to Doctor Nisar.

Nisar Ahmed started reading out the letter. 'Abba, I am going to Delhi in connection with the carpet export business. The broker who got me a big order from America came to see me at Pulwama where I was attending my friend's sister's wedding. He had already booked the ticket for me, and so I could not come home before leaving. Please forgive me for this lapse and

I entreat you not to worry about me. I will return after meeting the customer. Ghulam Qadir.'

Noor Mohammad was enraged. 'But he did not even go to Pulwama. He was at Gul Beg's house all these days. I am sure Gul Beg is luring him into some illicit trade.'

'Now all the dots will get connected,' said Narayan Joo to Malla Khaliq. 'Gul Beg's agent Lasa Tak was with him when he handed over this letter to our Mohi-ud Din who had gone to the airport to receive a guest.'

Hearing this, Malla Khaliq stood up, saying, 'I will go to DIG Prahlad Singh now and get Gul Beg apprehended.'

Narayan Joo held him back, saying, 'Why do you get swayed so easily? You are sticking your hand in a hornet's nest. If the police come to know about this incident, all of Srinagar will know that Malla Khaliq's son has fled his home. What will Parveen's in-laws say if they hear about it? It hasn't even been a week since her wedding.'

Malla Khaliq, like a wingless bird, dropped to the ground. 'What should we do then?'

Narayan Joo said, 'We must, first of all, try to find out his whereabouts in Delhi, and what he is doing there.'

Nisar Ahmed did not agree. 'But, Lala Sahib, Delhi is not our Gagribal that even if a needle is lost, it can be traced out. How will we find him there and who will do this?'

'I know all the fruit merchants in Delhi, even Gul Beg's merchant Gur Sain Mal. I will phone him and I am sure we will find out all about Qadir.'

Malla Khaliq lost track of time and hardly remembered how many days Qadir had been away from home.

Narayan Joo somehow managed to trace Qadir's whereabouts. But by then Gul Beg had already booked his ticket for Bombay. The apple trader Gur Sain informed Narayan Joo that two more traders were to have left with Qadir for Bombay. He reached Malla

Khaliq's house in the early hours of the morning to break this news to him. He assured him that Vijay Kumar was in Bombay and would certainly meet Qadir. Keeping his hand on his shoulder, he said to Malla Khaliq, 'Haji Sahib, you have taught me never to leave faith in God's mercy.'

'I feel numb and helpless. I feel lonely. Noor Mohammad has left to help his son Nisar set up his home and hearth. Ghulam Ahmed will also come soon and take away his wife to Pattan. Parveen has already moved out to prosper in her separate world. Only this Qadir was left behind with us. Who knows what snare he has fallen in? If something untoward were to happen to him, I don't know what Zeb would do. What will happen to Bilal?'

Narayan Joo scolded him, 'Why are you being such a cynic? Ghulam Qadir has left just to seek a livelihood, and here you are, God forbid, declaring him dead! What is wrong with you? If my sister Aziz Dyad comes to know, you know well what would happen to her.'

'Narayan Joo, Qadir's inclinations are not virtuous. And you know that the tourist season this year was a dud.'

Narayan Joo too was very anxious about the poor turnout in the tourist season, but he had entrusted all to God. By consoling Malla Khaliq, he in a way, consoled himself. 'There is still plenty of time, God will set everything right. Go and tell Aziz Dyad what we have come to know about Qadir. Give up this brooding, otherwise she will not believe what I say.'

Zeb sat with Aziz Dyad picking spinach. The moment Malla Khaliq and Narayan Joo entered the room, she picked up the basket of vegetables and was about to go into the inner room, when Narayan Joo stopped her. 'Sit here, my child. You must also hear the good news.' Then he turned to Aziz Dyad. 'Ghulam Qadir was in Delhi and has now left for Bombay in connection with his carpet business. He will stay there for a week or so, then return home.'

Aziz Dyad said to Narayan Joo, 'I think Vijay Lala is in Bombay; he must have told you about him.'

Narayan Joo was thrown, but he immediately regained his

composure and spoke so as to anchor her faith. 'Of course, he telephoned me.'

'May my Dastagir bless him! I was restless like a live fish in fire. And this daughter of mine was more worried than I. Thank God, all is well.'

It had been three days since Parveen had returned home. Her presence restored the old joys in the family. Ghulam Ahmed had returned from Pattan and Noor Mohammad, too, along with his wife. But whenever Malla Khaliq was alone, or with his wife, his fear about receiving some bad news from Bombay resurfaced. He cursed himself for lying every day for the sake of his wife.

When anyone asked him why Ghulam Qadir was not around, he would say, 'He has gone to Bombay to meet some important customer.' But when his relative Naba Kantroo heard it, he could not digest it. He said, 'Yes, I believe the customer is really very important. Otherwise why would Ghulam Qadir leave for Bombay without bidding farewell to his only sister?'

Malla Khaliq abhorred Naba Kantroo. The very thought of him made his mouth bitter. He picked up a bottle of water and drank it in one go. Then he heaved a long sigh and stretched himself again. He grazed Aziz Dyad's body and she turned over to face him. 'Are you still awake? Are you okay?'

'Yes, I am all right. I was just feeling thirsty.'

Aziz Dyad turned around and slept. Roving in the wilderness of fears, Malla Khaliq, too, slept.

Early next morning, Malla Khaliq took his boat to the shrine of Makhdoom Sahib after a long time. He ran into Narayan Joo at the temple of Maha Ganesh. As was the custom between them, he slapped Malla Khaliq on his back and said, 'Good morning! Alhaj Abdul Khaliq Sahib, the lucky man. I am delighted to meet you again here. All our sorrows and aches will get assuaged. I am sure.'

'I have never given up my trust in my benevolent saint. It was just that I was so caught in the vortex of my anxiety that I could not make it here for some days. Please wait for me near the Devi's shrine. We can go back together.'

'That is a good idea.'

'Did you hear from Vijay Kumar?'

'Yes, I did. He has not been able to get any information. Today he is going to the Kashmir Arts Emporium in Bombay. The airport people told him that Ghulam Qadir reached six days ago. Vijay traced his telephone number, but the call went unanswered. But don't worry, Vijay Kumar will find him soon, somehow or the other.'

Narayan Joo, chanting sacred verses, went towards the Maha Ganesh temple ahead of Makhdoom Sahib's Ziarat at the foot of the Hari Parbat hillock. Malla Khaliq climbed the stairs towards Makhdoom Sahib's shrine.

At home, Aziz Dyad sat brushing Parveen's hair. Then she turned Parveen to face her and asked her, 'All is well here. Tell me honestly if you are happy there. Don't try to lie.'

'You tell me, are you happy?'

'I am very happy.'

'Then I am also happy.'

'Leave my happiness aside and tell me if you are happy there or not.'

Parveen held her mother in a tight hug and said, 'Don't you see how happy I am?'

'Stay happy like this, always. May my Peer Dastagir fill your life with joys!'

Parveen cast a loving glance at her mother and asked, 'But Abba doesn't seem to be happy. Something's worrying him.'

'Since you left for your in-laws, he feels an emptiness in this house. He remains a little despondent. And then you know the tourist season this year hardly brought us any business, all three boats are lying empty.'

'Has Ghulam Qadir really left for Bombay to sell carpets or—?'

'The carpet business that he started last year seems to be taking off. That's why he had to leave for Bombay in such a hurry.'

'This too might be a cause for Abba's worries.'

'Yes, in a sense.'

'You get some rest here and I will go see Zeb in her room.'

'But make sure to return soon, for your father must be on his way back.'

Parveen left for the willow groves behind the house. She reached Razaq's shed. The door was locked, but the window was ajar. She stood up on her toes, bent forward and looked in. There was darkness inside. The trunk too was empty. She heaved a deep sigh and ambled through the willow groves towards the rear swamps where she would find the remains of her stifled desires. She stopped and looked all around. Everything was the same. She spotted the old carry-boat that belonged to the vegetable vendors. She moved closer to the water. One of the steps on the ghat had caved in. She slipped, but caught hold of a willow branch just in time. Just then, she saw the doll that she had given Razaq lying in the mud. She felt an iron grip clench her heart. Holding on to the willow branch, she bent forward and picked up the castaway doll. She sat on the ghat and washed the doll. She wiped it with her headscarf and held it close to her cheek; her eyes filled with tears. She murmured, 'So he did not know your value either?

Zeb's call brought her back to reality.

'What are you doing here all alone?'

Parveen started and hid the doll in the side pocket of her phiran.

'I know what you are searching for.'

She held Parveen's hand and said, 'Forget everything that once happened here. He was a sensitive and sensible guy and, as such, bearing the secret, left this house.'

Parveen looked agape at her sister-in-law. 'But I heard Abba saying that he has gone on vacation!'

'What else would he say? Razaq left in the middle of the night without giving notice. He did not even ask for his six months' salary. He tidied the whole house after your departure, and then left.'

'Who knows where he has gone!'

'All this was a dream, and I advise that you forget it all; you will otherwise lose yourself in a maze. Let's go. Abba must have returned from Makhdoom Sahib.'

Parveen felt gripped by a wild despair. Zeb stopped and turned to her. 'Wipe your tears. Look at me. I too had entrusted my fate in the hands of your brother, but all men are made of the same substance. They are always perfidious in love. Who knows who my rival is and how she ensnared him? And in comparison to me, you are fortunate. Forget him and repay the love of your husband.'

Parveen seemed to be listening to Zeb, but inwardly she was still trying to understand why Razaq had discarded the doll in that manner. *Did he abhor me to that extent?* she thought.

Malla Khaliq had returned from Makhdoom Sahib. Aziz Dyad asked him, 'Did you meet Narayan Joo?' When Malla Khaliq told her that Narayan Joo had assured him that his son Vijay Kumar was doing whatever he could to trace Qadir, she was somewhat calmed. Squatting near the window, he saw Zeb and Parveen outside the kitchen. He entreated his wife to remain calm. He had three cups of tea and then went out to the isle. Qadir's child Bilal caught sight of his grandfather and capered to him. 'See, I haven't plucked any flowers today.'

Malla Khaliq was overwhelmed by love and he took the child in his arms, kissed his cheeks and said to him, 'Not only today, but you should never pluck any flowers ever.'

'Then why do you cut so many flowers for the vases?'

The innocent question left Malla Khaliq speechless. Then he said, 'You little imp! Who can win against you!'

'Papa. He steps into the boat in one leap.'

Malla Khaliq felt his heart sink. He sighed and thought to himself, 'Those very leaps of his have ruined our peace.'

'Why are you silent now? Why do you cull flowers for the vases?'

'I cull only those flowers that are about to wither.'

'What is "wither"?'

'I mean flowers that are about to shed their petals.'

'But Mummy says plucking a flower is a sin.'

'True. It is a big sin.'

Holding the child in his arms, Malla Khaliq sat down. Just then, he caught sight of Ghulam Ahmed rowing towards the ghat. Bilal also saw him. He went romping towards the ghat yelling, 'Ama Toth is home, Ama Toth is home!'

Malla Khaliq's left eye started twitching. Ghulam Ahmed was not alone, his wife Zoon was with him.

Ghulam Ahmed asked the boatman to stop the boat. He and Zoon climbed up the steps and addressing Razaq's replacement he said, 'Subhana, will you please pass that attaché case to me?'

'All well? Why have you returned just within four days?' Malla Khaliq hastened to ask him.

Ghulam Ahmed placed the attaché case on the ground, and took the child in his arms. 'Yes, all is well, Abba. There was hardly anything to do there. I managed to load all the consignments of the fruit in the trucks, and settled the accounts with the broker who left for Delhi. I thought you might be feeling lonely here.'

Malla Khaliq laid his hand on Ghulam Ahmed's shoulder and said, 'I was just worried if everything was all right.'

Ghulam Ahmed kissed Bilal's forehead. 'Here, I brought some toffees for you.'

Bilal took the toffees and gave one to his grandfather. Then he stretched his little arms towards him. Malla Khaliq took him in his arms again, and Ghulam Ahmed lifted the attaché case and went into his room.

Bilal cast a piteous look at him and then turned to his grandfather again. 'When will my Papa be back, Abba?'

The question lacerated Malla Khaliq's heart. 'Yes, dear, he will be home soon.'

Fetching the hookah, Ghulam Ahmed said to Zoon, 'It would have been better if you had stayed back at your parents' house until I returned from Bombay. You could have also kept a watch over your darling son.'

Zoon, who never agreed with her husband, gave him a pat reply, 'You may be able to con other women, but not me. Abba is all alone here, and Amma is also starting to feel lonely here. Yet you advise me to relax and enjoy myself at my parents' house! You are going to Bombay to make money!'

Ghulam Ahmed pushed the hookah aside. 'Will you please lower your voice? If anybody comes to know that the business went bust, we will be ridiculed.'

'Then why are you being so stupid? I am quite happy staying here. You may go wherever you want to, but don't leave without informing Abba, like Qadir did. So far as your son is concerned, he is being held as mortgage by my father. As long as you owe him money, you don't have any right over him.'

Zoon was seething with rage because she knew that despite so much toil, Ghulam Ahmed could not earn anything over his daily wages and money for the bus fare; the broker had appropriated the profit. Having left over ten boxes of apples for Ghulam Ahmed, he had silently left the valley. The ten thousand rupees that he had given his father for Parveen's wedding was all the money he had. In addition to that he had entrusted over twenty thousand rupees to Zoon so that she could repay some part of the loan from his father-in-law. Zoon was angry again. 'Now why are you suddenly so silent? You won't gain anything by puffing the hookah with an empty tobacco pot. Think about what you will tell Abba.' Ghulam Ahmed did not want to annoy Zoon. He said ruefully, 'My wits fail me. Please tell me what I should tell Abba.'

Zoon entered the inner chamber, and took out twenty thousand rupees which the broker had given her husband to repay the debt to her father. She flung the bundle of notes at Ghulam Ahmed saying, 'Now go and give this money to Abba so that he is convinced that you too are not a fake coin. Then you talk about Qadir. You can later on tell him about Abdullah Shah's trip to Bombay.'

'And how will I pay your father?'

'We will think about that later. You better not come back from Bombay empty handed.'

'Who knows if I will earn anything there! Maybe I should borrow some money from Abdullah Shah.'

'Why borrow from him? You could claim some advance. Why should you undertake so much trouble for nothing?'

'Yes, I appreciate your wisdom. I will have a word with him tomorrow. Today let me make my Abba happy.'

Having decided all this, Zoon went to Aziz Dyad. Ghulam Ahmed also deemed it proper to sit for a while with his mother and find some occasion to talk about his going to Bombay. He, then, entered his houseboat and started dusting the cushions placed on the porch while waiting for his father to come.

In a short while, he sighted his father's trip-boat. He dropped a pillow on the steps of the houseboat so that Malla Khaliq would observe it and feel happy that he was tidying the houseboats. When the trip-boat touched the shore, Subhan hurried and pulled the prow of the boat to the ghat. Bilal came out of the boat and ran on the isle with a pinwheel in his hand. He ran into the kitchen to show it to his grandmother.

But Malla Khaliq was worried about what he had heard at Abdullah Shah's shop. He sat down and started gazing at the lake. Ghulam Ahmed sat close to him and started talking about Ghulam Qadir. 'Abdullah Shah's munshi told me that Ghulam Qadir went from Delhi to Bombay. Shah met one of Gul Beg's agents.'

Malla Khaliq cast a penetrating glance at him. 'And when are you planning to leave?'

This caught Ghulam Ahmed by surprise. He stammered, 'Me? I have to go to Delhi only for a couple of days.'

'And then from Delhi to Bombay. Abdullah Shah told me everything.'

Ghulam Ahmed tried to explain, but Malla Khaliq left him speechless, saying, 'Don't try to sprinkle salt on my open wounds by giving me false explanations. When will you give up this craft of duping people? How dare you tell Abdullah Shah that you have already sought my permission?'

'Abba, I never told him I have your permission. On the contrary, I told him that I will have to seek your permission. You know Abdullah Shah well.'

'And don't you know him? You know pretty well that he is a crafty cheater, and yet you decided to partner with him!'

'No one can cheat me. We have agreed that he will pay me twenty-five per cent of the total commission. I will take my share after every sale of carpets. He will bear all the investment. My job is only to carry the carpets to the exporters in Bombay. Didn't he tell you that?'

Abdullah Shah had tried to entice Malla Khaliq many times before and, having sowed the seed of doubt, he did not deem it proper to lengthen the argument. Feeling that the time was opportune, Ghulam Ahmed took out the bundle of twenty thousand rupees and offered it to his father. But Malla Khaliq cast a furious look at him and said, 'You are trying to bribe me so that I remain quiet, aren't you?'

'No, Abba, this was my share of the profits lying with the broker. I have not given my consent to Abdullah Shah yet and if you don't allow me, I will not go to Bombay. I thought that since the apple season is over and there is hardly anything to do at home, it would be better if I worked for Abdullah Shah to make some more money.'

Ghulam Ahmed held his father's hands and gave him the money. In a broken voice, he started imploring him, 'Abba, take this money. It is of course a small amount, but it is honest money nevertheless. I am not a rogue.'

Malla Khaliq melted a little. Placing his hand on Ahmed's head, he said, 'Give it to Zoon. Let us see what we can do after you return from Bombay.'

'No, Abba, I have reserved some for my expenses.'

Caressing his son's head, Malla Khaliq rose. The money fell on the ground. He bent down, lifted the money and put it into

Ghulam Ahmed's pocket. 'You have earned some honest money, and that by itself is a treasure for me.'

Ghulam Ahmed's eyes watered and he stared at his father's face with guilt bubbling in the pit of his stomach. Malla Khaliq mistook this for sadness at his refusal to take the money. He put his hand into his son's pocket, took out a hundred-rupee note and put it into his own pocket. 'I will accept this much and think that I spent all your money on this household.' Having said this, he started climbing down from the prow. Ghulam Ahmed gathered courage and said, 'So may I leave, Abba?'

Without looking back, Malla Khaliq replied, 'You all may go wherever you want.'

Parveen went back to her in-laws' house. When the cook and the tent-man did not bring their bills to settle expenses, Malla Khaliq grew anxious. He sent the money to them through Noor Mohammad, but they told him that Ghulam Ahmed had cleared their bills. When Malla Khaliq came to know about this, he called for Ghulam Ahmed. Before he could rebuke him, Ghulam Ahmed sought his forgiveness, saying, 'Why am I alone considered so worthless? Am I not obliged to do a little bit for the house? If I have done something wrong, you may kill me.' Malla Khaliq put his hand on Ahmed's mouth, and said, 'May God always keep you this responsible!'

Time moves like gushing waters; nobody knows what ravines and deserts it will carry one towards.

Malla Khaliq had inwardly started breaking, and he knew well that his time was running out. However, he made sure no one around him perceived this.

He gladly sent Parveen away with her husband to her in-laws', and on the very next day, Ghulam Ahmed left for Bombay with Abdullah Shah's carpets. Left alone, Malla Khaliq had no option but to work with vigour and determination. He entered the houseboat Gul and tidied its drawing room. The telephone in the corner began to ring as he was dusting the carpets. It was Narayan Joo. 'Is Haji Sahib there?'

'Where else would he be? Tell me without any ado if you have any information.'

'Ghulam Qadir was in Delhi with Gul Beg's broker till yesterday, but today he left for Bombay.'

Malla Khaliq's legs trembled and he sat down. 'What is he going to Bombay for?'

'Definitely to run some errand for Gul Beg.'

'With a consignment of hashish?'

Narayan Joo had the same apprehension, but in order to keep his friend calm, he said, 'I don't know what has happened to you. Why are you being so cynical? Gul Beg is not running just one business. Yet I will keep a tab. Vijay is there after all. He has acquaintances in every nook and corner of Bombay. If anything untoward happens, Bhonsley Sahib is also there.'

'So you also have the misgiving that he might be selling hashish for Gul Beg?'

'Again the same fears! Let us wait and see what God has in store for us.'

If Qadir was apprehended for drug trafficking, Malla Khaliq and his wife would surely breathe their last. He managed to get up, and made his way out of the houseboat. He looked all around. Dark clouds had enveloped the skies. The wind was getting fierce.

Whenever Malla Khaliq was in a quandary, he would take out his small boat and entrust himself to the vast expanses of the Dal Lake. The lake always showed him the way. He took out his rowboat and, beating the oar fast, he went behind the swamps towards the bigger Dal. The wind was turning into a storm and the ripples in the lake were getting wider. Yet Malla Khaliq felt that the tempest within him was wilder than the one raging outside. Maybe the only way to free himself from this unrelenting pain was to drown himself in the depths of the lake. He began to row fast towards the centre of the lake. The wind churned the water and smashing the waves against one another, made them rise towards the sky. Malla Khaliq then threw the oar aside. Each wave lifted his boat high and then dropped it down with a big splash. With his eyes shut, Malla Khaliq implored the Almighty to drown his boat and deliver him from the suffering.

Then as if a miracle happened, the wind started abating and the boat, too, began to settle. Malla Khaliq opened his eyes.

The stormy waters of the Dal had grown calm and the ripples became resplendent with a golden hue. The gloomy clouds had dispersed and the sun shone through. Malla Khaliq was transfixed. A strange voice whispered into his ears: 'Hey Khaliq! What has happened to you? You would get rid of your anxieties by ending your life, but did you spare a thought for your family's fate if you did so? It is a sin to seek riddance of cares like this.'

Cold sweat drenched his body. The sun again got enveloped by clouds. Malla Khaliq prostrated to God and sought absolution. 'Oh God, you show the way to all the lost ones, forgive me. Forgive me for all my sins! I was about to commit a blunder. Had You not shown me this miracle and held my hand, all the labour of my life would have gone to waste. Forgive me!'

He took the oar in his hands and turned the prow towards his houseboats.

Back on the isle, his entire family had started searching for Malla Khaliq. Zeb came running to Aziz Dyad. 'Abba is not here, and the little rowboat near the ghat is also missing. Sula Shoga says he saw him going towards the watercourses.'

Hearing this Aziz Dyad ran towards the prow, sat in a boat and rowed it towards the centre of the lake. Zeb was stunned to see how Aziz Dyad managed to reach the alcove near the houseboats that led to the deep water courses. Bilal came running and glued himself to her legs. She shoved him and he fell down. The child started crying loudly. Zeb sat down helplessly, with her head in her hands.

The clouds had almost thinned and the sun shone intermittently. Malla Khaliq diverted his boat towards one of the courses, laid down his oar and made as if to lie down.

GUL GULSHAN GULFAM

PART 2

He heard the sound of oar against water. Malla Khaliq turned in its direction, with a hand over his throbbing heart and saw Aziz Dyad coming towards him in her boat.

She held him in her strong gaze. Like a criminal, Malla Khaliq hung his head. 'I had got marooned by a whirlpool.'

'Were you really caught unawares in the whirlpool or did you decide to entrust yourself to the whirlpool because you couldn't bear to live with us any more? You did not even bother to think what would happen to your Azi!'

'Forgive me, Azi. Our situation has worsened to such an extent that I felt like there was no meaning in living any more.'

'And so you came here to end your life. You did not think about Zeb. About Bilal whom Qadir has deserted.'

'How can I explain myself to you? Had my conscience not reminded me of the wonderful family I have at home to take care of me, the family who are innocent and do not deserve to suffer, I would certainly have consigned myself to the Dal.'

'Remember how you have towed your boat through many a tempest. And now when your reckless son left for Bombay without your permission, you lost all your equanimity. He will return within a few days. Now let's go home. See how drenched you are. Paddle the boat, all will be fine soon.'

Malla Khaliq cast a piteous look at her face. He never wanted to keep any secret from Azi, but he knew that she would not be able to bear the shock. So he said to himself, 'I have to endure this venom all alone.'

After a week or so, Ghulam Qadir called his father from Bombay only to inform him that he was well and hoped to be home within fifteen days. Malla Khaliq was already quite furious with him and said, 'Whether you come after fifteen days or fifteen months, nobody here cares. You did not leave seeking anybody's permission, did you?' Qadir tried to explain his position, but Malla Khaliq put the receiver down. Aziz Dyad burst out, 'Why did you bang the phone down? You should have let me have a word with him. I would have at least asked him what was so urgent that he did not find time to keep us informed.'

Malla Khaliq cast a fierce look at her. His gaze could melt steal with his wrath. He somehow held his rage back. After a little reflection, he walked towards Zeb's room. She was busy arranging Bilal's clothes in the almirah. Seeing her father-in-law coming, she put the clothes down and went to him. 'You look quite perturbed, Abba. Why don't you come in? Is all well?'

'Yes, my daughter. It was Ghulam Qadir on the line from Bombay. He says he is coming soon.'

'Is he in Delhi or Bombay? You told me that—'

'Yes, my child, I told you that he has gone to Delhi. He then went to Bombay. You need not worry. He will be home soon.' Saying this, he went out.

Zeb shuddered. She could hardly stand. She sat down in a crumpled heap. The very word 'Bombay' rang a bell with her. Jane's face came to her mind. She was suddenly filled with hatred. She was sure that Qadir must be with her.

Malla Khaliq thought it proper to inform Narayan Joo about Qadir's phone call. Hearing the news, Narayan Joo was delighted. 'God has listened to our prayers. Where is he staying there?' But when Malla Khaliq told him that he was least delighted by the call and had, on the contrary, slammed the phone down, Narayan Joo lost his temper. 'You are an incorrigible fellow. Instead of interrogating him, you cut the conversation short. Tell me, how are we to find him now?'

Malla Khaliq was struck mute. He realized that he had committed a blunder. Narayan Joo tried to comfort him: 'It is all right. Qadir would know Vijay Kumar's address. He will finish his job and see him. You need not worry. I will also reach Bombay within the next few days.'

Malla Khaliq felt comforted. He went to share this news with his wife. Aziz Dyad said, 'Without Narayan Joo's support, you would keep making mistakes. Here, keep this kangri, see how badly you are shivering in the cold.' Having taken the kangri, Malla Khaliq sat down and cast a loving glance at his wife. 'Why only mention Narayan Joo when I would have lost my way long back if you were not by my side.'

'Come, come. Stop flattering me. Shall I get you a blanket? See how the sky is covered in clouds.'

'Yes, get me a blanket. The wind is cold. It must be snowing somewhere.'

'This is hardly the time for snow. The plane trees are still green.' Aziz Dyad went into the inner room and got a blanket for her husband. She placed one end of the blanket over her knees. 'I am afraid winter might come ahead of its time. Oh God, keep the weather warm until my children return home!'

Noor Mohammad and his wife Mukhta were facing a dilemma. They were happy that Nisar Ahmed had decided to marry Yasmeen, a girl from an affluent family. She was a doctor and her father was also a doctor who lived in Saudi Arabia. He ran a small nursing home and wished for his daughter to work there after completing her MD. When he met Nisar Ahmed in Srinagar, he liked him very much. He wanted the nikah to happen soonest. But Noor Mohammad knew well that his father was caught up in other problems at this point. But he did not have any other option. He said to Mukhta, 'There is no option but to have a word with Abba. Let us go there and return before evening.'

Malla Khaliq was engrossed in teaching Bilal how to read the Quran. He noticed Noor Mohammad and Mukhta coming through the isle. Touching the holy book to his forehead, he kissed little Bilal on his forehead and said, 'You may go and play now, my dear boy. Make it a habit to come to me as you did today. Taking the holy book from his hand, Bilal said, 'Let me keep it on the shelf.' He put the holy book in its case and, taking the support of the desk, he placed it on the shelf. Malla Khaliq fondly watched his movements. A smile appeared on his lips and his eyes filled with tears. 'I pray that you may thrive and flourish.'

Noor Mohammad and Mukhta entered the room. Bilal said salaam and then ran out. Aziz Dyad followed Noor Mohammad and Mukhta. Mukhta embraced her mother-in-law and said salaam to Malla Khaliq. Noor Mohammad squatted in front of his father with his head lowered. Malla Khaliq cast a searching glance at his face. 'Why are you so gloomy? Is all well with you?'

'Of course, Abba, all is well. You know Doctor Bhatt? He phones us almost every day. That is why I came here to take your advice.'

'What does he say?'

'He says that if Nisar Ahmed is not ready for marriage yet, we should at least finalize the nikah for now.'

'And what did you tell them?'

Noor Mohammad stammered. Mukhta helped him, saying, 'Abba, what could we tell them without consulting you?'

Malla Khaliq cast a glance at his wife's face. She said, 'When they are so insistent, we—'

Malla Khaliq intercepted her and said, 'We should not let go of their proposal. Is it not so? Yes?'

'Yes. That does not diminish the solemnity of the proposal,' said she.

A bitter smile appeared on Malla Khaliq's face. He turned to Noor Mohammad. 'Bhatt Sahib's daughter Yasmeen will complete her training and then her father will take her along to Saudi. People say he runs his own hospital there.'

'Yes, Nisar Ahmed also says so.'

'And then he will call Nisar Ahmed to Saudi as well, won't he?'

Noor Mohammad was struck dumb. Aziz Dyad sensed that her husband was about to lose his temper. She tried to cut the conversation short. 'See how you think so ahead of yourselves. It is still just a proposal, and you have already sent off Nisar Ahmed to Saudi!'

Malla Khaliq got angry. 'That is Bhatt Sahib's real scheme. Why should he implore so much otherwise? This way he will get two doctors without any effort to run his hospital.'

Aziz Dyad could not restrain herself and said, 'And what then? He has only one child, his daughter. Naturally he will want her to stay with him. And no doctor is willing to stay here. All of them are looking for ways to go abroad. Some go to Saudi, others to America and many others to Dubai. If Nisar Ahmed too aspires to go abroad and earn well, why should we blame him?'

Noor Mohammad grew restless and said, 'Please keep quiet, Amma. Why should we bother about others?'

Malla Khaliq could not hold himself back and roared, 'The poor people of our land are desperate for doctors, and the doctors abandon their parents, kith and kin to settle down in foreign lands.'

After a long silence, Noor Mohammad wearily said, 'All right, Abba. I will tell Bhatt Sahib that his proposal is not acceptable to us.'

Seeing the helplessness of his son, Malla Khaliq calmed down. Placing his hand on his shoulder, he said to Noor Mohammad, 'Look here, my dear son. We arranged for Nisar Ahmed's medical training, but never with the intention of earning wealth. In spite of our hardships, we sent him to Jaipur for further training. Why? We did all this with the dream that when he completed his training, he would return and serve our poor folks. I know he likes Bhatt Sahib's daughter. I am sure she is very nice. I will advise Nisar Ahmed to motivate her also to stay here and serve the people. And if Bhatt Sahib agrees to this proposal, I will have no objection to their nikah. If you don't have the courage to talk to him, give me his phone number, I will do it. I think he too nurses a love for Kashmir in some corner of his heart.'

The sky was overcast, and the air freezing. Having shut the doors and windows, Noor Mohammad and Mukhta sat brooding in their room. Mukhta said to her husband, 'Abba is right. If Bhatt Sahib really took Nisar Ahmed to Saudi, what would we do here? We have only one child after all.'

Noor Mohammad heaved a long sigh and started blowing the embers in his kangri. 'Let us sleep over it and see how things go from here.'

Malla Khaliq could not sleep. The room was ice cold, as if everything were covered in frost. The chilly wind outside had somewhat subsided. He turned prone and was again lost in the wilderness of anxieties. He tossed and turned till sleep finally overtook him in the last hour of the night. He could not get up in the morning until Zeb came to him with a fresh hot kangri. 'Give me the kangri, my child. Even if the sun forgets to rise some day, this daughter of mine won't forget to get me a hot kangri and wake me up.'

When he put his hand into the kangri to stir the hot embers under the ashes, Zeb chuckled. 'Abba, Nav Sheen mubarak! See, I am the first to give you the message of our first snow, so you have lost the bet.'

'No, no, this is called – what do the children of today say? Yes, April fool! This is cheating!'

'New-snow surprise, Abba, no April fool business,' said Zeb.

'Okay! I accept your new-snow surprise gift. Tell me, what do you want?'

'Really? Can you give me what I want?'

'Try me. I can get you even the stars from the sky.'

'I want Ghulam Qadir! Can you give him to me?'

'Ghulam Qadir? He will be with you as soon as he is free from his business trip.'

'No, Abba, no, I will never get him back now. He abhors me, and all this business is just a pretext. He is falling for strangers.'

'You need not worry, my daughter. If I have to, I will drag him back home; I won't dither.'

'Give me the cold kangri,' said Zeb after heaving a cold sigh. 'I will fill it with hot coals.'

Like a child, Malla Khaliq got up and strode towards the inner chamber with the kangri, saying, 'You stay quiet. I will claim a new-snow surprise gift from your mother-in-law. You may get me hot cinders in the kangri afterwards.'

Zeb followed him to enjoy the spectacle.

Holding Bilal to her chest, Aziz Dyad lay fast asleep. Malla Khaliq shook her awake saying, 'Why don't you get up? The sun is already well near our willow copse. Now please get up and give me my morning tea.'

Aziz Dyad calmly wriggled out of her quilt without waking Bilal. Malla Khaliq passed her the kangri. 'Warm up your hands before doing anything else.'

Aziz Dyad smiled at him and said, 'What is all this pampering for?' She put her hand into the kangri, and took it out immediately. Malla Khaliq let out a roar of laughter and said, 'You have lost the Nav Sheen bet!' Zeb also came in and paid first-snow greetings to her mother-in-law. Aziz Dyad would have said many stinging words to her husband, but seeing Zeb a little happy after so many days, she laughed too. She turned to her husband. 'You are already at the threshold of your eighties, and yet you remain so childish!'

'Do not try to change the subject. You lost the new-snow bet to us. Now tell us what are you going to cook for us?' With these words, Zeb nestled close to her mother-in-law. Moving her hand affectionately over her head, Aziz Dyad said, 'Whatever your heart desires.'

Malla Khaliq opened the window through which he could see the surface of the lake. Everything was covered with thick fluffy snow. He saw people in boats greeting each other. The tops of the boats, the willow groves, the surface of the Dal Lake – everything was enveloped by bright white snow. Kids of the vegetable growers living on the distant swamps were romping about on the fresh snow, with their dogs excitedly playing along. They called the first snow their 'maternal uncle'. Malla Khaliq stretched his arm out of the window to have a feel of the snowflakes. He withdrew his hand and shut the window. 'Oh! It has started snowing again. I have to fetch this month's ration from the ghat. What will I do now?' His wife said, 'There will be no one there at the ghat at this time.'

'I will keep my ration card in the queue. Otherwise poor Subhan shall have to keep waiting there the whole day.' Saying this, Malla Khaliq went out. The sight of snow filled his heart with joy for a moment, but then he grew anxious that if Qadir and Ahmed did not return soon, he would not be able to cope with the harsh winter. He entered Gul and took out the ration card from a drawer. He was about to lock the drawer when the telephone rang. It was Narayan Joo on the line. 'Hello! Houseboat Gul?' Malla Khaliq recognized the voice and tried to win new-snow bet from his friend. 'New-snow greetings! I won the new-snow bet!'

'Yes, I accept it.' The usual warmth and cheer were missing from Narayan Joo's voice. Malla Khaliq grew nervous. 'Narayan Joo, are you well? Why do you sound so low?'

'Who is there beside you?'

'Nobody. Has something happened?'

'How can I tell you about the calamity Ghulam Qadir has caused?'

Malla Khaliq stood rooted to the spot. Narayan Joo sensed this, yet he continued, 'I received a call from Vijay Kumar last night. He told me that the Bombay police have apprehended Ghulam Qadir. Karmakar of Delhi who used to meet Jane quite often was with him. The drugs were found hidden under the inner lining of his bag.'

Malla Khaliq shuddered. His eyes grew dim and he felt darkness closing on him.

'Now there is nothing to worry about. By some stroke of luck they landed in Bhonsley's lockup. Vijay Kumar will see him first thing today and find a solution to this.'

Malla Khaliq snapped out of his silence. 'I always knew this evil son of mine would bring great misfortune to this family. That premonition has always haunted me. He has brought shame on our entire dynasty. He has killed us while we are alive. Now tell me how to convey this message to my family. And what will I tell Zeb?' He gasped for breath and torrents of tears poured from his eyes.

'Why don't you talk? Tell me what I should do now.'

Hearing a cold sigh, Narayan Joo replied, 'That is what I am pondering over. I hope the plane arrives today. I have to leave for Bombay in two days. I will talk to Raina Sahib and implore him to grant me a ticket from the special quota, if not for today, for tomorrow. As soon as I arrive there, I will meet Bhonsley Sahib. You don't worry; let us see what God has decided for us. Don't tell anyone this. We will somehow have Qadir released.'

'Yes, please reach Bombay somehow.'

'All right, you keep calm. You may keep Noor Mohammad informed; I trust him as I trust you. Have faith and see how Mother Sharika alleviates our troubles.'

Malla Khaliq's face had turned dark as if smeared with soot. He felt as guilty and tainted as a criminal who was about to be sent to the gallows. With the ration card in hand, he stood petrified, like a statue. Aziz Dyad, who had been looking for him, entered the houseboat. When she found him standing there, clad in a thin phiran, she said, 'What are you doing all alone here in this freezing cold?'

Malla Khaliq stood looking melancholic. She said with much affection, 'I think you are anxious about Nisar Ahmed's marriage and Noor Mohammad's helplessness.'

Malla Khaliq paid no heed to her; he had forgotten everything. His heart was sinking. Then he let all his pent-up anger loose on her. 'Let them do whatever they like, you need not plead for them!'

'Poor Noor Mohammad too is caught up in a quagmire. Nisar Ahmed says that he won't marry any other girl. What can Noor Mohammad do?'

'Have all of you decided not to let me live? If I am a hurdle in everybody's way, why don't you slay me once and for all so that everyone is set free? That would surely release me too from this unrelenting suffering.'

Aziz Dyad had never seen her husband so angry and upset. She said, 'I don't know what has happened to you; every trivial thing infuriates you. You will freeze into an ice sculpture here. Come, Zeb is waiting with tea for you. You can do whatever you want later on.'

Malla Khaliq put the ration card in his pocket and cursed himself. 'I should not have rebuked poor Azi like that. The time is not far when I will run after every human being like a mad dog.' Outside, it had stopped snowing. He thought it proper to inform Noor Mohammad about Qadir. But if he left before having his tea, his wife would suspect that something was wrong. He therefore contained himself and walked to the kitchen.

As soon as he entered the outer gate of the lawn, Noor Mohammad, who was busy shovelling snow from the veranda, flung the spade aside and ran to meet his father.

Malla Khaliq said to Noor Mohammad, 'Let us go upstairs and talk.'

Noor Mohammad held his father's hand and helped him climb up the stairs. He made him sit down in the sofa. Climbing up had made Malla Khaliq's lungs gasp like bellows.

'What is the problem, Abba? Is Amma well?'

'I will tell you all. First give me a little water.'

Noor Mohammad ran to fetch water.

'Oh my God, have mercy on us!' Saying this, Malla Khaliq leaned against the pillow. Noor Mohammad came with a glass of water. He was followed by Doctor Nisar and Mukhta. Nisar did not lose any time in taking out his stethoscope. Trying to smile, Malla Khaliq said to him, 'My Doctor Sahib, I am perfectly well. Why do you take out your telescope?'

Nisar made him lie down and started examining him. After a while he said, 'There is no need to worry, it is a mild bronchitis. The mercury has dipped all of a sudden, and it has snowed much before it should. He has congestion.' He took out a bottle and a couple of tablets from his bag and made his grandfather swallow them with water. Finally he asked him, 'By the way, how come you came here so early on such a cold morning?'

'All is fine. In fact, I had gone to see Ramzan Joo because he had to go to Jammu. Then I wanted to see you and give you new-snow greetings.'

Noor Mohammad did not believe what he said. Malla Khaliq turned to his daughter-in-law. 'My dear daughter Mukhta, you have lost your new-snow bet. Tell me, what will you serve me?'

'I would certainly like to serve you a wild duck, but the government has banned killing of wild birds.'

'So am I to leave this rich home on an empty stomach?'

'Should I make you a pot of simmered turnips?'

'Yes, that should be fine. But remember to add mutton fat to it. Not today, but we will fix up another date for the feast.'

Nisar Ahmed remarked sarcastically, 'Yes, it is fatty mutton that has jammed your lungs.'

'Oh no, I was just joking with your mother. You may ask your grandmother how long it has been since we cooked any meat.'

Nisar Ahmed looked at his watch, and said to his grandfather, 'Abba, may I leave? I have to reach the hospital; we are running a camp there. I once again advise you to abstain from going outdoors as it is getting colder day by day. I think we must somehow or the other send Abba to Jammu or Delhi so that he is safe from the chill.'

Mukhta suggested that Abba go to Delhi to spend some time with Parveen.

'What? May I fill your mouth with candies for this suggestion! Do you mean that I should live at my daughter's house and eat her food? By the way, if I have to go anywhere, it will be to Narayan Joo's house in Bombay. He has been insisting that I live there with him during the winter months.' Malla Khaliq gave her a clear reply.

Nisar said, 'Of course, he might be going to visit his son soon. You could accompany him.'

'And what will happen to your old grandmother? Remember, I was fed pure milk and ghee in my youth; this chill cannot do me any harm. God save you! You may leave now.'

Mukhta followed Nisar Ahmed out and then went into the kitchen.

Noor Mohammad cast a searching glance at his father's face and asked, 'Abba, you don't look well. Have you received some bad news from Bombay?'

Malla Khaliq said, 'Shut the door first.'

'Abba, what should we do now? Bombay is no Kashmir where we could approach a Prahlad Singh, beg him to free Qadir by bribing the authorities.'

Narayan Joo was already packing his luggage when Malla Khaliq and Noor Mohammad reached his house. Narayan Joo cursed his friend for venturing outdoors in the cold.

Noor Mohammad said, 'That is what Nisar Ahmed advised him. He has contracted bronchitis. He advised us that we should send him to some warm place outside Kashmir, maybe Jammu or Delhi.'

Malla Khaliq got angry. 'Are we here to settle the issue of my cold or to think of some remedy for the thunderbolt that has struck us because of that scoundrel?'

Narayan Joo lost his cool too. 'Are you the only one who is anxious? Don't you see how I am already packed and waiting for the call from Raina Sahib? It is impossible to get a ticket for today, but he will certainly arrange one for tomorrow. I beseech you not to get so nervous.'

'Could Vijay Kumar go and see Bhonsley Sahib?' Malla Khaliq asked.

'Yes, he had gone to see him, but Mr Bhonsley is presently on a trip to Nagpur. He is back the day after tomorrow.'

Noor Mohammad nervously said to his father, 'So Mr Bhonsley might not know anything about this issue.'

'How does it matter?' his father asked him.

'If he were on duty nobody could torture Ghulam Qadir.'

Hearing this Malla Khaliq was aflame with rage. 'But I pray that they strip his skin off. They should chop him into pieces.' He started coughing violently.

Narayan Joo stood up, saying, 'I will get him water to drink; you please rub his chest till then. This is the result of some of our sins.' He went to the kitchen and Noor Mohammad held Malla Khaliq close to him and rubbed his chest. 'Nisar Ahmed has told you so many times that you should not get angry. You know how your blood pressure shot up just the day before yesterday.'

'Let my blood pressure increase and let my skull burst; I wish for relief from this perpetual agony.'

In the meantime, Narayan Joo brought water.

Passing the tumbler back to Narayan Joo, Malla Khaliq said, 'Qadir is a vagabond, a drug smuggler, and my other son is Naba Kantroo's son-in-law and a stooge of Abdullah Shah's. He did not even call us from Bombay.' Saying so, he became breathless again.

Narayan Joo said to Noor Mohammad, 'Your Doctor Sahib has rightly advised him to spend the winter in a warmer place. Haji Sahib, should I arrange for a ticket for you as well?'

Noor Mohammad seconded Narayan Joo. 'Abba, Lala Sahib is right. How long will you suffer like this? Sitting here you are imagining the worst. If you manage to meet Bhonsley Sahib in person, he will surely be lenient. He respects you a lot.'

'All that respect is now smudged by this drug smuggler of ours. How will I face Bhonsley Sahib in Bombay?'

Narayan Joo said, 'See, even if I succeed in freeing Ghulam Qadir, I may not be able to motivate him to come back. If he does not respect you, his father, why would he respect me?'

'Ghulam Ahmed is also there. I will find out where he is staying from his father-in-law.' Malla Khaliq said all this to save himself from going to Bombay.

Seeing his father being so stubborn, Noor Mohammad said, 'What are you saying, Abba? He used to play tricks with Ghulam Ahmed when he was here, think what he can do with him there in Bombay. If we don't act quickly, they will take Qadir to the gallows.'

'Let them hang him there, he deserves that. I will not go to rescue him.'

Narayan Joo lost his temper and said, 'All right, let his wife die here many times a day. And you can watch the apple of your eye Bilal wither away before his prime.'

Malla Khaliq grew quiet and finding himself helpless, said yes. 'I hope that my visit to Bombay will dispel the eclipse that has gripped Zeb's destiny. But how will I convince my wife Azi that I am going to Bombay only to get rid of my bronchitis?'

'Leave that to me. You go now. I will arrange for the tickets.'

Having made the decision, Malla Khaliq and Noor Mohammad left for home.

Malla Khaliq had no courage to face his wife, and he used Noor Mohammad as a shield. Noor Mohammad feigned anger and said to his mother, 'Why can't you stop Abba from going out in the cold. You should have seen him this morning. He is suffering from acute chest pain. He has contracted bronchitis.'

Noor Mohammad with his pretend displeasure convinced his mother that his father needed to go to Bombay along with Narayan Joo. She immediately said, 'You should follow what Nisar Ahmed has advised you to do.'

'But how can I leave you all here alone?' Malla Khaliq was still trying to seek an excuse to stay back, but Aziz Dyad said, 'Nobody is going to take me away.'

'What rubbish! I meant how will you cope with all the household work unaided?'

'I will come and stay here,' Noor Mohammad said.

Finally it was resolved that Malla Khaliq would accompany Narayan Joo to Bombay. All the kith and kin, including Parveen, were informed. Parveen came with her father-in-law to see him before his departure.

Seeing Parveen, Malla Khaliq looked around and asked Ramzan Haji, 'Was Parvez Sahib not able to come?'

'He has left for Delhi, Abba,' said Parveen.

'Some foreign customers are expected to arrive soon, that is why he had to leave in a hurry,' Ramzan Haji added. It had been decided that Parvez would take Parveen along to Delhi later on. Malla Khaliq gently asked, 'I think Parveen also was to accompany him to Delhi?'

'Yes. All of us are going together to Delhi, but after a month or so.' Ramzan Haji allayed his fears.

Malla Khaliq was now eager to reach Bombay. Never in his life had he kept any secret from his wife, but now he kept his head hung like some shamed criminal and he willed time to pass faster. Finally that day passed. Parveen was to stay for some days. In spite of that Malla Khaliq ate dinner earlier and retired to bed. If she had inquired about Ghulam Qadir, he would have no option but to lie; he considered lying the biggest sin.

Parveen was with her mother in the next room. She said, 'Some evil eye has jinxed our home. No one in the family has any peace of mind. Ama Lala or Qadir should have kept Abba's health in mind and postponed their trips to Bombay.' Her mother in her turn tried to assuage Parveen's anxiety. 'My dear daughter, what else could they do? It's not like they have any job here. You need not worry about me. Noor Mohammad will come to stay here until your Abba returns. You should forget about our problems. You tell me honestly if you are happy at your in-laws'.'

'They love me more than they love their own daughters.'

'And what about Parvez Lala?'

'I don't know. I fail to understand him. He blows hot and cold. He spends hours on the phone.'

'He has to, because his business is spread far and wide, even in Saudi. Your Abba says that these days most businesses are run on the phone,' Aziz Dyad said.

Parveen forced a smile on her lips. 'I told you, he takes me shopping, to the cinema, and does everything to keep me happy. But many a time, he sits aloof from me, as if he does not even know me.'

'Try to understand, my daughter, men have to cope with all kinds of problems. When there is some trouble in matters of

business, they get so upset that they don't want to talk to others. I
am praying that God bestows the joy of a child upon you. Then he
will worship you.'

⚓

Malla Khaliq woke up before dawn. After having his bath, he
entered houseboat Gul and offered his nimaz. Then he prayed, 'Oh
my Allah, with a heavy weight on my heart, I am leaving my home
because of my love for my offspring. Have mercy on me and help
me return with respect. Be kind to the one who has lost his way
and show him the right path. May his wife's destiny return to her
the joys of married life. I beseech you for nothing else.'

⚓

With a sad smile, Zeb looked at Parveen and said, 'Even if Abba
really succeeds in bringing Qadir back, he is not going to give up
his ways. You need not worry about me; I will seek refuge at my
Dastagir's feet. He alone will show me the right path. Whatever
Qadir becomes, I will still continue praying for him. Abba would
have finished his prayers by now. Give this bag to him.'

'What is in it?' asked Parveen.

'Dry morels. Qadir loves dry morels cooked with minced meat
balls.'

'Why don't you give it to him yourself?'

'No. I don't have the nerve to do this.'

Parveen took the small cloth bag from her and was about to
leave, but Zeb held her back. 'Oh yes, one more thing. Did you see
the *Srinagar Times* day before yesterday?'

'No, I did not. Did any news about Qadir appear in it? Is he
well?'

'The matriculation exam results have been announced in the
papers and Razaq has stood first. I would have never known who
that Abdul Razaq was if his photograph wasn't there beside the
news. See what good news I have given you this morning. He used
to study till midnight in his shed.'

Heaving a sigh, Parveen stood up. Zeb looked at her forlorn face. 'Are you not happy to hear this?'

'Extremely happy, and I know Abba will be happier than I am.' Parveen sat back down.

'Razaq always told me that he would come at the top, rise as high as the cliffs of the Zabarwan. And I always laughed at him and asked him to mind his job of scrubbing and cleaning. I sneered at him saying that he would remain doing the dishes till it was dusk and not be able to see even the Sulaiman Teng mountain far away.'

'My Dastagir will always help him.'

Parveen felt as if her heart was being crushed. Holding her tears back, she rose and left the room saying, 'What will I get from nursing such dreams? Once lost in life, one is lost forever. May others go on gaining scores, what does it matter to the one who has lost?'

These words struck Zeb's heart like arrows. She sat near the windowsill and was lost in her own worries. How can I tell this foolish girl that I have lost everything after I thought I had gained everything I wanted. Qadir, who said he was ready to sacrifice his life for me, deserted me after Bilal's birth. She recollected how Qadir once took her on a trip to Lolab. Her mother was alive then. He made an excuse to Abba that Zeb's mother wished to spend a few days with her. She remembered how he took her on that trip in a car borrowed from his friend. She remained lost in her memories and days of the past seemed to return in all their freshness. In her imagination, she roamed in the forests of love; Qadir was dressed like the heroes in films. Putting his arm round her waist, he walked her to the foothills. They saw children of the tribesmen searching for something amidst rocks. The thunders from the previous night had made the morels and black mushrooms pop up from the sandy earth. Qadir turned to Zeb and said to her in a filmy manner, 'What do you say, my darling? Why don't we go to collect a basketful of morels and present them to Abba?' Zeb had replied in an equally filmy way, 'My lord, the idea is not bad.' 'Then what are we waiting for?' he had said. Both ran towards the ravine. 'You please stay here while I search beyond the rocks.'

Zeb remembered how Qadir returned with a pile of morels in his shirt. 'This is called a real surprise. See how many morels I have collected. Where have you kept the ones you collected?'

Zeb showed him the four morels she had found. Qadir let out a big laugh and said, 'Only these few! Shame!' Zeb cribbed. 'Only these few were here, and what is there to laugh about? How did you find so many?'

'You know I am dark while you are milky white. It is said that morels are found only by people with a dark complexion.'

'What do the dark complexioned ones find then?'

'Nothing but fair complexion!' Saying this, Qadir held her in a tight hug.

Swimming in the memories of her past, Zeb felt her heart was wrenched; a torrent of tears poured forth from her eyes.

Malla Khaliq put the bag of morels in his attaché case. Qadir might begin loving Zeb afresh when he saw the morels. Noor Mohammad came very early to see his father. He said, 'Abdullah Shah has come to see you.'

'How did he pop up from the swamp so early in the morning? You should have told him that I am not free.'

'Abba, maybe we shouldn't avoid him. Perhaps he has come to know that you are not keeping well and are going to Bombay.'

Malla Khaliq went to houseboat Gulshan. Abdullah Shah was waiting for him in the drawing room. Abdullah Shah, who was known for his arrogance, stood up courteously, shook hands with him and then sat across from him. 'I came to know that you are not keeping well and are going to Bombay with Narayan Joo for treatment.'

'Yes, the Doctor Sahib is insisting I go there. You know winter has set in earlier than usual. This breathlessness is not leaving me.'

'Yes, it's true. All ailments get a new lease of life as it gets colder. I thought you might stay there for quite some time, and so came to see you before your departure.'

'But so early on such a frosty morning!'

'I was told that your flight leaves before noon. And I also have a small request. I have to send some carpets to Ghulam Ahmed. Since you are going there, I thought I could book the consignment in your name so that Ghulam Ahmed receives them well in time.'

Malla Khaliq was enraged to hear this, but repressing his anger, said, 'As you know Shah Sahib, I am indisposed. How can I take this responsibility? Whatever business is between you and Ghulam Ahmed is known only to God and you both. Besides, I hardly know where he stays in Bombay. I beg your pardon, I am not ready to shoulder this added responsibility.'

'There is nothing fishy in it, I assure you. If you—'

'I told you that I am not well. You may send it as you always send across such things.' Malla Khaliq did not let him complete his sentence. Then he called out to Noor Mohmmad, 'Please bring a cup of tea for Shah Sahib.'

Abdullah Shah stood up abruptly and said, 'No, so kind of you. I don't have much time. I thought ... All right, there are many other ways to send the consignment. *As-salaam-alaikum!*' He stormed out, fuming.

Malla Khaliq said, 'I told you that I did not want to see this evil person so early in the morning. See his gall! He thinks I am his father's porter that I should carry his load of carpets through the markets of Bombay!'

Aziz Dyad, Mukhta, Nisar Ahmed, Bilal – all of them were on the isle, waiting for Malla Khaliq. Subhan had already put his luggage in the boat. Aziz Dyad kept gazing at her husband, but he had no courage to look towards her. Bilal came running. 'Are you going to Bombay to meet my father? I will also go with you.' Malla Khaliq took the child in his arms, hugged and kissed him. 'You know you will start going to school soon. Let me go. I will be back soon. Once I return from Bombay, I will take you to school every day.'

Zeb came and took the child away from Malla Khaliq's arms and said, 'Abba will be back soon. He will get you many toys – motor, scooter, motorboat, everything.'

'And Daddy?'

'And Daddy, too,' Malla Khaliq said.

Noor Mohammad thought this farewell might become very emotional, so he told his mother, 'Now you should let Abba leave. We also have to pick up Lala Sahib on the way to the airport.'

Nisar Ahmed took his grandfather's hand and led him to the ghat. All of them followed him. Nisar Ahmed and Noor Mohammad sat beside Malla Khaliq in the boat. When the boat started moving, tears trickled down from Malla Khaliq's eyes. He kept gazing at his wife until his houseboats were out of sight.

From Delhi, Narayan Joo and Malla Khaliq took the evening train to Bombay. On their arrival at Victoria Terminus, they met Vijay Kumar who, along with his little son Vishal, was waiting for them.

Vijay Kumar said to his father, 'Let us move, otherwise we will lose track of the coolie.'

There was a huge crowd at the station. Malla Khaliq had seen Bombay railway station eighteen years ago while on his way to haj along with Aziz Dyad.

'There weren't so many people when I first came here,' Malla Khaliq said.

'Haji Sahib, eighteen years have gone by since then. Please take care of your pockets,' Narayan Joo said as they both hastened to follow Vijay Kumar.

While proceeding to Bandra, in the car, Malla Khaliq was growing impatient to know what Mr Bhonsley had told Vijay Kumar. Narayan Joo placed his hand affectionately on Malla Khaliq's shoulder and, in order to divert his attention, said to him, 'Haji Sahib, do you see how the world has transformed?'

'Yes, I see. This is the world of dreams which lures our new generation.' Vijay Kumar, who was driving, heard, looked back and said to him, 'If man does not have dreams to chase, how will the world move ahead?'

'Yes, that is true, but one must have the wisdom and courage to realize his dreams,' said Malla Khaliq.

'Uncle, you are absolutely right.'

In Vijay Kumar's flat, Malla Khaliq went near the window and looked out. He saw the ocean spreading as far as the eye could see. The evening sun was ready to go deep into the waters, making the water crimson red. Narayan Joo laid a hand on his shoulder and said, 'Haji Sahib, what are you thinking about?'

'I was watching the setting sun lighting the ocean aflame. I have been living on water all my life, and yet, God knows why, this vast expanse of water scares me.'

'This flat is on the twentieth floor, and looking down from such a height makes one nervous.'

'No. Seeing this fiery crimson of the sun makes me fear that I have to face something worse soon.'

Narayan Joo, trying to calm him down, said, 'But you have always loved watching the sun setting rather than the rising sun!'

'But not in this manner. God usually turns the waters of our Dal Lake a beautiful gold, not a fiery red like this. It seems ominous.'

'This is the colour of fire, which burns all impurities to ashes.'

'Panditji, this profound philosophy of yours is beyond my reach.'

'The secret of our destiny is known only to the One who has given us this life and breath.'

Just then, Vijaya, Vijay Kumar's wife, came to tell them that their tea was getting cold.

Then he turned to his father and said, 'When I met Bhonsley Sahib today, he said he had interrogated Ghulam Qadir separately. Thanks to Mother Sharika, the all-knowing goddess, Ghulam Qadir has told them the truth.'

Malla Khaliq felt like his throat was parched dry. His heart pounded in his chest and his brain was being hammered. He closed his eyes like a criminal who hears his death sentence with his own ears.

Vijay Kumar understood his pain, and very briefly told them all that had happened during Ghulam Qadir's interrogation. 'Mr Bhonsley has directed his staff to release Ghulam Qadir on two grounds: first, no hashish was found in his possession; it was the notorious smuggler Karmakar who was trying to operate through him; secondly, he has revealed incriminating information about the chain of smugglers. The police succeeded in apprehending the whole gang of smugglers.'

On hearing this, both Narayan Joo and Malla Khaliq heaved a sigh of relief. Narayan Joo held his friend's hands and said, 'Do you see, Haji Sahib, how your prayers are working?'

Vijay Kumar said, 'Daddy is right, Uncle. Bhonsley Sahib told me that he handled the case personally because Ghulam Qadir is the son of Haji Abdul Khaliq. Such cases are otherwise taken care of by his subordinates. If the case had been assigned to any of them, they would have not released him this easily.'

Malla Khaliq was drenched in sweat. He could not muster the courage to meet Vijay Kumar's eyes. 'But this wicked son of mine had secret connections with Karmakar right from Srinagar!'

Narayan Joo got irritated and stood up. 'You may go broadcast it throughout Bombay that your son is not innocent, and he is a hardened criminal! You are of course Raja Harishchandra of our time!'

Vijay Kumar made his father sit down and sat beside Malla Khaliq. 'I told you that Ghulam Qadir has told Mr Bhonsley everything. Mr Bhonsley is helping him because he said the truth.'

Cutting their conversation short, Narayan Joo asked him, 'When are they going to set him free?'

'Bhonsley Sahib will tell me that by tomorrow.'

Narayan Joo held Malla Khaliq's arm again and said, 'Come, let us phone my sister; she must be waiting impatiently for your call. Now get up. I hope God has finally set Ghulam Qadir on the right path. His repentance and truth will absolve him.'

Malla Khaliq got up to make a call to Srinagar.

Her sudden 'hello' startled Malla Khaliq and the receiver fell from his hand. Narayan Joo laughed, lifted the receiver and gave it to his friend. 'Haji Sahib, say something, poor Azi is waiting at the other end.'

'Hello! I am calling from Bombay. We arrived today. Just an hour ago – yes, we are with Vijay Kumar.

'How are Vijay Kumar and his wife?' asked Aziz Dyad.

'Yes, all are well. Are you well there? Yes Ghulam Qadir is also well. No, he has not come so far – yes, yes – you need not worry – Vijay Kumar knows where he lives—'

'Did Ghulam Ahmed come to see you?'

'He will also come soon. See how much you care about your sons. I wish you cared so much for me as well.'

Malla Khaliq nudged Narayan Joo and winked. Azi replied loudly, 'See what he says! You have your bosom friend with you to give you all the care you need. My poor sons are there in an alien land. Who knows how they are …'

'Why do you sound so low?'

Narayan Joo laughed and said, 'Haji Sahib, it is a call from a place fifteen hundred kilometres away.'

Malla Khaliq felt stupid. Azi said at a higher pitch, 'Is Narayan Joo near you? Tell him I can recognize his voice even in a crowd of thousands.'

Passing the receiver to Narayan Joo, he said, 'Here he is. Tell him yourself.'

Narayan Joo did not let Azi talk. He said to her, 'His soul lies there with you. He talked about you all the way.'

'I don't believe that. He did not love me when he should have. What is the point of all this love for me now? Now please tell me if he felt all right during the journey.'

'Perfectly fit.'

'You always say so. Is he still wheezing?'

'Absolutely not. I wish you could have seen how he climbed up the stairs like a wild goat.'

'Please tell him that Noor Mohammad wants to have a word with him.'

She passed the telephone to Noor Mohammad and left the room. Narayan Joo passed the phone to Malla Khaliq.

Malla Khaliq told Noor Mohammad about Qadir. Then he asked him to convey to Zeb that Qadir was fine and would be home soon.

'Abba, you do not have to rush back to Srinagar now. It is constantly snowing here. No flight could land for the last three days. The Jammu road is also closed. Please don't think of returning home for some time. Keep Qadir under close watch. *As-salaam-alaikum!*'

Malla Khaliq could not muster up the courage to meet Mr Bhonsley. But the next day, Narayan Joo and his son went to thank Mr Bhonsley. He said, 'There is hardly anything that merits thanks. I am sure that Ghulam Qadir was in league with Jane Lockwood. But there was no proof of his being an active smuggler.

'I am a great admirer of Haji Sahib for his wisdom, honesty and kindness. But had Qadir been apprehended carrying drugs or the hashish which was recovered from Karmakar, I couldn't have set Qadir free.'

Vijay Kumar was granted permission to see Ghulam Qadir in the police lockup.

Ghulam Qadir was crouching in a corner. Vijay Kumar tried his best to console him and cheer him up, but Ghulam Qadir, his eyes fixed on the floor of the cell, did not utter a word in reply. Finally, when he told him that his father had reached Bombay in search of him and that he would come to the police station to get him released and take him home, Ghulam Qadir trembled. 'No, no. How will I face him?' He begged Vijay Kumar to not bring his father there. 'I will kill myself well before that.'

'You have not murdered anyone.' But Ghulam Qadir knew what a grave crime he had been involved in. He said, 'I have committed a crime more serious than murder. I have really besmeared Abba's name in the city. I have ravaged his faith in me; I don't have the guts to face him. You please take me from here to some hotel.'

'Do not be so childish. My house is your own house, why should you stay in a hotel?'

'No, Lala Sahib is there. My Abba is there. I cannot go there. Please try to understand,' Ghulam Qadir continued pleading with him.

'Then we have another option. We have a guest room which is separate from our apartment. You can stay there for four or five days until you feel better about yourself.'

'How can I stay there and still hide from Abba's sight? Won't they see me when I enter?'

'The room has a separate entry. You just leave all this to me.'

Ghulam Qadir looked at Vijay Kumar suspiciously.

Vijay Kumar laid a hand on his shoulder and said, 'Trust me. And forget all this happened. Start a new life. Everyone will forgive you.'

'Yes, I have to. I have no option.'

'Good. Be a brave man.' Saying this, Vijay Kumar left.

Qadir was restless in the room. He shut the door and almost latched it from inside, but stopped. Then he sat on the bed, opened his bag and counted the money, and then, he put the envelope back into the bag. He kept it near his head and stretched out with his eyes closed. He remained still for a long time and then all of sudden, he got up as if he felt an electric current had passed through him. After reflecting a little, he went near the dining table. He removed the lids of the casseroles, served rice on to his plate, and helped himself to a spoonful of broth and then some stew on the rice. He was taken aback when he saw pieces of morels mixed with meat balls on the rice and a surge of affection and love filled his heart. He remembered Zeb. He forgot all his hunger, as if his mouth were filled with poison. He washed his hands again and dropped on the bed.

Then he opened his eyes and looked at his face in the mirror of the dressing table. He felt like a stranger was looking back at him. He saw his unshaven face, eyes sunk into the sockets and lips parched. He saw this stranger moving his lips, and then he heard himself saying, 'Do you see what shape you are in? What a millionaire you've become! The zeniths of the sky can be touched only by those who have strong wings to fly. Do you understand?'

He got nervous and started rummaging through his bag. He took out a notebook, kept it aside and started thinking again. He emptied the bag. An electric shaver dropped out. He put all his belongings back into the bag, kept the notebook under the pillow and ran to the bathroom. He shaved and then gazed at the platter of rice. The morels looked like a clot over a wound. He went over to the window. In the moonlight, the ocean looked like a fathomless abyss, and the waves roared like black serpents moving towards the shore. For a moment he though the tides would rise and engulf him. He shuddered. He shut the window, and moved towards the bed, but sat down on the floor. He imagined fresh morels springing all over. He heard the song of the shepherd girls that he and Zeb had heard while gathering morels in the woods. He jammed his ears with his hands and put his head between his knees. After remaining still for a while, he removed his hands from his ears, took the notebook and started writing something. Tears fell thick and fast on to the paper as he wrote. He dried the paper with his shirt. As he was writing, he heard the door opening. He hid the notebook under his pillow, switched the light off, and stretched out under the sheet. He lay with his back towards the door, listening for any sound in the corridor. There was a sound of light steps approaching which stopped near the door. Then there was complete silence. Qadir waited with bated breath.

Malla Khaliq softly opened the door and quietly walked into the room. Ghulam Qadir shut his eyes tightly. He felt his heart would burst. He yearned to fall at his father's feet, wash his feet with his tears and beg for forgiveness. But he did not have the courage or the right! He continued to lie curled up, still. He knew the sound of his father's footsteps since childhood.

Malla Khaliq walked to the side of his head. Seeing his son's face in the moonlight, his heart filled to the brim. He continued gazing at his face. He controlled his tears, bent forward to pull the sheet to cover Qadir from head to toe. Then Qadir heard the door closing. He got up from the bed, went near the door and put his ear against it. He heard Malla Khaliq's saying, 'Oh God, have mercy on us!' Qadir opened the door a crack and peeped out to see his father walking in the dark. When the door on the other side of the corridor opened, a shaft of light illuminated the corridor and Qadir saw that his father's back had bent a little more. A torrent of tears overflowed from his eyes. The light thinned and the door closed.

Ghulam Qadir also closed his door. He did not dare switch the lamp on.

Narayan Joo went to wake up Malla Khaliq. 'Haji Sahib, get up now. See, it is already broad daylight.'

Malla Khaliq got up abruptly. 'Oh my God! I slept like a dead man, after so many years; I even missed my morning nimaz. Oh God, have mercy on me!'

Narayan Joo asked the servant, 'Have we not got the newspaper yet?'

'Yes, I have kept it on the table.'

Narayan Joo started reading the paper. Vijay Kumar and he always had their morning tea together. Malla Khaliq joined them too. Malla Khaliq was still cursing himself for having missed his morning prayers.

'I hope you didn't find the room stuffy,' Vijay Kumar asked him.

'I slept so soundly after so long! Besides, the air conditioner was on, why would I feel hot?' Vijay's wife entered, bowed before the elders and started making tea. 'Did you send Ghulam Qadir his tea?' Vijay Kumar asked her.

'Yes, I sent Bahadur with the tray.'

While they were talking, Bahadur returned with the tray.

'Why? Is he still sleeping?' Vijay asked him.

'No, the door is wide open and he is not in his room.'

'He might be in the bathroom.'

'No, he is not in the bathroom either.'

Malla Khaliq almost dropped his tea cup on hearing this. Narayan Joo stood up, but Vijay Kumar stopped him. 'You stay here. He must have gone downstairs for a stroll. I will go and see.'

Vijay Kumar looked all around. He went and asked the watchman. He said, 'Yes, sir. I saw him leaving with a bag in hand. The man who was with you in your car last evening. He left early in the morning.'

Vijay Kumar rushed to the auto-stand. He inquired with the auto drivers and found out the number of the auto in which Ghulam Qadir had left for the railway station. While he was walking back towards the gate, the auto that had dropped Ghulam Qadir at the railway station returned. The first auto-driver called out to Vijay Kumar, 'Sir, the auto has returned from the station.'

Vijay Kumar ran to him. He asked him about Ghulam Qadir. The auto-driver replied, 'I don't remember what he looked like very clearly. He asked me to drop him at the railway station. But then he stopped me halfway and alighted. He gave me a hundred-rupee note, and when I was about to return the change to him, he did not take it and was soon out of sight. Has he stolen anything from your house?'

Narayan Joo was waiting at the door. He handed Vijay Kumar an envelope that Ghulam Qadir had left under his pillow.

'What is this, Daddy?'

'A pack of salt that the scoundrel has left behind to empty out on his father's open wounds. Read for yourself.'

The letter was brief.

'My dear Abba, I have committed so many sins that I don't know how to begin pleading with you for forgiveness. There is hardly any sin that I have not committed. How will I find the courage to fall at your feet? How will I show my face to my mother and my family at home? How will I face Lala Sahib who has loved me like his own child? It was on his insistence that I went to college. Now I am leaving to start my life afresh and make something of myself. I don't know my destination. But after thinking for many days and nights in the police lockup and the previous night, I came to the realization that there is still time to redeem myself. I want to prove that I, your Qadir, can achieve all that I had desired to since my childhood. But I swear on the dust on the soles of your shoes that I will follow the path of honesty. Kindly forgive me until I return to Kashmir with a face worth showing. Please don't waste your time searching for me.'

Vijay Kumar then said to his father, 'He has written that so that we will not search for him, and we have all accepted it! You need not worry; I can find him even if he is hiding in a raven's nest. I will approach the police commissioner; his son is a friend of mine. He will block all routes and let's see how he escapes from Bombay.'

Malla Khaliq stood up and said to him, 'It is a lost cause. Let him go wherever he wants to go. For me he died on the day we received the message that he was arrested by the Bombay police on charges of drug trafficking.'

Narayan Joo could not control himself, 'What nonsense are you talking? He is after all your own son. He is a piece of your heart even if he is bad. If he wasn't a family man himself, we could have considered letting him go. His destiny is connected with the life of an innocent girl and his little child. What will happen to them?'

Malla Khaliq felt as if all reasoning had failed him.

Vijay Kumar asked his father, 'What do you suggest? Should I leave?'

Narayan Joo remained silent for a little while and then he asked his daughter-in-law, 'What is your suggestion? Is it prudent to inform the police? If they apprehend him again, they will not only rob him of all his money, but also put him back behind bars.'

'Your Lala Sahib is right.' The mention of the police made Malla Khaliq quiver. He stopped Vijay Kumar.

But Narayan Joo was enraged and he said to him, 'What sort of a father are you? Can you imagine what'll happen to your family if they come to know that Qadir has deserted his family and fled?'

Feeling helpless, Malla Khaliq lamented, 'Then tell me what should I do and what calamities should I face?'

'We will find him. There are many private detective agencies in Bombay. We can seek their help.'

Vijay did not like the idea. 'No. Private agencies just complicate issues. I am sure he must have gone to meet Ghulam Ahmed.'

'Yes, Vijay is right. He was repeatedly asking about him and also had his address. I will go and find out if he knows anything about Qadir's whereabouts.'

This was Vijay Kumar's final decision. But Malla Khaliq alone knew that the two brothers had never kept in touch with each other.

Just then Ghulam Ahmed appeared. He greeted them more courteously than needed. Malla Khaliq said to Narayan Joo, 'Narayan Joo, why don't you welcome this guest with garlands? Why not hire musicians to welcome him? A business tycoon has graced us with his presence!'

Narayan Joo too was upset. 'How come the mighty magnate has found time to visit poor people like us?'

Ghulam Ahmed somehow mustered courage and said, 'Abba, I returned from Goa only late last night. Someone at my lodging informed me that Vijay Kumar had left a message that you have come to Bombay for treatment. Nobody in Srinagar told me even when I had called home.'

'Who would tell you from there, your Naba Kantroo or Abdullah Shah?' Malla Khaliq asked him sarcastically.

Narayan Joo stopped Malla Khaliq from dragging the argument by saying, 'What are we fighting over? Even if he did phone Kantroo Sahib, how does it matter? He is his father-in-law after all.' Then he said to Ghulam Ahmed. 'Look here, my son. We have been waiting for your call for a long time. If Abdullah Shah had not sent your letter, your father would not have left home. He was suffering from asthma there in the cold, so Nisar Ahmed advised him to come here for a couple of months.'

Malla Khaliq burst out. 'Why should we give him any explanation? Please just ask him about Qadir.'

Ghulam Ahmed looked at his father and said, 'He is now a very big carpet exporter, would he bother to come see me? A fortnight ago I had gone to the Gateway of India to hand over carpets to Abdullah Shah's partner, Rahim Sahib. He had seen Qadir coming out from the Taj hotel. A big Ford car was waiting for him. Rahim Sahib tried calling out to him, but he did not look back. He stays in big hotels and drives around in luxury cars. Why would he come to visit me?'

Malla Khaliq knew well that if Ghulam Qadir ever needed help, he would never approach Ghulam Ahmed. Nevertheless he asked, 'So, did he not come to see you?'

Ghulam Ahmed looked towards Vijay Kumar and asked, 'What is the matter? Is Qadir well? Has he got into trouble over here?'

Vijay Kumar led him to his room, saying, 'Come with me, I will tell you all.'

Malla Khaliq tried to stop him, but Narayan Joo said, 'Why are you getting so scared? Let Ahmed come to know all that has happened. How long can you hide this from your family?'

'I am sure this fool will spread the news to all corners,' Malla Khaliq said.

'No, he is not such a fool. He is sure to have the details of Gul Beg's associates. I am sure we will get some clue from them.'

In the next room, Ghulam Ahmed stood dumbstruck. Vijay Kumar asked him, 'Why are you silent? Why don't you tell me what we ought to do now?'

'What can I say? Qadir has never let Abba have even a minute of peace. In spite of my best attempts, I could not assuage my father's worries. Whatever business I tried to set up failed. I am just about to establish myself in Bombay and Qadir has again gotten into trouble. I will not have the credibility of a farthing in the business circles here when they come to know about my brother's fraudulence.'

These words enraged Vijay Kumar. 'You are lamenting over your business when Ghulam Qadir has not committed any theft. He has taken to hiding because he is suffering from a sense of guilt. It is our moral obligation to find him and help him start afresh.'

'Hah! Him starting a new life! He has developed a taste for illicit money. He is simply incorrigible.' Ghulam Ahmed firmly dissociated himself from the problem.

Vijay Kumar had great hope that he would help them trace Qadir. He knew that Ahmed had strong connections with the Kashmiri businessmen who had shops in Bombay. He stood up and said to him, 'It is all right, Ghulam Ahmed. But please don't talk like this in the presence of Haji Sahib. We must reassure him that we will find Ghulam Qadir.' After this, he went back to the drawing room where Malla Khaliq and Narayan Joo sat with their heads hung low.

Vijay Kumar gave them a little hope by saying that Ghulam Ahmed knew a lot about Gul Beg's accomplices whom Qadir stayed with when he was in Bombay.

Vijay Kumar and Ghulam Ahmed hurriedly had their breakfast and left in search of Ghulam Qadir.

They had hardly reached the gate when Noor Mohammad called from Srinagar. After the formal greetings, Narayan Joo handed over the phone to Malla Khaliq. His hand holding the phone shook. When Noor Mohammad asked him about Ghulam Qadir, he stammered but maintained his composure and said, 'Don't tell your mother or Zeb anything about him. We got him released, but he is not allowed to leave Bombay for some time. He is here, staying confined in the guest room. He has no courage to come near me. Let us see what God decides. Is your mother well?'

Noor Mohammad said, 'Here she is, ask her yourself. She is quite well but always worried about you.' After this he handed over the phone to Aziz Dyad.

It took her a little while to come to the phone, and on the other end, Malla Khaliq grew nervous. He said to Narayan Joo, 'Perhaps the line has gotten cut. Hello! Why don't you say something?'

Narayan Joo smiled and left the room saying, 'You worry too much! You chat with her until I return.'

Aziz Dyad did not have anything particular to say. After a few formal inquiries, she returned the phone to Noor Mohammad. 'Ask him if Qadir is well. Has Ghulam Ahmed visited him yet?'

Malla Khaliq heard every word that she said. He said, 'God will have mercy on all. I forgot to tell you, Ghulam Ahmed came to see me today. Yes, yes, he is well. His business is running smoothly. He told me that he had phoned you.'

'Yes, he did call. He also called his in-laws to speak to his wife. It was she who told Amma that he is doing well in Bombay.'

'So, that is all for this time. Take care of everyone at home, particularly your mother. *Wa-alaikum salaam!*'

Narayan Joo returned and asked him about everyone at home. He said in reply, 'As long as Noor Mohammad is there, I need not worry. I told you that Ghulam Ahmed must have phoned his in-laws, and now I found out that he did indeed call them.'

'What can be done about that? God has not created all human beings from the same mould. You just pray to Dastagir Sahib that we find Ghulam Qadir. I will bring him to his senses.'

'One who has lost sight of the righteous path cannot be redeemed. Just pray to God that he does not invite any new perdition for us.'

'Mother Goddess knows which direction he has taken!'

'I am no longer bothered about that. Let him go wherever he wants. I only want to find him for the sake of poor Zeb.'

But how could they find Qadir? He had alighted from the auto-rickshaw halfway and taken the bus which was headed for the seashore of Guraya. He had seen the bus from a distance and, after giving a hundred-rupee note to the auto-driver, ran to catch the bus. He had come to know about Guraya beach from Gul Beg's accomplices who frequented Bombay with the consignments. Steamers went from the beach to the old Portuguese colonies around Goa. The bus reached Guraya in the afternoon.

There were dense crowds there; people queued for the two steamers that stood anchored at the shore. Ghulam Qadir almost jumped from the bus and ran towards one of the queues. He found out from a person standing in the queue that the steamers were heading towards Daman–Diu. Ghulam Qadir knew that there were many Kashmiri traders in Goa. If he was identified by any of them, all of Kashmir would come to know about his new destination. He again asked the same person, 'What sort of place is that?'

'Diu and Daman? Very beautiful,' the stranger said in reply.

Ghulam Qadir thought that perhaps God had allotted a livelihood for him there. He ran and stood in the queue at the ticket counter. He got his ticket, saw the number of the steamer and placed the ticket in his pocket. He zipped his bag and ran towards the steamer.

The steamer was now far away from Bombay. Qadir did not know which shore his boat of destiny was going to touch. With his eyes shut, he continued ruminating over what evil spirit must have possessed him that he was swayed by a crook like Gul Beg. The voice of a woman singing pulled him out of his thoughts. He looked to his left and saw a European girl and a robust shepherd-like young man of the same age. The man was rubbing his cheek against the girl's, and was trying to coax her.

The European girl giggled and blushed, looking absolutely blissful. Qadir continued gazing at the girl. He remembered when he had once tried to please Zeb with his jokes. When the European girl noticed that Qadir was ogling at her, she blushed and looked away. Qadir felt like the girl resembled Zeb. She was thin and her face was apple red like Zeb's. After a long time, he felt an ache in his heart. He cursed himself. 'What happened to you, Qadir? You left behind a beautiful woman to follow that white slut like a dog!'

The girl was looking at Qadir and then looking away. He was afraid that she might be a sorceress like Jane. In order to avoid her eyes, he looked towards the ocean and soon started thinking about Zeb. He yearned to jump into the waters and swim back to her. But how would he face her after all that he had put her through?

Besides all of Kashmir probably knew that Malla Khaliq's son Qadir was apprehended in Bombay for smuggling hashish. Then he started consoling himself. 'Qadir, there will be a time when you will go back to your family with your head held high and they will warmly welcome you home. But now is the time for your real trial. It is time for you to prove yourself.'

Far away, through the dense coconut trees, the beautiful shores of Daman shone in the golden light of the rising sun. It looked like an island from fairy tales. When Qadir reached the shore, he saw the European girl waiting for her companion. But her eyes were fixed on Qadir. When Qadir walked past her, she said 'Hi!' but Qadir was now a defeated young man. Flinging his bag on his shoulder, he quickly walked ahead. Travel agents, hotel agents, shopkeepers and vendors came running towards passengers, each wanting to impress them. Ghulam Qadir was reminded of Srinagar airport where he once used to run after the tourists. Now he felt like a hapless fellow for no one approached him. He examined himself. The four-thousand-rupee shoes which Jane had bought him were covered with muck. His jeans were covered with so much dirt that its blue was not discernible.

He was very hungry. He walked to the nearby market, looked all around and took note of all the big hotels and shops. He did not venture into any of these hotels. He knew he had thirty thousand rupees in his bag. But seeing his dirty shoes and jeans, nobody would allow him inside anywhere. He continued walking and reached the other end of the market where he noticed a small hotel.

There were about eight to ten homeless people eating rice and fish outside the hotel. A hefty native woman approached him. 'Full or half?' Initially Ghulam Qadir could not make out what she was saying. Soon he understood that the restaurant served either rice with fish or roasted chicken, and he asked for rice and fish. He was not sure if the chicken would be halal.

'Madam, full plate,' he said.

Within no time a platter of rice and two pieces of fish and gravy in a bowl were placed before him. He washed his hands and started devouring the food. The fish gravy was very tangy and spicy, but he was too hungry to bother. The woman brought him a fork and a spoon. But when she saw him using his hands, she looked at him in amazement. Then she said to herself, 'Poor soul!'

Ghulam Qadir forced a smile on his lips and said to the woman, 'I like eating rice with my hands. It somehow makes it tastier.' The woman laughed and took back the fork and spoon.

After ordering and polishing off another half-plate, Qadir asked the woman if he could get a room in her hotel. She cast a bemused look at the shanty of a restaurant and asked him, 'Do you think this is a hotel?' Qadir nodded. Liza turned out to be the owner of the hotel. 'There are just two rooms, in a shambles. My man and I live there.' She advised him to seek lodging in the hotel that lay behind a grove of coconut trees some distance away.

It was a bungalow-type hotel for tourists.

Qadir trudged towards the hotel. He heard a man wailing from inside the bungalow. 'I will die, Reeny dear! I will die of hunger. Oh, I will die, my child!'

'Where will I get you food from? I have sold every utensil that I owned. I sold even the cups, don't you see? I am dying myself.'

'I will die, Oh God! Do something, Reeny dear.'

'What will I do? Tell me! Take that chopper and cut me into pieces, cook my flesh and eat it. But you have grown so fat that you cannot even move from your armchair. Oh Jesus! What will I do?'

Ghulam Qadir reached the veranda from where he could see directly into the bungalow. Old chairs and tables lay inside, scattered haphazardly. In the front, was the counter, perhaps of the kitchen. A little away from this counter, he could see an old rocking chair in which an aged and bulky man sat quite snugly, as if he were welded in place. He wore an old-fashioned pant with suspenders. Above his chair, there was an iron chain with a big leather grip suspended from the ceiling. This arrangement had been made perhaps to help the big man get up from the chair.

Reeny was walking about angrily, from one corner of the room to the other. She disinterestedly tried to tidy the scattered furniture every few minutes. She was around thirty. Her skirt and blouse were relatively clean. Qadir could not make out whether she was the daughter or the wife of this bull of a man. Her face was hidden behind her hair constantly being ruffled by the wind. Seeing the condition of the house and its inmates, Qadir was in a quandary whether to go inside or not. He finally climbed the steps of the veranda, just as the old man in the chair began screaming: 'Oh Mary! Oh Mother! Why don't you have mercy on me? I am dying of hunger and Reeny refuses to give me anything to eat.' Qadir felt pity for him. But Reeny went towards the old man like a ferocious lioness, and gesticulating with her arms, burst out, 'Yes, yes. I don't give you food. You have devoured everything we had and stored it in the fat of your body. You have grown so huge that even this chair cannot contain you.'

'Oh God! I have been asking you for so long to replace this chair. I am not huge, this chair is meant for a child! It is so small!'

Reeny could no more control her anger and said, 'Is it a kids' chair? Even the carpenter was taken aback when he was asked to construct this mammoth chair for you. It is so wide and big that even an elephant can rest in it, but you do not fit! Shame on you!'

Qadir was now on the veranda and Reeny saw him. She came running towards the door and started shouting at him, 'Hey, what are you doing there? Out! Out! Run away or this father of mine will devour you too. Get lost!'

Qadir was nonplussed. 'Oh my God! Have mercy! Is she his daughter! Has she no compassion for her ailing father?' Reeny shouted, 'Are you enjoying the spectacle? Run away for we have nothing to give you as alms.'

'He is just hungry. Please give him something to eat,' Qadir dared to entreat her.

'Are you going to leave now or should I call the police? Are you his son? I told you that if you don't run away, he is sure to eat you up. You thank your stars that he is unable to move out of his chair.'

Qadir cast a piteous look at the aged man. He thought that the noblest deed at that time would be to feed this hungry old man. He climbed down the steps and went to the motel where he had had his meal. He bought a whole tandoori chicken and five to six pieces of bread. Holding this food in a packet, he ran to the bungalow. He ascended the veranda and peeped inside. Reeny was not there in the hall. The old man was having a catnap. He walked in and took out the tandoori chicken and the warm bread. Smelling the fragrance of chicken, Reeny's father opened his eyes. He grabbed the chicken. He did not even wait to see the angel Christ had sent to quell his hunger. When Qadir gave him the hot bread, he held his hand and kissed it repeatedly. Chewing mouthfuls of bread, he prayed for him, 'My son! Oh my son! God bless you!'

In the meantime, Reeny came down the stairs. In his rapture, the old man yelled, 'See! See Reeny! Mother Mary has heeded my moans and sent this angel for me. See what a delicious roasted chicken he has brought me.'

Seeing the chicken and the bread in her father's hands, Reeny rushed in like a wounded lioness and snatched the bread away from his hands. 'Are you going to kill him? He will die! The doctor has strictly forbidden all this food. Where did you bring all this from? Get out! Who are you to be doing all this? Get out!' Then she took away the half-eaten chicken from her father's hands. 'You are sure to die, you glutton!'

The old man got angry. He held the suspended chain in front of him and tried to get out of the chair, cursing Reeny. But the chair moved up along with him. He crashed back into it. Reeny's eyes filled with tears. She wept and returned the food to her father. Then she sat beside him. She held her head in her hands and sobbed. After a while, she stood up and vented her rage on Qadir. 'Who are you? Why did you come here? Get out!'

Qadir hesitantly told Reeny that he had come seeking a room to stay and that he hoped to find some job. Reeny let out a venomous laugh and said, 'A room and a job! Here! Here in this broken house! You please go somewhere else. We have nothing to offer here.'

Qadir cast a sad look, looking at her face for the first time. Then he looked towards the old man. Reeny asked him, 'Why do you look at him? Do you think you can buy him over by giving him a loaf of bread?'

The old man swallowed the last piece of bread and let out a loud belch. He turned to Reeny. 'There is no one in the world who can buy Dallas De Souza. Not even that bitch, Liza Brigonza.'

Reeny lost her temper again and said, 'Shame on you! You lost even this hotel business to that woman! And now you say that no one can buy Dallas De Souza!'

Reeny immediately realized that she had disclosed family secrets in front of a complete stranger. She again shouted at him, 'Will you leave now or else …'

The old man yelled, 'No, this hotel belongs to Dallas De Souza. This boy will not go anywhere. Get your baggage. You will stay here!'

Father and daughter quarrelled with each other over this issue. Seeing this, Qadir tried to flee, but Dallas De Souza gathered all his energy, took the chain in his hand, and heaved his giant body out of the chair. 'This boy will stay here with us.'

It was finally decided that Qadir would spend the night in the veranda until he found a proper room to stay. Ghulam Qadir thought that it was a good opportunity, but told them that he wasn't a beggar, and he would pay them rent for staying there.

'You just go on serving me,' Dallas De Souza said to him.

Upset and agitated, Reeny went upstairs. Dallas De Souza managed to slide back into the chair again with Qadir's help. When he had caught his breath, he beckoned to Qadir. 'Don't get scared. My daughter is a little hot-tempered. You stick around. She will calm down soon. You just continue bringing me roasted chicken and bread. But don't buy anything from that cow Liza. Even if you do, don't ever let her know that you get it for me.'

They heard Reeny climbing down the stairs. 'You run away and sit in the veranda. She is coming.'

Ghulam Qadir ran out. The sun was setting and the sea looked golden. Qadir felt like going for a little swim in the tides. But he was too scared of losing his clothes and his bag in this alien land. He looked around and saw a water tap just behind the trees. He washed his shoes, then removed his jeans and aired them out. He change into the pants and T-shirt he was carrying in his bag. After washing his hands and face, he felt like a human being again. Placing his shoes in the sun, he calmly walked towards the bungalow.

Dallas De Souza was still trying to convince his daughter. 'If we can afford to let out a room to him in the house, he can be very helpful to us.' But Reeny did not heed his words and went out. Qadir was sitting on the steps. 'Why are you sitting here as if we owe you something? Move and make way for me.' Qadir rose and stood aside. Without looking back, Reeny took her bicycle and rode towards the sea.

Qadir walked into the hall and held the plump hand of Dallas De Souza and said, 'Thank you, Uncle.' De Souza looked at him in amazement and said, 'Who? Who are you?' and Qadir muttered to himself, 'Damn it! He is losing even his memory.' He reminded him of the tandoori chicken and said, 'You remember?'

'O! Yes, yes. Sweet boy!' Then he asked Qadir to sit on the arm of his chair and asked him his name and where he was coming from. 'Qadir. My name is Qadir.' He anglicized his name and told him that he worked as a businessman in Bombay. 'I suffered a huge loss in my business there. Now I have come to Daman to look for some ordinary job just to get by.'

'Bombay is no good,' De Souza said. Qadir tried to evade further inquiry, but the old man was alert now. 'What business were you running in Bombay?'

'Hotel business.'

'Hotel?'

'It was an eatery. I mean eating joint.'

When he felt that the old man was not looking convinced, he made his story more believable. 'It was a partnership. My partner cheated me.'

'Yes. There is no dearth of cheaters. I was also cheated.' He looked around and was about to narrate his tale, but hearing the bell of the approaching bicycle, he asked Qadir to go out.

The evening arrived quickly. Ghulam Qadir sat in a corner of the veranda. Reeny parked her bicycle in a corner of the compound. She untied the bag of vegetables from the handle of her bicycle and went into the bungalow. While walking in, she looked at the veranda. Qadir sat crouched there, but Reeny did not say anything to him.

Qadir saw Reeny walk into the kitchen. He stood up, took his bag in his hand, and calmly stepped in to tell De Souza that he was going to fetch some food for him. 'God bless you!' De Souza said.

Ghulam Qadir reached Liza's restaurant. He hurriedly filled his stomach with rice. Then he packed tandoori chicken and bread for De Souza's house.

Reeny had placed a tray of food on a small table almost over the protruding tummy of her father. She had cooked fish. There was a basket filled with baked bread. Her father had pounced on the food as if he had been hungry for months together. Qadir felt sorry for Reeny. He understood that this gluttonous elephant of an old man had driven her crazy. 'Who knows if this poor girl has eaten?' he thought. He felt an urge to go in and give the parcelled food to her. But seeing Reeny's grimace, he could not muster the courage. He again sat in a corner of the veranda.

De Souza finished the basket of bread within no time. Reeny came, took away the empty plate and went back into the kitchen. She reappeared, and took the tray from the table, and went to the window. She looked out and saw Qadir. She seemed like she was about to say something to him, but then went back.

Ghulam Qadir was still trying decide whether to hand over the parcel to De Souza or Reeny. In the meantime, Reeny appeared at the door. Qadir tried to hide the parcel, but Reeny caught sight of it. She came running and snatched the parcel away from his hands. She said angrily, 'What is this? Do you intend to kill him?'

Ghulam Qadir was flummoxed, but managed to say, 'It is for you.'

Casting a furious look at him, Reeny said, 'What?'

Qadir stuttered, 'No, no, for me.'

Reeny took the parcel and went in. De Souza caught sight of it and his mouth watered. 'That is for me. Give it to me.'

Reeny went back to the veranda, tossed it at Qadir and shouted, 'If you ever do this again, I will not let you stay in Daman, leave alone the veranda. Understand?' She went to her father. She pulled the chain and brought its leather grip near her father. 'Now get up. Time for you to sleep. Come on.'

She used all her strength to pull him out from the chair. Taking the support of the wall, De Souza moved to his room slowly, step by step. Before entering his room, he looked back at Qadir through the window, then said, 'Keep it up! Goodnight! We will meet tomorrow.'

Reeny shut the door. Then she came out, holding an old blanket in her hand. She threw it towards Qadir. 'Take it, or you will die of cold. But don't run away with the blanket.' Then she shut the door and switched off the lights. Qadir heard her climb up the stairs.

Then there was silence all around. The only sound that could be heard was that of the sea rising and falling under the bright moonlight. Qadir took out a cigarette and lit it. Then he used his bag for a pillow, and pulled the cotton duvet over himself and gazed at the moon which was visible through the coconut trees. It seemed as lonely and forlorn as he was.

Narayan Joo and his son Vijay Kumar searched all of Bombay, from Chandivali to Colaba, but they could not find any trace of Ghulam Qadir. In the evening, they sat near Malla Khaliq to discuss the next course of action. He said to them, 'It is a hopeless case. I am not worried about Qadir; if he is destined to ruin his life, let him do so. My only worry is about facing my wife and Zeb.'

'What will you say to your wife? She will feel like she has lost her son.'

'Is she alone going to suffer? I am not a stone, after all. Have I not lost a piece of my heart as well? Both of us will wail over the loss for a month or so and then get sucked into the routine household chores. But what will poor Zeb do? She has to live a long life with just her innocent child.'

Narayan Joo was also worried about Zeb, yet he was convinced that after many more failures, Qadir would finally return and prostrate himself at his wife's feet. But he felt that Aziz Dyad, who was already old and ailing, would not be able to bear the shock.

Vijay Kumar finally broke the silence by saying to his father, 'I think we should call Noor Mohammad and tell him all that has happened.'

Narayan Joo turned to Malla Khaliq, 'What is your opinion, Haji Sahib?'

'Where has Ghulam Ahmed gone?' he asked, instead of answering their question. He was sure that Ghulam Ahmed could never find a better opportunity to settle scores with Ghulam Qadir. He must have gone to call Naba Kantroo, he thought. Trying to dispel his fears, Vijay Kumar said to him, 'He received an order and left to attend to it.'

Narayan Joo said to him, 'What do think of Vijay Kumar's suggestion?'

'Well, we cannot hide it any longer.' Malla Khaliq heaved a deep sigh and continued, 'It is God's will. We have to anchor our boat in this fierce autumnal wind, otherwise everyone might drown.'

It was also decided that Ghulam Ahmed would return to Kashmir well before Malla Khaliq so that he could make his mother understand that Qadir had deserted all of them and had left for some unknown destination with his associates. Ghulam Ahmed would reassure her that Qadir, engaged in some big business, would return soon and take Zeb and Bilal with him. He would also convey that Malla Khaliq would return to Kashmir as soon as the severe winter ended. Until then they would try to trace Qadir's whereabouts.

Malla Khaliq's only worry was that Ghulam Ahmed might make a mistake and disclose everything to his mother. When

Ghulam Ahmed came back, he assured his father he would stick to the story.

Ghulam Qadir woke up with a start. He stood up and looked all around. The morning haze was gradually thinning and the steamers belonging to the fishermen were fighting with the strong tides of the ocean. He folded the blanket and peeped into the hall; it was all dark inside. He went to the bathroom near the water tap in a corner of the compound, and took a bath. Then he walked towards the shore. The steamers had halted quite a distance away from the shore. The colourful sails on the steamers waved cheerily in the breeze. A fleet of smaller boats rushed towards the steamers. The fishermen, who had toiled in the ocean all night, started filling the boats with basketfuls of fish. Suddenly there was a commotion all around. Ghulam Qadir went closer. He saw heaps of fish at the shore. The middlemen opened their registers and the auction began. There were many marts along the shore, and the din kept increasing. Qadir had never seen anything like this. He got nervous and walked back fast towards the bungalow.

The door opened just in time. He kept his bag in a corner near the window and covered it with the blanket that Reeny had given him. He began to think about his next course of action. Soon, Reeny came out with a basket in her hand. Ghulam Qadir greeted her, but she responded with a frown. She took out her bicycle and rushed to the market.

Qadir went into the hall where he found a pile of chairs in a corner. There were some tea-tables scattered in the hall, all seemed to be wailing over their bad luck. Qadir tidied the furniture by placing four chairs around each teapoy. Then he entered the kitchen where he found a cloth to dust and clean the furniture with. Hearing the sound of furniture being moved, Reeny's father, who was sleeping in the room adjacent to the kitchen, woke up.

'Reeny dear!' De Souza called out to his daughter.

Qadir hurriedly wiped the last chair. He heard De Souza calling his daughter again. 'Reeny, come, I need your help.'

Qadir hurried into the room. De Souza cast a glance at Qadir. 'Who? Who are you?'

Qadir forced a smile on his lips while saying, 'I got you tandoori chicken yesterday. Remember?'

De Souza's eyes bulged and stretched his eyelids. 'Oh, is it you? My angel! That means Reeny has not forced you to run away from here! Where is she?'

'She went away on her bicycle,' Qadir replied.

'Poor girl!' Heaving a long sigh, De Souza said. 'She must have gone to borrow more provisions. Come on, help me.'

Qadir held his hand, and De Souza walked towards the dressing table. He saw his face in the mirror. He straightened his tie and turned to Qadir, 'Come, let's go.'

Holding on to Qadir shoulder with one hand and the wall with the other, he managed to reach his armchair, sitting in which he could look at the ocean and pass his days. He observed the hall. He was amazed to see the hall and all the furniture neat and tidy as it had once been. He cast a look at Qadir and then surveyed the hall again which looked like a good restaurant, as it had once been.

'How does it look?' asked Qadir.

'Did you do all this?'

Qadir nodded.

'Good, very good. It looks like it used to during the good old days.' De Souza's eyes filled with tears that rolled down his swollen and stubbled cheeks. 'How well our business ran! And then she left this world.' He remembered his wife whose death had devastated him, as if she had taken away all his joys and comfort with her. While he narrated his tale of woe to Qadir, Reeny's bicycle bell was heard. Qadir tried to run out, but De Souza stopped him, saying, 'Just keep standing here.'

Reeny came in with her basket full of provisions. She was taken aback as soon as she walked in. Angrily tossing her basket on the table, she turned towards Qadir. 'Did you do all this?'

Qadir hung his head. Reeny moved closer to him. 'Did you do this? Why don't you reply?'

'Yes, he has done it,' De Souza intervened. 'I asked him to do all this. Understand?'

'You need space for your friends, don't you?' she sneered at her father.

Qadir intervened. 'I did it of my own will.' He continued, 'You have such a beautiful house, and that too in such a beautiful location, but it is lying vacant. It is a sin. That Liza's eatery is not bigger than the garage of this bungalow.'

Reeny scowled at him. 'Don't mention that whore. It is because of her that we are in such a miserable condition. If I had not thrown that whore out, Mr De Souza here would not have hesitated to place at her feet even this hut that he has inherited from his forefathers.'

De Souza implored her with folded hands, 'Stop it please, Reeny. Don't embarrass me in his presence. I beg of you.'

'Okay! Is that all? There will be no more mention of that witch.'

Qadir begged for her pardon, 'My fault, memsahib. I accept my fault. I will pile up all the chairs in that corner in no time. I thought we could collaborate on restoring this restaurant.'

'But how can you restore it? I think you have been deluded by Mr De Souza into believing that he has the key to some hidden treasure. Oh God! What is all this? Where have you come from to annoy us? Go, go away!' Saying this, she sank helplessly in a chair. Qadir felt that she was beginning to soften a little. He walked up to her and said, 'Please don't blame your father. *I* thought that this restaurant could be restarted.'

'We need money for that, right? It is an ordeal for me to manage our daily bread. But why am I telling my woes to you?'

'My Mother Mary has sent this angel to help you,' De Souza said in order to support Qadir.

'You shut up! You and your hallucinations!'

Qadir grabbed the opportunity. Perhaps God has ordained for me to do some good deed so I can absolve myself of my sins, he thought. Then he dared to go near Reeny again, and say to her, 'Reeny memsahib! I have some money with me. If you allow me—' Reeny grew furious again and stood up. She said, 'How much do you have? A thousand, two thousand – how much? Do you even know how much you need to run a hotel?'

Qadir could sense that Reeny secretly nursed a desire to restart the hotel. Qadir ran to the veranda and took out his bundle of money from his bag and then came in. 'I do not simply talk big. I have this much money with me. If we work hard together, it is not impossible to restart your hotel.'

Reeny cast a suspicious glance at him, trying to understand why this stranger was so eager to help. Qadir understood what she was thinking and hastened to say, 'I am nobody to do you any favours. I am only lending you this amount so that you may restart the hotel.'

God has sent me to this new place, he thought, to restart my ruined life. I could not have reached Reeny's house just by chance. He convinced her that he had sufficient prowess in hotel management, particularly in catering to tourists, and that nobody could surpass him in the art of persuasion. Thus Reeny began dreaming of restoring the old glory of her hotel, but she was very careful to hide her joy and hope. Qadir was adding new alluring colours to her dreams. 'Memsahib, you just say "yes" and see how the rusted and broken signboard of your hotel once again regains its old glory.'

Reeny smiled cautiously, yet Qadir was sure that he had almost won the dice. 'Once the hotel starts functioning and making profits, you may repay me in easy instalments. In return, I will never ask for anything more than shelter and bread twice a day. You may pay me some remuneration after the hotel finds its feet.'

De Souza was intently following their conversation. He said to Reeny, 'Say yes, my child. Saint Mary has sent him as our angel. Say yes!'

Reeny first looked at the bundle of money and then at Qadir's face. 'Mind it, I take this money as a loan from you.'

Qadir said, 'Of course, just a loan.'

'What is the rate of interest?' asked Reeny.

'No interest, just a small share in the profit, and that too only when the hotel starts making money.'

'And what if it does not take off?'

'Why won't it? I will make it, you just watch.'

She got up. 'Give me some time to think it over.'

'Great!' De Souza was elated. 'Now please give me something to eat. I have shown enough patience. I have not even had a dry toast since morning. Please, Reeny.'

Reeny cast an angry look at him. 'This hotel has not started functioning yet. You understand?' Saying this, Reeny walked into the kitchen.

At the door, she turned back and said to Qadir, 'Take care of these notes, lest the wind from the ocean blow them away.'

Qadir collected the notes. De Souza asked Qadir to come nearer. He clenched his hands and yelled in victory, 'Bravo! Keep it up. Now go and make preparations. But bear in mind that you shouldn't forget to get me tandoori chicken when you return. How well that whore roasts the chicken!'

'Which whore, Uncle?'

'You know who she is.' And then he laughed boisterously. Qadir laughed too and said to himself, 'This is called old man's love!' He put the money back into his bag and began tidying up the furniture. In the meantime, Reeny brought breakfast and placed it in front of De Souza. He ate the bread and the six-egg omelette in minutes.

When Reeny was about to leave, Qadir stopped her. He entrusted his bag to her, saying, 'Please keep it with yourself. The money now belongs to you. You may use it to restore your hotel.'

'What will I do with your bag? Business is business. I'll simply give you a written receipt. And tell you what to buy from the market.'

Qadir took out the money from his bag. 'Please count it for yourself.'

Reeny counted the money and then entered the room at the

end of the hall which once used to function as an office for the hotel. Then she came out with a receipt on the letterhead of her hotel.

'Now that you are my partner, you have the right to stay inside the house and have your meals here.' She led him to the office room. 'You may stay in this room until I get the room upstairs in order.'

Qadir walked into the room with his bag. The room was full of office paraphernalia: chairs, table, cupboards and a sofa set placed against the wall. Qadir thought it was a blessing for him. The sofa can function as a bed, he thought.

He spent the whole day with Reeny, cleaning and tidying the hotel. Then he got a long ladder made of bamboo sticks, which had been placed in a corner of the compound. He stood the ladder against the front of the bungalow and reached for the rusted board suspended with one rope. In the meantime, Reeny got two brushes and a couple of cans of paint. Qadir insisted on hiring a professional painter to write the signboard. But Reeny said, 'You just watch how I transform these blurred letters into a masterpiece. What can a painter do? I made this board with my own hands.'

De Souza dragged his chair near the window and watched them with delight. Then he yelled, 'Don't change the name! The original name is perfect. This name was suggested by your granny. HOTEL SOLACE. How musical, how soothing! HOTEL SOLACE.'

Qadir shouted back, 'It is great, really great.'

'Do you hear me, Reeny?' De Souza said.

'Yes, Papa!'

When the board was ready, she kept it aside to dry. After washing her hands, she came near Qadir. 'Now you deserve a cup of tea.' Qadir followed her inside.

Qadir lay awake late in the night. He tossed and turned on the sofa. He was beseeching his saint Dastagir to help him succeed in this enterprise so that he could proudly return to his family as a successful businessman. Every time he thought about Zeb and Bilal, he broke out in a sweat. He felt like a criminal.

The night was nearly over, and the din of the hooters of the steamers woke Qadir. He looked out through the window. The moonlight had dimmed and the morning light gave a silver tinge to the waves in the ocean. After having his bath, he came out into the veranda. The door of the hall was wide open. Reeny was touching the signboard. Qadir went near her. 'Is it dry now?' Qadir climbed up the ladder and hung it above the veranda. 'How does it look?'

'Fabulous!' she said.

Having sold their catch to the middlemen, a group of fishermen were walking towards town. They stopped upon catching sight of De Souza's bungalow. The signboard was shining brightly in morning light. They whispered to each other. Qadir approached them and asked, 'How does it look?'

'So Mr De Souza has finally disposed of his hotel?' The fishermen sniggered. Reeny yelled at them. 'No, we haven't sold off the hotel, but restored it.'

An old man from the group begged for pardon and said, 'Congratulations! When did it reopen?'

'Last weekend.'

They began to murmur again and turned to Qadir, but before they could ask him anything, he said, 'Me? I am her employee, a waiter.'

'He is the chef, waiter, everything,' Reeny said. 'Do you want to know anything else? '

The old fisherman was silenced.

'Now please go away, your wives must be waiting for you.'

Many more fishermen passed by the bungalow and stopped to have a look at the woebegone hotel with the bright contrasting signboard.

Reeny led Qadir inside the bungalow. They were amazed to see that De Souza had reached the window without any aid. 'Did you see? Just the signboard has attracted so many people. When the hotel is actually functional, think how popular it will be.'

Reeny held her father's hand, 'Yes, Papa.'

It was a Saturday, what the Europeans called a weekend. De Souza had driven his daughter crazy. She had opened the large trunk in his bedroom; it contained clothes that he had worn in his youth and in the days of his prosperity. Old shirts, double-breasted suits, neckties, waistcoats … But not a single piece would fit him now. Completely exhausted, Reeny sat on the edge of the bed and said to her father, 'Now tell me, what should I do? See what you have made of yourself. All these clothes are of no use. Not a single one fits you.'

'But we have to do something. I cannot attend the inaugural function of this hotel in these rags.'

'Yes. We have to do something.' Ghulam Qadir entered, bearing a navy blue three-piece suit on a hanger. He had hired the suit from some shop and dry-cleaned it. 'Take it, sir. Your hotel is to be inaugurated and you cannot sit in the function wearing these tattered clothes. How can this servant of yours allow that to happen?'

De Souza measured the coat against his shoulders and then held Qadir's hand and kissed it repeatedly. 'Oh my dear son! How many things you take care of! You are great. Do you see, Reeny? See, he is the one who will take good care of this bungalow. Now I can die a peaceful death.'

Reeny's eyes filled with tears. 'Stop this. Yes, now he is everything to you. I have shrivelled to a thorn serving you, but you just ignore that.'

She cast a miserable glance at Qadir for the first time and said, 'You are a sycophant!'

'This is not sycophancy,' said Qadir. 'This is how one should respect the elderly.'

De Souza put on the suit. Reeny looking at him lovingly

while he picked out a tie. She asked Qadir, 'Where did you get this suit from?'

'You know there is a market of second-hand goods for the fishermen. See how neatly it fits him. I am sure everyone will admire Uncle.'

'Come on. There are many other jobs pending.'

Before going out with Reeny, Qadir went to De Souza and said, 'Any more service, sir?'

'No. Thank you.'

The sun had hardly set when a brightly dressed band of folk dancers and folk singers arrived. They alighted from the bus and came running towards Reeny's bungalow to greet her. She looked at them in amazement. Qadir came out and showed the artistes to the space reserved for them.

Reeny stopped him. 'What is all this? Who has ordered this show?'

'It was my idea. Music and dance will attract crowds, publicize the hotel.'

'Did my father advise you to do so?'

Qadir nodded.

'But who is going to pay them?'

'He did not only give me their address, but also a letter addressed to their leader. He was very happy to receive the letter. He has come only to fulfil his duty as a friend.'

'What have you come to fulfil?'

'This is a friend's gift. Now you will have to arrange for their drinks and food. Understand?'

In the meantime, two artistes unloaded a big box from the bus. Qadir looked at Reeny. 'Do you see? This is true friendship. They have brought their provisions along.'

De Souza managed to come out of his chair and hugged and kissed his old friend the maestro Braganza. 'Old times have returned,' Braganza said, holding De Souza in an embrace. 'Old man!'

'Yes, Braganza, yes.'

After congratulating De Souza, Braganza came out. As soon as he took the guitar in his hand, all the artistes thronged around him. They started singing the symphony. The dancers began to sway too. Guests started coming in groups. Qadir, Reeny and a couple of hired attendants waited on the guests. Those who were familiar with De Souza went into the bungalow to greet him. Hotel Solace was relaunched with much pomp and splendour.

All the guests and the customers left by midnight. Qadir and Reeny sat down and assessed the expenditure incurred towards the function. De Souza who was falling asleep in his chair, his chin touching his belly. 'Oh God! We have been unmindful of Uncle! See how he has nodded off in his chair.' They got up and hauled De Souza to his bedroom.

Qadir felt proud. He wanted to tell Reeny that this success was made possible by him, but it was too soon to brag about his prowess.

The next day there was a rumour in the market that De Souza had won some lottery. How could he restart his hotel when he was almost a pauper? Business rivals were beginning to feel jealous of him. But those who knew what Reeny had endured since her mother's death were very happy for the daughter and father.

Within a month or so word about Ghulam Qadir's delicious kebabs, roasted rib-meat, and fragrant stew spread among all the tourist travel agencies. Reeny had to appoint four attendants to wait on their customers. Gradually, Qadir took the management under his own control on Reeny's insistence.

Reeny got the room upstairs furnished for Qadir; it overlooked the ocean. One day she came to his room and placed thirty thousand rupees before him. 'You once loaned this amount to me. Daddy will assess the interest due on it and pay you that as well.'

Qadir's heart almost sank. He hastened to say, 'Does it mean that I should leave this place now.'

'Are you crazy?' Reeny sat beside him. What will I do without you? You are now my partner. This hotel belongs as much to you as it does to me. As far as the bungalow is concerned, it belongs to my Daddy. He may even write that to you in the future.' She then laughed. 'So keep this money.'

'Deposit it back into the account,' Qadir said angrily. 'When I really need it, I will ask for it. The salary that I get is enough for me. We have to make this place the best hotel in the city.'

'Oh! You are a daydreamer!' Reeny smiled and took the money back.

Qadir put on his suit and went down to meet De Souza in his room. He was nicely dressed and waiting for him. Qadir helped him walk to his easy chair. Looking at Qadir filled his heart with a strange but sweet love. This love intensified whenever he saw Qadir and Reeny together.

Reeny and De Souza were happy, but Qadir sometimes seemed to get lost in his thoughts. The fear that he could get exposed made him gasp for breath.

One day he dreamed of his father and mother: They were stranded in the middle of the sea and were desperately calling out to Qadir. He ran helplessly on the shore, trying to respond to their calls, but his voice choked. He woke up with a start. Then he could not go back to sleep. He got up and stared at the tides in the sea. His conscience cursed him: 'Qadir! What kind of a son are you? You have been here for so long building your career, while your old and ailing father is in Bombay. You did not even bother to send word to him that you are well here and busy fulfilling the promise you made to him in the letter.'

He decided to write to his father. But if he sent the letter to Vijay Kumar's address, they would find out where he was on seeing the postal stamp. It would be better to send the letter through some tourist hailing from some far-off place.

Narayan Joo took Malla Khaliq again to the doctor. The doctor conducted tests and told him he was suffering from anxiety disorder.

Malla Khaliq remained quiet with his eyes shut until they returned to Vijay Kumar's house. They found Vijay Kumar impatiently waiting to see them. The moment his father took a seat, he handed the letter to him. 'See, I told you Ghulam Qadir would certainly send us some message!' Narayan Joo gave the letter to Malla Khaliq, but he said, 'You read it please, let me know what he has written so graciously.' Narayan Joo took the letter and started reading:

'I know the agony I have caused you. I am also as restless as a live fish in a hot pan. Nevertheless I know that one has to go through many ordeals and stay away from loved ones for a long time in order to get one's sins absolved and start life afresh. I want to make my family proud of me. Abba, God has bestowed his mercy on me and brought me to a place where I will certainly achieve my goal very soon. I will surely inform you about my location and my work, but all in good time. Kindly forgive me for all my sins and pray for me. Your worthless and sinful son, Ghulam Qadir.'

There was a lull in the room. Then placing an arm on Malla Khaliq's shoulders, Narayan Joo said to him, 'It is my firm belief that Ghulam Qadir has realized his mistakes and is surely trying to rebuild his life.'

'I also think so. What do you think, Uncle?' Vijay Kumar asked Malla Khaliq.

'It is hard to believe that he has mended his ways. However, there is the consolation that he is alive.'

Narayan Joo took the envelope from Vijay Kumar's hand. 'He has dispatched this letter from Tiruchirapalli. You see this stamp?' He passed the envelope back to Vijay Kumar. 'I have already examined the stamps.'

Malla Khaliq said to him, 'Do you know where Tiruchirapalli is?'

'It is far away from here, in Kerala,' Vijay Kumar replied.

Vijay Kumar compared the writing in the letter with that on the envelope. Neither the handwriting nor the ink matched. He arrived at the conclusion that Ghulam Qadir had not posted the letter himself because he took every precaution possible to ensure that they did not trace his address.

In the evening, Ghulam Ahmed returned from Goa in a steamer. He told his father that he met many Kashmiri businessmen in Goa. He told him that these businessmen were so busy that they hardly had time to talk to anyone. 'Abba, there is a big bazaar of Kashmiri vendors.'

Malla Khaliq could not hide his irritation any longer and said jeeringly, 'Then why didn't you set up shop there? Why did you come back? We are here, waiting for word about your brother, but you are happy to have met every Kashmiri vendor there is in Goa!'

Narayan Joo intervened, 'You tell us if you found any clue about Ghulam Qadir in Goa.'

Ghulam Ahmed fell silent. Malla Khaliq roared at him, 'Why don't you answer?' Then he raised his head and looked towards Narayan Joo. 'I inquired from every shopkeeper, I searched in every hotel there, but I found no trace of him.'

Malla Khaliq cut him short. 'How would you get any information from Goa? He has gone to some remote corner of Kerala to hang himself.'

Vijay Kumar gave Qadir's letter to Ghulam Ahmed.

The business of Hotel Solace continued to expand. Reeny and Qadir kept busy from dawn to dusk. They became very close friends.

One day, while Reeny was making coffee for her father, De Souza smiled at her and said, 'What is your opinion of Qadir? I mean—' Reeny held the cup of coffee in her hand and said, 'Your coffee is getting cold.' De Souza took the cup from her and answered his own question. 'I know you like him. I know that Mother Mary has sent him for you.'

'Not for me, but for you, so that he gets you fatter by plying you with tandoori chicken.'

De Souza almost choked with laughter. 'Oh, you naughty girl! That is now an old story. Now my own fairy is also a part of the story. Now, my pretty girl, tell me, do you like him?'

'Yes, he works very hard.'

'When is he going to propose to you?'

'Do not live in dreams, Mr De Souza. Please have your coffee. I have a lot of work to finish.' Then she went out of the room. De Souza looked at the icon of Christ in the hall, and thanked God for their good fortune, crossing himself.

Time passed as if it were flying on wings. Ghulam Ahmed returned to Srinagar and for the first time in his life, showed some sense of responsibility and seriousness. He made everyone believe that Ghulam Qadir had been approached by a business tycoon and that he had started a new business in collaboration with the businessman in Saudi. His father-in-law tried his best to get the truth out of him, but Ghulam Ahmed did not yield. Naba Kantroo finally said to him, 'Everything will come to light sooner or later. Nothing can be kept from me for long.'

Ghulam Ahmed got annoyed, but preferred to control his anger and left with his wife for his home. His son, entrusted to his father-in-law, was waiting at the stairs. The child pleaded to go along with them. Naba Kantroo called him, 'Mukhtar Ahmed, what are you doing there, my darling? Your tutor is about to arrive. Come in now and go to your room.'

Mukhtar got frightened as though caught in a misdeed and scurried away to his room. Ghulam Ahmed caught hold of his wife's arm and said to her, 'We should leave now. Your father will not let our son put even a handful of earth on our graves.'

When they were home, his mother asked him, 'Ama Lala, why have you not brought Mukhtar back? My heart is about to burst from this separation.'

Neither Ghulam Ahmed nor his wife had an answer. Aziz Dyad grew furious. 'Tell me, have you given your son up for adoption to Naba Sahib? Let your Abba come back, I will take him along and get Mukhtar released.'

Ghulam Ahmed tried to evade the issue. He took out the bundle of notes that Narayan Joo had given him. Handing over the bundle to his mother, he said, 'Ten thousand rupees. You please give it to Zeb. Qadir gave it to Abba for Zeb before he left for Saudi.'

'I'll pray he prospers. May my Dastagir Sahib bless him with great success!'

Having handed over the money to his mother, Ghulam Ahmed said to his wife Zoon, 'You come with me; bring me my sweater, I am shivering.'

Zoon followed him to their room. As soon as they were well inside the room, he burst out with rage at her. 'You were at your father's house for so long, why did you not talk to him about Mukhtar? I have repaid him every penny, then why doesn't he let my son come here?'

Zoon also grew angry. 'Does he lay diamonds there at my father's house? You talk as if my father has held him as mortgage. He has great concern for his welfare. Didn't you see how much attention he pays to his studies? What will you be able to provide him with over here?'

'Why do you jeer at me like that? How about Nisar Ahmed? Did he become a doctor on the expenses met by his mother's parents?'

Zoon was silenced. But to avoid fighting further with her husband, she said, 'Now listen, and do not shout. I will have a word with my father to allow our Mukhtar to come here occasionally.'

When Aziz Dyad gave Zeb the money, she did not even touch it. She did not believe a word of what Ghulam Ahmed had said. She said to her mother-in-law, 'Amma, I have nothing to do with this money; I hardly need any. Noor Mohammad has never let me or Bilal feel any want.'

'This is your husband's earning, you should not refuse it.'

'Where will I keep it? You please keep it. If I ever need it, I will ask you for it.'

In the evening, Noor Mohammad and Ghulam Ahmed went to the deck of the houseboat on the pretext of examining its condition. They talked about what they would do if the truth of Qadir's disappearance reached Kashmir before Malla Khaliq's return. Then Noor Mohammad was lost in many apprehensions and stood mute. Ghulam Ahmed asked him why he was so glum.

'He was destined to ruin himself, so he is ruined. But there is a more serious problem that we have to tackle now. Last week, Parveen phoned Nisar Ahmed from Delhi. Parvez looks gentle and decent, but he is extremely nasty behind closed doors. He does not return home before midnight and has been having an affair with some girl from Hyderabad from even before the marriage. It is said that he has married her and the girl is pregnant now.'

Ghulam Ahmed felt as if the ground had slipped away from under his feet. 'Does Ramzan Sahib know about this?'

'Parveen says perhaps he doesn't. Their house is so huge that nobody knows where the other is or what he is up to.'

'Why doesn't she tell Ramzan Sahib or her mother-in-law?'

'Parvez has not confessed. She came to know from her maid who used to wash the Hyderabadi woman's clothes when she came to stay at their Delhi house. Amma doesn't know, but if she comes to know, she is sure to die. Only Nisar Ahmed and I know of this. He has already booked a flight ticket for Delhi. Let him come back, and then we can decide what to do.'

Ghulam Ahmed was enraged. 'What should we do? I think we may have to get Parveen divorced from Parvez. He is a wolf in sheep's skin! I will accompany Nisar Ahmed. We will resolve the issue as soon as possible.'

Noor Mohammad begged him to stay calm until Nisar Ahmed returned from Delhi.

In Delhi, there was a heated argument taking place between father and son. Haji Ramzan was a thorough gentleman and honest in his business. He almost suffered a stroke when he found out that Parvez had consummated his marriage with a Nawab-girl named Marriam Qazalbash. She was the only daughter of her parents and owned a big estate in Banjara Hills in Hyderabad. Parvez was taken in by her wealth. Besides, she was incredibly beautiful. This secret affair was uncovered by a shawl merchant from Kashmir, Abdul Rahman Naqash, who saw the two lovers in the swimming pool of a five-star hotel where he had gone to show his old kani-shawl to a European tourist.

Haji Ramzan had a well-established showroom in Hyderabad, Bombay, Calcutta and Madras. Many old nawabs of Hyderabad and other rich people were among his customers. Ramzan Haji often sent Parvez to Hyderabad because he was a mature and educated salesman. He had met Marriam for the first time on a flight to Hyderabad. When Haji Ramzan found out, he summoned Parvez back to Delhi. Parvez had the gall to tell him that he had not done anything that was not allowed in his religion. 'I can give you many instances of men with three or even four wives,' he told his father.

Ramzan was enraged. He would have killed him if his wife and Parveen had not intervened. Parveen led her husband to their room, latched the door and said to him, 'It is not a sin to love anyone. But deceiving someone like this is a sin that cannot be forgiven by God. Whatever had to happen has happened. Henceforth you follow your path and I will follow mine. God has set me free. You need not worry about me. Nisar is coming here tomorrow, and I will go back to Kashmir with him.' Parvez was about to say something, but Parveen stood up, unlatched the door and left the room.

In the living room, Ramzan Haji and his wife sat horror-struck. Parveen sat beside her mother-in-law, who was wailing, wanting to end her life because of her son's sins. Parveen held her close. 'Do not weep, Amma. It is my misfortune that I'm having to leave behind the affection and care of parents like you. Don't worry about me. I only need your blessings.'

Ramzan Haji held her head close to his chest and said, 'You need not worry. I will disown him legally. How can he take the liberty of being our only child and smear my honour with shame? I will deprive him of every penny. I will declare all my property in your name. Let him go wherever he wants to.'

Parveen remained silent.

The next day Nisar Ahmed reached Delhi. He took Parveen back to Srinagar.

Noor Mohammad, Ghulam Ahmed and Nisar Ahmed decided that until Malla Khaliq returned to Kashmir, they would not let anybody know that Parveen had returned permanently from her in-laws' house. Aziz Dyad was delighted to see her. Parveen took care that her mother did not find out the truth about her marriage. She was happy to have returned to her family and house on the lake.

The month of March ended, and with the beginning of April, Malla Khaliq grew restive. Narayan Joo had also begun to get bored in Bombay. He went to Malla Khaliq's room and found him sitting near the window staring at the sea. 'What are you engrossed in, my lord?'

'The winter is over. Do you remember you used to quote verses of Ghalib in your letters: from walls as well as doors, verdure springs up.'

Narayan Joo sighed and completed the verse: 'I languish in the wilderness, while spring has ushered in back home.'

'The intensity of this verse has been driving me mad since this morning when I saw greens sprouting from the walls and crevices of those shanties of the fishermen. Does every withered straw of Bombay grow green with the advent of spring as we see in Kashmir?'

Narayan Joo laughed. 'Here in Bombay, one hardly feels or notices the end of winter and beginning of spring. The greenery that you see on those huts is moss. It appears because of water leakage from kitchens or toilets.'

'The musk willows would have bloomed with the end of the long winter.'

'Yes, almond buds must also be about to bloom. One can see the mustard bloom all along the road leading to Shalimar.'

'And I am pining away here, waiting for that ill-fated rascal! I am simply wasting my time waiting for him here in this awful weather.'

'This is what I wanted to tell you. We must go back to Kashmir. We can think of resolving Qadir's problem there.'

'You are right. Yesterday I received a call from Noor Mohammad. He told me that the weather has improved. The tourist season too is about to begin.'

'Good. I'll ask Vijay Kumar to book our tickets.'

The tourist festival had started with much fervour in Daman. There was hardly any place for more guests, even in the residential quarters. Reeny and Ghulam Qadir had already worked out a solution to this rush. They erected two long tents in the large garden beside their bungalow. The rooms on the upper floor were already booked. They had made all the necessary arrangements in the tents for the comfort of visitors.

The tourists spent their days on the beaches, and as soon as the sun set, they came back to performances by dancers and musicians. The indigenous drink of Goa and Daman, 'feni', was served in plenty. Qadir had never seen such a great festival before. After the day's work, he would sit with De Souza in the evening who would ask Qadir to get him a mug of feni.

'No, Dad, no alcohol. The doctor has forbidden you.'

'My child, feni is not alcohol; it's made of cashew nuts. It is good for health. You get a mug for yourself too.'

'I told you many times that I don't drink. And I am not going to allow you to have it.'

'See how everyone relishes it. Look, people are offering it to Reeny as well.'

Ghulam Qadir stood up and said, 'No, she should not drink it either.'

He ran to the lawns where a group of girls and boys were dancing around a bonfire. Reeny was surrounded by tourists who offered her feni. Qadir rushed in. 'No. No. You should not compel anybody.'

Reeny was taken aback. It was an old tradition of the place. But when she looked at Qadir's red face, she followed him to the bungalow.

'Let's go in, Daddy is waiting for you.'

Reeny liked this roguish, admonishing, possessive style of Qadir's. Qadir went to De Souza and said, 'Did you see, Reeny did not drink, and so, you will also not drink, okay?'

Reeny affectionately held his hand, asking for forgiveness. 'Sorry, Qadira. I'm sorry.'

'Damn your doctor! It is a festival, my son,' De Souza groaned and sank deeper in his armchair.

By midnight, the din of the tourists abated. When Qadir, Reeny and the waiters were busy cleaning up, De Souza somehow managed to get up from his chair. The hall was empty and everyone was busy tidying the garden, and seeing the guests off. He slowly walked, taking the support of the wall, towards the storeroom where the feni and other drinks were kept. He picked up a couple of bottles and took them to his room and hid them under his mattress. Then he returned and forced his body back into the chair.

Qadir and Reeny came back to the hall accompanied by the caterer. Qadir sat at De Souza's feet, held his hands and said, 'Sorry, Uncle, I am doing all this only for the sake of your health.'

'I know, I know, my boy. I agree. It made me feel a little dispirited but it's all right. Don't worry. Now I want to sleep. I am very tired.'

Reeny came running and asked him, 'Are you not going to eat anything?'

'I am not hungry.'

'It is not possible. I'll warm up your food.'

'No, no. I am not feeling hungry. You have dinner. My son must be famished.'

'All right. You go to your room. I will send some food there.'

De Souza was on pinpricks. Holding the chain, he pulled himself up. Qadir assisted him to his room and said, 'You change, I will go bring you dinner.' Having said this, he went out and closed the door.

De Souza hurriedly changed his clothes, took out the bottle of feni hidden under the mattress, dragged himself to the bathroom and finished half the bottle in no time. He hid the bottle behind the towel stand. There was a knock on the door. He wiped his moustache with his sleeve and returned to his room. The waiter had placed the tray of food on the table.

'Please enjoy the food; chicken tikka, sizzling hot!'

'Thank you, you may take the tray back in the morning. Has everyone gone to bed?'

'Yes.'

'All right, you also go to sleep. Close the door after you.'

The waiter left. De Souza latched the door from inside, went back to the bathroom, and got the half-empty bottle. He poured the contents into a glass, sat on his bed, and said to himself, 'Now let me enjoy.'

He emptied the glass in no time and gobbled up all the chicken in the bowl. Then he stretched himself out on the bed. Within no time he was fast asleep.

Everyone in the house had worked late into the night, and Reeny and Ghulam Qadir slept till noon the next day. De Souza alone woke up feeling rejuvenated. He showered and got dressed in the three-piece suit. He also wore a butterfly necktie as if he was going to a party. He hid the empty bottle under his bed and walked to the dining hall. The waiters were already busy with their daily chores.

Seeing De Souza smartly dressed, the chief chef said to him, 'Good morning, boss! Going somewhere?'

'Get me a hot cup of coffee. Send Johnny to clean my room. Go, why do you stare at me?'

He almost fell down as he said this, but the chef held him. De Souza shoved him and walked to his chair. Before he could sit in the chair, he stumbled again. The chef came running to him, but De Souza growled at him, 'I can manage. Why don't you get me my coffee? Go, make it hot.'

The chef went away. De Souza sat in the chair and started to croon and play with his necktie. When the chef returned with his coffee, he found De Souza snoozing in the chair, his chin touching his protruding stomach. He gently nudged him and said, 'Here is your hot coffee. I got you some cookies too.' But De Souza did not move. The chef touched his arm. 'Sir, here is your coffee. Sir?' But De Souza did not respond. The chef tried to wake him up, but De Souza's still body dropped to one side of the chair. The chef let out a scream. 'Johnny, come here quickly. Boss is unconscious.' He ran up the stairs and yelled, 'Reeny memsahib, Qadir Sahib, come downstairs, quickly.'

Reeny and Ghulam Qadir came out of their rooms and ran down to the hall. Reeny phoned the doctor. In the meantime, all the servants in the house gathered and tried to get him out of the chair, but all their attempts failed. Ghulam Qadir ran to the garage and brought a hammer and a saw. Reeny was walking to and fro between the hall and the gate, waiting anxiously for the doctor.

Ghulam Qadir cut the arms of the chair and with the help of attendants, managed to get De Souza out of the chair. They laid him carefully on the carpet. The chef brought a tumbler of water. Ghulam Qadir tried to make De Souza swallow a sip of water, but he did not and the water trickled down from the corners of his mouth.

The doctor arrived. He examined De Souza and said to Reeny, 'Sorry, my child. He is gone. He suffered a cardiac arrest.'

Reeny stood still, like a lump of clay, gazing at her father's face.

The doctor wrote the death certificate. He took Ghulam Qadir aside and explained to him all the funeral rites and rituals. 'Obviously the people of the community will perform all the rituals. Since he has no relative in the neighbourhood, you may have to stand by her as her only support. He was a noble soul. May he rest in peace. God bless you.'

The doctor went to Reeny and placed his hand on her head. 'Be a brave girl. I had told him not to touch alcohol, but he is reeking of feni.'

Reeny looked at the doctor and then at her dead father. The doctor sighed and said, 'I shall go to the church and inform the father.'

Qadir asked the attendants to help carry De Souza to his room. He knew all his friends, other hoteliers and traders would come to see him one last time.

De Souza was buried the next morning in the cemetery of Daman with full honour. Reeny, clad in a black dress, sat near the grave with her eyes closed, praying for her father's soul. Tears flowed down her cheeks.

After the funeral, the padre went to Reeny and advised her to show fortitude and forbearance. The mourning procession slowly came out of the cemetery. Near the outer gate, Reeny individually thanked and bade farewell to all the people who had come. Ghulam Qadir and the attendants of the hotel stayed with Reeny.

Ghulam Qadir took out his handkerchief and gave it to Reeny. 'Let us go.'

Reeny wiped her tears, heaved a long sigh, and said, 'Let us go.'

No one entered the pantry.

Four days had passed since De Souza's funeral. After attending the last of the prayers, Reeny and Qadir entered the hotel. She looked at the chair which lay in a corner, as if still wailing. She went near the chair and held the handle of the suspended chain in her hand. Qadir went near her and said, 'Let's move forward, it is of no use now.'

She began to wail loudly. All the waiters and servants came and stood around her. He sat near her, and hesitantly placed his hand on her shoulder. 'Please stay strong, Reeny.'

'Now what will I do, Qadira?' Saying so, she rested her head on Qadir's chest. Qadir's eyes brimmed with tears.

The noise of the sea had subsided and the sun was slowly submerging in the golden waves. The glare of the setting sun on their faces was getting dimmer, and they hardly knew when the day was over.

Their employees, sitting still in a corner of the hall, looked like transfixed shadows; no one had the will to switch the lights on.

The chief chef finally switched on the lights in the veranda. The light of the lamps entered through the windows and filled the hall. Qadir said to Reeny, 'Let us get up now. It was God's decree, what could we do?'

'Daddy left me all alone in such a vast world. All is finished—'

'No, all is not finished. If you give up like this, Uncle's soul will never forgive us. Let's get up. I am here with you, you know that.'

Reeny cast a hopeful glance at his face, then got up and walked slowly towards the stairs.

Ghulam Qadir accompanied her upstairs. While climbing up the steps, he turned and said to the staff, 'Why is it all dark? Switch the lights on, and make preparations for dinner. People will be here soon returning after their ride on the steamers.'

All the lights were switched on, and the walls of the hotel were bright again. The workers began to work again.

Ghulam Qadir entered Reeny's bedroom for the first time. He was holding her hand. He made her sit on the bed and was about to leave, when Reeny tugged at his hand and made him sit down beside her.

'No, Qadira, stop. I don't know what is happening to me. Don't leave yet.'

'But there is a lot to be done downstairs.'

'They will do it on their own. You sit here with me. I am feeling scared.'

'All will be fine again. You have to persevere.'

Qadir sat beside her. Reeny closed her eyes. He felt every second was getting heavier than the last. Before he could utter another word, she said, 'Qadira, promise that you will never go away from this hotel.'

'How can I go away, Reeny memsahib?'

'Never abandon me, I will die of loneliness.'

'Don't talk like that.'

The days of mourning were over. Joseph Farera, De Souza's advocate, arrived, and handed over an envelope to Reeny. 'The last will and testament of my friend De Souza.'

Reeny, who had almost overcome her grief, received the envelope and was about to open it when Joseph Farera stopped her and advised her that he read the will in Ghulam Qadir's presence as there was a mention of him in it. Reeny handed the envelope to Farera.

Farera opened the envelope and turned toward Ghulam Qadir. 'This is the last will of De Souza. Please pay close attention to what he has written – 'I, De Souza, with all my five senses alert, deed my Hotel Solace over to my daughter Reeny and her partner Qadir.'

Ghulam Qadir was flabbergasted. He protested, 'No, no. The hotel is Reeny's property. I came here only to lend a hand. I have no right over it.'

Farera smiled. 'Let me read through the whole deed. "It is my heartfelt desire that after my death Qadir support my daughter for her whole life. They get married and keep my name alive. Mother Mary herself sent Qadira like an angel to me when our boat was about to sink. It is my firm belief that he will fulfil my last wish. If they do not agree to this deed, the hotel may be donated to the orphanage of the church – my dear children, I request you to agree. I am sure your life will be replete with joys and happiness."'

Reeny fondly looked at Qadir, but he felt frozen.

'So I am leaving. You reflect on De Souza's decision which he arrived at after much deliberation. Qadir Sahib, he loved you more than his own son. When he came to me to request my counsel, he became very sentimental. I request you to respect his last wish. Goodbye.' Then Farera left.

Reeny said, 'Now you are a prisoner, sir. How will you escape?'

'Marriage is not child's play, memsahib, we will have to think it over seriously.'

'I have already thought for myself. Now it's your turn to think.' Qadir felt defeated and wearily walked out.

Qadir did not sleep a wink. Reeny was really in love with him. He was not the man he used to be, otherwise he would have taken pleasure in the fact. He wanted to get reunited with his family and call Zeb and Bilal here. But now if he did not marry Reeny, the hotel and other property would go to the orphanage of the church. And if he married Reeny, his Zeb and his son would have no shelter. 'What will happen to my Abba and Ammi?' he thought.

He would finally tell everything to Reeny.

In Srinagar, Noor Mohammad had been summoned by the bank to meet the manager. He was terrified at the thought of some new trouble coming their way. On the one hand he faced the dread of Parveen's plight being discovered by others in the family, and on the other, he felt burdened with the guilt of lying to Zeb and Aziz Dyad about Qadir. He was eagerly waiting for his father to return and resolve all the problems. He went to the deputy manager who handed him a transfer order of fifty thousand rupees from the Bank of Chennai in the name of Malla Khaliq. Noor Mohammad was flummoxed. He could not remember any tourist who might have come from Madras to stay in their houseboats. 'I think this is the money that Haji Sahib has received as an advance from some customer in Bombay. Abba has left from Bombay and is expected to reach Srinagar in a couple of days.'

When he returned his mother gave him a letter that the postman had delivered. He ripped the envelope open with trembling hands. It was a typed letter from some Swami from Madras. After a formal salaam and good wishes, the letter conveyed that he owed over one lakh rupees to Ghulam Qadir in connection with his carpet business. Qadir had instructed him in Bombay that the money be paid to his father.

Mr Swami had further written that he had to urgently leave for America and that he would pay the balance amount immediately on his return.

Aziz Dyad had become nervous after receiving the letter; she asked Noor Mohammad if all was well.

'Yes, all is well. Ghulam Qadir has sent fifty thousand rupees to Abba.'

'God bless him! Has he written anything about Qadir's coming home?'

He thought, so Ghulam Qadir is now in Madras! No, no, there is still some mystery to be solved. Wrapped up in a blanket, he sat on the deck of the houseboat. Zeb got him a hot kangri and asked him about the letter. 'It was from Ghulam Qadir's partner. He has sent fifty thousand rupees to Abba. He is still in Saudi, perhaps,' Noor Mohammad lied to her.

Zeb sighed and went back. On reaching the pantry, she overheard Aziz Dyad and Parveen arguing. Parveen was weeping. 'Why don't you understand? I have nothing against my in-laws. But why should I call them? You need not worry about me. Let Abba come home; only he can solve my problem.'

'Why don't you tell me what actually happened there? Your in-laws have phoned you so many times, you should have spoken to them to ask after their well-being.'

'I will surely call them, but only after Abba is home.'

Zeb did not think it proper to interrupt the private conversation. Parveen had told Zeb everything. But she had requested her not to divulge Parvez's second marriage to anyone until Abba returned. On hearing the argument between Parveen and her mother, she thought that perhaps Parveen had told her mother.

Seeing Qadir's indifference, Reeny was gradually losing hope, while Qadir could not muster the courage to convey his decision to her. He quietly finished dinner and went upstairs to his bedroom. Reeny left her meal half finished and listlessly went to her room.

Qadir stretched out on the bed and fell asleep in no time. It was midnight when the strong wind from the ocean threw the window open. Qadir shivered with cold. He got up to shut the window but then he saw someone sitting crouched in an armchair in Reeny's balcony. He called out, 'Who is there?' But there was no reply. He went out into the balcony. Reeny sat weeping. Qadir walked up to her and sat before her on his knees. 'What has happened, Reeny memsahib? Why are you sitting here all alone in the cold?'

Reeny turned to Qadir. 'Why did you come here? If you hadn't, I wouldn't have been reduced to such misery. My days were passing by somehow. Why did you come? Go! Leave me. Get away.' She cried and stood up. Qadir gathered courage and held Reeny's arm. 'Let's go in. You will fall sick in this cold.'

'Why are you making me suffer? Six days have gone by since the lawyer came, and during these six days, you have not bothered to talk to me even once.'

'I am sorry. Please forgive me. How can I explain what I am going through?'

'You thought I was forcing you to shoulder my responsibilities by enticing you with the possession of this hotel. How can I make you understand that you are the only person in this world besides my father whom I trust? How can I bring myself to tell you that – I cannot live without you? Hotel or no hotel, Dad's property, or no property!'

Qadir squatted on the floor at her feet and kissed her hands. 'I cannot leave you and go anywhere else. And I cannot hurt Uncle's soul. If I am destined to undergo this trial, I will not dither. I have received so much love from you people. You have shown so much trust in me. I cannot be so ungrateful as to leave you alone and escape. And even if I wished to do that, where would I go? How?'

Ghulam Qadir gasped for breath. This was the first time in his life that he was overwhelmed with emotion. Reeny got out of her chair and sat on the floor beside him. She held Qadir close to her chest as if he were a frightened child. Qadir finally got up and helped Reeny up. 'You better call the advocate.' Reeny was about to say something to him, but Qadir stopped her. 'Before you say anything more, I want to talk to you honestly. I will abide by what you decide after that.'

'Neither you nor Uncle ever inquired about my past. You did not even try to find out who I was and what I did. I feel obligated to tell you everything about myself before we take any decision.'

He told Reeny about his parents, his brothers and sister. He did not hide the episode with Jane and about his trip to Bombay. But he did not tell her about Zeb, nor did he tell her that he had a son in Kashmir. He had resolved that in order to save Reeny's property and to gain her faith, he would tell her the rest at the right time.

Reeny was overcome with compassion for him. 'Now you can visit your family with your head held high. You can invite all of them on our wedding.'

'No, there is still a lot to be done. This is not even the time to tell them where I am. That is why I am sending them money from Madras.'

The very next day they called upon De Souza's lawyer and informed him about their decision. He advised them to register their marriage in the court so that all possible hassles over them belonging to different religions could be avoided.

Reeny was ecstatic, but Qadir felt guilty. Reeny ran towards the Ford car which was reminiscent of De Souza's days of prosperity. She had got it repaired and painted after having restarted the hotel. She opened the door to the driver's seat and said very courteously to Qadir, 'Come, drive me home!' Qadir cast a bittersweet smile at Reeny and sat in the car. Reeny looked at him and said, 'It is a custom that the ladies take their seat first. And then – anyway, all can be pardoned for today.' Qadir drove fast along the shore towards Hotel Solace. Reeny exclaimed in joy, 'Ah, this is our beginning!'

Malla Khaliq's return to his home was no less than a festival. The whole family assembled at the isle well before his arrival at the airport. Ghulam Ahmed left with a taxi to receive Narayan Joo and his father.

All the plateaus of Wompore were burgeoning with almond bloom. Seeing the stunning panorama of early spring at the Wompore plateau, Narayan Joo said, 'Wow! Haji Sahib, do you see how Kashmir has worn a new bridal dress to receive you?'

'Yes. This is why I was pining to return to the lap of my mother Kashmir. But now I feel as if life has been wrung out from my body.'

Ghulam Ahmed consoled him. 'All will be fine again. Qadir must also be worried about us. He sent fifty thousand rupees through some businessman in Madras. He has written saying he is going to Japan and will send us fifty thousand more on his return.'

'See, I told you many times that Ghulam Qadir will sooner or later realize his mistakes,' Narayan Joo said to Malla Khaliq. But Malla Khaliq was simmering with anger and anxiety. 'Don't mention that vagabond. If he had indeed returned to the right path, he would not continue playing hide-and-seek with us.' The taxi driver looked curiously at them and Narayan Joo stopped speaking.

Ghulam Ahmed said to the driver, 'Brother, first we must drop Panditji at Barzula, so turn the taxi in the opposite direction.'

On reaching home after dropping Narayan Joo, Malla Khaliq forgot all his pain when he saw Noor Mohammad, Nisar Ahmed and the rest of his family gathered around to welcome him. He embraced each of them one by one. His eyes were searching restlessly for Bilal. 'Where is Bilal?' he asked Noor Mohammad.

'He was sitting there on the stairs waiting for you. I don't know where he is hiding now.'

Malla Khaliq left all of them and walked slowly towards the willow grove; Bilal suddenly appeared and ran away from him. Malla Khaliq caught up with him. He lifted him in his arms saying, 'You imp! Why were you running away from me?' Bilal held him in a tight hug and Malla Khaliq kissed him many times over. Aziz Dyad and Zeb came near them. Aziz Dyad looked fondly at the two. 'He was angry with you. He said that Abba did not call him even once.'

Malla Khaliq kissed Bilal's forehead and said, 'Oh, I could rip apart my chest to show you how deeply I missed all of you.' Aziz Dyad's eyes brimmed with tears.

Bilal turned his grandfather. 'Is Daddy not coming?'

Everyone fell silent. Malla Khaliq caressed the child's head and said, 'He will be home within a month's time.' Zeb's heart sank.

Noor Mohammad and Ghulam Ahmed went to their father's room at midnight. Aziz Dyad asked Malla Khaliq, 'Why don't you say something? They have told you the whole story about Ramzan Haji's son.'

'What can I say? I only want to know what sins of mine merit this retribution. In Bombay I kept trying to reassure myself that Ghulam Qadir will soon realize his misdeeds, come out of hiding and shoulder the responsibility of his family. I did not know that there was yet another lightning waiting to strike me.'

'We must think of some immediate measure to resolve this issue. Our poor Parveen will otherwise keep dying every moment there,' Ghulam Ahmed said.

This enraged Malla Khaliq. 'So much has happened here in my absence, and you did not even bother to inform me! Had I known earlier, I would have stayed in Delhi and taken Ramzan Haji to task.'

'You were already so burdened with despair there, how could

we trouble you further? Besides it was an alien city, people would certainly start rumours.'

Malla Khaliq could no more control his anger. 'Who would start rumours there, Narayan Joo, Vijay Kumar or his wife? They feel the pain when even a thorn pricks us.'

Aziz Dyad was in tears. 'Your poor helpless sons were so worried about your well-being, I have no words to tell you. They had concealed this news even from me till a couple of days back. I came to know only when Ramzan Haji's wife called Parveen a dozen times and requested me to send her back. I was almost persuaded to do so, but Parveen threatened to kill herself. That is how I came to know about the whole affair.'

'All right, let me ask Parveen myself if all this is true. If it is, we will not send her back.'

Noor Mohammad who had been quiet so far, said to his father, 'Abba, whatever Parveen told her mother is absolutely true. Nisar Ahmed verified everything in Delhi.'

Malla Khaliq said to Aziz Dyad, 'Don't shed any more tears. I will summon Ramzan Haji to the public court. I will settle the whole matter in one sitting. They don't know with how much love and affection we have raised our daughter.'

'Nisar Ahmed says that Ramzan Haji and his wife did not know anything about Parvez until Naqash Sahib saw Parvez and that woman from Hyderabad together in a hotel in a swimming pool.'

'How simple-minded you are, Noor Mohammad! Were their eyes closed until their son got that Hyderabad woman pregnant? I will send for Ramzan Haji in the morning. This is sheer deceit.'

Aziz Dyad said to her two sons, 'Your Abba is right; we should not delay this matter. They will blame us otherwise. It's past midnight. Let's go to bed. Let us see what God has in store for us.'

Ghulam Ahmed and Noor Mohammad left.

But Malla Khaliq and Aziz Dyad kept waking up every half-hour till the first crowing of the cockerel. This was the first time they had lived away from each other for such a long time. They slept side by side and kept consoling each other. When the cockerel let out its last call, Malla Khaliq turned towards his wife and held her head close to his chest.

'Azi, this chest of mine has grown heavy like a stone. Every second that passes makes me feel that the rock of time crushing me is getting heavier. For all these months I waited to see Qadir return and hoped that he would fall at my feet and ask for forgiveness. But he did not turn up. I had promised Zeb that I would bring him back. But he ran away and is now absconding. Today I could not even make eye contact with that innocent girl.'

'He might not have had the courage to appear before you. And then he must have become absorbed in his business in Saudi. He will surely come back after making something of himself.'

'I have only one grudge against him – that he deserted such a lonely wife and beautiful son to live in some alien land.'

'I think he might have reformed himself by now. Otherwise he would not have sent you money.'

Malla Khaliq was about to reveal the details of Qadir's escapades to his wife, but stopped because she was already crushed by her daughter's disastrous marriage. And if she came to know about Qadir's wrongdoings on top of that, she would not be able to bear it. 'Yes, yes, I think so too. Let's wait and see what God has decided for us.'

'That is all right, but don't forget to phone Ramzan Haji in the morning.'

'Yes, I will call him after returning from Makhdoom Sahib. You better sleep now.'

'What is the time now?'

'It is already four-thirty in the morning.'

Aziz Dyad turned on her side and fell asleep. Feeling tired himself, Malla Khaliq too shut his eyes.

Haji Ramzan did not give Malla Khaliq any time to call and complain. He came over to Kashmir the very next day, and the two met in Narayan Joo's house. He was repentant and begged for Malla Khaliq's forgiveness with folded hands. Malla Khaliq was accompanied by Ghulam Ahmed and Noor Mohammad. Noor Mohammad was full of resentment, but when he found Haji Ramzan already despondent, he listened to his apologies without reacting.

Malla Khaliq, Narayan Joo, Noor Mohammad and Doctor Nisar were convinced that Haji Ramzan and his wife were not guilty. Haji Ramzan stood up, placed his cap at Malla Khaliq's feet and said to him, 'I swear by Dastagir Sahib that I did not know the truth. This evil son of ours deserves death for shaming us to the extent that we cannot face the world. How can I make you understand that I have lost all respect in my community? Please punish me as you see fit for I am a sinner.'

Malla Khaliq made him stand up and said, 'All this is okay, but you please tell us what to do. Do you think our name is intact? Even if we forget about our respect, what will our darling daughter do now? Where is she to go?'

It was Narayan Joo's turn to speak. 'Look here, Haji Sahib. We accept every word that you said as true, but please answer Malla Khaliq's question.'

Nisar Ahmed was firm in his decision and said, 'I have the answer. Under such circumstances, prudence suggests that Parveen be granted legal divorce. In no case can she live with their son.'

Ramzan Haji heaved a long sigh and said, 'Doctor Sahib has understood what perdition we were caught in, in Delhi. Yes, the situation demands that we agree with Nisar Ahmed's decision.'

Narayan Joo intervened and said, 'It is not only your decision that counts. You let us know what your son's decision is.'

'He has agreed to set Parveen free. How can I even begin to tell you how this cuts my heart as if with a sharp knife! It is certainly our misfortune that we will be parted from such a good-natured daughter-in-law. But we don't want her life ruined. I have doubled the promised alimony and deposited it in her name with the bank.'

Malla Khaliq's heart felt like it would erupt in rage. 'To hell with your money! How can money compensate for the losses we have suffered?'

Nisar Ahmed wished to end this argument and said, 'Abba, there is no point in lengthening this dispute. I have already sought Parveen's opinion and she wants nothing other than divorce.' He then turned to Ramzan Haji, saying, 'Please send us the divorce papers along with a written confession from your son, so that we can start the formalities.'

Ramzan Haji begged for forgiveness from Malla Khaliq, his sons and Narayan Joo. Then he left.

Narayan Joo heaved a long sigh of relief and said, 'God has finally resolved this problem in a proper manner; you deserve congratulations.'

Malla Khaliq grew furious. 'What do you mean, Narayan Joo? Do you think this merits congratulations? What will happen to our daughter now?'

'You watch how my Goddess Mother fills her life with flowers.'

Aziz Dyad finally conceded to getting Parveen divorced. When Malla Khaliq told her that everything had been resolved amicably, she felt relieved.

Reeny and Qadir got married in court in accordance with De Souza's will and subsequently the hotel and his other assets were written to Reeny and Qadir. Reeny threw a party for her friends and the businessmen she worked with. The guests were served champagne and feni. Reeny made all the arrangements for the party. Ghulam Qadir was careful not to let his quandary mar Reeny's happiness. He remained beside her the entire time.

When the guests were raising a toast to the bride and groom, Ghulam Qadir was served champagne which he had to drink in one shot. Then Reeny's girlfriends kept refilling Ghulam Qadir's and Reeny's glasses with red wine. Ghulam Qadir tried his best to avoid drinking, yet he had to have three glasses. He had never touched alcohol before. Soon he got tipsy and started dancing with the guests.

Finally at midnight, Reeny's friends led her to the nuptial room which they had decorated with roses. Then they returned to the hall and escorted Ghulam Qadir. They pushed him in and closed the door.

Three months had passed since Parveen's divorce. Nevertheless, Malla Khaliq and Aziz Dyad continued to worry about her. They were eagerly waiting for the *ilat*, the period of abeyance after divorce in Muslim jurisprudence, so that Parveen could start her life afresh. Whenever Aziz Dyad talked to Parveen about remarriage, Parveen would leave the room, annoyed. She told her parents that if they compelled her to get married again, she would jump into the lake. Malla Khaliq, therefore, restrained his wife from talking about another marriage.

The days passed in quick succession, and the new tourist season arrived. Noor Mohammad took charge of Gulshan which Ghulam Qadir used to run. Meanwhile, they kept receiving Qadir's money orders from different locations. Zeb consoled herself by telling Bilal that his father would come soon with a suitcase full of new clothes and toys for him. And when that promised 'soon' passed and a new month began, she would get irritated with the child's persistent inquiry and want to give him a sound thrashing.

Malla Khaliq stood at the ghat waiting for Narayan Joo. Bilal came to him crying. He picked Bilal up and tried to calm him down. 'Look here, my child, your father is extremely busy with his business. When a man is too involved with his work, there is no time to spare. The moment your father is free from his work, he will come back to you.'

'No, he is not coming. He has fled the house,' Bilal said, still crying.

'Don't talk like that. You know we were in Bombay. He sought my permission to go to Saudi. Don't be so impatient. You are a grown-up boy. You should not annoy your mother like this.'

In the meantime, Narayan Joo's shikaarah approached the ghat with some tourists. Bilal spotted the boat before Malla Khaliq did. He stopped crying and yelled, 'Abba, Lala Sahib is here!'

Malla Khaliq walked down the steps to receive the tourists. A party of European tourists. He was amazed at how quickly they reached from the airport.

'How did you reach so soon?' he asked Narayan Joo.

I will tell you later, first meet your guests and escort them to the boat. Keeping his right hand on his chest, Malla Khaliq went ahead to welcome the tourists. 'Welcome to our humble abode, sir.' Narayan Joo introduced Malla Khaliq to the tourists. Noor Mohammad came running, and took their luggage. There were two groups. They were led by Ghulam Ahmed to Gulshan.

After escorting the guests to their rooms, Narayan Joo and Malla Khaliq returned to the isle. Aziz Dyad came and greeted Narayan Joo with a tray of tea. 'Should I serve tea to Lala Sahib or would he like to help himself?'

'We brothers have transcended all old barriers of formality by living together in Bombay for so many months.'

'May Dastagir always bless you!' She served a cup to Narayan Joo and then to her husband. While drinking their tea, Malla Khaliq asked Narayan Joo, 'You did not tell me how you managed to bring the guests from the airport so soon.'

'I have seen many miracles of my Devi, but the miracle that I witnessed at the airport today was hard to believe.'

'When the party of our tourists reached the counter, I raised the placard to give them a signal. When I raised the placard a couple of times, a young police officer came and stood before me and he continued looking at me. When I was about to sit down, he greeted me with a smile and said, 'Didn't you recognize me? I am Abdul Razaq.' He raised his uniform cap. He was very much the young man who once worked in your house.'

'Was he really Razaq?' Aziz Dyad could not believe what she was hearing.

Malla Khaliq was elated. 'Yes, it must have been Razaq for I was sure that the young man would one day become a big officer. I don't remember another young boy so engrossed in his studies.'

'"I am a police inspector now." he said to me. "You please stay here; I will complete their registration myself."'

'This is how we did not lose any time at the airport. What an impressive young man he has become! He accompanied me to the car. He asked about you. I told him that you are back home and suggested that he visit you. He said he did not have the courage to face you.'

Malla Khaliq's eyes filled with tears. He turned to Aziz Dyad. 'See, this is goodness. Now compare him with Parvez, that wretched son of Ramzan Haji's!'

Aziz Dyad was dumbfounded. She lifted the tray and went to the kitchen.

Malla Khaliq asked Narayan Joo, 'Is he posted at the airport?'

'Yes. I know why you are asking me this. Don't waste any time. I have got his phone number.'

'May he prosper more and more,' said Malla Khaliq.

When the family sat down for dinner, Malla Khaliq proudly announced that Abdul Razaq had become a police inspector. Parveen's wounds started aching again. Zeb said to her father-in-law, 'Abba, he always stood first in all his tests.'

'And you know how your brothers-in-law used to call him names,' Malla Khaliq said, looking at Ghulam Ahmed.

He retorted, 'If we are not strict with the servants, they are sure to get spoilt.'

Noor Mohammad knew that this would turn into an argument, and so he changed the topic.

'Abba, the Europeans told me that they wanted to spend a few days in Ladakh and asked me to accompany them.'

'There is no harm in that.'

'Only two to three days.'

And they again got busy with their day's work and further mention of Abdul Razaq was avoided.

In the evening, when Malla Khaliq and Aziz Dyad were about to go to bed, Malla Khaliq mentioned Abdul Razaq. 'What a lovely boy he was! But alas, my bad luck!'

Aziz Dyad asked her husband, 'Is he married?'

Malla Khaliq smiled at his wife's naivety. 'What nonsense you talk! He is such a big officer now, how could he have not married? Destiny might have ordained some fortunate girl to him. You sleep now,' he said and turned on his side. Aziz Dyad remained awake late into the night. She knew that her ill-fated daughter was being consumed by flames.

Two days passed. Narayan Joo called Malla Khaliq and told him that Abdul Razaq was eager to meet him.

'Then you should have brought him along,' Malla Khaliq told him. 'Bring him here for tea this evening.'

'I already invited him without seeking your permission. I hope I was right.'

'Why are you being a stranger? Is my home not yours as well?'

'While talking to him, I came to know that he is still unmarried. So I thought of initiating Parveen's proposal with him.'

Malla Khaliq fell silent, but inwardly he prayed to God, 'Let the separated lovers unite this time.'

Narayan Joo nervously asked Malla Khaliq, 'Why are you silent? Did I say something wrong?'

'You have never said anything wrong till date. In fact, I have also been thinking on similar lines. But time has defeated us. Abdul Razaq is now an officer, and you know our Parveen is—'

Narayan Joo interrupted and said, 'There is no harm trying.'

'If he refuses, Parveen shall suffer doubly.'

'Then I really made a mistake in asking him to come.'

'No, not at all. Please bring him here. You cannot even guess how dear he was to me.'

Malla Khaliq put down the receiver. Aziz Dyad had overheard him in the kitchen. She hurried to her husband and said, 'What did Narayan Joo say? Why did you name Parveen while talking on the phone?'

'He harbours the same dreams as you.'

'What dreams do I harbour?'

'Did you not ask me repeatedly if Razaq is married?'

'There is nothing wrong in asking.'

'Then listen. Narayan Joo was telling me that Razaq is eager to come here. He is getting him here tomorrow evening.'

'What are these "dreams" that Narayan Joo sees as I do?'

'Abdul Razaq is not yet married, and Narayan Joo wishes we get Parveen married to him.'

'To be honest, I was also thinking about that.'

'Yes, let's see if God approves of the plan and reunites the two separated lovers.'

'But I don't see how we can initiate this.'

'Why should you ask for his charity? You better seek Narayan Joo's counsel; he knows how to approach these problems.'

When Zeb told Parveen that Razaq was to visit their house, she felt her heart flutter out of control. She held Zeb's hand tightly and squeezed it. She was shivering. Zeb held her close to her chest and said, 'I can understand the tempest raging in your mind. On the one hand you ardently want to have a glimpse of your estranged lover, and on the other you are afraid that he might have forgotten those sweet old days you spent together.'

'He could have forgotten me a long time ago. Otherwise he would have tried to find out what befell me.'

'If he had forgotten you, he wouldn't have stayed unmarried, would he?'

'How idle your thoughts are, my Bhabi? You think he would have waited all these years just for me?'

Zeb had no answer, and she thought it better to change

the subject. She said, 'Entrust yourself to God and see how He saves you.'

How could Abdul Razaq afford to forget Parveen? He had promised her that he would continue his studies and make himself worthy of her. Though he had lost her to another man, he did not forget his promise. He had kept track of all the events in her life. He had resolved that he would never let any other girl occupy the place in his heart where Parveen always lived.

On the next day, when he and Narayan Joo were rowing towards Malla Khaliq's houseboats, Narayan Joo very nimbly raised the issue of the misdeeds of Ramzan Haji's son, Parvez. Abdul Razaq said to him, 'The news of his crimes is already rampant here, especially among the traders.'

'That is why Haji Sahib is in great pain. What a lovely daughter he has! Pure and pretty, like a lotus in the Dal Lake. That wretched boy did not know her value.'

Abdul Razaq fell silent and just looked at the row of houseboats which were coming closer. Narayan Joo then said to Abdul Razaq, 'Razaq Sahib, now that you are quite settled in your life, you should think of selecting a good girl and marrying her. This is the right time for a man to build his home and family.'

Abdul Razaq replied with a smile, 'You have so much experience and so wide is the circle of your acquaintants, do me the favour of finding a good girl for me.'

The boat touched Malla Khaliq's isle, and their conversation remained unfinished. Noor Mohammad had seen the boat advancing from a distance. He sent a message to his father through Bilal. Ghulam Ahmed had also seen the boat, but he preferred to hide. He came out through a window of houseboat Gulshan and ran towards his own room. He caught hold of his wife's arm as she was picking spinach while sitting on the rear prow. 'You are hurting my wrist – where are you dragging me off to?'

'Razaq is coming here along with Lala Sahib!'

With a jerk, Zoon freed her wrist. 'Leave me, I also want to see how he looks in his police uniform.'

Tormented by the fire of jealousy, Ghulam Ahmed shoved her and said, 'Go die. I am afraid he could get us all handcuffed.'

The chairs were already kept ready on the isle. Malla Khaliq was urging Abdul Razaq to sit in a chair. But Abdul Razaq desisted. 'How can I ever have the cheek to sit in a chair in your presence? My place will always be at your feet.'

Narayan Joo forced him to sit in the chair. 'You please sit in the chair, so that he will sit in peace.'

Everyone sat down comfortably, but Abdul Razaq sat on the edge of the chair. Abdul Razaq still considered himself the same old waiter 'Razaqa' in the presence of Malla Khaliq and accorded him the same respect.

In the meantime, Bilal ran to his mother who was busy ironing clothes with Parveen. 'Mummy, Mummy! He has come.'

Zeb left the clothes and ran towards the kitchen. 'Switch off the iron, Amma is all alone there,' she said to Parveen. Bilal followed her. Parveen switched off the iron and went near the window. She drew the curtain to one side and looked out towards the isle. Abdul Razaq was sitting in the chair directly facing the window. She could hardly believe her eyes. Was this the same Razaq who used to wear a four-cornered conical cap and serve at their house?

Holding the curtain in her hand, she sat down. Her heart fluttered so fast that she felt it would rip open the cage of the ribs. All her repressed love surged forth again and a torrent of tears flowed from her eyes. She shut her eyes, and held her heaving breast; her lips quivered. 'Oh my God! Why are you doing this to me? Why did you send him back to add to my pain?' She heard a big guffaw from Narayan Joo. She wiped her tears and started to peep out to see what had made them laugh so loudly. She saw Bilal wearing Abdul Razaq's uniform cap and walking round them saying 'left-right-left-right!' Abdul Razaq held him close, kissed his forehead and tried to make him sit beside him in his chair. But he stretched out his arm for a handshake and said, 'Thank you. I will also study a lot and become a police officer, just like you.'

Malla Khaliq was very happy. He said to Abdul Razaq, 'Now he can speak English better than I can.'

Noor Mohammad caressed Bilal's hair and said to Abdul Razaq, 'All this is the result of Zeb's perseverance.'

Meanwhile, the waiter brought them tea, and Aziz Dyad followed carrying a basket of bread. Seeing her, Abdul Razaq stood up and tried to touch her feet. Aziz Dyad withdrew, saying, 'Oh no! What is all this for? Please sit, my son. May my Dastagir help you grow more and more.'

While offering a cup of tea to Abdul Razaq, she said, 'How this Haji Sahib of yours missed you after you left! And when he came to know that you are now a police officer, he was delirious with joy.'

'How can I repay his favours? It was only his love that showed me the path to make something of myself.'

Malla Khaliq said, 'But I did not teach you to leave all your possessions here and flee in the night.'

'Yes, that was my fault for which I could never dare face you. Today I am here to beg your pardon for that mistake.'

Narayan Joo smiled. He said to Malla Khaliq, 'Do you remember, Haji Sahib, I once narrated the story of the "prodigal son" to you while we were walking on the roads of Bombay?'

Abdul Razaq looked at Malla Khaliq and said, 'Please forgive all my sins, just as the prodigal son was forgiven.'

'But I am the real sinner, my dear son. You still came here, that is your greatness,' said Malla Khaliq.

'Your tea is getting cold, my son,' Aziz Dyad interrupted. The waiter stood at a little distance, uniformed and ready to obey any command, as Razaq had once stood at the house. Razaq had looked intermittently towards him. He thought that it might be the same uniform that Malla Khaliq had given him many years back. The waiter felt nervous and moved away and stood behind a willow tree.

After an hour or so, Abdul Razaq sought their permission to

leave. Walking beside him towards the ghat, Aziz Dyad said to him, 'Now, remember to visit us whenever you find time.'

'Why not, for it is his home,' Narayan Joo seconded Aziz Dyad. Abdul Razaq looked at him and said, 'Surely, provided they have really forgiven me.'

Holding his hand fondly, Malla Khaliq said to him, 'In fact, we ought to seek your forgiveness because we did not even try to find you and congratulate you when we heard about your success in the matriculation examinations. The fact is that we were mired in misery at that time.'

'In case I could be of some help to you, I would consider myself fortunate.'

'I pray you always be in great health and good spirits.'

'So, I take your leave now.'

'God bless you!' Malla Khaliq led him and Narayan Joo to the steps of the ghat. While walking down the steps, Abdul Razaq looked towards the isle and the kitchen, hoping to catch a glimpse of Parveen. She had walked around the back the house and reached the drawing room of houseboat Gulfam. She could clearly see the boats waiting there. She continued to gaze at Abdul Razaq until his boat drifted away behind other houseboats in the lake.

Whenever Abdul Razaq returned from the airport and drew closer to his house, he often called on Narayan Joo. He frequently referred to Ramzan Haji's son and gave a new list of his offences. This made Narayan Joo infer that Abdul Razaq was actually interested in finding out about Parveen's fate. So one day he mustered the courage and brought up the proposal. Razaq lowered his gaze with modesty and said to Narayan Joo, 'This is equal to throwing a rope to lasso the sky. I once worked as an attendant at their house. How will they agree to marry their daughter to a waif like me?'

'You just tell me if you are agreeable.'

Abdul Razaq nodded. 'I once longed to say this, but did not have the guts.'

'It is okay. I shall initiate the subject with Haji Sahib.'

'They will never reject your opinion.'

'You just have faith in God for He alone will fulfil your heart's desire.'

Malla Khaliq could hardly believe his ears. The whole family rejoiced. Zeb went running to Parveen and held her in a tight embrace. 'See how Dastagir Sahib has blessed you! It is a miracle. I wish you had seen how ecstatic Abba, Amma and Lala Sahib are. Tears flowed from Noor's eyes, and Ghulam Ahmed who had hid himself on Razaq's first visit came running and hugged Abba.'

Parveen gaped at her. Zeb said to her, 'Why don't you say something? Did you hear what I told you?'

Parveen heaved a sigh. 'I heard. I heard everything. Oh, I wish it had happened a long time ago. I am not worthy of him any more.'

'If you were not, why would he come with the proposal? You stupid girl, true love stands every test and triumphs. You just forget your fears and thank God for His mercy. Come on now, Amma is waiting for you.'

'No, I won't go there right now. How can I face them?'

'All right, let Lala Sahib leave and then you come.'

The engagement had taken place. The tourist season was over. Whenever there was a rush of tourists, there was some kind of disturbance in the valley, and the tourist season would suffer losses. The tourism industry had grown used to this fitful nature of the trade. Then autumn set in and as usual weddings were in full swing. Malla Khaliq held the nikah celebrations of Parveen and Abdul Razaq with much gusto. The separated lovers were reunited and everyone was happy. Zeb was so delighted she forgot her own miseries. After Parveen was sent off, she silently walked behind the willows and reached her own room. She looked at Ghulam Qadir's photograph that was fixed on the wall facing the door. She felt pained that Parveen's brother had missed this important event in her life. She gazed at it. Then she started crying. 'Where do you keep hiding? Spring is over, summer has faded away, trees are withering – how much longer should I remain waiting for you? If you did not worry about me, why don't you feel some pity for your parents? Are you not bothered to know about your sister's plight?' She sat down with her head between her knees and sobbed.

After her father's death, Reeny had never trusted anyone as she trusted Qadir. She felt that she had been born again. She only nursed the grouse that Qadir was so busy with work that he hardly spent any time with her. She did not know that Qadir did it on purpose because he did not want to have the time to face the truth. He wanted to stop thinking about his past. It haunted him doggedly. Whenever Reeny asked him why he couldn't relax a bit, he would say he wanted to make her Hotel Solace the best hotel in Daman.

One day she got irritated and said to him, 'Why do you always call this only my dream? You know this hotel belongs more to you than me. You are the one who sowed the seed of this dream in me. This belongs more to you than me. Be honest, is it not so?'

Ghulam Qadir squeezed her arm and said, 'Yes, it is. That is why it is necessary that we work hard so that we are able to live a comfortable life.'

'Then you can finally take me along to Kashmir and proudly introduce me to your family,' Reeny said with much enthusiasm. The words struck Ghulam Qadir's heart like a dart, and he stood up. 'Oh God! I have to go to the market and arrange for things needed for tomorrow's party.' Having said this, he entered the garage and reversed their new Maruti car.

Instead of going to the market, he drove behind the hotel and stopped at a secluded place on the seashore. He started reprimanding himself, 'What a perdition you are marooned in! Now there is only one exit from this mess and that is to be so rich that no one will have the courage to ask you why you married a second time.'

He looked at the ocean extending far and wide before him. He saw a small boat battling with the tides to reach the shore. The boat was sinking and rising again; but the boatman did not lose his resolve. When the boat got closer to the shore, Ghulam Qadir thought the boatman seemed to resemble his father; the same upright back, the same arms with thick brawn. He began sweat heavily. He started the car and drove fast to the market.

Having finished shopping, he returned to the hotel. Reeny was in the backyard, discussing something with her advocate. Seeing the advocate, Qadir grew nervous. He asked the chief chef to take out the goods from the car, and strode over to Reeny. Reeny said, 'We were waiting for you. See what a good proposal the advocate has got us.'

The advocate shook hands with Qadir and said, 'One should not lose this golden opportunity.'

'I don't understand,' Qadir said.

'A big hotel at Panjim in Goa is on sale. It was constructed just last year. With very little effort, it can be transformed into a five-star hotel.'

'That is all right, but why are you here?'

'We were just considering the proposal,' Reeny replied.

'But why here in this barren backyard?'

'Let's go inside and talk about it.'

They went into the drawing room where the advocate explained every detail of the proposal to Qadir. Having assessed all the aspects of the proposal, Ghulam Qadir's desire to acquire more property was kindled, yet he felt like he was building castles in the air. He said to Reeny, 'The proposal is excellent, but how will we manage to get all this money?'

'That is what we were discussing in the backyard before you arrived. You know the whole stretch of land is lying without any use, and there are many people who have their eyes on it.'

'Some traders have started offering me a handsome amount for the land,' the advocate added.

'We can sell this piece of land and purchase the hotel,' Reeny

said. 'You don't know how keen I am on extending our business
to Goa.'

Ghulam Qadir started making calculations and he knew that
even if they sold the land, they would fall short of money. The
advocate suggested that he could easily arrange for the remaining
money on loan from a bank.

After a few visits to Goa, the deal was finalized. The hotel had
been constructed by some Marwari who had died along with his
son and wife in a car accident. The company that had financed the
businessman had no option but to put the hotel's up for auction.

After having purchased Hotel Sea Waves, Ghulam Qadir grew
oblivious of everything other than managing it. He worked day in
and day out and succeeded in reviving the hotel's old glory. Upon
seeing the success of the hotel, Reeny went back to Daman because
the tourist season was about to begin over there. She would come
to Goa to spend a few days with Ghulam Qadir, or he would go to
Daman. And so both hotels continued to flourish.

It was a record tourist season in Kashmir. Malla Khaliq, Noor
Mohammad and Ghulam Ahmed worked relentlessly to serve the
tourists and hardly found time to think about Qadir. But how
could Aziz Dyad and Zeb forget him who lived in some unknown
place! Only the money that he regularly sent to Malla Khaliq from
Madras, Kochi, or some other place in the south vaguely hinted at
his location. Whenever Malla Khaliq received the money, his anger
knew no bounds, and he quarrelled with his family members on
every trivial issue.

One day when the postman delivered the mail, there was a big
envelope addressed to Ghulam Ahmed. It was a pretty envelope
which bore stamps that showed sea waves and children playing
in it. In a corner at the bottom was the name of a firm, 'Kashmiri
Carpet Museum, Panjim, Goa'. The name piqued Malla Khaliq's

curiosity, and he thought to himself, so there is a branch of our Arts
Emporium in Goa too. But Ghulam Ahmed never mentioned this.
Maybe he did not remember. But who had sent this letter to him?
He called Ghulam Ahmed and passed the letter on to him. 'The
people from the Emporium have sent you this letter. Have you ever
delivered any carpets to them?'

'When will you start trusting me, Abba?' Ghulam Ahmed asked
him while opening the envelope. 'I hardly have anything to do
with the Emporium.' Then he suddenly yelled, 'Abba, this may be
a clue of Qadir's whereabouts!'

'What?' Malla Khaliq was alert to hear more.

'It is a letter from Mohammad Ismail of Gojwara. He has a
big shop of carpets in Goa. When I once went to Goa to inquire
about Qadir, he took me to each and every Kashmiri businessman
working there to get some clue about Qadir.'

'Tell me what he has written.'

'He writes, "There is hot news in Goa that a Kashmiri has
purchased Hotel Sea Waves of Goa. His name is Qadir Damanwala
as he has a hotel in Daman as well. He might be your brother
Ghulam Qadir. They say that he usually remains confined to his
hotel premises. It is better you come and ascertain for yourself."'

'All nonsense! Maybe there is a big businessman with the same
name Qadir Damanwala! If our loafer Qadir had that much talent,
why did he waste it all here?'

'Abba, there is nothing wrong in going to Goa to find out the
truth. I have a feeling that he might be our Qadir. Otherwise how
is he managing to send you so much money every month?'

Malla Khaliq's suspicion was stirred. He consulted Noor
Mohammad and also called Doctor Nisar. They decided to send
Ghulam Ahmed to Goa.

When Abdullah Shah heard about Ghulam Ahmed's going to
Goa, he felt delighted. Ghulam Ahmed called at his house and he
said to him, 'See how God has paved the way for your benefit. If
Ghulam Qadir really has such a big hotel in Goa, we can rent a
showroom in the hotel and start our carpet business there.'

Ghulam Ahmed's greed too raised its head. 'How can I be in such luck? How can an empty-handed person like me strike gold so easily?'

Abdullah Shah was such a deft businessman that he could count even the feathers of a flying bird. He knew well that Ghulam Ahmed had purposely come to his house. He looked at him. Ghulam Ahmed wished to take full advantage of the opportunity and continued to say, 'It may take me a week to reach Goa and all the showrooms will have been booked by then.'

'No. Why? You better travel by air. I will book you a ticket today. You should take some sample carpets along with you.'

After travelling partly by air, and partly by train, Ghulam Ahmed reached Panaji. He went straight away to Mohammad Ismail of Gojwara. He showed him the road leading to Hotel Sea Waves and advised him, 'Please go inside cautiously for they do not allow vendors to enter the hotel. You should first make a thorough inquiry about this Qadir Damanwala before going ahead.'

Ghulam Ahmed took a turn and got his first glimpse of Hotel Sea Waves, and he was stunned. He stopped at a distance from the gate. He waited for the right time to enter. He pleaded to his Saint Dastagir that the owner of the hotel might come out to the lawns so that he could see whether Qadir Damanwala was really his brother or someone else. Just then a big car came from the market side, and the gatekeeper opened the gate immediately. Ghulam Ahmed could now see clearly up to the porch of the hotel. He moved closer. The car stopped at the portico. The gatekeeper went running and opened the door of the car. Ghulam Qadir's heart pounded in his chest when he saw his brother getting out from the car. Unable to control himself, he ran across the lawn calling out to his brother. The gatekeeper tried to stop him. Ghulam Qadir turned around and saw his brother weeping and running towards him. Even he could not hold himself back and welcomed his brother with open arms.

The two gatekeepers looked at each other with surprise. Ghulam Qadir held Ghulam Ahmed's hand and took him to his room. He closed the door behind him, and made his brother sit down. The two brothers sat nervously before each other, each about to burst forth with words but each anxiously waiting for the other to start the conversation.

Ghulam Ahmed had resolved that he would berate and unmask him in the presence of his employees. But having seen what a big hotel he owned, and seeing the change in his station, he could not muster up the courage. As soon as he entered the hotel, he had seen many resplendent showrooms which kindled hope in him. But he ensured that he did not say anything that may quell his dreams. He did not want to lose the opportunity of working in this splendid hotel. It was Qadir who broke the silence. 'Why don't you say something? Why don't you get up as you used to in the past and curse me for all the sins that I committed all these years? All of you might have thought that Qadir has been interred in an abyss of sins and will never come out, and that is why he continues to hide from his family. The fact is that I was so ashamed of myself that I fled from Bombay to seek some way to start a chaste and dirt-free life. God was kind to me and all that you see around here is only because of His mercy. Believe me there is not even a farthing of illegal money in what I have built.'

Ghulam Ahmed did not even realize the passing of time. Ghulam Qadir went on narrating his tale and he listened intently. He questioned him every once in a while so that he could ascertain every detail. His story of success was no less interesting than the tales in the Arabian Nights. While Ghulam Qadir related his story minute by minute, he did not divulge the details of his marriage with Reeney.

The two brothers would not have realized that it was already evening if Qadir had not received a call from the reception. On hearing that Reeny had phoned him twice from Daman, Ghulam Qadir stood up abruptly. He went to the next room to call her back.

'I am sorry, Reeny. My elder brother Ghulam Ahmed has arrived here in search of me.'

'This is such good news! Please let me have a word with him.' She was really delighted to receive this news. Since Qadir had mentioned his family members repeatedly, she really wanted to go to Kashmir and meet his family.

'Of course, I will let you talk to him, but this is not the right time. You need to be patient.'

'Okay, as you wish. But please do not quarrel with him. You should treat him well.'

'Surely I shall. We Kashmiris are unmatched in hospitality, you know.'

'What a strange language you speak in today!'

'Yes, this is my reply to what you said. Don't worry. I will take good care of him. Bye!'

He returned to Ghulam Ahmed. Seeing the cordless telephone in his hand, Ghulam Ahmed said to him, 'Since the phone is already in your hand, please call up Abba. He has been on tenterhooks about you.'

'No. Not today. You talk to him first, only then will I get the courage to talk to him. Take this phone. I will go downstairs to close today's accounts. Besides, you might hesitate to talk to Bhabi in my presence.'

He went out of the room. Ghulam Ahmed rose, closed the door, and dialled home.

Malla Khaliq rarely trusted Ghulam Ahmed. He noted down the telephone number of Hotel Sea Waves, consulted with Noor Mohammad and then went to Barzul to see Narayan Joo. On hearing what Malla Khaliq told him, Narayan Joo connected him with a partner of his in a travel agency in Goa. He got the details about Hotel Sea Waves, and then turned to Malla Khaliq and Noor Mohammad.

'Congratulations, Haji Sahib! Every word of Ghulam Ahmed's is true. Your son Ghulam Qadir is now rolling in money.'

Malla Khaliq was dumbfounded. Words failed him. Narayan Joo nudged Malla Khaliq and said, 'What thoughts are you lost in, sir? If you don't trust me, take this phone. I shall connect you directly with Ghulam Qadir.' He dialled the number of Hotel Sea Waves. 'Hello, Hotel Sea Waves? May I speak to your proprietor?'

'Mr Qadir? Yes, one moment.'

Then he handed the phone over to Malla Khaliq, but he refused to take it. 'No, no. He may be the wealthiest man in the world, but to me he is a sinner who is never to be pardoned.'

By then Ghulam Qadir came on the line. 'Hello, who is it?' Malla Khaliq hastened to return the receiver to Narayan Joo, as if there was a serpent in his hand. Narayan Joo did not waste any time and said, 'Dear Ghulam Qadir, we forgot all our anger and misgivings when we got to know about you. Here is your Abba, talk to him.'

'No, no. Not now. I can hardly talk to you. I cannot muster enough courage to talk to Abba. Even being able to talk to you feels like speaking to my own father. Kindly tell him that his Qadir cannot lay his head at his feet unless he brings him a good name.' Qadir got very emotional.

Narayan Joo had placed the receiver close to Malla Khaliq's ear. When he heard Qadir's words, he could not restrain himself. A torrent of tears flowed from his eyes and he instinctively replied, 'My dear son, how long will you keep all of us drowned in pain?'

'Abba!' This was the only word Qadir could utter before he broke down. In the meantime, Ghulam Ahmed entered the room. Seeing Qadir crying with the receiver in his hand, he went running to him. Ghulam Qadir handed over the receiver to him. 'It is Abba on the phone.' Then he went and sat in the other corner of the sofa, holding his head in his hands. Ghulam Ahmed said to his father, 'Abba! He has no words to speak. He is devastated.'

Malla Khaliq's heart was surging with love and he struggled to find words. 'Let him prosper. I pray that he has more and more successes in life. But please tell him that while he lives in luxury, there is a lonely girl pining every moment for her husband.'

'He need not be reminded of that. Please don't be so worried for he will be home shortly. I shall bring him.'

Noor Mohammad and Narayan Joo were straining to hear what they were talking on the phone. Finally Noor Mohammad could not stop himself and he asked his father, 'Abba, what does Qadir say?'

'It is Ghulam Ahmed. Qadir is mute. You talk to him. He may be able to talk to you.'

Noor Mohammad took the telephone. 'Ghulam Ahmed, will you please hand over the phone to Qadir?'

In a little while, he heard Qadir's sobs. Noor Mohammad said to his brother, 'Nothing will come out of weeping. Remember that your entire family is at home, dying to see you. Now for God's sake forget about the past and come back just once to Amma. She has reduced to a skeleton. If you come, you will heal the wounds of your mother, and your wife.'

'I am also longing to see you all. I have a couple of urgent jobs to do, then I will come back and beg for your forgiveness. Ama Toth can stay here till then. Is Amma there? I—'

'No, we are at Lala Sahib's.'

'Give the phone to Lala Sahib – Lala Sahib, pardon me for having sneaked away from Vijay Kumar's house without letting anyone know.'

'Dear son, you just return to us. All the snow will melt and the gardens will bloom again.'

'I need nothing but your blessings.'

The family was sitting together, and Zeb nestled close to Aziz Dyad. When Narayan Joo, Malla Khaliq and Noor Mohammad entered, Aziz Dyad sprang up. Before she could utter a word, Narayan Joo congratulated her. 'Dear sister, you must offer the sacrifice of a lamb, for your son is now the owner of a big hotel.' Aziz Dyad looked agape at him to see if he was joking. Then he went to Zeb and said, 'My dear daughter, why are you still brooding like this? Winter is over, the ice has melted and spring has returned. Now get us a big samovar of tea.' Her Qadir was now a big businessman; she trembled from head to foot.

'Did you have a word with him yourself?' Aziz Dyad asked Narayan Joo to be sure.

'I did. Should I have engaged an advocate for that?'

Noor Mohammad made his mother sit down, and he recounted every detail of the conversation with Qadir. In the meantime, Inspector Razaq came along with Parveen. He had got all the information about Hotel Sea Waves through the Goa police.

Abdullah Shah spoke to Ghulam Ahmed on the phone. When he saw Malla Khaliq and Noor Mohammad coming happily out of Narayan Joo's car, he thought the time was opportune to be the first one to pat Malla Khaliq's back. Noor Mohammad phoned Doctor Nisar and the festivity started in the houseboats. The news spread among all the houseboat owners and the shopkeepers of Dalgate.

There in Goa, Ghulam Ahmed was growing impatient to find an occasion to ask Ghulam Qadir for a showroom. He was enjoying the services and the luxuries in the hotel as the most important guest. Finally he found the occasion he had been eagerly waiting for. He asked for Ghulam Qadir's permission to clear the accounts of Abdullah Shah with the carpet dealers of Gojwara. Ghulam Qadir said to him, 'You need not bother; let me call one of them here.'

'No. I think I will have to go there myself. I have delivered some new carpets to them, and I have to seal the deal.'

'How is Abdullah Shah's business running?' Ghulam Qadir asked him.

'Foreign tourists are very interested in silk carpets. I have also been involved in his business.'

'I have a suggestion. I have constructed a new wing for showrooms near the entrance of the hotel. You take one of the showrooms and start your own business. I am sure Abba won't object.'

This was the chance Ghulam Ahmed had been waiting for. He just hung his head and muttered, 'But one must have strength to do that. One has to buy a showroom and then decorate it with attractive goods.'

'You need not worry about that. We could run this hotel as a partnership so that Abba doesn't think I have done you any favours.'

'What about Reeny Madam who you said is your partner? She may have some objection.'

'You leave that to me. You go select the best showroom. We can get it decorated as you like.'

Ghulam Ahmed was sneaky and he initially feigned lack of interest, but when Ghulam Qadir almost entreated him, he selected a big showroom just near the entrance of the hotel. Then made a call to Abdullah Shah. He broke this news to his father as well as his father-in-law.

Ghulam Qadir was happy on two accounts: he could finally do something for his family, and he was sure that he could have Ghulam Ahmed on his side so that he would not reveal the secret of his marriage with Reeny to anyone.

Reeny came to Goa to spend some weeks with Ghulam Qadir. So he then divulged his big secret to Ghulam Ahmed. But Ghulam Ahmed remembered Zeb's helplessness and his fervour for becoming a big businessman petered out. He yelled, 'Ghulam Qadir, what a big sin you have committed!'

Ghulam Qadir told him that the circumstances did not leave him much choice.

'Does this Reeny Madam know that you already have a wife in Kashmir?' Ghulam Ahmed asked Qadir, but Qadir again lied that he had told everything about his past to Reeny. Ghulam Ahmed was not convinced but because of his greed for the showroom, he did not stretch the issue.

Reeny was happy that Ghulam Qadir's elder brother had arrived from Kashmir. She was happier to know that her husband had made his brother agree to start a business within the hotel. She respected him so much it completely overwhelmed Ahmed. She even supervised the decoration of his showroom. But Ghulam Qadir was worried that he might tell her about Zeb. Perturbed, he walked restlessly from one hall of the hotel to the next and strolled in the lawns. Reeny perceived his anxiety. One night, she woke him up and asked him what was bothering him so much and why suddenly he had started to seek excuses to stay away from her. Ghulam Qadir ended up telling her the truth about his wife Zeb back home.

Reeny turned cold as ice. 'Qadir, what a lightning have you struck me with. Oh God, what treachery! You have wronged not only me but even your first wife. How could you do that, how?'

Qadir fell at her feet and said, 'I know that I have sinned. I have committed a crime which merits retribution beyond limits. But believe me that I did all this only to save your property. Otherwise—'

'Otherwise I would have had to beg for a living, isn't it?'

'Whatever I did, I did only to repay the new lease of life that you and Daddy gave me. Now I am torn in two halves, and each half bleeds. Please have mercy on me. Before we got married, I tried many times to tell you about Zeb, but I could not muster the courage; I did not want to shatter your dreams. Now I will accept whatever punishment you deem fit for me. I am ready to leave this house right now, and never return to show you my face. I will pass all my shares in the property to you, and prefer to get swallowed up by the same darkness from which you and Daddy once saved me.'

'You cannot get rid of me so easily. If I ever loved anyone in my life, Qadir, it is only you and you know this well. I have suffered so much in my life that I have no strength to endure any more. I don't want to steal anybody's rights. If there is even a little love for me in any recess of your heart, then you go to Kashmir and bring your wife and son along. I will love them like my own. This is the only retribution for your sins.'

Qadir rose, held Reeny to his chest, and started crying.

'Neither of us will cry any more. You go back to Kashmir, gather all the strewn fragments of your life and return to me.'

'I cheated you. I—'

'I am not going to listen to even one more word. I will arrange for your journey to Kashmir tomorrow.'

Having said this, she switched off the lights.

The night was no less painful than doomsday for Ghulam Qadir. From the next day, he started playing hide-and-seek with both Reeny and Ghulam Ahmed. Ghulam Ahmed could see that some kind of dispute was afoot between the husband and wife. They had their breakfast as well as dinner without speaking a word to each other. On the third day when they finished their breakfast, Reeny said to Ghulam Ahmed, 'I have an important issue to discuss with you. Please come to my office for a while.'

Ghulam Ahmed felt worried hearing those words from her. He wondered if she had changed her mind about allotting the showroom to him. He followed her to her office. Reeny opened the drawers and took out two air tickets. 'This is your ticket to Srinagar; you will fly back tomorrow.'

Ghulam Ahmed felt his ripe crop was being destroyed by a hailstorm. He looked intently at her face. But when she told him that there was also a return ticket from Srinagar, he found the nerve to ask her, 'But, why should I go to Srinagar so soon? I still have to settle accounts with a few clients.'

'You could do that after you return. You are not going alone; Qadir Sahib will go with you.'

'But—'

Reeny did not let him argue and hastened to tell him why she wanted Qadir to go with him. Ghulam Ahmed was taken aback and he understood why Ghulam Qadir had been so evasive recently. He said, 'That means Ghulam Qadir never told you that he is already married and with a son.'

Reeny did not want her husband's name to be tarnished in the eyes of his brother and covered up for him. 'Yes, he had told me everything about his life. Since our business is running smoothly now, he can bring Zeb and Bilal here.'

Ghulam Ahmed suddenly found himself looking at Reeny with new-found respect. 'You are really a very generous and progressive human being.'

'Please go and prepare for the journey.'

All this time Ghulam Qadir had been peeping into Reeny's office through the curtains. The moment Ghulam Ahmed came out, Reeny called Ghulam Qadir. 'Qadir, I have given Ahmed Sahib his tickets, and your ticket is with me. I have made him understand everything. Don't be scared, I did not tell him that you kept me in the dark. His presence will make it easier for you to face your family. The ticket for your onward journey is confirmed but the return ticket is open.'

Having said this, she disconnected the phone, and sat still like a wall. After a while, she heaved a long breath and stood up to go out. 'God help me,' she said.

Ghulam Ahmed's phone call stirred the languid atmosphere in Malla Khaliq's house. The family started making preparations to receive Ghulam Qadir.

The news revitalized Aziz Dyad who had been reduced to a mere skeleton. She could not stop crying. Malla Khaliq too felt that his old wounds were finally beginning to heal. He sent a message to Parveen and Abdul Razaq. Noor Mohammad was happy to see that his father was again making all the arrangements himself. Noor Mohammad's wife, though, was worried about Aziz Dyad. She phoned her son. 'Nisar Ahmed, when are you coming here? Amma is not able to contain herself, she is constantly shedding tears.'

'You need not worry; she is just overjoyed. Make her swallow a pill from the strip of yellow tablets. I will be there when I return from duty. Is Abba well?'

'He is absolutely fine. I wish you could have seen how he changed his phiran and sat on the prow of the boat as if Qadir was arriving today.'

Parveen arrived and the house was filled with more joy. All were happy except Bilal who was going through a sensitive age; he was in the third standard. He had grown so courteous that no child could beat him. He was doing extremely well at the Burn Hall School, always at number one in the junior group – not only in his exams, but also in boating, races and other games.

Festivity was in full swing in the house. Everyone except Bilal was rejoicing. He had taken a fish line and sat near the rear swamps. He had slowly lost all his love for his father. He remembered how he had ill-treated his mother over every small thing. He had been observing all these years how Zeb shed tears endlessly, sitting confined to her room.

Zeb herself did not look happy even when Parveen congratulated her for being the wife of a big hotelier. The wounds inflicted by Qadir were so deep that they could not heal so easily. But when she thought of Bilal's future, she would start nurturing new hopes.

Reeny spent the remaining days with Ghulam Qadir and Ghulam Ahmed buying gifts for their family. Yet Ghulam Qadir did not dare look at her in the eye or talk to her. But Reeny had finally come to terms with everything and was going about happily with a smile on her face as was her habit. On the day of Ghulam Qadir's departure for Srinagar, she gave him an envelope containing traveller's cheques. She sat calmly in a chair in front of him and spoke with perfect equanimity. 'I have a lot of sympathy for you. I can understand your predicament. But if you speak honestly and convince your family that Reeny is not a bad woman to usurp anybody's rights, I am sure that you will succeed in bringing Zeb and Bilal here. If this really happens, our life will start afresh. I will keep praying for your success. Now get up and prepare to leave.

I have got you cheques for more money than you had asked for. Who knows when you will be in need there?'

Ghulam Qadir was dumbstruck; he could not say more than 'I love you.'

Reeny gave him a sour smile and went out of the room.

Ghulam Qadir felt that his whole being had frozen. He did not know how he would face his family. He could not make out how he would persuade Zeb and Bilal to come to Goa. If Ghulam Ahmed had disclosed his secret, Qadir would not even be allowed to cross the threshold of his house. The thought made him shudder. He stood up abruptly. Ghulam Ahmed opened the door and came in. Qadir felt his presence as a glimmer of some hope. He made his elder brother sit near him and said, 'Have you completed your preparations?'

'But tell me why you are still so slow? It will get late.'

'Sit for a while, it won't take us more than half an hour to reach the airport.'

Ghulam Ahmed said, 'Okay, tell me what you want to say.'

'What can I say to you?' Ghulam Qadir heaved a sigh.

'Tell me frankly, what is wrong with you? You don't seem to be happy about going home.'

'What do you mean? I wish I could rip my chest apart to show you how restless my heart is to have the bliss of being under the soothing shade of Abba and Amma again. There is just one woe—'

'How will you tell them about your second marriage here, isn't it?' Ghulam Ahmed interrupted. Ghulam Qadir had no answer. 'Leave that to me,' Ahmed said.

But Ghulam Qadir was sharp enough to have understood his brother's ambitions during his stay in Goa. He hadn't changed. He had the same impetuosity, the same crookedness. He said to him, 'No, you don't say anything to anyone there. I will wait for the right time to tell them.'

'Yes, that would be proper.' Ghulam Ahmed was happy that he was saved from getting tangled in the situation. He wished to reach Srinagar in one dash and tell his father-in-law that he was no longer a worthless fellow; he had a big showroom in a grand hotel. He told Ghulam Qadir, 'Now stand up. Our Dastagir will help us out. Come on now.'

Reeny went to the airport to see them off. Before they proceeded towards the plane, Reeny took Ghulam Qadir aside and said to him, 'When you reach your homeland, don't forget that there is someone waiting for you here in Goa. I will be counting every second, keeping the lamp of hope lit, to see you back soon.'

Qadir moved closer to her, but Reeny turned to Ghulam Ahmed who was eagerly waiting for Qadir to come along.

Boarding was announced again and Ghulam Ahmed, carrying Ghulam Qadir's bag, ushered him inside. 'Come now. All the passengers are already seated in the plane.'

Ghulam Qadir looked back at Reeny. Her eyes were fixed on him.

Noor Mohammad and his son Doctor Nisar were already at Srinagar airport to receive them. Abdul Razaq was also on duty there, but he had taken leave for the day so that Ghulam Qadir wouldn't feel that he was there to browbeat him as a police officer. Narayan Joo also wanted to accompany Noor Mohammad to the airport, but Malla Khaliq held him back, saying, 'Is he someone superior to you that you should go garland him? If you had not got him released from the police station, he would have been languishing behind bars till date.'

Ghulam Qadir was a changed man. He wore very simple clothes so that his people wouldn't think he was being a show-off. Noor Mohammad forgot all his rancour and held him in a tight embrace. Both brothers wept like children. Doctor Nisar looked around and saw people watching them. He drew them aside. 'No more, Papa, no more crying now. Let us sit for a while.'

Ghulam Ahmed had gone to collect their baggage. He came

pushing the trolley. 'Let's move now. Everyone must be eagerly waiting at home.'

Noor Mohammad wiped his tears, stood up, and asked Ghulam Ahmed, 'Did you get everything?'

'I carried nothing, except this worn-out trunk. The two big attachés belong to Ghulam Qadir. Did you carry anything else, Ghulam Qadir?'

'Nothing more.'

'So you take the baggage out and I will get the car.'

Abdullah Shah's employees spread the news in the whole of Dalgate that Malla Khaliq's son Ghulam Qadir was now a wealthy hotelier in Goa. Even the boatmen knew that he was returning. They thronged to the ghat to see him. All of them knew him. Many of the younger ones were Qadir's childhood playmates. Everyone imagined what he would look like now. Seeing these folks sitting idly at the ghat, Sula Tancha rebuked them, 'You idlers, get to work. The people in your home might be waiting for a little rice to cook their meals.'

'You come here and see how he looks. Wearing an Arabian dress, he will look like the hero of the Arabian Nights,' a young boatman gave a repartee to Tancha.

'Yes, I know him. I remember all about him – he would not spare even one egg in my pen.'

'Come, come, I know that limping hen of yours always brooded,' the young boatman teased.

Sula Tancha would have chased him, if a boatman had not yelled – 'There comes Doctor Sahib's car!'

Hearing this, everyone stood up and jostled against one another to reach the steps of the ghat and wait for the car.

The excitement of seeing Ghulam Qadir petered out when the boatmen and their children saw him in a simple shirt and trousers. They were all the more disappointed when Ghulam Qadir met and hugged them one by one.

Malla Khaliq's old employee Subhan was waiting in his shikaarah at the ghat to carry them across.

Ghulam Qadir climbed down the steps to embrace him. Subhana was about to come out from his boat to welcome him, but Qadir said, 'Be careful, Subhan Chacha, you might slip.' But Subhana dashed out and held him to his chest. 'Are you well, Chacha? Are all your children well?'

'Now that you are back, the eclipse is over,' the boatman replied.

In the meantime, Ghulam Ahmed and Doctor Nisar put the baggage in the shikaarah. Ghulam Ahmed said to Subhana, 'It is enough for now. You may express your love later at home.'

Subhana turned towards the houseboats. When they left, the boatmen in the crowd started gossiping about Qadir. Seeing Qadir's demeanour, they could not believe that he was now a big hotelier. Sula Tancha, in particular, refused to believe it because Qadir had not met him even after seeing him there. 'Why are you adamant to make your throats soar? Maybe he has a small eatery somewhere, and has come here to show off.'

A vendor who was in the bevy heard him and said, in order to silence him, 'Tancha, you are greying now, and yet you do not give up your envy.' All the boatmen guffawed when Sula Tancha could not even utter a word in response.

Everyone except Malla Khaliq, Bilal, Zeb and Aziz Dyad were standing at the isle waiting to receive Ghulam Qadir. The moment Subhana fastened the boat to the bank, Parveen ran down the steps barefoot. Ghulam Qadir jumped out of the boat and hugged his sister. Mukhta said, almost shouting, 'Come, come! He kept us waiting till we lost our eyesight, and now he is here to show off his love.'

This made Ghulam Qadir realize his guilt. He let Parveen go and ascended the steps of the ghat. Zoon advanced towards him and said, 'Don't be dismayed. This sister-in-law of yours has tied so many votive cloths for your safe return.' Ghulam Qadir went and held Mukhta's hands in his, kissed them and said falteringly, 'Bhabi, please forgive me for I have sinned against all of you.' Mukhta could no longer hold herself back and she wept aloud. 'Do not shed your tears for this worthless fellow,' he said to her.

Noor Mohammad and Ghulam Ahmed came near them. Noor Mohammad said to his wife, 'Are you going to settle all your grudges here in the open? Let's go inside; Amma is waiting for him.'

'Where is Abba?'

'He is in the drawing room in Gul. Amma is also there.'

Doctor Nisar asked Subhan to take the two big attachés to Ghulam Qadir's room, and the third one to Ghulam Ahmed's. Then he went to houseboat Gul.

The atmosphere in the houseboat was grim. Ghulam Qadir sat holding his father's feet, and Malla Khaliq sat motionless with his eyes closed. Aziz Dyad did not have the courage to break the silence. Finally Narayan Joo sat beside Malla Khaliq. Keeping his hand on his shoulder, he said to him, 'How long will you remain silent? God pardons even the most heinous crimes when the sinner repents.' But Malla Khaliq was unmoved. Aziz Dyad scolded him, 'Open your eyes and see how all of us here are begging for your pardon on his behalf.'

'Abba, if you don't want to absolve my sins I will go back right now,' Ghulam Qadir said.

Tears trickled out through Malla Khaliq's closed eyes. Using a corner of her headcloth, Aziz Dyad wiped the tears from his face, and said, 'This is quite childish of you.'

'Let him lighten his heart,' Narayan Joo said. Ghulam Qadir could not stop himself and he embraced his father and started crying. Finally Malla Khaliq, after all a father, touched Ghulam Qadir's back and addressed Narayan Joo, in his typical English, 'See the return of the prodigal son.'

'The prodigal son had returned after losing everything and failing in every game of life, but this one has returned after winning and making an honest man of himself. Now let us all get ready, and go get the blessing of Dastagir Sahib. I also tied a votive thread at the Devi's shrine. I will go untie it.'

'Lala Sahib, it is already very late today, we will go there tomorrow before dawn,' Noor Mohammad suggested.

When the ice had been broken, the festivities started. The news spread among all the neighbours, and all of them thronged on the isle. Everyone congratulated Malla Khaliq and Aziz Dyad and shook hands with Ghulam Qadir. Many rejoiced in his success, but many more were consumed by an unexpressed jealousy, yet they feigned joy and took part in the celebrations.

Amidst all this, no one remembered Zeb and Bilal, who were in their room, away from all the festivities. Bilal was enraged and said to his mother, 'If you are keen to go, you can go see him. I will never go to his house; never shall I leave my Abba and my Ammi.' Zeb crouched in a corner of the room and vented all her anger. 'Why are you driving me crazy? He has yet to ask us to go back with him.'

'This has been the only subject of discussion here in the house for the last few days. I have told Abba that I will never go with *him*.'

'And what did he say?'

'He smiled and then cried. He will also miss me if I go along with *him* – that owner of a hotel.'

'No, this does not suit you; he is after all your father.'

'I don't consider him my father and I have no qualms in admitting this to everyone.' Having said this, Bilal was about to go out, but Zeb closed the door and made him sit. 'All of Gagribal has assembled there. What will they say?'

Bilal sat down again but his anger was not abated. He started pulling out hairs from the felt mat.

'What did that mat do to you? If you want to pull out somebody's hair, pull out mine.'

Bilal stopped. He nestled close to his mother and said, 'Don't say that, Mummy.'

The two would have remained in the room for much longer, but Parveen came looking for them.

'What are you doing here? Come out. Abba wants you there.' She switched the light on.

'Where is Abba?'

'He is in Gul. Now come out, because everyone has left and only our family remains.'

'No, I am not going there. Take Mummy.' Bilal sulked and went to the inner room.

'He will follow you, just come out.'

Parveen went to the door of the inner room and said to Bilal, 'Come out and see pictures of your Papa's hotel.'

'Didn't I tell you I am not coming?'

After much persuasion, Parveen made Zeb change her phiran. With her head lowered, she shyly followed Parveen to houseboat Gul.

There in the drawing room Ghulam Ahmed had set up a full exhibition of advertisement posters and post cards of Hotel Sea Waves. Like a typical salesman, he went on praising every aspect of the hotel. The moment Parveen led Zeb in, the air in the room froze again. Aziz Dyad stood up and made Zeb sit beside her. Ghulam Qadir was drenched in sweat. He could not even raise his eyes to look at her. Ghulam Ahmed perceived there was too much tension in the air. He turned to his wife and said, 'See the gorgeous showroom Ghulam Qadir has allotted to us in his hotel. You go and show it to your father who never considers anyone his peer.'

Malla Khaliq got irritated and said to him, 'Now keep this office closed for some time. Let us talk first and then you can show off your cleverness.'

Ghulam Ahmed was struck mute and he hastily collected the photographs.

'Where is Bilal?' Malla Khaliq asked.

'He must be here somewhere,' Parveen replied on behalf of Zeb.

Aziz Dyad naively said, 'He has been keeping to himself for the last few days, I don't know why.'

Noor Mohammad tactfully said, 'He had to complete so much school work. Should he constantly sit in your lap?'

Malla Khaliq cast a glance at Zeb who sat limply behind Aziz Dyad looking down. 'My dear daughter, all of us have forgiven him, not because he is now a wealthy person, but because he has sought absolution for all his sins and has returned to the right path. You too may forgive him now. God says that if a wrongdoer finally returns to the righteous path and entreats for forgiveness, he should be forgiven. I can only advise this for the sake of your happiness.'

'Do you think she needs to be told all this? She is such a wise girl after all. Do not worry, my daughter, by Dastagir's grace, our withered garden is in bloom again. Now get up, it is already late. We will have dinner together, as a family. Or should I send you your plates here?'

'No, Amma. Let us eat together, just as we did in the old days,' Ghulam Qadir said, with an extra stress on 'together' so that everyone felt that he was one them again.

Malla Khaliq said to Parveen, 'What time will Abdul Razaq get here?'

'Abba, he had to leave for Handawara for something urgent.'

'That is why he was not at the airport. Ama Lala had told me that his duty is at the airport, and I wished to see him there. I am keen to see how nice he looks in a police officer's uniform,' Ghulam Qadir said, looking affectionately at Parveen.

Aziz Dyad said, 'He looks just like a hero, a real hero.'

'When is he to return from Handawara? I owe many apologies to him as well. I have never talked to him in a friendly manner.'

'Now you may make it up to him by inviting him to Goa.'

'Why should he travel so far? I will do all I can here in Srinagar; you just watch.'

Enjoying this warm conversation, they moved over to the living room. While walking over, Ghulam Qadir once, just once, dared to raise his eyes towards Zeb. Zeb hurriedly walked ahead of them to the kitchen. All of them sat in the living room to have dinner as they used to in the good old days.

There was a casual reference to Doctor Nisar's marriage. The father of the bride had told them that the couple would stay in Kashmir and not go to Dubai.

Malla Khaliq was reassured that his family would not disintegrate now. Ghulam Qadir was consciously labouring to talk as genially as he had in the earlier days, but whenever he glanced at Zeb, he stammered and lost his nerve.

Noor Mohammad had succeeded in persuading Bilal to come out to have dinner with the family. Sitting beside Malla Khaliq, he sat quietly, having his food. Seeing Bilal's cold detachment, Qadir could not find the courage to talk to his son. Aziz Dyad wished that he had sat beside his father, but Malla Khaliq cued her to be quiet. He knew how angry Bilal was with his father. Bilal hurriedly finished his food and left the room.

Among all of them Zeb was most anxious about Bilal. She knew well that Bilal was not like other boys his age, to get mollified with candies and toys. She went after Bilal to her room, but he had already taken his bag of books and tiptoed to his grandfather's room. Zeb looked at Ghulam Qadir's attachés and she shivered. The presence of those attachés there indicated that he would soon come to her room to sleep.

Zeb had lost all her nerve since she heard about his life in Goa. On the one hand she was very happy that he was finally settled and successful, but on the other hand, all her old bruises had starting aching afresh. When Ghulam Ahmed had phoned that he was coming along with Ghulam Qadir, the old wounds had started bleeding again. Then the terrifying thought that her love who had deserted her would come and lay claim her again, sent tremors up her spine. 'Oh my God! A fresh ordeal!' she whispered.

She heard Ghulam Ahmed and Noor Mohammad outside the room. Noor Mohammad was urging Ghulam Qadir to enter his room, and Ghulam Ahmed boosted his courage.

'Noor Sahib, he has come here to take Zeb and Bilal along, why should he hesitate to enter his own room?'

'Houseboat Gul is empty, I will sleep there for the night and see what can be done tomorrow,' Ghulam Qadir insisted.

Noor Mohammad roared at him, 'What nonsense do you talk? If Abba comes to know about it, he will never forgive you.'

'But ... but I don't know how to face my wife.'

'Go ahead, enter the room and you will find the nerve. Poor Zeb must be in a vortex of anxiety right now. You go in and save her, and make her have faith in you once again.'

Ghulam Ahmed shoved the door ajar with his foot. Ghulam Qadir saw Zeb glued to the wall. He also stood still like a statue at the door. Both his brothers went to their rooms. He had no option but to walk in. He calmly shut the door, and languidly walked in and sat down on the floor. Zeb quivered, even more than she had on her nuptial night. As if some stranger had broken into her room.

Outside, the wind was blowing through the thicket of willows. Apart from that all was still and silent. This quiet frightened her all the more. Every second seemed as heavy as a rock pressing upon her. Ghulam Qadir also groped for words in vacuum for some way to open the conversation. When he did not utter a word, Zeb stood up and was about to go away to the inner chamber. But Ghulam Qadir held her hand. He slowly pulled her down and made her sit beside him. 'Even if I get as many as ten rebirths to beg for forgiveness, I will still be short of time.'

Zeb sat silently. The venom Ghulam Qadir had filled in her life made every word feel hollow. She had no trust in him now. She lost track of time. Ghulam Qadir continued to narrate all his ordeals to her. She sat still like a lump of mud. Finally when Ghulam Qadir could no more bear her silence, he held her hand in his. 'Why don't you say something? Why don't you unleash all your repressed wrath on me? Zeb, say something. If you don't fogive me, what does anyone else's forgiveness mean to me? I will die while living.'

'How can one who is dead in life, forgive the other? You might think that using the money you've been sending, I could cross this fierce ocean of life. All your money is safely placed in the almirah. I would have not even touched it, had Abba not been obstinate. In order to make him happy, I used to take it from him and keep it safely in the almirah. Let my Dastagir make you roll in wealth which made you desert me and everyone in your family. You won all that you desired, but there is one who has lost everything in the bargain. Now what can come out of this idle talk?'

'I know well that I have been very cruel to you, yet I entreat you to grant me just one chance, and I will repay all that I owe you.'

'When there is no claim, what is all this talk of owing and repaying? You should sleep now; you must be tired. I have made your bed in the adjoining room. Will you go or shall I go out and lie down in the veranda?'

When Qadir did not show any signs of moving, Zeb got up and was about to walk out of the room, but Qadir stopped her saying, 'All right, let it be so. But before going to the other room, please understand that during all the time I was trying desperately to find some escape from the whirlpool of my destiny, there was hardly any moment when you and Bilal were not in my heart. Nobody can escape the forces of destiny which simply left me wounded. Now the only salve I care for is you. If you forgive me, I will be freed from this unrelenting perdition.'

Qadir waited, but when Zeb did not say anything, he went into the inner chamber. She stood up and switched the light off. They spent the night tossing and turning in separate rooms.

Zeb inwardly cursed herself for being so harsh because even though he had come back after a very long time, he had still come back to her. She reasoned that if he had not cared about her and Bilal, he would not have sent so much money every month. But the hurt that Qadir had inflicted on her during his absence could not be easily forgotten. The thought made her get up abruptly, and she moved closer to the door of the inner chamber and peeped in through the rent.

Qadir sat still near the window, staring into the dark. For a long time, Zeb continued to gaze at him, and waited to see when he would take a cigarette out of his pocket. But when he did not light up, she was convinced that he had changed. After some time, Qadir got up and moved towards the door. Zeb dashed to her bed and wrapped herself up in the quilt. Qadir also peeped through the rent. Zeb steadied her breathing. When Qadir was sure that she was fast asleep, he returned to the window. He prayed that Ghulam Ahmed would not spill the secret about Reeny until they went back to Goa with Zeb and Bilal.

He had faith in Reeny's goodness and generosity. He consoled himself that Reeny would surely win over Zeb's heart; then Abba and Dyad and the rest of the family would also accept the truth. Money covers all flaws after all, he thought.

With the first crowing of the cockerel, Ghulam Qadir came out of the room and went to the isle after having a wash. Malla Khaliq was already there as if waiting for him. Ghulam Qadir said salaam and sat down near him in the boat. Subhan had already decked the boat with cushions. God had perhaps intimated to him that Ghulam Qadir might go along with his father to the dargah. Noor Mohammad came in another boat from the opposite direction; he placed a big basket full of oven-fresh bread on the prow of Malla Khaliq's boat and then sat down beside him. Aziz Dyad and Mukhta had also woken early and they came out to the isle to see them off and pray for the fulfilment of their wish. Aziz Dyad stayed there, watching them and praying for them until they were out of sight. Then she returned to the kitchen where Mukhta had already busied herself with the cooking. She told Mukhta, 'You please attend to the tea. I will go to wake Zoon, or she will remain in bed till the sun rises.'

'Let her sleep a little more. Ama Lala has returned to her after such a long time.'

'So please hurry. I will cut the vegetables. I hope they return soon, we will have a lot of visitors today. I hope Abdul Razaq also returns from Handwara today. He alone is yet to meet Ghulam Qadir,' Aziz Dyad said to Mukhta.

'I think he has not gone to Handwara or anywhere else. He must be waiting for Parveen's call. She might have wanted to assess Ghulam Qadir's behaviour first,' Mukhta replied.

'He is after all a police officer. He will come after assessing everything.' Parveen came in.

Aziz Dyad laughed and said, 'Now keep this wit to yourself; you cannot compete with him in prudence.'

'Did you realize this now? Abba had recognized it long ago, but all of you doubted him.'

Aziz Dyad was at a loss and so she deviated from the issue by throwing away the potato in her hand and cursing the vegetable vendor, 'Damn these potatoes, not a single one is good.'

Mukhta smiled mischievously.

The festivities were in full swing at Malla Khaliq's house. In the afternoon, Narayan Joo brought Abdul Razaq with him. Razaq took the path behind the willows and entered the kitchen. He changed, and then went to his mother-in-law. In the meantime, Parveen came with a tray containing tea and cookies for Narayan Joo. Abdul Razaq received the tray from her. His mother-in-law said to him, 'Oh no. What is all this? Why should you take the trouble?'

'Ghulam Qadir Sahib may also be there. Let me serve him his tea as I once used to.'

'Parveen, take this tray away from his hands. There are outsiders in the room.'

'He is not going to agree.'

Abdul Razaq did not pay any heed to what they said. He went ahead. Like a well-trained waiter, he sought permission before stepping in. It was Ghulam Qadir who looked at him first and he was stunned for a moment before he recognized Abdul Razaq. He stood up and hurried to take the tray from his hands. He passed the tray to Ghulam Ahmed, who felt embarassed to see Abdul Razaq walk in like a waiter. Ghulam Qadir stretched his arms towards Abdul Razaq.

Malla Khaliq glanced at Narayan Joo. He smiled and said, 'The winter is finally over and the snow has thawed. Let us go to Badamwari to enjoy the almond blossoms.'

'There is time. Besides, where is that Badamwari of yore, and those verdant almond trees? The greed of our people has ruined every good thing.'

'Let them go to hell. Enjoy this spring in your own family.'

Ghulam Qadir made Abdul Razaq sit beside him. Bilal watched the scene unfold, hidden behind a curtain in the room. He jumped into the rear end of the houseboat and capered to the kitchen. He held Parveen's hand and said to her, 'Come on, I will show you how he hugged Abdul Razaq and made him sit beside him.'

'Who do you mean?' Aziz Dyad knew who he was talking about, yet she wanted him Bilal to take his father's name.

Bilal got annoyed at this and said, 'It is all right, don't come. Come on, Mummy, you come.'

Parveen stood up and followed him out of the kitchen.

It took some more days for the ice to thaw completely. And then one day, when everyone had assembled after dinner, Ghulam Qadir asked for his attachés. He unlocked them and took out all the presents that he and Reeny had bought. Everyone was happy and prayed for the health and wealth of Ghulam Qadir. Bilal, however, was still sulking a little. He stood up and went out to sit at the prow. Ghulam Qadir watched him go out, his hand frozen over Bilal's gift. Aziz Dyad said to Noor Mohammad, 'You please see where Bilal is hiding.'

Ghulam Qadir sighed and said, 'He is yet to trust me.'

'He will surely trust you when he sees what his father has got for him.' Ghulam Ahmed tried to sound witty, but when he glanced at his father, he was struck dumb. Malla Khaliq watched Bilal through the window. He was crouching in a corner as if trying to hide himself from his own eyes. Having given all the gifts, Qadir locked the attachés and handed the keys to Zeb.

'What am I to do with these keys?' Zeb said to Aziz Dyad loud enough for Ghulam Qadir to hear.

'You can use them to pack your things. You keep the keys please. The time of your departure is fast approaching.'

The topic of Zeb and Bilal going along with Ghulam Qadir to Goa followed. Noor Mohammad asked Narayan Joo, 'Lala Sahib, are their tickets confirmed?'

'I have booked them for coming Monday. Ghulam Qadir insisted on Sunday, but as per my faith one should not travel south on Sundays.'

Malla Khaliq cast an affectionate look at his friend and said to his own sons, 'Do you see how much he cares for you?'

'After all they are like his own sons,' Aziz Dyad said, looking at Narayan Joo. In his eyes she could see his love for their family.

Ghulam Qadir and Noor Mohammad saw him off at the ghat. Then Noor Mohammad returned to houseboat Gul. Ghulam Qadir saw Bilal sitting alone in a corner. He went and sat down beside him. Malla Khaliq and Aziz Dyad watched them through the window. Malla Khaliq held his wife's hand and she cast a hopeful glance at him. Her face brightened and tears sparkled in her eyes.

Malla Khaliq was hopeful that Bilal's ties with his father would soon revive.

Qadir cautiously placed his hand on Bilal's shoulder, and said, 'My dear son, you alone are Abba's true disciple. When everyone in the family including your mother has forgiven me, why won't you?'

Bilal turned to him, with all the pent-up bitterness rushing to his fiery eyes, and said, 'Can my forgiving you return all those years to my mother that she spent weeping?'

'I will try to return every moment to her.'

'I can never forgive you.'

'Does that mean there is no relationship between you and me?'

'You are my father. Who can deny that, but—' Overcome with emotion, Bilal stood up and walked away. Qadir's hopes petered out, yet he felt proud that his son who was a babbling toddler when he had deserted him was now almost a grown-up.

Later that night, when Ghulam Qadir started describing Goa to Zeb, she said to him, 'What is so spectacular about this place you own in Goa, which you and Ama Lala are constantly bragging about? What does your wealth mean to me if Bilal does not accompany me there? You know I cannot live without him. You may talk to Abba for only he can make him agree to go there.' Having said all this, Zeb went into the inner chamber to sleep.

Even sleeping in the same room could not give Ghulam Qadir the courage to move closer to her.

The bitter secret that he was hiding in his heart made him numb. He sat by the window all night.

Bilal finally agreed to go to Goa. But he placed a condition that he would return to Kashmir after a month or so. Malla Khaliq was glad at this decision; it was impossible for him to survive without his grandson.

Ghulam Qadir started preparing for the journey. He asked Ghulam Ahmed to go to Narayan Joo's office to confirm four tickets for them. Ghulam Ahmed was very excited that he would soon be in Goa to start his new business. But he was plagued by the worry that if Qadir did not reveal the secret of his second marriage before going with Zeb and Bilal, Malla Khaliq would burn him alive for his deceit.

This was the first thing that Ghulam Ahmed had kept from his wife and this was making him very restless. One day before his onward journey, he was caught in a position that helped him relieve himself of the burden. He seemed nervous while packing. His wife noticed this and after her persistent probing, he revealed the cause of his predicament. Zoon looked as if she had been struck by a thunderbolt. 'How cruel of you! Don't you feel ashamed of yourself for cheating on that poor woman who has suffered so long? Your heart has turned into stone!'

'Please don't shout; listen to me first. If I wanted to cheat on Zeb, why would I tell you? I was only worried about Amma. If I had told her about this, she would have died.'

'Do you think she is going to jump for joy whenever she comes to know? Do you still want to hide this from Abba and Amma?'

'Do I have another option? I swear by Allah that Qadir promised me that he would reveal everything about himself to Abba when he reached Kashmir.'

'If he had done so, do you think Abba would have agreed to send Zeb and Bilal with him?'

'What do you suggest I do?'

'What can I suggest now? If you want to save yourself, you go and tell Abba. If you don't have the guts, I will tell him. I don't want to shoulder the sin of keeping Zeb in the dark.'

In the evening, when the entire family was sitting together, Aziz Dyad made Zeb sit close to her on one side and Ghulam Qadir on the other. She held Qadir's hand and said to him, 'Now, my son, forget all that has happened. Promise me that you will make it up to this daughter of mine.'

Qadir was drenched in sweat. He was looking for the right words, when Zoon turned to her father-in-law. 'Abba, has Qadir really told you all about his life in Goa?'

Qadir felt his soul draining out of his body. Malla Khaliq asked Zoon, 'Why do you ask me this?'

'You first tell me if he has told you everything.'

Ghulam Ahmed trembled, but tried to end the issue. 'Of course, he must have told Abba everything.'

'Has he told him then that he married the woman with whom he is running the hotel?'

Zoon's pronouncement struck the family like lightning. Malla Khaliq asked Qadir, 'Is she right?'

Qadir bowed his head and remained silent. Malla Khaliq turned to Ghulam Ahmed. 'You tell me, is it true?' He also remained silent, but Zoon was quick to take her husband's side. 'What can he tell you? Qadir has strictly told him not to say anything; he had promised to tell you everything himself. But when Qadir did not, he told me.'

Zeb stood up and dashed out of the room. Bilal slowly stood

up, turned towards Malla Khaliq, and said in a voice quivering with rage, 'I knew this swindler came here only to destroy us further.'

Malla Khaliq stood up, thundering over everyone in his rage and, catching hold of Qadir by his arm, dragged him to the door, saying, 'Get out, you charlatan. Get out of my house without wasting another second.'

Noor Mohammad intervened. 'For God's sake, Qadir, have mercy on us. Please release us from the burden of your wrongdoings.'

Malla Khaliq looked as if some giant spirit possessed him. His grip on Qadir's arm was as firm as steel. He dragged him out into the open on the isle. Seeing this fight, Aziz Dyad fainted. Zoon and Mukhta ran to make her drink a little water. Ghulam Ahmed remained cowering in a corner.

Noor Mohammad entreated his father.

'Abba, leave him now and go in. I will kick him out right now. Amma is ill. Please go in. Please.'

He called Subhana, who came running. 'Take out the shikaarah immediately and drop this man at the ghat across.'

Malla Khaliq loosened his grip on Qadir and sat down. Qadir was about to say something, but Noor Mohammad held him back and said, 'For God's sake, let us live in peace. Don't you see what you have done?' He forced his father to go in.

Qadir stood all alone on the isle. There had been a power failure and the house lay pitch dark. He heard the splashes of oaring; Subhan had come with the shikaarah. Qadir once again looked at his room, and then started climbing down the steps of the ghat. He slipped and was about to fall into the waters, but Subhana held him just in time. He had yet to turn the prow of the boat when the sound of someone coming over the planks was heard. It was Bilal, carrying the two attachés that Qadir had brought. He stepped down the stairs and flung the attachés at Qadir. One of the boxes opened and all the gifts Qadir had brought were strewn about the boat.

'Take all this stuff along, you may need them there for your Mem and your children?' Bilal said with all the contempt he could muster.

Subhan pushed the boat ahead. Qadir stared at the silhouette of his son, who disappeared into the darkness without looking back.

Having reached the Boulevard, Qadir went up the ghat. 'Subhan Joo, please pass the two attachés to me.'

Subhan lifted the two attachés and ascended the steps. Qadir took out a bundle of notes and pushed it into the pocket of Subhan's phiran. He could not control himself, and held Qadir in a hug and cried. Qadir who was already crying said, 'Not a single soul in the whole family bothered to think where I would go in the middle of this dark night. Why should you shed tears? Go back and take care.' He crossed the road and walked into Hotel Asia Brown.

The family was awake for the entire night grappling with the tragedy that had befallen them. Noor Mohammad kept sitting near his parents, who lay in bed, eyes wide open and hurting. He thought about people coming to know; his family would have no place to hide.

Bilal sat with his mother. 'And you were looking out for him, the swindler! I can't believe you even tried to kindle love for him in my heart!'

Zeb's heart had turned into stone. She sat with her eyes closed and did not utter a word. Bilal was fuming with rage, but she did not try to douse the fire. When she remained unmoving, Bilal got frightened. He touched her shoulder and said, 'Mummy, why don't you say something? Mummy, just look at me, open your eyes. I am with you. Your son. I will go on to become a much bigger businessman than him. You just wait and watch. Abba is here. We should not lose hope. Mummy, open your eyes.'

Zeb opened her eyes and cast a long, empty glance at his face. Then she hugged him. She said to him with resolve, 'My darling son, I will not wail and die. We will gain nothing by cursing him and calling him names. I was just praying to Allah to show the right path to the person who has lost his way.'

Bilal took both his mother's hands in his and said, 'You are great, Mummy, bravest of all.'

'Do you know where I am drawing this courage from? You and those books you get for me from the library. You should not worry about me. You just watch how I start a new life now.' Zeb's face was glowing like fire.

At Goa airport, Reeny stood waiting to see if Ghulam Ahmed would come out with Zeb and Bilal. But when all the passengers came into the lounge, she sank in the nearest chair. Ghulam Qadir came, his eyes brimming with tears. Reeny looked at him, 'What happened?'

Ghulam Qadir took her hand and said, 'I have lost, Reeny.'

The talk about Qadir's going back to Goa in such unpleasant circumstances grew stale in Srinagar. But no matter how old the news became, it still stayed fresh in the minds of Ghulam Ahmed, Malla Khaliq and Aziz Dyad. Ghulam Ahmed felt all his plans had been washed away. As for Malla Khaliq and Aziz Dyad, there was a cindering brazier before them in the form of Zeb.

Ghulam Ahmed was advised by his wife to lie low for some time.

Seeing Aziz's condition, Malla Khaliq said to Noor Mohammad, 'You go and tell Narayan Joo all that has happened here. He might give us some advice.'

'Abba, Lala Sahib is in Kolahoi with tourists.'

'Then whom can we consult?'

Aziz Dyad whispered to her husband, 'What is there now to consult about? We must first of all settle the issue of Zeb. She has been confined to her room all these days.'

'Amma is right,' Noor Mohammad seconded his mother. 'We can consult Lala Sahib later on, for we must first see to Zeb. Who knows what condition she is in?'

This enraged Malla Khaliq. 'Do you think your father was waiting to comply with your orders? I already went to her room. She deserves praise for the way she is bravely handling this situation. Instead of me consoling her, she was comforting me! "Abba, forgive him," she said to me. She has somehow made Bilal also accept the reality. He is still angry but not as furious as he was.'

'That is fine, but this young girl has a long life ahead of her. How can your comforting words do her any good?' Aziz Dyad asked.

It was finally decided that they would go together to Zeb's room. When Zeb saw her family walking towards her room, she got scared. She quickly went to the inner chamber where Bilal was studying. She said to him in panic, 'Bilal, something has happened. Everyone is coming here. I am afraid if your father—'

Bilal did not wait for her to complete her sentence and went out. Malla Khaliq, Aziz Dyad and Noor Mohammad entered her room. Bilal asked his grandfather, 'Abba, is all well?'

'Yes, all is well. Where is my daughter, Zeb?'

Zeb came out and said salaam to Malla Khaliq.

'Let's sit down, my daughter.'

All four of them sat down on the floor. Zoon and Mukhta also came to see what was happening. Ghulam Ahmed had no more courage to interfere in any way. There was complete silence in the room and everyone waited for Malla Khaliq to begin. It was Aziz Dyad who broke the silence.

'My dear daughter, this Abba of yours has been restless like a live fish in a frying pan for the last few days. He is worried about how you are going to spend your life all alone.'

'I have reached the conclusion that I will get you divorced from our worthless son so that you can start a new life.' Malla Khaliq tried to shorten the conversation. Noor Mohammad continued with his father's suggestion. 'And our jurisprudence also grants this.'

Zeb bowed her head. Silence filled the room as everyone waited to hear what she would say. She finally said to her son Bilal, 'Do you understand what Abba and Amma are suggesting?'

Bilal nodded.

'And what do you say?'

'What could I say? Only you must take the decision.'

'That means you also want me to leave this house?' she asked Bilal. Malla Khaliq and Aziz Dyad felt hurt by her words.

'My daughter, who would ever think like that over here? We are all concerned about your well-being as we are of Parveen's. I need your consent to give you freedom from that trickster. I will see your palanquin off from this house as we did that of Parveen.'

'Please remember, Abba, that it will not be my palanquin leaving this house but my coffin. It will be my final farewell and it will arrive only after I have seen all your grandchildren grown up to my heart's content. This is my final word. But in case I am a burden to anyone in this house, I will arrange for my own departure. Abba, you have taught my Bilal to stand on his own feet, and he in turn has taught me the same. You need not worry about me. I will engage myself in such work that will bring you a good name.'

Bilal hugged his mother and said, 'You are really great, Mummy!'

Aziz Dyad and Zoon stood dumbfounded. Malla Khaliq sat in front of Zeb and Bilal. 'Nobody will talk about this any more.'

Narayan Joo came to know about Qadir when he returned from the Kolahoi glaciers after four days along with a party from Sweden. When Malla Khaliq narrated his woes to him, his heart grew heavy. He held his friend's hand tight and said, 'But this marriage was no promise to the Mother of the Universe! I will go tomorrow to Goa and set him free from that witch!'

Noor Mohammad said, 'When our own blood is bad, how can we blame others?'

This emboldened Ghulam Ahmed to speak up. He said, 'It isn't Reeny's fault. Qadir never told her that he was already married.'

Any word from Ghulam Ahmed was unbearable for Malla Khaliq. 'Who asked you to interfere in this matter?'

'Maybe what Ahmed says is true,' Narayan Joo said.

'Even if I am very evil, God is always watchful. She is very righteous and gentle.'

This enraged Malla Khaliq further. 'Don't you hear me? I am telling you to keep quiet. I know why you are pleading her case. You might have an eye on her wealth.'

Ghulam Ahmed stood up in fury and said before leaving, 'Will you ever trust me?'

Narayan Joo tried to pacify Malla Khaliq. 'You are taking out all your frustration on him when the focus of the problem lies somewhere else. Please be calm and listen to me. If you allow me, I can take Noor Mohammad along and go to Goa to verify the truth.'

'No, not at all. He is dead to me now.'

'But, my dear friend, think of poor Zeb.'

'I will take care of that.'

Reeny's behaviour was changing. She had become irritable and rebuked her employees over small things. All of them were amazed to see this change in her. Then one day when she was rude with the general manager of the hotel, Qadir entered her office, slammed the door and made his displeasure known for the first time. 'If you are angry with me, which you have every right to be, please take it out on me. Why are you being so cruel to these poor chaps? They might leave us one by one.'

'Let them go to hell. And don't teach me how to deal with my staff.'

'Reeny, please, have mercy on me. I have been abandoned by the whole world, just for one mistake. Oh God, grant me a release from this world! Reeny, I did all this only for you, for your future.'

'Yes, yes. You cared so much for me that you did not tell me about your past. Who knows how many more secrets you have kept hidden from me?'

'Please trust me. I have told you everything. I swear by the Almighty, that except for Zeb and Bilal, I have given you an account of every second of my life. Now you have not even given me a chance to say what happened in Kashmir.'

'Do you think I should have laid my head at your feet? Qadir, tell me how did your family treat you?'

'When they came to know that I had married a second time, they simply threw me out of the house at midnight. My son Bilal hurled all the gifts in my face which you had bought for all of them. Now, I am a forlorn, dejected and broken person who has come back to you. Don't cast me away, Reeny. If you also kick me out, where will I go?'

'This house, this hotel, and the whole estate belong to you. How can I force you to leave when I myself am a hapless woman?' She held the corner of the table for support. Her hands shivered. She somehow managed to sit down on the sofa, and started crying. Qadir gathered courage and sat beside her. He tried to hold her hand but Reeny withdrew. 'Don't touch me.'

'All right, if I have lost even the right to touch your hand, I am finished.'

Reeny muttered while crying, 'How can he understand that I was eagerly waiting for him to bring his wife and son here. I have been waiting and praying desperately for good news from his family. The two brothers might have made their parents believe that Reeny is a wicked woman. But she is not a home-breaker. She is blameless in all that happened. How do I tell this double-dealer now that I am going to be the mother of his child? What is the point of telling him? All my dreams have been shattered.'

Ghulam Qadir froze. For a long time he could not decide whether to go crazy with joy or lament over his destiny.

Reeny continued wailing. 'This stone-hearted person only wants to know where he can go if I kick him out. Now the forces of the Universe have left me in such a fix that I cannot sever relations with him, even if I wanted to.'

Ghulam Qadir could not hold his feelings back and he held

Reeny close to his chest. She was shivering terribly. Then she became still. They hardly knew how long they remained there like that.

After staying in Goa for a fortnight, Reeny left for Daman to manage Hotel Solace.

Returning to Daman was an excuse to be away from Ghulam Qadir for some time. She wanted to ascertain if she still loved Ghulam Qadir as much as she had before the unravelling of his secret. But Ghulam Qadir was worried that Reeny might divorce him. This fear of being deserted by all his loved ones started breaking him bit by bit.

Malla Khaliq and his family were gradually coming out of their distress and their life was changing.

Zeb had got a new lease of life. She decided to complete her education that she had left halfway. Malla Khaliq encouraged her even more than Bilal.

Ghulam Ahmed alone remained brooding. On the one hand, he was harassed so much by Abdullah Shah for debts that he did not dare pass through Dalgate, and on the other hand, his own father-in-law persistently avoided him. Seeing the changes in the destinies of others, he felt tormented. He wished to go to Goa, prostrate at Ghulam Qadir's feet and beg for his forgiveness. He was sure that he would forgive him and give him the showroom, decked with carpets. But he was at a loss for how to seek Malla Khaliq's permission to go.

With every passing day, pressure from Abdullah Shah's increased and finally one day he approached Malla Khaliq. With folded hands, he said to him, 'No one can equal you in kindness, gentleness, and uprightness. Keeping this in view, I have come to entreat you to let Ghulam Ahmed go to Goa, settle all the accounts there and bring my carpets back.'

Malla Khaliq who was already furious with Ghulam Ahmed, was about yell at Abdullah Shah, but the latter was shrewd enough to interrupt him. 'I know all about your family. But try to understand; Ghulam Ahmed also stands marooned in a storm. I pity him. If he did not have a cash crunch, why would he have gone to Goa?'

'You know, Abdullah Shah, I am not interested in your personal problems. Who am I to stop Ghulam Ahmed from going anywhere? If he thinks it's right for him to go to Goa, let him go.'

'That is enough for me. I am not a dishonest businessman as you know, and I have never been dishonest particularly with Ghulam Ahmed. I was happy that because of Ghulam Qadir his boat too set sail in the right direction and by extension, my fortune as well. Nevertheless, it was not conceded by God, for it needs the luck of the person. So let me go. I will discuss the issue with Ghulam Ahmed.' Having said all this, Abdullah Shah threw his shawl over his shoulder and left.

Malla Khaliq called Noor Mohammad in. 'Abba, Ghulam Ahmed swears by the holy book,' said Noor Mohammad, 'that he knew nothing about Qadir's second marriage until they were ready to return to Kashmir. He is really in a quandary as he has left behind some carpets belonging to Abdullah Shah in Goa for the showroom.'

Hearing this explanation, Malla Khaliq began to think that if he allowed Ghulam Ahmed to go to Goa that might help revive relations with Qadir.

It was finally decided that Ghulam Ahmed would be allowed to go to Goa. This could help him repay his debts to Abdullah Shah. But he was told not to have any association with Qadir.

After reaching Goa, Ghulam Ahmed stayed with an old friend. He opened his showroom in the morning and went back at the end of the day.

One day while Ghulam Ahmed was coming to open his showroom, he passed Ghulam Qadir in the new wing of the hotel. Ghulam Ahmed started to explain his position, but Ghulam Qadir stopped him saying, 'Ama Lala, I have no grudge against you. Whatever you did was your duty. But why have you distanced yourself from me? I have allotted this showroom to you. Even Reeny is party to this decision. You may do whatever you want to do with it. You have severed all relations with me and that is my misfortune. But the relation I have with all of you shall abide until my death whether you believe it or not.'

He lowered his head and walked back towards his office.

Time does not wait for anyone. It was nearly a year since Ghulam Ahmed had returned from Kashmir. Around this time, Ghulam Qadir went to the bank and sent a draft of one lakh rupees for Zeb's personal expenses, but he sent it in Noor Mohammad's name for he did not dare send it to his father. When over a month had passed and there was no reply, he understood that they had finally forgiven him; otherwise they would have sent the draft back. He went again to the bank to send the second draft, but the bank manager informed him that his first draft had remained uncashed till date.

After a few days, he got a letter from Bilal in which he had attached Qadir's latest draft as well as a draft for all the money he had sent to Zeb earlier. The letter was brief: 'Haji Abdul Khaliq's family has never lived off illicit money, and never will until he lives, and after him, I. Don't repeat this again. Bilal Ahmed.'

This was so devastating a blow that Ghulam Qadir could not endure it. For days he remained despondent. He wanted solace and took to drinking. Whenever Reeny called him up from Daman, he sounded distant. The slight crack that appeared in their relationship gradually became bigger. With every passing day, he grew more and more bitter about being banished from home, his wife and only son. He felt that he had been dragged out of not only his home, but also his native land. The bitterness changed to unbearable restlessness. Many times he was driven to such extremes that he wished to end his life.

One night, when he was almost ready to drown himself in forgetfulness, Reeny called him up. 'Sorry, Qadir, for disturbing you at this hour. I am going to the hospital tomorrow to get admitted. Come here after a few days to manage all the hotel work.'

'Why are you getting admitted?' Qadir had lost his wits.

'Wake up, Qadir, don't you understand? I am going to the hospital to give birth to your child. Idiot!'

Reeny then switched her phone off. The intoxication of alcohol had subsided. He entered the bathroom and placed his heavy head under the cold tap. When he had regained composure, he called his manager and asked him to immediately arrange for a speedboat for him to go to Daman.

Qadir went straight away to St Mary's Hospital. Reeny was amazed to see him. She had not expected Qadir to come and that too so quickly. She broke down and began to shiver. Qadir sat beside her on the bed, and said, 'Forgive me, Reeny. Please forgive me.'

Reeny hugged him. 'You came so late in the night, battling the monsoon tides! That too for an arrogant girl like me! If anything had happened to you, where would I go?'

'I have tormented you a lot. Please forgive me.'

'Now you have come back to me, all my worries have left me. You leave now, the doctor might be coming. I am absolutely fine. The doctor says that I should go into labour by evening. There is still a lot of time. You please go to the hotel and come back after having breakfast.'

Ghulam Qadir kissed Reeny's forehead and went out.

Reeny forgot all her rancour. Her eyes were wet with the sweetness of happy tears.

She reclined against a pillow, shut her eyes and started talking to the baby. It moved in her womb. 'Yes, he has come. Your Daddy has come back.'

From midnight to dawn, Reeny remained in labour, in the throes of birthing. Ghulam Qadir paced the corridor all night, and for the first time since his return from Kashmir, pleaded to Dastagir Sahib for Reeny's health. It was Sunday, and the moment the church bell rang to summon people for Sunday mass, Reeny safely delivered a baby boy. The nurse came out to congratulate Ghulam Qadir who forgot all his pain and tried to enter the delivery room. The nurse stopped him with a smile and said, 'Have a little patience, we will let you see him very soon. The baby is being washed. You keep a gift ready for me till then. Okay?' She smiled and disappeared into the labour ward.

Ghulam Qadir stood eavesdropping near the door of the delivery room and heard the cries of the newborn baby. It all seemed like a dream to him, until the nurse led him into the room to see Reeny, with the baby by her side. She turned to Ghulam Qadir and said with a weak but radiant smile, 'Now your bonds here are all the more difficult to break; you cannot escape. Why are you keeping this distance from me? Come closer. Don't you want to have a good look at your child?'

Ghulam Qadir took the baby in his arms and held him close to his heart. Seeing this, tears sparkled in Reeny's eyes. She said to him, 'He is still very delicate; easy, easy, darling!'

The news of Ghulam Qadir's becoming a father spread throughout Daman. A party was thrown in the hotel. The general manager of Hotel Sea Waves in Goa, in the meantime, had been eagerly waiting for the news, and when the manager of the Daman hotel called to break this news to him, he was beside himself with joy. He called all the employees and shared the good news with them.

Ghulam Ahmed was busy showing carpets to a party of Europeans, but hearing the noise outside, he came out to see what the matter was. The general manager spotted him from a distance and greeted him loudly. Ahmed asked him, 'What are the greetings for?'

'You are an uncle now; our boss is the father to a baby boy. We just received the news from Daman.'

Ahmed was flummoxed. What is this new calamity that we have to face? Now what should I do? I have to see Reeny and Ghulam Qadir to congratulate them. If I don't, it won't be right. She allotted this showroom to me even before Qadir's consent. If I don't go to Daman, I will have to greet her on the phone. And if I phone her, what will Ghulam Qadir think of me? If people back home come to know about this, they will simply disown me. On top of it all, Lala Sahib's son Vijay Kumar is arriving here day after tomorrow; he will also come to know about it. On second thoughts, his arrival may be a blessing in disguise. He can be the one to inform everyone in Kashmir that Ghulam Qadir has had a second son. Let me ask the general manager for the phone number of the hospital.

In the evening, he made a phone call to Daman and Reeny received it; Ghulam Ahmed thanked his luck. After thanking him Reeny said, 'Don't you want to congratulate your brother? He is sitting beside me. Here, talk to him.'

Ghulam Ahmed congratulated Qadir as well. He could make out that Ghulam Qadir had not liked his calling Reeny.

Ghulam Qadir forgot all about his past for some weeks. Reeny felt assured that some miracle had revived all her withered roses and life seemed in full bloom to her. But after a fortnight or so, the general manager of Hotel Sea Waves phoned to tell her that Narayan Joo's son was coming there along with his family the following week. Ghulam Qadir felt like he had been hurled down a mountain.

Vijay Kumar had told him many weeks ago that he would spend a couple of days in Goa. He in his turn had insisted he come there along with his family.

He had thought that Vijay Kumar was the only link between him and his family, and was eager to host him. But when he heard that he was coming all of a sudden, he got worried. He said to his general manager, 'Did you not tell him I am not in Goa?'

'I did. I even broke the news of the arrival of our little boss to him.

'It is okay.' Clenching his teeth, he put down the receiver. When he told Reeny about Vijay Kumar's impending visit to Goa, she looked happy. 'So after a few days you will have to go to Panaji. The baby will be a month old by then. You should leave after celebrating his first-month birthday. I would love to come along with you to see him, but the doctor has asked me not to leave Daman for some time.'

After celebrating the first month of his child, Qadir returned to Panaji.

A week after that, Vijay Kumar reached Goa with his wife. Ghulam Qadir was prepared to face Vijay Kumar. Vijay Kumar had seen the worst of him. He had treated Qadir sympathetically all those years ago in Bombay. He hadn't labelled him a sinner. He took the couple sightseeing in Daman and to meet Reeny. He was sure that after meeting Reeny, Vijay Kumar might suggest that Narayan Joo meet her. If Narayan Joo liked Reeny, he would convince Malla Khaliq and the others to forgive him.

Vijay Kumar and his wife loved Reeny. They assured Ghulam Qadir that time would heal all wounds. Before returning to Bombay, Vijay Kumar promised Ghulam Qadir that he would tell his father everything. Ghulam Qadir embraced him and said, 'I have been cast away by my own brothers, but you, my brother, will certainly take my boat across. If you can make your father believe that all that happened in the past happened because of the unavoidable fate that held me captive, he might persuade Abba to forgive me.'

'You need not worry. I will convince my father to speak to Haji Sahib.'

When Ghulam Ahmed came to know that Vijay Kumar and his wife had returned to Bombay, he heaved a sigh of relief. He had been hiding away from them. Ghulam Qadir had shown Ghulam Ahmed's showroom to Vijay, but he hadn't shown up.

Ghulam Ahmed heaved a long sigh and said to his salesman, 'Peter, go upstairs and fetch me a cold Coke from the hotel. And throw in some ice as well.' Peter ran up the stairs and Ghulam Ahmed sat down on the sofa. 'Oh my Dastagir! I wish to lay down my life at your feet for this great mercy on me!' Peter brought him a bottle of Coke and poured it out into a glass. 'Put some ice into it.' Peter held out the glass to him and he guzzled it in one go. 'Ah! Now my heart feels a little cool and calm.'

'Sir, what did you say?'

'Go and have some Coke yourself. I have been spared from telling anyone anything. Let Vijay Kumar tell them everything.'

Vijay Kumar phoned his father. 'Daddy, now it's up to you to mend the broken relations.' Narayan Joo kept quiet for a moment and then said to him, 'I think you have also become enamoured of Qadir and his Mem like Ghulam Ahmed. Tell me, what will happen if, God forbid, you abandon your wife and marry some other woman? Would I ever forgive you? No, no. I cannot plead his case. But yes, I cannot hold back the news that a second son has been born to Ghulam Qadir. He may do whatever he chooses to with that information.'

When Narayan Joo nervously passed the news on to Malla Khaliq, all his wounds began to bleed afresh. He cast a scathing smile at Narayan Joo. 'You deserve a lot of greetings! Come! Let us rejoice and announce this news to all of Kashmir! Instruct the chefs to prepare a feast, why don't you?! Now why are you silent? You know we have already severed all relations with that unfortunate boy. Then why did your darling son go to him? Answer me.'

Noor Mohammad, Aziz Dyad and Mukhta overheard the entire conversation from the kitchen. Aziz Dyad nervously said to Noor Mohammad, 'Go pacify your Abba; he is furious. I am afraid he might spew more venom on your poor Lala.'

Noor Mohammad lost no time. 'What is all this, Abba? Do you think that the world should stop spinning? Vijay Kumar's job demands that he travel from city to city; he is after all a businessman. He might have gone to Goa on business and met Qadir by chance. Is he supposed to dig out his eyeballs to refrain from seeing him?'

Narayan Joo interrupted, 'Noor Sahib, the anger that plagues your Abba plagues me as well. He did not say anything wrong to me.'

Malla Khaliq felt bad for his rudeness. He held his friend's hand and said, 'Please forgive me; I don't know what has happened to me.'

'It is not only you, something has happened to all of us,' Noor Mohammad said. He had argued with his father for the first time in his life.

Narayan Joo touched Noor Mohammad's shoulder and said, 'My dear son, circumstances took such an ugly turn that they outwitted even the bravest of men.'

The fire was still raging in Malla Khaliq's veins. He turned to Narayan Joo. 'See this person did not tell us anything about this!'

'Maybe he did not know *anything* about it.' Noor Mohammad tried to plead for his brother.

'How could he not know about it? He might be busy in garnering the oats of Qadir. It is also possible that they might have strictly told him not to divulge anything to us.'

Aziz Dyad tried her best to hold back her anger, but when she sensed that the argument was unending, she came in and burst out. 'You just sit here and pass judgements without even knowing what is happening there!'

'Congratulations, your darling son there has had one more son. Ready yourself to go greet him.' Saying this, Malla Khaliq tried to silence her.

'I heard it, I heard everything. Please don't broadcast the news now.'

'What are we going to get by stretching this issue?' Narayan Joo silenced her. 'Ask your daughter-in-law to get me a cup of tea.'

Aziz Dyad went back to the kitchen and the argument stopped. Nobody mentioned Qadir or his second son after that.

Noor Mohammad was feeling angry with Ghulam Ahmed. In the evening he made a call to him from Doctor Nisar's house. After reproaching him, he said, 'You deserve much applause for forgetting all of us after reaching Goa. Even if you had not told anybody else, you could have at least confided in me that Ghulam Qadir had had a son. You will never change.' Noor Mohammad forcefully put the phone down.

Qadir held on to Vijay Kumar's promise that time was the greatest healer. That was the only hope that he had left. But when nobody in Kashmir contacted him for several months, his hopes faded. He once again began to seek solace in drinking.

Reeny stayed in Daman for most of the time, and there was nobody to stop Ghulam Qadir from drinking or take care of him. She spent most of her time nursing her child, yet she never forgot to call her husband every evening.

Neither Ghulam Qadir nor Reeny could decide what to name their son. Ghulam Qadir finally left it to his wife with only one request: that his name should not indicate his religion or caste. Reeny wanted to select a name that would have some connection with Kashmir for she still nursed the hope that Qadir's family would welcome them home some day and embrace her son as their own. But Ghulam Qadir could not come up with a Kashmiri name. They therefore fondly began to call the baby Tinkoo. But when they decided to celebrate the child's first birthday, Reeny felt silly writing 'Tinkoo' on the invitation cards. She said to Ghulam Qadir, 'If you don't suggest a proper name, I will not get the invitation cards printed, nor shall I invite anyone.'

Ghulam Qadir unwittingly uttered 'Sulaiman'. 'But if you want the name to be in keeping with your own religion, you could call him Solomon,' Ghulam Qadir said.

'Does the name have any connection with Kashmir?'

'Yes, it does. There is a mountain just in front of our houseboats, called Sulaiman Teng, the Hill of Solomon. At the top of the mountain, there is a two-and-a-half-thousand-year-old temple called Shankaracharya. When we wake up early in the morning and open our windows, the hill is the first thing that is visible. It looks splendid in the morning. I am sure my Abba will admire this name.'

'Okay. Sulaiman! The name sounds good!'

She looked at the baby lying on the floor playing with his toys. 'So, Tinkoo Sahib, you shall be called Sulaiman from this moment. How do you like it, Sulaiman?'

Sulaiman's first birthday was celebrated with much pomp and show in the hotel at Daman. Without Ghulam Qadir's consent, Reeny invited Ghulam Ahmed as well. But how could he gather the courage to go to Daman? He wished Reeny on the phone. Ghulam Qadir had sent a card to Vijay Kumar also and entreated him over the phone to come. He kept waiting for Vijay Kumar even after the party ended. But when he did not turn up, Qadir felt very sad. He went upstairs and started drinking in his room.

After putting Sulaiman to bed, Reeny found Ghulam Qadir drinking. 'What is this madness? I did not stop you while the party was on because we were celebrating, and so I let you have your fill. But you continue drinking even after the party is over, like a drunkard.'

Qadir had started to slur and he said, 'What do they think of themselves? Have I committed a murder? They expelled me from my own house and severed all relations with me! Okay. Let them do so, but there was still one bond left ... Vijay Kumar, a brother of mine, how much he cared about me – and then his father, our own Lala Sahib, he has also disowned me – Oh God, I am feeling stifled! Now tell me what I should do ... I try my best to forget everything, but cannot—'

Reeny sat beside him, and held him close. 'I can feel your pain. I know that even after having achieved all that you had yearned to, you feel like you have lost everything. You don't know how much it hurts me to see you in this wretched condition. But only cowards take the aid of alcohol. Please don't repeat this madness in future. I am always with you. Let us fight together, and I am sure we will be able some day return to our dear ones.'

'Everything's finished,' he said and then started wailing over his destiny. Reeny held him tighter and made him lie down beside her. 'Now get some sleep. Time heals all wounds.'

Ghulam Qadir was fast asleep within no time. After that day, Ghulam Qadir kept looking forward to the day when time would actually heal all his wounds, but his wounds turned into irremediable gangrenes. Five years went by. Many things happened in those five years.

Ghulam Ahmed understood that he had lost all his respect among his employees, and so did not want to continue living in Goa. Ghulam Qadir's attitude towards him influenced other Kashmiri businessmen and they all looked down upon him because he lived in a rented room even though he was related to a big hotelier. When he was free from Abdullah Shah's debts, and had saved sufficient money, he sent the key of the showroom to the general manager of the hotel. He also wrote a letter to Ghulam Qadir in which he expressed his reasons for returning to Kashmir.

All these years Ghulam Qadir had expected that Ghulam Ahmed would come closer to him and share in his sorrow. But when Ghulam Ahmed did not deign to make any effort, he convinced himself that this was good riddance. When Reeny came to know about this, she said to Ghulam Qadir, 'You keep Ghulam Ahmed's showroom vacant. I am sure that he will return.'

Malla Khaliq was happy that Ghulam Ahmed had repaid all his debts and was home never to go away again. He was all the more glad when Ghulam Ahmed gave him sixty thousand rupees that he had earned from his business in Goa. The rest of the money he kept with himself to repay what he had borrowed from his father-in-law.

When Naba Kantroo came to know that Ghulam Ahmed had returned from Goa and had resolved not to go back, he became furious. He vented his rage on his own wife. 'You get up and call Zoon. Tell her to come here along with that worthless fellow. Get up, why don't you? Get up, and do what I say.'

Just as his wife came out of the room, she heard the compound gate opening. She peeped out through the window and saw Ghulam Ahmed and Zoon entering the gate.

When Naba Kantroo saw his wife coming back, he reproached her again, 'Are you afraid? You sit here, I shall go and drag him in. He has ruined my daughter's life.'

His wife warned him, 'Sit silent, they are coming here. You hear him out and then do whatever you want to do.'

Ghulam Ahmed and Zoon stepped in. He was carrying a huge bag in his hand. He greeted his in-laws and calmly sat down. Naba Kantroo responded to his salaam rather grimly, but his wife was very polite and said, 'Are you well, dear Ama Lala? We are seeing you after so many months.'

'I had some business compulsions and could not visit Kashmir as often as I would have liked.'

Naba Kantroo lashed out at Ghulam Ahmed saying, 'He was so overwhelmed with his business that he did not find time to phone us! Then why did you shut your shop there? To take charge of your estate here? Or have you sold away even your shop?'

Zoon got angry with her father. 'Daddy, why are you always scolding him so harshly for no reason? He has come here to see you after so long and you are insulting him!'

Ghulam Ahmed held his anger in check, but seconded his wife. 'They are used to poking fun at me. Why are you getting so agitated?' He then took out a big envelope from his bag, and held it out to his father-in-law, saying, 'This is the money you had entrusted me with, along with the interest.' Then he passed the bag to Zoon, saying, 'There is also something for your mother in it.'

Zoon took out a few suits and a few kilos of cashews from the bag and gave them to her mother. 'These suit pieces are for you and the cashews are for Daddy. You may sneer at him, but I alone know how deeply he loves you.'

Ghulam Ahmed said to his father-in-law, 'I have not sold my shop there, nor have I given up my business. I value Abba's honour more than anything else in the world. I stayed there so that I could repay the money and the interest that I owed you, and to Abdullah Shah who had entrusted his carpets to me so long ago.' Then he turned to Zoon. 'Let's leave now.'

'No, this is not proper, my son. How can I let you go without having lunch?'

'We are quite full. Haji Sahib served us lunch as soon as we entered his house. Please let Mukhtar Ahmed come back with us. He can go to his college from there.'

Hearing the sarcasm, Naba Kantroo could not hold his anger in, but he reflected a little and reined in his tongue. He changed his tone. 'You are getting irritated. Look here, dear Ama Sahib, whenever I say anything to you, I say it only for your own good. I had come to know from Abdullah Shah that you ran your business quite successfully. You know your father does not talk to me. Both of us were happy, but when Abdullah Shah told me that it was your father whose fear made you wind up your shop and come back to Kashmir, I was really angry.'

'No, I did not return because of my father. I have returned of my own accord. Abba, of course, has his own principles which everyone admires. I returned only to safeguard those principles.'

Naba Kantroo got more furious on hearing this. 'Yes, we all know about your father's principles. He does not understand that times are changing. Had he been wise, he would not have forced his millionaire son to leave his house. Qadir had only done what every rich person does. Is it a sin to take a second wife?'

Ghulam Ahmed did not think it proper to argue further and he said to Zoon, 'Get up now. The issue is getting unnecessarily stretched. Get up and let us leave.'

Zoon got up and followed her husband, but before crossing

the threshold, she said to her father, 'Please send Mukhtar Ahmed home as soon as he returns from college.'

'Yes, we shall send him. Why won't we? We will surely send him to serve that Bilal there who has been made the heir apparent by your father.'

'You need not worry about that for it is our personal matter.' Having said this, Ghulam Ahmed left, followed by his wife, his head held high.

After they left, Naba Kantroo's wife reproached her husband. 'They had kept silent so far because you had them under your thumb, because they owed you money. How will you control their lives now? And tell me, how long will you keep Mukhtar Ahmed separated from his parents? Why don't you let him go back to his home?'

'Yes, I think so as well. We must send him back otherwise his share of the property will be usurped by others. This is something your precious princess and your stupid son-in-law don't understand. I will take Mukhtar Ahmed and make them write over his share of the property to him.'

Naba Kantroo's wife looked at him, utterly horrified. He in fact grudged Malla Khaliq because he was the only person who didn't attach any importance to his wealth. This was the reason he used many a ruse to upset Malla Khaliq. Today, when his own wife was becoming bold enough to talk back to him, he silenced her with his intentions.

The next day was Sunday. Naba Kantroo took Mukhtar Ahmed along and reached the ghat of Gul, Gulshan and Gulfam. Malla Khaliq and his family were sitting in the open enjoying the pleasant autumnal sunshine. All three houseboats were lying vacant. The tourist season in which Bengali tourists thronged Kashmir was yet to set in. Mukhtar Ahmed went running to the isle. Malla Khaliq hugged him. He was looking for his grandmother. Aziz Dyad was resting in bed; she had been unwell for some days. Mukhtar's mother took him to her. Malla Khaliq stood up to shake hands with Naba Kantroo and said, 'Today all my ill feelings have been washed away. Come here and take a seat, please. Noor Mohammad, go and arrange for tea.'

'The autumnal sun does not suit me, let's sit indoors,' Naba Kantroo said.

'Yes, why not. Noor Mohammad, send the tea there,' Malla Khaliq said and led Naba Kantroo to the drawing room of houseboat Gul. There was silence for some time. Malla Khaliq knew that Naba Kantroo's visit was not devoid of purpose. How could he come there with Mukhtar Ahmed without some hidden motive?' He looked at Naba Kantroo. 'Is everything well at home? Do you get letters from your son in Dubai? Is he coming this year?'

'We are not as lucky as you are. But you know, people do not abandon their business to come home. You might have been relieved from your anxiety because of Ghulam Ahmed's return—'

'But we were hardly anxious about him. He would have told you the real reason for his return when he visited you yesterday.'

'Now all is well. But you know Mukhtar Ahmed is now an adult and he must also get settled in life. He could start some business of his own, but you know that needs a lot of money. I wish he could know his position in the house, so that we might plan for his future.'

A deep furrow appeared on Malla Khaliq's forehead. Then he said, 'Who are you talking about, Ghulam Ahmed or Mukhtar Ahmed?'

'I don't need to worry about Ghulam Ahmed. I want you to settle something for Mukhtar Ahmed.'

'But what is there to settle for him? Let him come and start business in collaboration with his brother. God has been gracious to us. There is so much to do in the family that we never have an idle moment,' Malla Khaliq said while taking care to control his anger.

'Yes, yes, I can totally see it with my own eyes.'

'Why are you not being frank?'

'The thing I am concerned about is that Mukhtar Ahmed should not have to suffer or serve anyone here after being so well educated.'

'Please don't talk in riddles and tell me straight what you want to say. But first of all, may I know in what capacity you are pleading for Mukhtar Ahmed? He is after all our scion and we are the ones to take care of his well-being.'

'You can ask him this. I have spent my sweat and blood bringing him up, and educating him.'

'So you are here to ask for the honorarium for your labour?'

'Not my honorarium, but the share that is due to him. Ghulam Ahmed is so dim he has no courage to talk to you directly. I am the only one looking out for Mukhtar Ahmed.'

Malla Khaliq reflected for a while and then called out to Ghulam Ahmed. 'Ghulam Ahmed, would you please come here?'

Ghulam Ahmed and his wife had seen Naba Kantroo coming so they were standing nervously in earshot. But when Malla Khaliq called him sounding angry, Ghulam Ahmed had no option but to come running. 'What, Abba?'

'If you were so keen to claim your share, why didn't you tell me directly? Why did you send your father-in-law to plead for you?'

'What are you talking about, Abba?'

Then he turned to Naba Kantroo. 'When did I ask you to interfere in our personal affairs?'

Naba Kantroo almost shouted at Malla Khaliq. 'Why are you asking him? Just talk to me. I want you to give Mukhtar Ahmed his rightful share of the property. This worthless son-in-law hardly knows anything about his share. How will he ask you for this?'

Ghulam Ahmed grew so angry that his tongue started failing him. 'I still have some regard for you, otherwise—'

Malla Khaliq called Zoon as well.

Hearing the noise, Bilal also came running. Mukhtar Ahmed came in tow. Then Noor Mohammad and Mukhta.

Malla Khaliq called Zoon again, this time in a louder voice, 'Why don't you come in, Zooni?'

Aziz Dyad quivered as usual. She almost crawled up to the window to see what was happening.

Zoon came running, and Malla Khaliq said, 'Your father has come to demand Mukhtar's share.'

'Share? Share in what?'

In the meantime, Naba Kantroo had come out into the open on the isle. He came face to face with Malla Khaliq and said, 'I did not come with the intention to pick a fight. Why are you getting angry with this poor girl?'

Bilal could not hold himself back. He would have attacked Naba Katur, but Noor Mohammad held him back. When the squabble did not show any signs of dying down, Malla Khaliq pulled Naba Kantroo by the hand towards houseboat Gulfam and then to Gulshan. 'Look here, Kantroo Sahib, these two houseboats are the fruit of my own lifelong toil and I can give them to anyone I like. I inherited Gul from my father. If they mean to divide it among themselves, then you need to hire saw-men to slice it into parts, and take away the splinters of wood in a wheelbarrow. Do you hear me, Ghulam Ahmed?

Ghulam Ahmed got agitated. 'I swear by my son Mukhtar Ahmed, he will get buried in clay if I or my wife ever talked like that. My father-in-law does not like us being united and living together under one roof. Zooni, why don't you say something?'

'What can I say? He has come to smear my face with shame.'

Naba Kantroo shouted louder, 'Ghulam Ahmed has resolved to make you paupers. But I am here to see that Mukhtar Ahmed is not denied what is rightfully his. I will go right now and hire an advocate. I will show you that I mean business!'

'We have known what kind of person you are since I married into your family,' said Ghulam Ahmed. He folded his hands and said, 'Please go away and have mercy on us.'

Noor Mohammad noticed that people from other houseboats were starting to get curious and he said to Naba Kantroo, 'Please go. See, the neighbours are coming out to enjoy the spectacle.'

Naba Kantroo held Mukhtar Ahmed's hand and said while pulling him, 'Let's go, Mukhtar Ahmed, I will show them what will happen if they deny you your share.'

With a jerk Mukhtar Ahmed freed himself and said, 'I am not going back with you. You are driving me mad. My home is here; I don't need your bungalow.'

Bilal stepped forward and held his hand.

'Do you see the pull of our blood?' Malla Khaliq said to Naba Kantroo.

Naba Kantroo left, muttering to himself. He cursed them before leaving. 'If I don't make the blood in your veins turn to ice, I am not Naba Kantroo!'

'We will see about that, you can leave,' Ghulam Ahmed said to him, following him to the ghat.

Bilal and Mukhtar Ahmed went to their grandfather, who hugged them. Then suddenly Zeb cried out through the window, 'Abba, Amma has fainted.'

All of them rushed in. Noor Mohammad ran to ring up Doctor Nisar who left his work unfinished and rushed home.

Aziz Dyad was lying unconscious. Mukhta rubbed the soles of her feet. Zoon got some water and poured some drops into her mouth with a spoon. Bilal brought the medicine that Doctor Nisar had prescribed earlier for such emergencies. He somehow managed to make her swallow it. After a while, Aziz Dyad showed signs of recovery. Ghulam Ahmed began to curse his destiny. Malla Khaliq held her hand. Doctor Nisar gave her an injection.

After giving her the injection, he asked everyone except Bilal Ahmed and Malla Khaliq to leave the room. 'Abba, she will be all right. But she needs some rest. There is nothing to worry about. Bilal Ahmed, you stay here. Let us go upstairs.'

He led Malla Khaliq out and Malla Khaliq narrated the whole event to him. Nisar Ahmed got furious, but he held his anger in check. They entered his room where they saw Ghulam Ahmed hitting his head repeatedly against the wall and saying, 'All this is my fault. I alone am to be blamed for this. What a blunder that I went to see that swine!' Noor Mohammad was trying to calm him down. 'This had to happen sooner or later. Why are you beating yourself for it?'

Ghulam Ahmed was fuming. He stood up all of a sudden and shouted, 'Zooni, mind it, I will not let this dirty Naba Kantroo escape unscathed. If, God forbid, something happens to my mother, I will raze his house to the ground. Do you hear me?'

Malla Khaliq slapped him. 'Stop this buffoonery! Your mother is recovering. She will die if she hears you shouting like this.'

Ghulam Ahmed was completely dumbfounded.

Nisar Ahmed went back to his grandmother's room again. After a little while, he came back. He saw Mukhtar Ahmed hiding behind the door.

'What are you doing here, Mukhtar Ahmed?' Nisar Ahmed said to him. 'Our grandmother is all right. You go inside and sit there with Bilal Ahmed.'

He was happy to know that Mukhtar Ahmed was home again. He assured all the family members that Aziz Dyad had recovered for the time being.

Next day, Aziz Dyad had another severe stroke and Nisar Ahmed got her admitted to the hospital. It was so severe that everyone had given up hope. But she survived. After a month or so, she was brought back home.

All through this time, Narayan Joo remained by Malla Khaliq's side. He had suffered the loss of his wife. He knew well what the loss of a spouse meant. Besides, Aziz Dyad was like a sister to him. And Aziz Dyad had looked after his wife during her ailment; even her own mother would not have done so much.

Even after bringing Aziz Dyad back home, Narayan Joo spent most of his time at his friend's house. Malla Khaliq knew for certain that Aziz Dyad could fly away any time, leaving him behind. He, therefore, hardly left her bedside. Aziz Dyad would say to him, 'Are you going to give up working for me? I won't die without letting you know. You go, take out your rowboat and ride through the watercourses. Autumn is about to end. All the watercourses will soon freeze.'

Malla Khaliq would smile and keep sitting there. The days continued slipping by.

Narayan Joo coaxed Malla Khaliq into paying a visit to the shrine of Mata Sharika on Hari Parbat. Each of them prayed at their respective sites of faith for Aziz Dyad's health; Malla Khaliq at Makhdoom Sahib's and Narayan Joo at the temple of Sharika.

When they went home, Aziz Dyad seemed to look better. She sat waiting for them, propped up against a pillow. Noor Mohammad, Ghulam Ahmed, Bilal and Mukhtar were standing around. Doctor Nisar had tea with the family after examining his grandmother. He did not want to tell them that she was not completely out of danger. Then Parveen walked in as well.

Feeling relaxed after a long time, everyone went to bed early. But Malla Khaliq and Aziz Dyad kept awake. He tried to persuade her to sleep, but she insisted on talking to him. 'Yes, I will sleep; but I have been sleeping for all these days. I keep remembering our happy old days. How long we struggled to reach this stage of our lives. I wish God helps us lead our boat safely into the life after.'

'Yes, He has to, for we have never wished anyone ill ever. You just close your eyes and sleep. '

'As soon as I close my eyes, all the days of our past flash in my mind in quick succession, just like a talkie film. I distinctly remember how your father constructed Gul after many ordeals. But do you remember bringing me as a bride to that old barge of a boat with all its planks rattling like a toy rattle. Yet I was on cloud nine for I had found my amazing life companion.' Having said this, she broke into laughter.

'What makes you laugh at our penury?'

'I just remembered an event. Do you recall, we were newly married, and your father had gone to his in-laws' house and we were completely lost in each other. A thief sneaked in through the rear door and started picking up the utensils in the kitchen. While I cowered in fright, you shouted at him, "Hey, my dear, I am a little busy now, otherwise I would come over to the kitchen to help you rummage through these earthen pots." The rascal ran away, but broke one pot with a bang at the prow of the boat, and then jumped into the lake. You were such a jolly guy!'

'What about you? You were so aloof.'

'True. But I always lost my poise when I looked at you. I used to swoon and feel listless.'

'Yes, those were the days. But when my father passed away and I had to shoulder the family responsibilities, it was then we realized that life is not all fun and frolic; those were trying times.'

'Yet we sailed through, although we were quite young. One night you stared at me in the light of a lamp, and then all of a sudden you blew the flame out. I asked you if you had taken edible oil from the kitchen to put in the lamp; otherwise why would you blow it out? And you told me—'

'Yes, I remember, and I remember that night every time I look at you. I told you that we should spare some oil for the next evening, because I could not do without seeing your beautiful face in the dark.'

'Do you remember that flood in the fifties when the embankment of Sonawar was washed away and Club Nala got submerged? A houseboat had overturned near the racing track and broken into pieces. But we saved our own houseboat, spending the whole night changing the knots of the ropes.'

'I remember everything. Our boat was at Chinar Bagh then. A party of European tourists had come. You had as much energy as I had. If you had not worked alongside me, what would I have done? I would have drifted about aimlessly all my life.'

'That's not true. There is no one in this world as sharp and wise as you. You just lifted me from the dust and made me worthy. Don't I know how hard you worked to build this house inch by inch? You never went to anyone asking for help.'

'That is not entirely true. I went penniless many times. How many times I had to seek help from Narayan Joo. Do you remember?'

'Somehow, with the help of God, we managed to live our days quite happily. Drop this topic now and talk about something else.'

'Now you try to sleep. Nisar Ahmed has said you need rest more than the medicines. Sleep now.'

'I will. Nothing will happen to me, don't worry. It is such a relief to be able to talk this way with your soulmate. Now all is well. I have only one request to make of you: please give up anger and grudges.'

Malla Khaliq interrupted her. 'Now please stop there. I know what you want to say.'

'If you really know, just forgive him.'

'It is not possible to lick one's own spit. Do you hear me? Now sleep. Don't mention him again.'

Having said this, he switched the lamp off and stretched himself out.

The night passed, but in the morning, when they were having tea, Aziz Dyad had another stroke. The teacup in her hand dropped. She became breathless and got drenched in sweat. Everyone panicked and Malla Khaliq said to Bilal, 'Bilal, phone the doctor and tell him!'

Nisar Ahmed soon appeared in a motorboat. He rushed to the room and asked everyone to leave. He called up the hospital for the ambulance, and kept consoling the family until the ambulance arrived. 'There is nothing to worry about.'

'Where has your Abba gone? My last hour is here, call him in. Noora—' With these words she lost consciousness again.

Malla Khaliq stood trembling in a corner; he did not have the courage to come near her. When she fainted, he was about to exclaim '*Inna lilaaha*', just as one would say on someone's passing. But Doctor Nisar covered his mouth with his hand and said, 'Abba, I have injected a sedative. She will be all right, you need not worry.'

Aziz Dyad was carried to the ghat where she was placed in the motorboat. On the other side of the lake she was carried on a stretcher and into the ambulance.

Four days had passed since Aziz Dyad had been brought to the hospital. She was still struggling for her life in the ICU. She regained consciousness on the fifth day. However, Doctor Nisar told his father it was merely her will to live that had revived her. 'I must keep you informed that her heart is not functioning well. She needs an operation, but she is too weak to survive it.'

Noor Mohammad warily asked Nisar Ahmed, 'So there is no hope...'

'Let us wait for a week or so. If she shows signs of recovery, we can consult the heart specialist.'

No one was allowed to enter the ICU, but Aziz Dyad's obstinacy made them allow Malla Khaliq to sit near her for a while. She held his quivering hand and stared piteously at his face.

'Why do you look at me like this?' Malla Khaliq asked her.

'You have stared at my face for your whole life, now if I stare at you just for a little while, is it a sin?'

'But you want to tell me something. I can see it in your eyes. Say it, please.'

'I know if I ask for something, you will not agree to do it. So what is the point of saying it out loud? I had a dream last night; I found myself all alone, walking over the frozen Dal Lake. There was snow all around, heaped on the ice crest. Zabarwan hill was shrouded in shining white clouds, and I was wearing a white phiran. Then I felt my legs and feet slowly turn into icicles. I looked around but no one was there. Then I saw many people emerge from the white clouds, all wearing white clothes, and signalling me to go with them, but my legs felt weak. The frost under my soles cracked and I tried to cry out, but was unable make any sound. I might have woken up screaming, because I felt someone touching my shoulder. I opened my eyes and saw the nurse. What does this dream mean?'

'What can I say? They say that in dreams we see what we keep thinking about in the deepest corners of our mind.'

'No, many of my dreams have come true. I am not scared of death, but I don't understand the meaning of this dream.'

'It could be that you went near those angels who appeared in the white clouds so that they could carry you along. But when the snow thawed, you came back to the waters of the Dal. You returned to us. Nisar Ahmed told me that you were out of danger.'

'It is a false consolation, I am not stupid. I am telling you that my time to leave this world has come. And I have no unfulfilled desires; you never left any wish unfulfilled. Now please accept my last request. Please forgive Qadir. I want to see him, just one last time. I will otherwise die with this yearning and you will keep repenting.'

Malla Khaliq covered her hand with his.

In the meantime, Doctor Andrabi, accompanied by Doctor Nisar, came in and examined Aziz Dyad. After looking at the reports, Doctor Andrabi said to Aziz Dyad, 'Our mother is much better today. You should continue with the medicine and take the injections on time. Most importantly, you should not worry too much. God will help us, and you will recover quite soon.'

But this was not acceptable to the Almighty. In spite of the doctors' unrelenting care, her condition worsened day by day. Her heart was calm, but her body was dwindling. Even in her unconscious state, she muttered, 'Has he not come yet?'

Everyone knew whom she was waiting for, but nobody dared to tell Malla Khaliq that he was being unreasonably obstinate during his wife's last days. Everyone sat in the waiting room, weighed down by a terrible gloom. Noor Mohammad came out weeping from the ICU and said to his father, 'Abba, her eyes are fixed upon the door.'

Narayan Joo reprimanded his friend. 'This is not merely stubbornness, this is sheer foolishness. Don't you see how she has given up food and water? You may not agree, but I too hold some right over my sister. I will phone Ghulam Qadir right now and tell him to come.'

Malla Khaliq cast a glance at Zeb, who was softly chanting holy verses for her mother-in-law's life. She stopped and said to Mukhta, 'We must do what Lala Sahib suggests, our mother's spirit will never forgive us otherwise.'

Malla Khaliq heaved a long sigh and rose saying, 'It is God's will.' Hearing this, Narayan Joo also stood up, and took Ghulam Ahmed along to call Qadir.

The message that his mother was in the ICU, battling for life, struck Ghulam Qadir like a bolt of lightning. Reeny had moved to Goa because she wanted Sulaiman to go to a good school. She had gone to bring their son from school when Ghulam Qadir received the phone call. When she came to know that his mother was very ill, she immediately called the travel agent and got a ticket on the first flight out for Ghulam Qadir. Sulaiman threw a fit saying, 'I will also go with Papa! Granny will be happy to see me.'

Ghulam Qadir tried to make him understand, but he refused to yield. 'No, if you don't take me along, I will not let you go. Papa, I have not seen Kashmir, and you grew up there. You have told me many stories about Kashmir. Please, Papa, take me along.'

Seeing the child's persistence, Reeny said to Ghulam Qadir, 'Take him along. This time they have invited you on their own so there is no need to fear. And I'm sure when Amma sees Sulaiman, she will find a reason to live. Your father also change his mind. Take him.'

Ghulam Qadir thought Reeny was right. He was convinced that when they saw the innocent child, they would not treat him badly. Reeny booked a ticket for Sulaiman as well.

Ghulam Qadir and his son reached the hospital. The family was gathered in the waiting room when he entered, but no one spoke to Ghulam Qadir except Noor Mohammad. Malla Khaliq was sitting inside the ICU near his wife. Without looking at his face, Noor Mohammad said to Qadir, 'Come with me and see how her eyes are fixed on the door, waiting for you to walk in.'

The moment Ghulam Qadir entered the ICU, Malla Khaliq

stood up abruptly and Nisar Ahmed also moved away. With her
listless eyes, Aziz Dyad looked at Qadir. Ghulam Qadir held her
hand. Aziz Dyad tried to speak through the oxygen mask, but her
words came out in a faint incomprehensible whisper. Tears flowed
out from the corners of her eyes.

Not able to bear the scene, Malla Khaliq was about to go out
when Nisar Ahmed said aloud, '*Inna lillah wa inna ilaihi raajiuun!*'
(We all are God's creation and bow to Him.) Malla Khaliq turned
back and came running to the bed. Noor Mohammad sank at the
foot of the bed. Ghulam Qadir tried to move away when he saw
his father coming nearer, but he collapsed on the floor. A nurse
came running inside. Malla Khaliq stood still like a wall; his gaze
had frozen on the face of his dead wife.

Nisar Ahmed helped Ghulam Qadir up and the nurse held him
by his arm and led him out.

The rest of the family began wailing in the waiting room.
Doctor Nisar held his grandfather close to his chest. Malla Khaliq
said to him, 'She has flown away, leaving me behind all alone! Will
she not return?'

What could Doctor Nisar tell him? Malla Khaliq cast a glance
at Aziz Dyad's face and said again, 'This was not our tryst.' Doctor
Nisar could not control himself any longer, and started to sob. The
door of the ICU opened and the rest of the family entered.

Ghulam Qadir sat on a bench outside. Sulaiman kept standing
beside him in the deserted waiting room. Looking at his father and
then at the door of the ICU, he finally went into the ICU and near
the bed of his dead grandmother. He gazed at her face. Aziz Dyad's
face looked so calm that the child thought that she was asleep. Her
silver hair framed her face. He had almost reached the bed when
Ghulam Ahmed noticed him. He placed his hand on the boy's
shoulder and said, 'Come, my son, come with me.'

'Let me see my granny,' Sulaiman said.

All eyes turned towards him. Noor Mohammad firmly said to
him, 'Take him, why don't you take him outside?'

Ghulam Ahmed led the child out and left him with his father.

Sulaiman hugged his father and cried silently.

The nurses came with a stretcher to take Aziz Dyad's body out.

The days of mourning were over, but Malla Khaliq was yet to return to reality. He kept sitting outside houseboat Gul, looking vacantly at the lake. The whole family was worried for him. Narayan Joo alone consoled them that time would heal him. He came daily and stayed by his friend's side. Noor Mohammad had taken charge of the house. Bilal and Mukhtar ran all the errands. Ghulam Qadir had confined himself to a room in Gul, moping over his misfortune, but could not muster the courage to go near his father.

Ghulam Ahmed and Zoon managed the affairs of the houseboats Gulshan and Gulfam to host the tourists.

Abdul Razaq was posted at Udhampur. He did not want to take Parveen along, but everyone insisted, 'How can you stay all alone in a new place?' He agreed and then the couple approached Malla Khaliq for his permission. He looked at them as if he was seeing them after a long time. Then he said, 'So you are leaving? You may go, God bless you. Don't be burdened by worry.'

He accompanied them up to the ghat. Parveen and Abdul Razaq were struggling to hold back their tears. Noor Mohammad and others followed them to the ghat. Parveen turned around and looked towards Gul. Ghulam Qadir was sitting near the rear window watching them. Seeing this Parveen felt her heart would burst out with pain. Ghulam Qadir waved goodbye. The boat glided away and the family returned to the house. Malla Khaliq went to houseboat Gul where Narayan Joo was waiting for him. Life had worn Malla Khaliq down. Once a tall, strong-built man he now hunched over while walking. Narayan Joo stood up to support him. He said, 'Stand upright. What is this hunchback all about?' Climbing the staircase of the prow, Malla Khaliq said, 'When my greatest pillar of support is lost, how can I help being hunchbacked?'

Soon everyone got busy with routine chores. Sulaiman alone stood on the isle feeling very lonely. No one in the family had spoken a word with him. Zeb, who had already started living a new life, sat near the window absorbed in her studies; she was preparing to take her BA examination. She looked out for a moment and noticed Sulaiman; seeing him standing all alone, her heart filled with pity. He was innocent after all. Poor boy! How forlorn he looked! Qadir should not have brought him along.

She suddenly realized that she must not think about the boy and his father and immersed herself in her book again.

Malla Khaliq, sitting at the prow of the houseboat, also looked at Sulaiman. He was also moved with compassion. He said to Narayan Joo, 'Is that illegitimate boy still here? Why doesn't he leave now?'

'He will surely leave; he will not stay here.'

'Please send him away as soon as possible. Seeing him worsens my pain.'

'He is your own blood after all. It is only natural that you feel for the child.'

'You want me to go crazy and tear my clothes!?'

'No, no, no. Please don't think so.'

Malla Khaliq was getting worked up. He looked towards the isle; Sulaiman had climbed down the stairs of the ghat and reached the lowest step.

Zeb looked at Sulaiman again. 'What sort of a woman is his mother! She knew that the child's grandmother was dying. She should not have sent the innocent boy here. Women of other lands hardly think about others.'

Sulaiman was watching the waters lapping gently against the step, and also the small fish at the bottom of the lake chasing one another through the weeds. He dipped his arm into the water and tried to catch the tiny fish. He suddenly lost his balance and fell headlong into the lake. Seeing this Zeb screamed out, 'Bilal, the boy is drowning! Bilal!' And she ran out towards the ghat. Hearing Zeb's screams, Bilal, Mukhtar, Ghulam Ahmed, Noor Mohammad, Mukhta and Zoon rushed out. The din made Malla Khaliq and

Narayan Joo come out. Bilal jumped into the water and brought out Sulaiman who was struggling for breath. Mukhtar caught hold of his hand and pulled him on to the ghat. Ghulam Qadir also came running. Bilal flung a venomous barb at him, 'If people don't know how to take care of their children, they should not beget them.'

Hearing such harsh words, Ghulam Qadir did not dare move ahead. Bilal and Mukhtar laid the child on the ground and pumped Sulaiman's chest to squeeze out the water from his lungs. Zeb rushed in and got a towel. Then Bilal took the boy in and changed his clothes.

Ghulam Qadir, like a smoked rodent, went away without being noticed. He phoned Narayan Joo's office to book his return ticket.

The mishap shook Malla Khaliq out of his gloom, and he came back to the world of possible contingencies.

After changing Sulaiman's clothes, Bilal and Mukhtar took him to the deck of the houseboat and made him sit in the sun. Malla Khaliq was also sitting outside in an armchair after Narayan Joo had left. He looked at Bilal and Bilal said to him, 'He is shivering. Needs some sun.' Malla Khaliq did not reply. Sulaiman, shrunken with fear, squatted before Malla Khaliq and said to him, 'Sorry, Grandpa!' Malla Khaliq stayed silent.

Subhan got a samovar of qahva and poured it into the cups. He held out the first cup to Malla Khaliq. He said to Subhan, 'Pour some qahva for this boy as well.' Sulaiman dithered, but Malla Khaliq said to him, 'Have it. You are cold.' Sulaiman looked at Bilal who with his hands indicated that he could take the cup. While sipping the qahva, Malla Khaliq's gaze kept returning to Sulaiman. He could no more hold his emotions in and said to the child, 'Don't you know how to swim?'

The cup in Sulaiman's hand shook, as he said, 'No.'

'You are the son of a boatman and yet you don't know swimming!'

Sulaiman started sweating; he lowered his head and said, 'Mummy does not allow me to step into water. One of her cousins drowned, so she is afraid of water.'

Having said this, he put the cup aside, wiped his mouth and looked all around at the vast expanse of the Dal. He said to Subhan, 'Uncle, does this lake stretch up to those mountains?'

'Yes, from the foothills of Zabarwan to those mountains in the distance,' Subhana replied.

'It is beautiful!'

Malla Khaliq felt something stir in his heart. 'Has nobody taken you on a trip of the lake?'

'Papa does not come out of his room. He keeps weeping. He must be missing Granny.'

'You take him for a trip in the shikaarah tomorrow,' Malla Khaliq said and stood upto leave.

The next day Subhan returned to the houseboat after having taken Sulaiman for a trip of the lake. Yet no one in the family showed him any warmth. Ghulam Qadir got ready to leave. After begging for forgiveness from all his family members, he and his son crossed over to the Boulevard where a taxi from Narayan Joo's travel agency was waiting. As they were leaving, everyone began to feel overwhelmed with sadness, but no one dared tell Malla Khaliq anything or to look towards the ghat at the time of Qadir's departure. Bilal alone followed them up to the ghat and said to Sulaiman, 'When you are home, you should learn swimming or you might drown.' This sarcasm felt worse than death to Ghulam Qadir, and he vented all his anger on the boatman. 'Why don't you leave, Habba?' Habba rowed the boat quickly. Ghulam Qadir did not look back even once. But poor Sulaiman continued looking back at his grandfather's houseboats until they were out of sight.

Two months had passed since Qadir returned from home after getting humiliated again. All this time, Sulaiman never stopped talking about Kashmir and the Dal Lake. Reeny was tired of listening to him. Something was eating her from within.

Ghulam Qadir seemed like a shadow of his former self; he had left behind his heart and mind in Kashmir. He as usual rose early in the morning, got ready for work and worked like a machine. The private time he spent with Reeny was no more than an obligation to him. Every day after completing his work, he returned to his room, sat in the balcony and drank until the bottle was empty. But it was impossible to get rid of his yearning for the lost days. His nostalgia sometimes assumed the melody of the songs of the nymphs of Parimahal and gave him wings to soar over the summits of the Zabarwan hills or to glide through dense pines. But many times it appeared like venomous serpents which stung him and caused terrible pain. The days kept drifting.

In Kashmir the dust had somewhat settled and life had returned to its normal pace. All three of Malla Khaliq's grandchildren, Nisar Ahmed, Bilal and Mukhtar, had helped him forget his sorrows and pain. Whenever the memories of his wife grew intense, he, despite Doctor Nisar's protests, quietly climbed up the Sulaiman hill and reached the level land where his Aziza was buried in the family graveyard. He would sit for a long time near the gravestone and pour his heart out to her departed soul. He was sure that his Azi heard everything.

The nature of his business, like that of the weather of Kashmir, was whimsical, now hot and then cold again. And everyone had finally forgotten Qadir Damanwala as well.

Bilal had even removed the photograph of his father from his mother's room and buried it deep amidst a heap of old waste paper. Zeb never asked him where the photograph went.

Whenever she was free from domestic chores, she either read or enjoyed the songs of mystic poets. She sometimes wrote a diary. She hid it from the family. But one day when Bilal was rummaging around in the trunk, he found her diary. He read the songs one by one. He could hardly believe that his mother was such a good poet. He could not hold himself back and took the diary to show it to his grandfather.

Malla Khaliq was changing the covers of the sofa in houseboat Gul, but Bilal made him drop the work. 'Why are you so happy? Have you dug up some treasure?'

'This is definitely a treasure! Sit down and I will show it to you.'

Malla Khaliq sat down and patiently waited for Bilal. With a flourish, Bilal took out the diary and showed it to his grandfather. 'Here is the treasure that made me so happy.'

'What is all this about? What is so special? Is there some old tale written in the diary? Or is it some rare manuscript?'

'You just listen to this.'

He read out the songs written by Zeb to his grandfather. Malla Khaliq, who loved poetry and art, heard every verse intently. He finally stopped him and asked, 'Tell me, when did you write these poems?'

'You first tell me honestly what you think of them, Abba. Please be very frank!'

'They are just beautiful! I am not a connoisseur of poetry, but your words are really soulful. Tell me what inspired you to become a poet?'

'Abba, these are not mine. These are my mother's.'

'What, these are Zeb's?'

'Yes, Abba.' Then he told him that his mother had hidden the diary under clothes in her trunk. Hearing this, Malla Khaliq was filled with pride. He hugged Bilal and said, 'This is also a result of your hard work. Had you not helped her walk towards the truth, she might have been still living a life full of tears.'

Malla Khaliq then touched the diary to his forehead and said, 'My dear, you take this diary and keep it where you found it. Don't let her know that you have seen it; that might hamper her creativity. There will come a time when she herself will recite these to us.'

In Goa, Ghulam Qadir and Reeny's business continued to expand, and they rented out their hotel at Daman on lease. This made it possible for Reeny to move to Goa. Many businessmen approached

Reeny to rent the showroom they had given to Ghulam Ahmed and they offered an attractive rent, but hoping that Ghulam Ahmed would return, she did not let anybody have it.

Ghulam Qadir avoided passing by Ghulam Ahmed's showroom because whenever he did, he felt his old wounds hurting again and it also reminded him of the bitterness of his failure. Even Ghulam Ahmed, who was considered the most ungrateful and worthless son by Malla Khaliq, had rejected help. The showroom became a bone of contention between Ghulam Qadir and Reeny, yet she did not let any businessman occupy it. She made Sulaiman repeatedly write letters to Bilal so that the severed relations between Ghulam Qadir and his family could be restored, but they never received a reply. She was helpless because with every passing day, Ghulam Qadir was becoming more and more aloof. He worked all the time like a soulless robot.

One day, feeling utterly exasperated, she made Sulaiman call Bilal, but when Ghulam Qadir came to know of it, he got angry like a rabid dog. He snatched the telephone from Sulaiman's hand. After a very long time Reeny's patience gave way. 'What is this madness? That son of yours there once saved our son's life, and the poor child wants to thank him and you—'

'Do not force this innocent boy to become a part of the horrible vortex I am stuck in. They just hate him. They hate you, they hate me. And still you yearn to forge relations with them!'

'I am desperate to forge relations with them because you are severing relations with me! I want my Qadir back, that is all.'

'What? When did I sever relations with you? What nonsense are you speaking?'

'Yes, of course, I am shattered, and I hold myself responsible for that. Please give me some more time to gather the broken pieces of my life.'

'Till you do that, you plan to continue drowning yourself in alcohol? Have you looked at yourself in the mirror lately? See what you have made of that handsome face. For God's sake, don't ruin yourself, Qadir, please!'

'I work from dawn to dusk like a blindfolded bullock in an oil mill. You know how much I have expanded your business. Yet you're saying that I am ruining myself.'

'You work all the time because you can't bear to spend time with me. I don't need this business. I need nothing but my own Qadir.'

Qadir felt sorry for Reeny, and he held her in a hug. He promised her that he would not touch alcohol again.

But the damage had been done. He was losing his appetite with every passing day. The pain at the right side of his chest was become unbearable. Yet he never let Reeny know. When the medicines he took for over a fortnight did not give him any relief, he consulted his family doctor who advised him to undergo a couple of tests. When the doctor saw the test reports, he went pale and said to Qadir, 'I will run the tests again immediately for a confirmation.'

Ghulam Qadir became anxious. 'Is there anything serious, doctor?'

'You need not worry. The tests are not very clear.'

When reports of the second round of tests came, the doctor went quiet. He said to Ghulam Qadir, 'I will call Reeny and ask her to come here.'

'No, doctor, no. For God's sake don't disclose anything to her.'

'Why shouldn't I tell her? You have to get admitted in the medical institute of Bombay and have a thorough investigation done. It is imperative. We do not have such facilities here and you need treatment immediately.'

'So you suspect that I—'

'I cannot say anything for certain yet. Your liver is not functioning well. But we can only verify this in Bombay. Since you cannot go alone, Reeny must accompany you.'

'No, doctor, she will simply die of shock. I have a brother in Bombay. I entreat you not to tell anybody about my illness.'

After promising secrecy, the doctor contacted a couple of doctors at the Tata Memorial Medical Institute, prepared Ghulam Qadir's case history, and forwarded the file to them.

Reeny was happy that Ghulam Qadir had begun spending most of his time with her and loved her as he used to. After a week or so, while having breakfast, he told her that his friend Vijay Kumar had sought his council in connection with a big business deal, and he would have to go to Bombay for a few days. Reeny felt happy that Narayan Joo's son was trying to seek some excuse to restore their severed relations. She saw Qadir off to Bombay the very next day.

On reaching Bombay, Ghulam Qadir went straight away to Vijay Kumar's office. Vijay Kumar was surprised when his secretary handed Ghulam Qadir's visiting card to him. He got up and went out to meet Ghulam Qadir who had never thought he would be received so warmly. Vijay Kumar led him in and asked his secretary to send them coffee.

'No coffee please, I would like just a glass of water. Coffee does not suit my system.'

Vijay Kumar asked the secretary to get them tea. Then there was a little silence. Vijay Kumar said, 'Please forgive me for not even responding to your invitation card. The circumstances were such that I could not. But I swear by my father that my love for you has not lessened by even an ounce.'

Ghulam Qadir looked at him innocently and said, 'If I did not trust your love and friendship, why would I come here without giving you any notice?'

The tea was served. Vijay Kumar asked his secretary not to allow anybody inside.

Vijay Kumar asked Ghulam Qadir, 'Now tell me why have you come here to see me? Are you interested in some hotel here?'

Ghulam Qadir smiled and said, 'Yes, I am. I am interested in the Tata Memorial.'

'Don't be silly.'

'But I am not joking.'

'What do you mean?'

Ghulam Qadir took out the medical reports. Looking at the case history, Vijay Kumar's hands began to shake. He got up and stretched his hands out to Qadir. 'There is nothing to worry about. This is only a preliminary test. I will call Doctor Arvind Koul today. He is the head of the pathology department. God forbid, even if there is anything serious, it can be treated here. Times have changed, and there are many new remedies for every disease. Everything will be all right. Where are you staying? And where is Reeny?'

'I came straight away to your office. I haven't told her yet. She has already suffered a lot of because of me. If she comes to know that I am here to undergo a medical examination, she will die of the shock.'

'But if, God forbid, there is anything serious, we will have to tell her.'

'Let me undergo all the tests and then we can inform her.'

Malla Khaliq and Narayan Joo went to Hari Parbat as they did every day in the morning to pray to their respective gods and saints for everyone's health and prosperity. When they were done praying, they met each other in the middle and walked down through the Kathi Darwaza, the huge gate in the rampart that was built by emperor Akbar around the hill known as Hari Parbat. They were reminiscing the happy days of their youth when they used to walk through groves of almond trees and orchids and participated in all rituals and festivals together.

'Very soon people will not spare even these walking tracks. They destroyed such a beautiful valley to erect brick and stone walls all around!'

Malla Khaliq stopped at Kathi Darwaza to catch a breather, and turned to Narayan Joo. 'Emperor Jahangir died with an unfulfilled desire to see almond blossoms. He raised such a huge fortification to keep his almond garden safe from encroachment, yet he could not reach here in time for the almond blossoms. But see how people have ruined it to grow hashish.'

Narayan Joo made a concluding remark, 'Let us walk ahead. How many misfortunes will we lament over – the dwindling

Dal Lake, the fast vanishing pine forests, or the withered almond orchard? Now please get up, otherwise I will be late to the airport.'

Malla Khaliq held his knees and said, 'My knees feel weak. I feel a strange something gripping my heart.'

'It is age, old man, it is nothing but age!'

'On the one hand you reprimand me for walking with a hunch, and on the other, you tease me saying I am getting old. You are impossible.'

'I was just kidding. It is your hard work and courage that helps me continue this business of living.'

'It is okay. Let us fix up a time to have another of our debates on who is encouraging whom. Let us get moving or you will never reach the airport. You shoulder so much of your business single-handedly. Such an inspiration.'

Narayan Joo stood up, looked back to have a parting glance at the hill, heaved a deep sigh, and said, 'All this is the Devi's wish.'

Vijay Kumar's wife could hardly believe that Ghulam Qadir had finally put all his grudges aside. She remembered how well Ghulam Qadir and Reeny had hosted them when they visited Goa and Daman. Vijay Kumar did not let his wife know about Ghulam Qadir's illness.

The tea and snacks were placed on the table and Vijay Kumar took Ghulam Qadir to the dining room. They had hardly started drinking the tea when a tall young man entered and went straight up to Ghulam Qadir. He held out his hand to him for a handshake. 'Good evening, Uncle!'

Ghulam Qadir responded to his greetings unsurely.

'I think he doesn't recognize me, Daddy. That is why I had insisted on coming to Goa with you.'

'You!' Ghulam Qadir realized that the young man was Dilip Kumar, Vijay Kumar's son.

He had seen him many years back when Vijay Kumar had bailed him out from jail. He got up and gave him a warm hug.

'Oh God! Do you see, Vijay Kumar, how time has flown like a galloping steed? May God bless you, son.'

They had their tea together. Ghulam Qadir continued to look fondly at Dilip Kumar. He was lost in his memories of Kashmir; he felt like he had returned after so many years. His conversations with Vijay Kumar and his family in Kashmiri seemed sweet like honey to him. Looking at Vijay Kumar's son, he imagined Bilal's face. Tears flowed from his eyes. Then the telephone rang and the moment passed.

Vijay Kumar received the call; it was Reeny. He handed over the phone to Ghulam Qadir, and took his wife and son to the next room. There he told his family the real reason for Ghulam Qadir's sudden visit. There was a lull in the house.

Ghulam Qadir kept talking about Vijay Kumar, his son and his wife on the phone. After assuring Reeny that he would return soon, he put the phone down and went into the drawing room. When he saw all of them looking upset, he tried to restore the cheer that had been in the air a little while ago.

'Reeny was happy to hear that we have been reunited here.'

Vijay Kumar said, 'I think we must tell her why you are here, otherwise she will never forgive us.'

'No. Qadir Uncle is right. Let us see what the tests say and then we can tell her,' said Dilip Kumar. 'Dad, I think you should call Doctor Arvind Koul and make an appointment. You know how busy he is.'

'Thank you for your advice, my father.'

'You see, Dilp Kumar is a replica of his grandfather,' Vijay Kumar's wife said. 'He talks like him and always gives us advice. Like his grandfather, he repeatedly says, "Daddy, what are you doing here?"'

'Yes, I do say so. What is here for us? Everything is artificial. I have told you that I will go back to Kashmir and work alongside Lala Sahib. We can modernize the tourist industry there. Having visited the whole of Europe, I realize what an abundance of culture and landscape God has given us.'

'Okay. We will discuss this issue some other time. You first make sure that your uncle's baggage is kept in his room. In the meantime, I will fix up the time with Doctor Koul.'

Next day, Vijay Kumar took Ghulam Qadir to the Tata Memorial Institute. Doctor Arvind perused the reports of the tests conducted in Goa. After seeking council from other doctors, they decided to admit Ghulam Qadir without any delay. Vijay Kumar had no option but to inform Reeny over the phone. Ghulam Qadir tried his best to dissuade him. 'Let me undergo the surgery, and then we can tell her.' But Vijay Kumar told him that it wasn't right not to inform her.

Reeny shuddered to think that Ghulam Qadir was suffering from cirrhosis of the liver. First she refused to believe it, but when Vijay Kumar told her that Ghulam Qadir had made up the excuse of coming to Bombay on business, she was furious. She went to her family doctor and screamed at him. But the doctor said, 'Ghulam Qadir had made me promise that I would not tell you about the tests.'

'And you went with it?! How could you!'

The doctor tried to explain his position further, but Reeny stopped him, 'Enough. Please tell me what to do now. I don't have much time.'

'I have been in touch with the doctors in Bombay. They are quite hopeful that after the surgery they will succeed in stopping the disease from spreading. If you agree, I am ready to accompany you to Bombay.'

'Thank you. Let me go first.'

Reeny was furious with Ghulam Qadir, but when she found him lying helpless in a hospital bed, her anger petered out. 'We will fight it out. We shall not give in. You just get well and I will repay all that I owe you.'

Ghulam Qadir was overwhelmed. 'Forgive me, Reeny. I have caused you a lot of pain. I deserve this punishment. I have been a source of pain for everyone including you, you who love me so dearly.'

The next day Ghulam Qadir was taken into the operation theatre.

They waited with bated breath. The light on top of the door of the operation theatre shone red, and all eyes remained fixed on it. Every hour of waiting seemed like a high mountain to climb. Reeny was constantly on the phone with Sulaiman in Goa.

After six long hours, the door of the theatre opened and Doctor Gujral and his other associate surgeons came out. Doctor Arvind took Vijay Kumar to his room. He said, 'A big portion of his liver is still safe. We have tried our best to render the infected portion inactive, yet we cannot be sure that the disease won't come back.'

Then he added, 'You please call his wife in, I want to tell her the diagnosis myself.'

Vijay Kumar got up and called Reeny in. Her legs were unsteady with fear. Vijay Kumar tried his best to assure her that the operation had been successful, but she could not believe him for she knew that cirrhosis of the liver was a fatal condition, and only a few patients could be cured. Shivering with fear, she entered the doctor's room. The doctor did not conceal anything from her. 'We tried our best and froze the atrophied part of his liver which was badly affected. But I cannot guarantee that your husband is completely cured. Since God is the greatest doctor, I will take His name and prescribe medicines and will also write the necessary instructions.'

It was over a month and a half since Ghulam Qadir and Reeny had returned to Goa. Ghulam Qadir had recovered noticeably during this time. Their family doctor visited them every day to examine him and then passed his report on to the doctor in Bombay.

One day, while Reeny and Ghulam Qadir were engrossed in sweet memories of the past, Ghulam Qadir held her close and said, 'I don't know how much longer I will get to share this life with you. I want to tell you some truths that I had buried in the past.'

'I do not want to hear anything. You first get well and then I shall lend my ears to your secrets. You have been sitting for quite long today, it is better you sleep now. I am afraid your back might hurt again.' Reeny was about to get up, but Ghulam Qadir stopped her.

'Nothing will happen to me. The burden of some truths is crushing my soul with its weight, and I will have no peace until I share them with you.'

'All right, tell me. Have I ever won against your obstinacy?'

'You know, my shattered life brought me to your threshold like a worthless beggar. You insulted me and forced me to leave your house, but I was so weary that I had no energy to go anywhere else. Do you remember when you took pity and flung an old blanket towards me before slamming the door, saying, "You might feel cold, so wrap yourself up with it?" That little gesture told me volumes about your kind heart hiding under your apparent sternness. That little gleam of hope gave me strength to start a new life. I promised you that I would regain my lost life with honour.'

'I know all this. You don't have to remind me,' Reeny interrupted. 'And then you invested all your savings in restoring our hotel and you became my partner. And then Daddy passed away, which brought us close to each other. Then we got married, and I gave birth to Sulaiman. You went to Kashmir to retrieve your lost life, but there – now that's enough. Let us end this old tale there. If you want to tell me anything else, go ahead. Otherwise you better get up and stretch out on the bed.'

'I married you, but in spite of my best efforts, I could not forget my past.'

'This too is not new to me. Get up now, please.'

'For God's sake, let me speak, please. I married you not because I was in love with you, but because it was an obligation for me. I felt it was necessary to save your honour and the property we had worked so hard for. I did all this only to repay the trust that your Daddy had placed in me.'

'I know. I know all this.'

'But you don't know this. In a very short time, you won my heart and I fell in love with you. The birth of Sulaiman sanctified our relationship. But in spite of all this, I could not forget Zeb. I honestly tried to. That girl loved me from the core of her heart and entrusted her entire being to me. She suffered for no fault of hers.'

'Yes, you are right. There is no fault in her. I alone became the villain in this story. But then I pushed you to visit Kashmir so that you could reassemble your scattered life and make amends. We are all puppets in the hands of destiny. Destiny steers us in whatever direction we are preordained to travel. I therefore implore you never to think that I bear any grudge against you. But I surely have one complaint, for which I may never forgive you, and that is your choice of such a fatal retribution for your sins. What right did you have to play with your life? You knew that your life is entwined with mine. Now let us stop this. I have already forgiven you for the rest. If I have ever loved anyone in this world, it is you, Qadir.'

'You have forgiven me, but she has not forgiven me. My soul shall, therefore, always remain restless. I did not find anybody there who sympathized with me. The pain in my heart changed into the cancer of my liver, which remains gnawing at my insides. Please take me back to Kashmir; I don't want to die here. Please, Reeny, take me to Kashmir.'

'You get well and I promise you I will take you to Kashmir. We will take Sulaiman along as well. But please get well first.'

'I will be able to recover only there near the waters of the Dal Lake where I took my very first breath in this life.'

Ghulam Qadir continued to entreat her. 'Please, Reeny, don't make excuses and leave on the pretext of some chore or the other.'

Feeling helpless, Reeny phoned Vijay Kumar and requested him to come to Goa.

Vijay Kumar consoled her by saying he would come to Goa but only after consulting Doctor Arvind.

Doctor Arvind told Vijay Kumar that if Ghulam Qadir was insisting on going to Kashmir, he should be allowed to go. But he must undergo some precautionary tests before going there. Then he said to him, 'Ghulam Qadir might get re-energized in Kashmir and find the strength to fight his condition.'

Reeny's doctor consulted Doctor Arvind Koul and both of them agreed that since Ghulam Qadir's cirrhosis had spread and his days were numbered, it would be sensible to send him back to Kashmir where he could spend the remaining days of his life in the company of his family.

Reeny entrusted the business to her general manager and started preparing to leave for Kashmir. But Vijay Kumar was still at a loss as to whether he should keep the secret to himself or tell his father. He sought Ghulam Qadir's opinion. 'Now it is no secret. We must inform Lala Sahib that we are returning to Kashmir. But—' Then he fell silent, but Vijay Kumar knew why he could not complete the sentence. 'Why are you silent? If I tell my father, he will surely pass on the news to Haji Uncle.'

'That is the trouble. I don't want to seek sympathy from anyone. I have been dead to them for a long time. They should not come to know about my disease.'

'So should I tell my father or not?'

Ghulam Qadir shivered and said, 'Oh God, what a terrible quandary you have put me in! Can't you let me live even my last days in peace?'

'Okay. I will not tell them. Although you do know that the secret cannot remain hidden for too long.'

'So—'

'So we must divulge it to Lala Sahib at least. Don't worry, I will entreat him not to tell Haji Sahib.'

'All right. I will also implore him to help me get my boat out of this whirlpool.'

The news was such a shock to Narayan Joo that he lost his balance and almost fainted. Vijay Kumar was frightened. 'Lala Sahib! Lala Sahib! Why don't you speak? Lala Sahib!'

After regaining his consciousness, he muttered, 'What can I say? Does Malla Khaliq deserve to bear another tragedy now? You have left me shattered. I am not able to move even a step.'

'Sorry, I am sorry. But I had promised Ghulam Qadir that I would call you in the morning. Lala Sahib, there is very little time left. Ghulam Qadir wants to spend his remaining days in Kashmir, that too on the banks of the Dal.'

'He is not the first to desire this. Whoever was born in this paradise has yearned to dedicate his last moments to this land, especially if they were distanced from it.'

'He wants to be in Kashmir as early as possible, but he does not want anyone to know about his illness, especially Haji Uncle.'

'How is that possible? Tell me, how is it possible. Oh my Mother Goddess! What a dilemma! Today we had decided to go to Nigeen Lake after visiting Hari Parbat to offer condolences to the Shoga brothers whose mother just died. How will I spend the whole day with Malla Khaliq and keep such news from him.'

'We have to do something about it. Qadir longs to beg his family for forgiveness. But he doesn't want anyone to know. He told me that he would also like to talk to you.'

'No, no. I don't have the strength to talk to him. Let me see if my omniscient Goddess shows me some way out.'

Having said this, Narayan Joo put the phone down.

He decided not to go to the Parbat, but was at a loss about the excuse he could use to convince Malla Khaliq. If he told him that he was not feeling well, he would immediately come to see him. Therefore, with the Devi's name on his lips, he got up and went to Hari Parbat. While they turned towards Kathi Darwaza after coming out of the Devi's temple, Malla Khaliq cast a glance at Narayan Joo, who languidly ambled towards the car waiting outside the gate. 'Why are you so silent? Is everything all right? You look weary.'

Narayan Joo was struck mute. In order to evade further inquisition, he said, 'This is nothing but age. A minor trouble.'

'But you are younger than me! Don't lie to me. Tell me the truth. Is all well with Vijay Kumar and his family in Bombay?'

'They are absolutely fine.'

'What is it, then?'

'I told you, this is just my old age giving me trouble, nothing else. I was pondering how long my legs would be able to support me. It will be absurd to leave at the end of autumn, and stay away from mother Kashmir for the whole winter.'

'This going and coming is of your own accord. I suggest you don't leave this winter.'

'Yes, it has been long since I won a Nav Sheen bet. Yes, I seriously think I won't go to Bombay this year. One cannot be sure about one's life. I was born here, I grew up here, and now I wish to die here.'

'You are scaring me with such words. Why are you jinxing the day by talking about such sad things early in the morning? If, God forbid, anything happens to you, I shall die before you. Don't talk of death and dying.'

After offering their condolences to the Shogas at Nigeen lake, Narayan Joo dropped Malla Khaliq at Gagribal and went straight to his office. His manager Ahmedullah was amazed to see Narayan Joo coming directly to office after visiting the Parbat.

He asked, 'Is any special party coming today that you came here so early?'

Narayan Joo trusted Ahmedullah. And his mind was heavy with anguish and he wanted to unburden himself. He also wanted to seek counsel. He took Ahmedullah to his room and asked him to close the door. Narayan Joo's face was pale. Very cautiously Ahmedullah said to him, 'Have I committed any mistake?

Narayan Joo reassured him warmly, 'Ama Saeb, it is I who always commit mistakes and you are always there to set everything right. I am terribly sad today. Khaliq Sahib's son Ghulam Qadir is very ill. Vijay Kumar phoned me early in the morning, and told me that Ghulam Qadir wishes to spend his last days on the banks of the Dal Lake next to his own family and houseboats. He has entreated us not to divulge this secret to Malla Khaliq or anyone else in the family. This is tormenting me. I think that Malla Khaliq and his family should somehow know about this. I am entrusting this secret to you so that you can give me some advice on how to handle this situation.'

Ahmedullah looked stricken. He sighed and said, 'This is all God's dispensation. He lifted him up from the dust, carried him to such heights, and see now—'

'This is what torments me. He became a millionaire, and now he craves for a little patch of earth.'

'This is the essence of life. Well, what have you decided to do? If you allow me, I can gently break the news to Haji Sahib.'

'If that were the solution, I would do that myself.'

'You are right. Let us call Noor Mohammad in, and you tell him everything.'

'Yes. This is what I also want to do.'

Ahmedullah then phoned Noor Mohammad and asked him to come collect the details of the season's accounts of the travel agency so that he could file for income tax returns.

Noor Mohammad reached Narayan Joo's agency. Ahmedullah was impatiently waiting for him at the door. Seeing him so anxious, Noor Mohammad sensed something was up. Ahmedullah led him straight to Narayan Joo. When Narayan Joo told him about Ghulam Qadir's illness, he was left speechless. And when Narayan Joo told him that Ghulam Qadir wanted to live his last days in Kashmir, Noor Mohammad could no longer contain his grief. He cried and said to Narayan Joo, 'Is this the last nail in the coffin? Lala Sahib, how broken my father will feel! And Zeb, who has just started her new life, will again get engulfed by gloom.'

Narayan Joo consoled him, 'Look here, my son, you are the only one who can support your father as well as everyone else in your family.'

'So you have abandoned us, left us to the mercy of God!' Noor Mohammad exclaimed.

'Yes, my son, all of us depend on God's mercy. How can I tell you about my suffering since this morning? While driving from the

Parbat to Gagribal, I was about to break the news to Malla Khaliq, but my courage failed me.'

'Do you think I have the courage to convey this to him? No, I cannot do it.'

'Someone has to take the onus. Whatever happened is now in the past. Ghulam Qadir is your blood brother. He has played in my arms as well as a child. Whatever he did, right or wrong, he is bearing its consequences. We must forget everything and forgive him so that he can live his last days in peace.'

'I am at a loss as to what to do now.'

'There is no other option but to be brave. You have a word with Ghulam Qadir. Your voice may alleviate his pain.'

'What about Abba?'

'I will convince him. Shall I connect you to Ghulam Qadir?'

'Not yet. I will talk to him later. Ghulam Ahmed will have his number.'

'I don't think it is proper to phone anyone else right now. I have Ghulam Qadir's number; let me write it down for you.'

Noor Mohammad reached Doctor Nisar's house in a daze. Doctor Nisar had just returned from his night duty in the hospital. When he saw the pallor on his father's face, he anxiously asked him, 'Papa, what has happened? Why do you look so pale?' Noor Mohammad shut the door and told him about Ghulam Qadir's illness. Nisar sank into the chair in shock. Then he pulled himself together and told Noor Mohammad, 'Let me talk to Vijay Kumar.'

'He has left for Goa. He might be staying at Ghulam Qadir's hotel. Lala Sahib has given me his Goa number.'

When the receptionist at the hotel heard that he wanted to talk to Ghulam Qadir, he wanted to know who he was. He exasperatedly said, 'I am his elder brother, Noor Mohammad from Srinagar.'

The operator uneasily dialled Ghulam Qadir's room and Reeny

answered the phone. She eagerly shook Ghulam Qadir awake and said, 'Darling, wake up, it's your brother!'

'Who, Ghulam Ahmed?'

'No, it is Noor Mohamamd.'

Hearing this, Ghulam Qadir snatched the receiver from her. His hand trembled. He tried to stay calm, but his heart was about to burst with grief and sorrow, and the pent-up tears flowed from his eyes.

Noor Mohammad, too, could not utter a word. Having collected himself, he said to Ghulam Qadir, 'Look here, Ghulam Qadir. Please talk. You just see how God will take away your pain and sorrow. Come to Kashmir, come home. Everything will be absolutely fine.'

With a shudder, Ghulam Qadir said, 'What home do I have left after you forced me to leave in the dead of night? Not once but twice. You did not even have pity on my innocent child. To you I am already dead. Are you now going to let my corpse in through the door from which you threw me out when I was alive? It cannot be, never. I had entreated Vijay Kumar not to divulge the secret of my illness to any of you.'

'He is blameless; he told only Lala Sahib who did not tell anyone but me, even though he was with Abba this morning.'

'I know. God has made you a pious human being, who means everyone well. If there is still some love left for me in some corner of your heart, I entreat you – book me a houseboat far from your houseboats, so that I can breathe my last in the soothing breeze that blows over the Dal.'

Noor Mohamamd started to cry. He tried his best to persuade Ghulam Qadir, but he did not yield. Finally Doctor Nisar took the phone from his father and said to Ghulam Qadir, 'You need not worry. You may stay wherever you want. We shall arrange for that. No, we will not tell anyone else in the family. I alone will visit you there.'

'Thank you. You have lessened the burden on my heart.' He put the receiver down and told Reeny, 'Now in perfect peace I shall—'

Reeny silenced him by keeping her hand on his mouth. There was a knock on the door and Reeny opened it to see Vijay Kumar standing on the threshold. Ghulam Qadir sat up against the pillow and started complaining. 'You see, the news has been broadcasted everywhere. I had requested you to tell only Lala Sahib and nobody else. Noor Mohammad called up.'

'Don't you trust me? I have not spoken to anyone, except Lala Sahib. I will call up Lala Sahib and you can talk to him yourself. I have not told anyone, understand?'

Reeny could see that Vijay Kumar was getting upset, and she said to Ghulam Qadir, 'Relax. You know Vijay Kumar so well. He can never lie. He has talked to Narayan Uncle, and Uncle did whatever he thought wise. Besides, everyone will hear this sooner or later. It cannot be kept hidden forever.'

'Thank you. Lala Sahib might have thought it was the right thing to do. Yet I request you that if they wish to make my last moments easy, they should not forcibly take me to Abba's house.'

'That has already been decided,' Vijay Kumar assured him. 'I will ask him why he told Noor Mohammad in spite of my insistence.'

Reeny was trying to make out what they were saying in Kashmiri. But when she could not understand much, she asked Vijay Kumar, 'What is he saying?'

'He is saying that he will not go home no matter what.'

'Tell me, how could someone with any shred of self-respect go back to the home that threw them out?'

'I agree with you.'

Vijay Kumar went to his room with the intention of calling his father. While he was dialling his number, Jankinath of Dhars, his cousin, was with Narayan Joo. He had come with the proposal of Hradaynath's daughter for Vijay Kumar's son. Though Narayan Joo was distressed, he did not think it feasible to reject the proposal outright, and so he said instead, 'Look here, my dear Jana, times have changed. I cannot order Vijay Kumar's son to get married to the girl I point out to. The boy has come back from Switzerland only day before yesterday. I don't yet know what he plans to do now. Tell me, how can I give you his horoscope?'

Jankinath was yet to answer when the phone rang. When Narayan Joo heard Vijay Kumar's voice, he did not want to talk in the presence of Jankinath. He told Vijay Kumar, 'My dear, there seems to be some problem, your voice is not clear. Please hold the line, I will talk to you from the next room.'

Vijay Kumar complained to his father, 'Did I not implore you not to tell anyone about Ghulam Qadir's illness? But—'

Narayan Joo interrupted, 'How could I not tell them that Ghulam Qadir is terminally ill? This secret cannot be concealed for long. Besides, we should try and reunite Qadir with his family in his last days. You need not worry, Noor Mohammad, I am sure, will be able to handle Malla Khaliq better than you or me. You just tell me, is he in a position to travel?'

'The joy of going back to Kashmir has revived him a bit.'

'Yes, this is the miracle of the love for the motherland. Man, however far away he may have gone, finally seeks his roots.'

'He has so much wealth here and everything that could bring a man happiness, yet he is unmindful of everything and is readying himself to reach Srinagar.'

'Mother Kashmir calls him. This is her magnetism. Don't you constantly hear that call?'

'Now stop this, please. I have many urgent tasks to attend to right now.'

Narayan Joo let out a bitter laugh. 'Everyone is running after tantalizing images of wealth and fame. But everyone will finally return and crave to be home.'

'Lala Sahib, I am getting late. Tell me if you have booked a houseboat for Ghulam Qadir, or shall I request someone else?'

'Noor Mohammad's son Nisar is making all the arrangements without letting Malla Khaliq know. Tell me, when will he get here?'

'I will tell you later.'

After hanging up, Narayan Joo returned to the room where

Jankinath was waiting for him. 'I am sorry, I don't know why the phone in this room did not work all of a sudden.'

'Oh no, you have hung up! I wanted to have a word with Vijay Kumar. I would have asked him to send the horoscope.'

'How will he arrange for the horoscope there? I told you that we must first know what the boy wants to do. We can discuss this only after that.'

'That is okay. But please don't give his horoscope to anyone without letting me know.'

'I give you my word. Now tell me is Nabir Kaka's family well? It has been a long time since I saw them.'

'You have almost stopped visiting us downtown. How will you see them?'

'This is due to my old age. Are they all fine there?'

'Yes, absolutely fine. Do come to our side sometime.'

'You keep rogan josh ready for me and I will surely come.'

'That's easy! I will take your leave now. But please don't forget what I said. Namaskaar!'

Narayan Joo led him to the door. Then he returned to his room. He thought, Jankinath is right that I have stopped going downtown. But how could I make him understand how loneliness has drained my body and soul? Then Vijay Kumar phoned again.

'Yes, my darling son, what is it now?'

'Ghulam Qadir's tickets have been booked. He, along with his family, will reach Srinagar airport at 1 p.m. the day after tomorrow.'

'Okay. I shall arrange for their stay today.'

'Nisar has already done that. He will be at the airport to receive them. Dilip will accompany them; I have a very important meeting to attend. I might come later.'

'Okay, I will send them the driver.'

'There is no need for that. He told me that he will come home only after seeing that they are settled in the houseboat.'

Doctor Nisar did not think it proper to meet Ghulam Qadir directly; he did not want Qadir to think that people were pitying him. At the airport, he introduced the son of the owner of houseboat

Glacier, Abdul Jabbar, to Ghulam Qadir. He had imagined that they would have brought him in a wheelchair, but he was amazed to see him walking out of the airport with the support of Vijay Kumar's son. Abdul Jabbar's son went running, showed his card to Reeny, and made the coolie put the luggage in the car. Doctor Nisar watched all this while hiding at a distance. Satisfied that they had been properly received, he left for the city.

At home, Noor Mohammad was anxiously waiting for him. The moment Nisar entered the compound, Noor Mohammad asked him, 'Has he arrived?'

'Yes, he has.'

'How did you bring him from there? You should have arranged for an ambulance.'

'Actually, he walked to the car. Lala Sahib's grandson has accompanied them.'

'That is fine. May Dastagir help him recover soon. Are you going there to examine him?'

'It is better that you see him first.'

Noor Mohammad was exhausted and he, like the day before, was late by three to four hours reaching home. Malla Khaliq wondered where he had been. He went to Bilal's room which they had constructed on the isle for their office. He sat in the chair and told Bilal, 'Sit down, you need not stand up. Sit in your chair.'

Bilal sat in the chair and Malla Khaliq asked him, 'Do you know what Noor Mohammad is so preoccupied with? No one knows when he comes and when he leaves.'

'He might be busy with some work for Doctor Sahib. You know his private practice has grown fast.'

'No, that is not the reason; he would have told me that. Ask him about his present engagements, will you?'

'Yes, I will.'

Malla Khaliq came out of Bilal's office. He came across Ghulam Ahmed's son Mukhtar Ahmed with a bundle of letters in his hand. He salaamed his grandfather. 'I went to the post office to get the mail.'

'That is good. God bless you.' Saying this, Malla Khaliq walked away to sit in an armchair in the open, and gazed at the lake. He noticed that algae and other weeds had spread all around their houseboats. The interlaced creepers seemed like a huge serpent shrinking and expanding with the ripples in the lake and that made him nervous. With a shudder, he got up and went to his room.

Houseboat Glacier was in a grove of willows in the greater lake towards Kotar Khana. The lofty Zabarwan hills stretched in front of it and their reflection appeared to be kissing the bed of the lake. Towards the right side, the Shankaracharya temple overshadowed the Boulevard. When Reeny came out on the prow of the houseboat holding Qadir's hand, she forgot her sadness for a little while. 'Beautiful!' Then Vijay Kumar's son took Ghulam Qadir inside. 'You must be feeling tired, you should get some rest first.'

'I am soon going to be resting forever,' said Ghulam Qadir. 'Don't you see how these silvery ripples of the Dal beckon me? You also sit here for a while in this soothing breeze that comes to us after touching the snow on the lofty peaks of Mount Harmukh.'

Dilip Kumar sat down beside Qadir and asked, 'Which one is the Harmukh?'

'You cannot see the whole mountain from here, but you can see the summits there, behind those smaller hills.'

'Yes, I can see. Is it snow that shines over the peaks?'

'It is snow, of course. What else could it be? How can I tell you what a splendid place it is! I have climbed up twice; first in my childhood when I was studying in Biscoe School, and then once again when I led a party of foreign tourists to the peaks.'

'They say the Harmukh Ganges originates from there. My grandpa told me.'

'Yes, there are two large lakes at the bottom. The water of the two lakes flows out, and in confluence runs into a very large lake.'

Reeny and Abdul Jabbar, the owner of the houseboat, came out. She said to Ghulam Qadir, 'Everything is set.'

'Jabbar Sahib has taken care of every comfort. No one but him could have done all this for us. He is a brother of ours after all.'

Ghulam Qadir looked towards her with a pained smile. Reeny laid her hand on his shoulder and said, 'Now get some sleep.'

He got up with a long sigh. Before going in, he turned to Dilip Kumar and said, 'Gangabal and Harmukh! No place in the world can compare with them. You must visit them.'

Dilip Kumar knew well that this was the last burst of a bright flame on the waning candle. Nevertheless, even in those last moments, Ghulam Qadir wanted to breathe the serenity of his Mother Kashmir into every pore of his being. When he stretched out on the bed and looked through the window at the Zabarwan, he said to Reeny, 'Do you see my paradise, darling?'

'Exquisite!'

'Please remember, when I breathe my last, don't close my eyes for you will find my paradise frozen in them. I will carry that vision as my only wealth to the other side.'

Reeny turned the other way to hide her tears. Then she pulled the quilt over Ghulam Qadir, and went to the drawing room where Dilip Kumar was waiting. 'We will have to arrange for a doctor to give him daily injections.'

Dilip Kumar told her that Doctor Nisar would be coming daily.

'Yes, Doctor Nisar spoke to me, but he did not make any such statement,' Reeny said.

'Then let us ask him.'

'No, we need not ask him; please arrange for a good doctor and a nurse who could stay here with us.'

'All right, I will discuss the issue with Doctor Nisar. We have got sufficient stock of medicines with us. If you need anything else from the market, please let me know.'

Noor Mohammad remained anxious. He was in his home, yet lost in some wilderness. He kept looking intermittently towards Kotar Khana where the houseboat Glacier stood. Malla Khaliq noticed how fidgety he was. He suspected something was wrong. He went out on to the isle where Noor Mohammad sat.

'Noor Mohammad, is all well? You have been brooding for the last few days and I find you rather distracted. What is the problem?'

Noor Mohammad was at a loss. He controlled his nervousness and said, 'I am just anxious about my daughter-in-law for she is pregnant for the second time.'

'But what is there to be worried about? She is with her parents in Dubai. And her father is a reputed doctor. She herself is an able gynaecologist. I spoke to Nisar only yesterday. He told me that all was well.'

'Yet I am quite perturbed, I don't know why.'

'Now you go inside; the wind is chilly tonight. Dastagir Sahib shall bring us succour. Now go in.'

'Subhan, where is he? I want him to take me across. There is no one at Nisar Ahmed's clinic to allot numbers to the patients.'

'Shall I take you across?'

'No. Here comes Subhan. You please go and rest inside.'

Thus Noor Mohammad lied to escape the situation. When he was sure that Malla Khaliq was inside, he sneaked away towards the Gagribal ghat. There he rented a boat and reached Glacier. When Abdul Jabbar saw Noor Mohammad's boat touching the ghat, he went running, greeted him and took him aside. 'They are sleeping right now. You come to the doonga and have some tea.'

They were about to go towards the doonga, when they heard the call-bell. Abdul Jabbar said to Noor Mohammad, 'It is the bell from his bedroom. You stay here until I return. Maybe he needs something.'

Abdul Jabbar he knocked on the door.

'Come in, the door is open,' Ghulam Qadir said.

Abdul Jabbar walked cautiously into the bedroom. He found Ghulam Qadir sitting up against a pillow and looking out through the window. 'Who was it in the shikaarah?' he asked Abdul Jabbar.

On hearing Noor Mohammad's name, he started sweating. In the meantime, Reeny also woke up in the next room. Without disturbing Sulaiman, she came into Ghulam Qadir's bedroom. When she came to know that Noor Mohammad was there to see

Ghulam Qadir, she said to Abdul Jabbar, 'Why didn't you show him in? What will he think about us? You please show him in.'

Abdul Jabbar went out and said to Noor Mohammad, 'You please go in. How courteous is this memsahib of Ghulam Qadir's! She scolded me for making you wait outside. Come this way.'

When Reeny saw Abdul Jabbar showing Noor Mohammad in, she went to the door. Ghulam Qadir stopped her saying, 'Where are you going? Please stay here. I don't have the guts to face him alone.'

'No, I am a stranger to him, and he thinks me a sinner. He might hesitate in talking to you in my presence.' She went to the other room.

Abdul Jabbar led Noor Mohammad into Ghulam Qadir's bedroom and walked out.

Noor Mohammad stood still, and frozen like a criminal. Holding the side of his bed for support, Ghulam Qadir got up and lay at his feet. Noor Mohammad could not restrain himself. He helped him up and held him in a hug. Tears poured from their eyes. Neither of them could speak.

Reeny was in the adjacent room, trying to listen in. When there was a long silence, she woke Sulaiman. 'Get up. Your Daddy's elder brother has come.'

'Who, Noor Uncle?'

'Yes. They were talking to each other some time back, but there is pin-drop silence now.'

'Stop, Mama. Listen! They are talking again.'

Reeny was curious to know what the brothers would say on meeting each other after so many years. She leaned against the partition between the rooms and tried to hear. Sulaiman got angry and said, 'What is this, Mama? Let me also hear.'

'I will listen and tell you.'

He sat down and Reeny tried to connect words with one another and make out what they were talking about in the next room. Noor Mohammad repeated the word 'maafi!' intermittently, and this was enough to make her believe that he had come there to seek forgiveness from Ghulam Qadir.

Noor Mohammad sat on the edge of the bed, holding Qadir's hand. 'Look here, Ghulam Qadir, if you could just once say a word to Abba on the phone, all the grudges will wash away. Then he will take you to your own house.'

'No, I had begged for forgiveness by lying at his feet. I did that when I was a worthless waif, and again when I was of some worth. Now what is left for me to gain? Having made a lot of money, name and fame, I have come back, losing the most important gamble in life, and now I am here to play with potsherds. I will lose this game as well soon and everything will be over.'

Noor Mohammad was speechless. He knew that his father wouldn't forgive him because he hadn't even mentioned his name all these years. Having let go of Ghulam Qadir's hand, he said to him, 'Vijay Kumar's son had come to Nisar Ahmed's clinic and asked him to arrange for a full-time doctor for you. But Nisar Ahmed himself is such an able doctor; is he not allowed to come here?'

'Have we bolted our doors from inside? All these arrangements were made by Nisar Ahmed. Who can stop him from coming here?'

Noor Mohammad got up and said, 'You get some rest. I shall send Nisar Ahmed here.'

'Please wait a while. Let me ask Reeny if she has asked Vijay Kumar's son about the doctor.' He pressed the bell, and Abdul Jabbar came in. Ghulam Qadir asked him to send Reeny in. After a little while, Reeny came in, her head covered with a scarf, and courteously paid her salaam. Noor Mohammad was taken in by her manners. Ghulam Qadir gently introduced her to Noor Mohammad. 'This is Reeny De Souza.'

'No. Reeny Qadir!' she corrected him. 'I am your unlucky Bhabhi.'

Noor Mohammad said, 'When our own son is a good doctor, what is the need for calling any other doctor in?'

Reeny explained to him that they needed a doctor and a nurse who could stay with them in the houseboat, to meet any eventuality that may arise. 'So as far as Nisar is concerned, he will be frequenting the houseboat.'

'All right, I will go and send Nisar here.' Then he placed his hand on Ghulam Qadir's head and prayed for him. He said to Reeny again, 'Where is Sulaiman?'

'You will not recognize him. He has grown quite tall, taller than us.'

'I have only seen Ghulam Qadir, Ghulam Ahmed and you. What can I say about others in your family? Yes, I am sure he has grown taller than all three of you,' Reeny said with a smile.

'May God protect him. So I will take my leave now.' Saying this, he went out of the room. Reeny followed him. He passed Sulaiman who was in the corridor. He was about to go into his room, but Reeny stopped him. 'Why are you running away? This is your Noor Uncle.'

'I know. *As-salaam-alaikum.*'

'*Wa-alaikumsalaam!* You have really grown very tall!'

'Do you remember after how many years you are seeing me again?'

Noor Mohammad went quiet.

'Eight years have passed since then. I have kept a record of all the events that have taken place in this time,' Sulaiman said.

Noor Mohammad felt a bit embarrassed. He remembered how he had forced him along with his father to leave home. Nobody in the family had spoken even a word with him. 'May God bless you. So I take my leave now.'

'Thank you for coming and showing us a little support,' Reeny said. Sulaiman said in Kashmiri, 'Let me see you off. Come this way.'

Noor Mohammad was amazed to hear him speaking in Kashmiri. Reeny said, 'His Daddy has taught him many things. I alone, like an aged parrot, failed to learn anything.'

Sulaiman held Noor Mohammad's hand and helped him sit in the shikaarah.

Noor Mohammad's shikaarah left and Sulaiman and Reeny continued watching it move away until it had vanished from sight. Then they returned to Ghulam Qadir's bedroom. He sat near the window gazing at the cliffs of the Sulaiman mountain.

Sulaiman went to him and said, 'What are you gazing at? Noor Uncle has left.'

'I was not watching him. I was looking at your namesake mountain, Takht-i-Sulaiman, and the two-thousand-year-old Shankaracharya temple at its summit.'

'I know, Daddy. You once told me about this.'

Reeny also joined their conversation. She said to Sulaiman, 'Do you see the lake at the bottom of that mountain? Your grandfather's houseboats are somewhere there.'

'They are surely there. Daddy has told me about them – Gul, Gulshan and Gulfam.'

The sun was about to set. Dark clouds had gathered around the peaks of the Apharwat towering over Gulmarg in the west. The golden gleam of the setting sun gave a crimson blush to the waters of the Dal. Reeny sat beside Ghulam Qadir near the window. He raised his head and stared at Reeny's face. 'What are you looking at?' she asked him.

'I am looking for the reflection of this panorama in your eyes.'

'You are crazy. Why don't you say that you want to see my reaction to this amazing vista?'

'Let it be so. Tell me what you think?'

'It is marvellous. Sunsets are beautiful in Daman as well, but they cannot match the ethereal beauty of this farewell of the sun by these splendid mountains. But the ocean of Daman is a million times larger than this lake.'

'What about it? The enchanting grandeur of our Kashmir is such that it has become the meaning of beauty for me. I will never forget it. I am not scared of death, but the thought that I will not find my Kashmir in the other world gives me much pain. Can there be such beauty anywhere else?'

'You talk of death again! Don't talk like that, please.'

Before Ghulam Qadir could say anything further, Sulaiman came in, after knocking on the door. He said to his mother, 'How long will you make him sit here? The sun has set. A cold breeze has started blowing and he might catch a chill. Now get up, please.'

He helped his father up and led him to his bed. The fatigue of the day intensified his pain and Sulaiman and Reeny made him swallow his analgesic. Reeny said to Sulaiman, 'I don't know when Dilip will bring the doctor here; we badly need one.' Sulaiman pressed the bell. When there was no response, Sulaiman went out and angrily called out to Abdul Jabbar. He was at the ghat holding the anchor of the boat that had arrived. He saw Doctor Nisar, another man, and a girl stepping out. Nisar could not recognize Sulaiman at first, but when he went closer, Sulaiman said, 'Doctor Uncle, please walk faster. Daddy is in a lot of pain.'

'Relax, Sulaiman. All will be well. I am sorry that I could not recognize you. You have grown taller than me, Sulaiman.'

They walked fast towards the houseboat. Doctor Nisar introduced the two people to him. 'This is Doctor Dullu, and Nurse Miss Nancy. They will stay here with you.'

They entered the houseboat. When they were in the drawing room, Sulaiman said to Doctor Nisar, 'Just a minute, I will be back. *Bas aas!*' Then he ran in. Doctor Nisar was amazed and looked at Abdul Jabbar. The latter said to him, 'He speaks Kashmiri better than you and I.'

Sulaiman returned and said, 'Please come in, Mummy is also there.'

Doctor Nisar asked Doctor Pushkernath Dulloo and the nurse to wait, and walked into Ghulam Qadir's bedroom.

Reeny stood up when Doctor Nisar entered. She paid her salaam to him and stepped aside. Doctor Nisar sat on the side of the bed near Ghulam Qadir. He tried to sit up, but Doctor Nisar stopped him. 'No. Please don't get up.' But Ghulam Qadir could not stop himself. He held Nisar's hand against his cheek and wept. Then he tried to say something, but Doctor Nisar said, 'I know. I know how all this happened and I know the pain you are in. Vijay Kumar told me everything. I bear no grudge against you. These issues will be settled later. Our first and foremost concern is your health.' He turned to Reeny and said, 'Why are you standing? Please sit down. Have faith in Allah. Where are his reports?'

Sulaiman lost no time in taking out the file. When Doctor Nisar saw the reports, he went pale. He called Doctor Dulloo in and showed the file to him. Then he said to Ghulam Qadir, 'The medicines prescribed are as per the latest research. We might not get them here.'

'Don't bother about that; we have brought the full course with us,' Sulaiman said.

'Then we need not worry,' Doctor Nisar said to Reeny. 'Doctor Dulloo is an experienced doctor. He will stay here to attend to him.'

Through all this, Ghulam Qadir looked morosely at Doctor Nisar. Holding on to one side of the bed, Ghulam Qadir rose and propped himself against the pillow. Doctor Nisar went near him, caressed his back and said, 'Don't worry. You will soon get well because you have come home.'

'True, this pain will end one day, but what can I do about the pain that torments my heart?'

'That too has a remedy. Just shift to your own houseboat. I mean, Gulshan, your own Gulshan. Then see how quickly you recover.'

'No, that is not possible. I know well my destiny. You are a doctor, such a big doctor, and you know as well as I do that my days are numbered. When I breathe my last, I entreat you to request them on my behalf to forgive me. I have hurt them so much that even if I lived for many years and repented for my sins, I would not be able to compensate them for their suffering. So returning to the houseboat is out of the question.'

Instead of going home, Nisar turned his boat towards his grandfather's. He found the whole family sitting out in the open under the light of an electric lamp. Malla Khaliq was furious. Nisar surmised that his grandfather had come to know about Ghulam

Qadir's return. He ascended the steps and heard Noor Mohammad explaining his position. 'Abba, I swear by my son Nisar Ahmed that I was about to tell you everything.'

'But you did not have the guts to do so. If Ghulam Rasool of Wangnoos had not told me, I would not have known for months together. He had seen that millionaire accompanied by his Mem crossing over to Jabbar's houseboat. He also saw you going there.'

Noor Mohammad lost his cool and said, 'Abba, don't you have faith in me? Have I ever hidden anything from you? All this happened because it was an emergency.'

Malla Khaliq grew angrier. 'Yes, yes. Everything happened all of a sudden! Qadir arrived in Srinagar and you received the information through a telegram! How about the fact that he is staying in Jabbar's houseboat? Did you come to know that through—'

'Abba, let Noor Mohammad finish what he wants to say and then—' Ghulam Ahmed tried to douse the fire. But Malla Khaliq silenced him, 'You shut your mouth! I know all of you were in league with that swindler.'

Zeb watched through the window of her room. She could not clearly make out what the issue was, except that Ghulam Qadir was in Srinagar with his new wife and child. She got scared seeing Malla Khaliq yell and went outside. Walking behind the willows, she hastened to the isle.

Doctor Nisar stepped out of the shadows and went up to his grandfather. 'Abba, the nature of the contingency was such that Daddy could not tell you anything. You ask Narayan Joo.'

'So he knew as well? Vijay Kumar would have also known then. I alone was in the dark.'

'Abba, Qadir Uncle is ill, very ill. Having seen his condition, Vijay Kumar had requested his father to let Qadir Uncle come home as it was his last wish. He wants to spend his last days on the lake.'

Zeb's head began to swim, and she held the trunk of a willow. Bilal was confounded and could not decide what to do. He saw his mother and went and sat beside her. 'Mummy, Mummy, look at me.' He held her hand. Her hands were trembling and she began to sweat heavily.

Everyone thronged around Zeb. Malla Khaliq tried to comfort her. 'My daughter, why are you trembling? I will plead to the Association and get him thrown out of Jabbar's houseboat. You go in. Mukhta! What are you waiting for? Take her in.'

Bilal and Mukhta took her to her room. Doctor Nisar led Malla Khaliq to the drawing room and said, 'Abba, Qadir Uncle is not well.'

'How many more times are you going to tell me that he is not well? What do you want me to do about it? How can I forget what he has done? Don't you see the condition Zeb is in? No, no. I will certainly have him removed from the Dal tomorrow. The sahib is here to boost his health! Let him stay in some hotel, then. There are so many luxurious hotels here. Have all the hotels been razed that he's come to stay in a houseboat to worsen our anguish?' Malla Khaliq continued spewing fire.

But Doctor Nisar, fully aware of his grandfather's health, did not think it wise to tell him that Ghulam Qadir had cancer. 'Abba, you need not get agitated. If you force him out of the Dal, people might mock you. There are many tourists staying in the houseboats. Let him stay there as one of them. We must not drag this issue.'

Malla Khaliq's rage was quelled to some extent. 'All right, but tell your father that if I come to know that he visited Jabbar's houseboat again, I will lose one more son at that very moment. Tell him.' Having said this, he went to his room.

The night fell like doomsday for Malla Khaliq's family. Malla Khaliq moped in his room. No one could gather the courage to go near him. In the other room, Bilal reproached his mother, 'What are you weeping for? You know how much he tormented us. Why don't you say something, Mummy?'

But Zeb neither looked towards him nor did she say anything. This irked Bilal all the more. 'You just get up. If you still have some attachment with him despite all his cruelty, I will escort you to Jabbar's houseboat right now.'

Zeb cast a glance at her son and said, 'God forgives every sinner if he begs for His pardon.'

'But did he ever come to beg for your pardon? He is here in Kashmir, yet he did not show up. Did he ever phone you all these years to ask after your health? Tell me now, why don't you?'

Zeb was struck mute again.

'Please go and get some sleep now. If he had any concern for you in any hidden recess of his heart, he would not have brought that Mem here on whose leftovers he has become a rich man. Now, please get up and go to bed. I have to wake up early in the morning.'

Zeb went to the inner room. Bilal switched the light off and went off to sleep. But Zeb kept waking and praying to God, 'Oh my Allah, you will lose nothing if you cure his illness. My family has excommunicated him, but please do not cast him away. Oh my God Almighty, cure him.'

Everyone stayed awake in Houseboat Glacier as well. Ghulam in Qadir kept writhing in pain; no painkiller could mitigate his suffering. As a last resort, Doctor Dulloo decided to give him an injection of morphine, but when the nurse moved towards Ghulam Qadir with the injection, he said, 'How many more needles are you going to pierce through my bones? They have already punched so many holes in me.'

Doctor Dulloo tried to cajole him. 'Just one more injection and it will let you sleep soundly.'

'This will not work. My pain will end only when my life ends.'

Doctor Dulloo took the syringe from the nurse and emptied it very carefully into Ghulam Qadir's skin. At the same time, he said to him, 'All pains intensify during the night. You will have perfect sleep till morning, I am sure.'

The next day, well before dawn, someone came knocking at Narayan Joo's gate, and then the bell rang. Malla Khaliq stood there.

'Where is the Pandit?'

'Janak! Who is there?' Narayan Joo asked his servant from his bedroom.

'Haji Sahib is here.'

A sudden pallor came over Narayan Joo's face. He came out and greeted Malla Khaliq, '*As-salaam-alaikum*! What brings you here so early?'

'How craftily you feign ignorance! Swear you know nothing, Look at me. I could never think that you could be so cruel as to destroy all the bonds and promises of our lifelong friendship.'

'Look here, I am not one to understand these riddles of yours.'

'Yes, yes! You are just a toddler after all, aren't you? I was under the delusion that even if the whole world deceived me, I will always have a friend to rely upon, my very own Narayan Joo.'

'Haji Sahib, tell me openly what you want to say. What blunder have I committed?'

'Bravo! Who brought Qadir here? Who booked Jabbar's houseboat for him?'

'So this is the issue! I thought something very serious had happened. You please sit down. I will tell you everything.' Narayan Joo narrated the chain of events. But Malla Khaliq strode out of the house saying, 'Narayan Joo, you have not been fair to me this time.'

Narayan Joo followed him, but Malla Khaliq slammed the gate after him. Sitting in the taxi, he said to the driver, 'Let's leave now.'

The taxi left and Narayan Joo stood at his gate, feeling heavy with sorrow. This has never happened even once in the last sixty years, he thought.

In the meantime, Dilip woke up. He opened the window to see who had come so early to meet his grandfather. When he noticed him standing at the gate, he ran down the stairs. He first met Janak Raj, the servant. He told him that Haji Sahib had come in a bad mood and left looking angry. Dilip rushed to his grandfather.

'It is my misfortune. Haji Sahib had come here to quarrel with me saying we all conspired to bring Ghulam Qadir and Reeny to Kashmir.'

'But why are you so perturbed? He would have come to know sooner or later. Did you not tell him how seriously ill Qadir Uncle is? You should have also told him that Uncle insisted that we should not tell him.'

'Yes, I told him everything, but that made him angrier.'

'Did you not tell him that Qadir Uncle has been diagnosed with cancer?'

'This is the only thing I could not tell him,' Narayan Joo interrupted him. 'Yesterday evening I received a call from Noor Mohammad and he also could not muster the courage to tell him that Ghulam Qadir is in the last stage of cancer.'

Having said this, he abruptly got up with the resolve to see Malla Khaliq without delay and tell him the truth about Qadir's condition.

'Where are you going?' Dilip Kumar asked.

'Gagribal. I will tell Abdul Khaliq everything in detail, and I am sure that when he hears that Qadir has cancer and won't live too long, his anger will go away. Only then will Qadir die peacefully.'

'Let me accompany you.'

Doctor Nisar reached Glacier early in the morning. He found Reeny pacing the front lawn. As soon as she saw Doctor Nisar stepping out of the shikaarah, she ran towards him. She said to him, 'Doctor Sahib, I was waiting for you. I can hardly tell you how we spent the night.'

'Doctor Dulloo told me everything.'

'He gave him an injection, but his pain refused to diminish. He was mumbling strange things in Kashmiri in his sleep. He was in immense distress.'

'Where is Doctor Dulloo?'

'He has just gone to have a bath. He also spent the whole night wide awake. Come in, please.'

They entered Ghulam Qadir's room where he lay in bed. After a while Doctor Dulloo joined them. He led Nisar to the adjacent room and showed him the night's report. 'Ghulam Qadir kept repeating the whole night: "Hasn't the boat come here?" He also intermittently asked about his mother and father. Poor Reeny was very stressed. She does not know which boat he is waiting for.'

'What else can it mean but his family? He is still not ready to give up. But how can he help his unconscious from speaking up?'

'I think he is slipping away slowly. I think it's time for you to inform your family and make them come over to him.'

'That is the problem. You know the condition of Haji Sahib's health. He has already come to know that Qadir Uncle is here and he is not well. He is still not ready to come here to see him.'

'But Qadir's last wish should not remain unfulfilled.'

While they were talking, Ghulam Qadir came to. In a broken voice, he called out to Reeny. Reeny went running to his side. 'I am here, darling,' she said to him.

'Has Vijay Kumar arrived? He had told me that he would come soon after completing his pending work.'

Doctor Nisar said to him, 'He is trying to come on today's flight. He called me this morning.'

'I have very little time left; he should have come by now.'

'He is coming. Just close your eyes and sleep a little more.'

'He should come quickly otherwise there won't be any point in coming.' Saying this, Qadir closed his eyes.

Doctor Dulloo said to Reeny, 'Madam, you also get some rest. You have spent the whole night away sitting.'

Doctor Nisar also said, 'We are here. You go to bed, please.'

Reeny stood up on weak legs that were threatening to give way and went to Sulaiman's room.

While agony gripped Ghulam Qadir, the news of his illness had caused havoc in Malla Khaliq's house. Soon after breakfast, Narayan Joo went to Malla Khaliq's house.

'Why are you here? Have you come to rub salt over my wounds?' Malla Khaliq asked him coldly.

Narayan Joo stayed calm. Bilal also joined them. Noor Mohammad tried to pacify his father. 'Abba, this is Lala Sahib, our own Lala Sahib.'

'Yes, he is my dear brother, I know. That is why he conspired with all of you.'

'What conspiracy? Why doesn't it dawn upon you that Qadir is critically ill? Lala Sahib and his family are more worried about him than we are!' Noor Mohammad tried to show some sense to his father.

'He reckons us his enemies now. Don't stop him. He came to my house early in the morning to quarrel with me.' Narayan Joo also started losing his calm. 'Had I not taken his poor health in consideration, I would have given him the details of Ghulam Qadir's illness.'

Bilal, who stood silently listening to the heated exchange, said to Narayan Joo, 'Look here, Lala Sahib, we have nothing to do with anybody's health, especially of someone who has no relations with us. He may come over to Kashmir or go to Ladakh, but before getting involved in his affairs, you should have consulted Abba.'

'Do you think he would have allowed us to extend any kind of help to Qadir? Why don't you understand that he will be in this world only for a few more days?'

'Let that be. How can we help it?' Bilal was unyielding.

'Mukhta, Zoon and Mukhtar were all there, standing behind the willows, but no one dared come forward. Sneaking behind the rear prow, Zeb entered houseboat Gulshan. She hid behind a window curtain to hear what they were saying.

When Narayan Joo heard what Bilal said, he shouted, 'No one but my Mother Sharika can help him! He is suffering from cancer, that too in its last phase? Do you understand? We are trying to fulfil his last wish. Is he not your own? Is he not the dearest son of my sister Azi? If you are not ready to forgive us even then, that is our misfortune. But I will not have the courage to see my sister in the afterlife, after her family refuses a dying man's last wish.'

Bilal fell silent. Zeb felt like her own life had been sucked out of her. Mukhta, Zoon and Ghulam Ahmed broke down. Narayan Joo's resolve encouraged Noor Mohammad and he started coaxing his father. 'Abba he is in the clutches of death. He is about to breathe his last. He is only waiting for you. Now, for God's sake, forgive him.'

'Yes. That is why he is staying there in Jabbar's houseboat to humiliate me. Even in his last moments, he is here to take revenge on all of us and to show off his wealth.'

'All right, you keep holding on to your ego, but I will go right now to be by his side. Come on, my boy, show me where Glacier, is.' Having said this, Narayan Joo held Dilip's hand and walked towards the ghat.

Noor Mohammad followed him, saying, 'Wait, Lala Sahib, I will also come with you.'

All three sat in the shikaarah which turned towards Kotar Khana.

Mukhta and Zoon started wailing loudly. Bilal tried to comfort them while he looked around for his mother. Mukhtar came near him and said, 'Who are you looking for? Zeb?'

'Yes.'

'I saw her entering Gulshan.'

Bilal dashed to Gulshan. He found Zeb sitting in a chair, resting her head on the edge of the dining table. Bilal placed his hand on her shoulder. Zeb gave a start. He saw a deep pallor on her face; she looked like she had aged many years in minutes. She said, 'They are saying he is suffering from cancer, and yet no one has any sympathy for him—!'

'Abba has taught us that we should never be unfaithful to our principles, even if our life is at stake,' Bilal retorted.

'But it is your same Abba who always says that if a sinner confesses to his sins and asks for pardon, we should forgive him.'

'But did he ever come here to beg for pardon?'

'He did come. Not once but twice.'

'He came for his own selfish interest. Now tell me if you thought he had come to seek forgiveness, why did you not return with him?'

Zeb stood up and went out of the room. Without looking back, she said to Bilal, 'Whether he openly asks for forgiveness or not, we must forgive him in his last hours.'

'You are, as Lala Sahib always says, a Devi. You may forgive him, but I will never forgive him.' Saying so, he went out to the isle.

In Ghulam Qadir's bedroom, Narayan Joo and Noor Mohammad sat on either side of the bed. Qadir was feeling a little better since morning. Reeny entered, carrying Ghulam Qadir's small bag in her hand.

Ghulam Qadir opened the bag and took out two envelopes from it; he handed one to Narayan Joo, saying, 'I request you kindly to pass this envelope on to Abba when I am gone.'

Narayan Joo tried to interrupt, but Ghulam Qadir said, 'No, please don't say anything. I entrust this letter to you, Noor. Do you know why I feel better today?'

Noor Mohammad had nothing to say. But Ghulam Qadir answered his own question. 'It is because Lala Sahib came here to see me. You don't know what he, his son and his grandson have done for me.'

'Are you not as good as my own son?' Narayan Joo said.

'Even if Abba could not come, Lala Sahib came to see me. He has forgiven me.'

The nurse entered to give him his scheduled injection. Ghulam Qadir said to Reeny, 'Please stop all this now. Please take her away. There is more that I want to tell them. Time is of the essence.'

Reeny took the nurse out with her.

Ghulam Qadir took out the second envelope and handed it over to Noor Mohammad. 'When I cease to be and Lala Sahib gives the first one to Abba, please give this one to Bilal's mother. Don't ask me anything, please. You will find the answers to all your questions in these two envelopes.' Then he turned to Narayan Joo and said, 'At what time is Vijay Kumar's plane to land?'

'It must have landed by now. In half an hour he shall be here.'

'It was nice of you to send Sulaiman along with Dilip. They alone must carry our legacy on.'

Malla Khaliq did not come out from his room even to have his food. A Japanese family was expected to arrive that day to stay in Gul and Gulshan. Bilal was worried about his mother and so Ghulam Ahmed took Mukhtar Ahmed with him to the airport to receive the guests.

Bilal went to his grandfather and asked him, 'Abba, are the Japanese tourists a family of two or three? And will you please come with me to see which room we should keep ready for whom?'

'How much longer do you want to keep giving trouble to this old man? Go and do whatever you want to.' Malla Khaliq had become distant. When Bilal did not move, he became furious. 'Now, what are you waiting for? Just look at the list kept in the office and make the necessary arrangements.'

Bilal went out feeling dejected. He looked towards the Boulevard; the Japanese visitors had already arrived at the ghat. Mukhtar Ahmed and Ghulam Ahmed were loading their baggage in the shikaarahs.

Bilal went to the kitchen. Mukhta, Zoon and Zeb sat huddled together, looking grief-stricken. Bilal reprimanded them saying, 'While you sit here with your limbs crossed, the Japanese tourists have already arrived. Go heat the food and be ready. '

The shikaarahs touched the isle; Ghulam Ahmed held the ropes in his hands and steadied the boats. Bilal went forward to assist Mukhtar Ahmed in unloading the baggage. He scolded the cooks who stood waiting. 'Why are you standing here? Take the baggage out from the shikaarahs.' He took out the list from his pocket and handed it over to the leader of the party. He directed them to keep the luggage in the allotted rooms.

Ghulam Ahmed went to his father to apprise him of the events at the airport. 'There was a great rush at the airport. We met Lala Sahib's son Vijay Kumar there. That is why we got a little delayed in coming here. While I was talking to Vijay Kumar, Rajab Dandur's son tried to grab this party of tourists from us, but Mukhtar Ahmed was alert and warned him off.'

Malla Khaliq listened to him but did not say anything. But when Ghulam Ahmed told him that Vijay Kumar went straight away to houseboat Glacier, he felt his veins starting to smoulder. He started scolding Ghulam Ahmed, 'I heard what you said, I heard it all. Now please go and see to it that all the arrangements have been made.'

Ghulam Ahmed discerned that the mention of Vijay Kumar agitated his father. He quietly went away to the isle. He called Bilal and said to him, 'My dear son, your Noor Chacha has gone with Lala Sahib, and Abba sits confined to his room. You take Mukhtar with you. You take care of the Japanese guests. Abba will simply kill us otherwise.'

When Ghulam Qadir saw Vijay Kumar, he sat up. He said to Sulaiman, 'Where is his father?'

'He is sitting outside, in the lawn.'

'Please go and ask your Mummy to come here,' he said to Sulaiman.

Reeny came in with coffee for Vijay Kumar. He took a sip and then opened his briefcase and took out a file. Reeny asked him, 'Have you discussed everything with the lawyer?'

'He has gone through it with a fine-toothed comb.'

'All right then, let us sign the papers,' Ghulam Qadir said.

After signing the papers, Reeny returned the file to Vijay Kumar. Ghulam Qadir stretched himself, rested his head against the pillow, and said to Reeny and Vijay Kumar, 'Now the last pending job is finished. I can die in peace. All my dreams have been realized except one. But how can one undo one's destiny?'

He turned to his side, but feeling the strain in his abdomen, he cried, 'Oh my mother! I am dying.'

Reeny held his back, but his pain only increased. Vijay Kumar closed his briefcase and went out to call the doctor. The nurse came running. The doctor also came. He looked at his watch and asked the nurse, 'How much time has passed since the last injection?'

'Four hours.'

'Then prepare the next injection. Quick!'

Narayan Joo stood outside. He did not have the courage to enter the room. After standing there for a while, he went out to the lawn. In the meantime, Noor Mohammad arrived with an amulet from Rahim Sahib of Baba Demb. While climbing out of the boat, he noticed Narayan Joo standing in the lawn. Narayan Joo asked him, 'Did he give you the amulet?' He still hoped that God would grant them some miracle and Ghulam Qadir would recover. Even the amulet given by Rahim Sahib was a gleam of hope to him amidst all the despair. Noor Mohammad said to him, 'I felt as if Rahim Sahib was waiting for me to come. I did not have to say anything to him; he said everything himself: "Has the hawk returned after having flown far away to find his own nest?" I said, "Yes, he has, but with his wings broken. He is in great pain. He is quite near his nest, but is not blessed enough to enter it." On hearing this, he got up, went inside his shrine and came out with this amulet. He said to me, "Go and put this around his neck. All his suffering will end. He will stretch his wings, and fly to his original abode."'

Narayan Joo understood what Rahim Sahib had said. He knew that Ghulam Qadir was now ready to fly away to his ultimate abode in the heaven above and the amulet was sure to free him from the shackles of life. But he remained silent. Noor Mohammad said, 'Why don't you say anything?'

'You go in, my dear, and put it round his neck. His condition has worsened; the amulet might give him some relief.'

Noor Mohammad went inside the houseboat. He was convinced that the amulet would save Qadir.

After much pleading, Vijay Kumar succeeded in making his father agree to go home. 'There is nothing for you to do here. You have not eaten anything. You are not very fit yourself. All of us are here to take care of Qadir.'

Vijay Kumar said to Abdul Jabbar, 'Please take him across. But please send the boatman back without fail.'

Narayan Joo held his knees to stand up. His mind remained in a turmoil. He took out the letter that Ghulam Qadir had given for Malla Khaliq and wondered what to do with it. He finally said to the boatman, 'My dear son, after dropping me at the ghat, please go to houseboat Gulfam and deliver this letter to Haji Sahib.'

'You mean Malla Khaliq ?'

'Yes. But do not hand it over to anyone else.'

The shikaarah touched the Gagribal ghat. Narayan Joo paid the boatman and insisted again that he should not forget to hand over the letter to Malla Khaliq. Then he sat in his car and left for home.

⚊⚊

Malla Khaliq stood on the isle with the Japanese tourists. He disinterestedly whiled away his time answering their questions. The tourists were getting ready to go to Ladakh the next day. The boatman tied the boat to the ghat and came over to the isle. Seeing him there, Malla Khaliq asked him what he wanted.

'I want to have a word with you.' He took Malla Khaliq aside and handed the envelope to him. 'Narayan Joo Sahib asked me to give this to you.'

Taking the letter, Malla Khaliq went to his room. He hastily opened the envelope and saw the stamp of Hotel Sea Waves on it.

His hands shook as he read the letter. Qadir had narrated all the sweet and bitter events of his life, from his childhood to the moment of writing the letter. Malla Khaliq felt as if his heart was about to burst out from his chest. His knees felt very weak all of a sudden and he had to hold on to a chair and sit down. 'Oh my God, what should I do now? Show me the right path.'

⚊⚊

Bilal, who was feeling tired after having attended to the Japanese tourists the whole day, entered his room late in the night. He saw his mother sitting in darkness near the window which looked on to the lights of Kotar Khana. He did not deem it proper to switch the light on. He went sat near his mother and said to her, 'How long will you remain here by this window? You have not eaten properly either.'

Zeb turned to him, saying, 'I was not feeling hungry. Have you eaten?'

'Do you think I should also have remained hungry? Tomorrow I have to work hard again. I must have sufficient energy in my limbs. Now you get up from here, please. Nothing good will come of sitting here. Whatever has to happen will happen. Don't kill yourself like this.'

When Zeb started getting up, he said to her, 'Keep the window shut; the sky is overcast. If it rains, water will come in.' He went into the inner room, shut the door and made his bed.

Zeb again sat down near the same window and gazed at Kotar Khana in the distance. Her heart felt like it had been stabbed by Bilal's words: 'Nothing good will come of sitting here. Whatever has to happen will happen. Don't kill yourself like this.' The poor boy cannot be blamed; he never knew his father's affection. How would he have any compassion for him? But I—? How can I forget that I loved him will all my heart? I entrusted my being to him.

Lost in such thoughts, she was drowning in the memories of her youth. She felt as if a wildfire was raging in her mind and soul and she was getting consumed by it. 'Allah! I stand marooned in a tempest. Show me the way out. Let him live, even if it is to go back to strangers. My own love for him and hope for him are enough for me. Forgive him all his faults! Forgive him.'

She was about to shut the window, when she noticed that the light in Malla Khaliq's room was still on. Malla Khaliq was still awake so late into the night. She sat near the window again with her eyes fixed on Malla Khaliq's room. The curtain of the window was drawn, yet she could clearly see him through the curtain. He was restlessly pacing his room. However stubborn Abba might be, he is his own blood! He too has been restless like me for the last few days. He is also fighting a battle with himself.

Malla Khaliq had finished his late night prayers. Qadir's letter had hurled him in a whirlpool which left no exit for him. He felt very tired. He remained curled up in bed, but he could envision his dead wife imploring him, 'Khala! Qadir is in deep pain. Don't you see the daggers slashing my heart? I have already forgiven him, why can't you?'

Malla Khaliq was drenched in sweat. He suddenly got up, switched the light on and started pacing the room. Aziz's voice echoed in his mind. Her voice faded away only to be replaced by Noor Mohammad's voice saying, 'Abba, he is in the clasp of death. He is looking for release, but he cannot unless you go see him. Now pardon him, please Abba.' Finally it was Narayan Joo's voice that told him: 'How can I make you understand? He is suffering from cancer and that too in its final stage. Why don't you understand? Is he not your own offspring? Is he not the dearest son of my sister Aziz?' Malla Khaliq felt his head spinning. Holding it in his hands, he sat down on the bed, and closed his eyes. But Aziz Dyad's voice did not leave him: 'Khala! He is dying. If you don't hold his head against your chest in his last hour, I will never forgive you. Get up and give up your ego. Time is running out. You will repent otherwise.'

Malla Khaliq was at war with himself. He remembered everything one after the other: his principles, the hurts caused by Qadir, Zeb's haplessness, the restlessness of Aziz's soul, Noor Mohammad's revolt, Narayan Joo's imprecations. Finally he caved in.

Zeb continued watching him from her open window. When she saw that he was going towards the ghat, she came out of her room, and reached the isle. She tiptoed after him. Malla Khaliq untied the boat. It was the same boat in which he had once strayed away to kill himself. He sat in the boat and turned its prow. Zeb got frightened. Before Malla Khaliq could push the boat away from the ghat, Zeb quietly stepped into it and crouched in a little space. Malla Khaliq looked over his shoulder and saw her. For a moment he was flummoxed, but he did not speak. He rowed towards Kotar Khana.

The windowpane of Zeb's room slammed in the wind and woke Bilal up. He went into her room and switched the light on. When he did not find his mother in the room, he went out and looked around. Hearing the sound of oaring, he went to the ghat. He could see a boat in the distance, moving towards Kotar Khana. He ran to Malla Khaliq's room. He was also not in his room. He hurriedly went to the swamps, took out another boat and rowed fast towards Kotar Khana. There was a deathly silence all around. Malla Khaliq's arms felt limp and lifeless and he oared slowly. Zeb feared that he might change his mind any time and turn the boat back. She knew that Malla Khaliq was still battling with himself, 'Allah, please give him strength.'

Even after being given the strongest permissible dosage of morphine, Qadir remained in pain throughout the night. He was delirious and continued babbling: 'Yes he must be coming – the boat is coming – yes, there it is – splashing – there, there – can't you hear—' He tried to turn towards Reeny, but his eyes closed, and he was unconscious again. Noor Mohammad and Doctor Dulloo sat in a corner of the room, watching Ghulam Qadir's condition worsen by the minute. Vijay Kumar had left for Barzul to change into clean clothes, but had left his son Dilip with Sulaiman who sat in the lawn near the ghat.

The clouds had thinned and the moon shone bright in the sky. The two young men continued to watch the silvery ripples in the lake.

'It is quite beautiful, isn't it?' Dilip said.

Sulaiman said, 'You know, I had thought if Daddy recovered, we could open a big hotel on top of that mountain.'

'No, not a big hotel,' said Dilip, 'for that would ruin the environment. In Switzerland, they have these small but modern hamlets for tourists. I have done a lot of research and collected reading material from there.'

'That is not a bad idea. The Spice Village of Kerala is like that. You must see that,' Sulaiman suggested.

'Yes, I shall surely go there and see it. Let Qadir Uncle get well.'

'Yes, he is suffering so much. Let me go check on him.'

Sulaiman stood up, but Dilip stopped him. 'Look, a boat seems to be coming in this direction.'

Noor Mohammad also heard the sound of oars disturbing the stillness of the lake. He had dozed off for a short while and the sound awakened him. The sound was coming nearer and nearer. He got up and looked through the window. Reeny and Doctor Dulloo also woke up. Reeny said to him, 'Who is there in the boat?'

Noor Mohammad recognized his father in the moonlight. The beating in his heart quickened. He whispered to her, 'Perhaps it is Abba.' He went out for a closer look. The boat was touching the ghat. She asked Doctor Dulloo, 'Who is that woman with him?'

'She must be his daughter-in-law.'

Reeny froze. She looked at Ghulam Qadir. He lay with his eyes wide open. He said to Reeny, 'They have come – they have come to take me home! Yes, they—'

Reeny was fidgeting like a caged bird. Qadir tried to sit up. He said to her, 'See, they have come to take me ... I ... I will not go ...'

'No, no one can take you away. You just keep lying.'

Noor Mohammad came in panting. 'Qadir! Ghulam Qadir, your Abba has come to you, yes, your Abba!'

Reeny shuddered. She drew the curtain of the dressing room attached with the bedroom and hid behind it as if she was a thief.

Noor Mohammad pulled the curtain of the bedroom to one side, and Malla Khaliq walked in followed by Sulaiman. Zeb dithered; she did not have the courage to go in. She stood at the door. Noor Mohammad said to her, 'Zeb, why don't you come in?' Sulaiman also requested her to come in, but her eyes remained fixed upon Ghulam Qadir's cadaverous face. He was reduced to a skeleton.

Malla Khaliq stood near the head of the bed. Noor Mohammad nudged him awake saying, 'Dear Qadya! Ghulam Qadir! Open your eyes. Look, your Abba is here.' Ghulam Qadir started, and opened his eyes. Malla Khaliq was overwhelmed. He held Qadir's hand, sat at the edge of the bed, and held him close to his chest. Ghulam Qadir's pain subsided a little. An unrestrained cry came out from him. 'Abba!' Malla Khaliq held his hand close to his own face drenched with tears. 'No, Abba, don't shed your precious tears for this good-for-nothing son of yours. Abba, please!'

Reeny, hidden behind the curtain, felt like a stranger intruding on someone's personal moment.

Wiping his tears, Malla Khaliq looked at Zeb. 'If you did not hesitate in coming here with me, why are you hesitating now to come nearer?'

Zeb moved forward and stood near Ghulam Qadir's feet. Her tears had run dry. She stared blankly into Ghulam Qadir's face, softly chanting sacred verses for his absolution. Ghulam Qadir could hardly make eye contact with her and said to his father, 'I know I have wronged her.' Then turning to Zeb, he said, 'Please forgive me.'

'Allah alone can forgive mortals like us. We all should bow before Him for forgiveness.' Having said this, she sat down on the floor. But Sulaiman got her a chair. She sat in it and continued reciting verses from the Quran.

Qadir started closing his eyes when Bilal's brisk steps were heard. He was heard asking someone outside, 'Where is he? In that room?' Qadir woke up again. Malla Khaliq, Zeb, Noor Mohammad and others there looked towards the door as Bilal stepped in.

Reeny moved the curtain to one side and looked into the room. Bilal had come in fury, but when he saw everyone there aghast, he held his anger back.

Ghulam Qadir looked at his father's face and said, 'I know that Bilal will never forgive me. But Zoon Bhabhi, Mukhta, Parveen, her husband Abdul Razaq – where are they?'

'They will come tomorrow morning. Parveen and Abdul Razaq are in Udhampur.'

'When? When will they come? My time to leave has come, yes ...'

'Don't say that. See, all of us are here praying to Allah for your recovery.'

Malla Khaliq tried to comfort him, but Qadir started shivering. He held his father's hand firmly and began to gasp desperately. 'Abba – hold me – hold me closer, hold me, close—'

Zeb sobbed loudly, yet continued reciting the holy verses. Malla Khaliq said to Ghulam Qadir, 'Take Allah's name, take His name—'

But Ghulam Qadir's breath refused to support him, his body became limp and his eyes were riveted to the roof. Noor Mohammad and Bilal poured a little water into his mouth. Malla Khaliq held him close and tight to his chest and recited: '*Inallalu wa inaa ilaihi raajauun.*' On hearing these words, Reeny came out running, flung herself on Qadir's body and started wailing loudly.

Doctor Dulloo was still holding his wrist to feel the pulse, but his face clouded over. He gently closed Ghulam Qadir's eyes and got up.

Noor Mohammad was about to faint, but Bilal held him. Zeb continued to recite sacred verses and tried to comfort Reeny. Vijay Kumar's son Dilip held Sulaiman to his chest as they wept. Malla Khaliq went out and sat in the portico of the houseboat. The night had ended and dawn was almost here. Far away the loudspeakers at Hazratbal began to play hymns which mingled with the breeze of the Dal. The tolling of the bells at the Shankaracharya temple seemed to be bestowing eternal rest on Ghulam Qadir's soul.

Vijay Kumar's son Dilip entered the drawing room, and looked out to the prow of the houseboat. He saw Malla Khaliq bent in prayer. He quietly picked up the telephone and called his father to inform him about Ghulam Qadir's death.

Narayan Joo sank in the sofa hearing the news. He said to Vijay Kumar, 'So he left with the unfulfilled desire of meeting his father.'

'No, Daddy, Dilip told me that Haji Sahib was with Qadir in his last moments. Zeb Bhabhi was also with him. The two were followed by Bilal Ahmed. Dilip told me that Ghulam Qadir breathed his last in his father's arms.'

Narayan Joo turned to the wall where a photograph of the sacred site of Tulmul was hanging. 'Oh Mother! I lay down my life at your feet. You ultimately showed the right path to that stubborn brother of mine. Qadir's departed soul would otherwise haunt him always.' Then he turned to his son and said, 'Start the car. The driver is not expected here before nine.'

The news of Ghulam Qadir's passing spread throughout Malla Khaliq's fraternity and throughout Dalgate. A caravan of shikaarahs and canoes left for houseboat Glacier.

Malla Khaliq received all the mourners and did not break down even when Narayan Joo, Vijay Kumar, Parveen and Abdul Razaq arrived.

All of them wept but Malla Khaliq sat aside like a lump of clay. Reeny remained confined to her room. She sat still with her eyes shut. Zeb too sat silently near Mukhta. The time for the burial was running out, yet no one dared ask Malla Khaliq where to perform the rites.

Noor Mohammad said to him, 'From where should they carry the body away, Abba?' He cast a listless glance at him. 'While he lived, he did not enter his house. Should you carry him home now that he is dead?'

Ghulam Qadir had expressed his last wish to Noor Mohammad that his body should be interred near the foot of his mother's grave.

Abdul Jabbar, the owner of houseboat Glacier, was standing beside Noor Mohamamd. He said to him, 'You need not worry. This too was his house. All the rites shall be performed here.'

Bilal Ahmed, who chanced to hear Abdul Jabbar, was about to express his resentment, but Malla Khaliq stopped him with a gesture of his hand. Vijay Kumar took him aside and said, 'Since Sulaiman and his mother are also here, it is perhaps for them that Haji Sahib has taken this decision.'

Narayan Joo sat beside Malla Khaliq. He was at a loss as to how he could revive his friend from his state of numbness.

By afternoon all the arrangements had been made. The sky was overcast with dark clouds when Qadir's body was placed in a big boat. A procession of boats followed it. All the mourners were reciting '*laa illaha illalah*' in unison. Ghulam Qadir's last journey ended in the waters of the Dal where he had opened his eyes for the first time. He was placed for his final rest in the foothills of the Shankaracharya mountain where his mother was buried.

All the women remained at the ghat until the funeral procession was out of sight. Ghulam Ahmed had stayed back to look after the family. He made arrangements for sending the women back to the houseboats. When everybody had left, Reeny sat all alone. Abdul Jabbar's wife and his daughter-in-law went to her. The daughter-in-law said to comfort Reeny, 'We can feel your pain, Madam. Please don't think that you are alone. We are here to share in your grief.' Reeny thanked her. 'You took care of all of us throughout this period of suffering. Even my own people would not have been able to help us as you did. Never in my life shall I forget your kindness.'

'No, Madam, we did not do a favour to you. Allah had assigned this task to us and we were honoured to fulfil it.'

'Which direction is the graveyard where they carried the body to?'

'It lies there behind that mountain. Qadir Sahib's mother is also buried there. It is there, where you can see the crowd gathered.' Reeny got up, went into the houseboat, and climbed the stairs to the deck from where she could see the funeral procession. The sun came out from behind the clouds; it had already touched the summits of the Apharwat mountain. The light started gradually diminishing at the foothills and the people gathered there also grew invisible. Reeny closed her eyes. She felt like she was drowning in an endless ocean of darkness.

Next day in the evening, Noor Mohammad and Mukhta found Zeb
sitting at the window from which she could see Kotar Khana. On
noticing them, she moved away and sat in a corner with her head
bent. She felt nervous as if she had been caught doing something
wrong. Noor Mohammad took out the letter which Ghulam Qadir
had entrusted to him for her. Holding out the unopened envelope
to her, he said, 'My dear sister, I kept this envelope safe with me for
the last few days. Ghulam Qadir had asked me to give this to you
after his passing. What he has written is between you and him. We
are here only to entreat you to forgive him now. Whatever had to
happen has already happened. Please ask Bilal also to forgive him.
Only then can his soul find eternal rest.'

'I forgave him long ago. If I had not forgiven him, why would
I go in the dead of the night with Abba to see him? As far as Bilal
is concerned, give him some time. He too will forgive him. Time
will heal his wounds. He was his father after all.'

Zeb opened the envelope. Her hands quivered. She felt like Ghulam
Qadir was speaking to her. 'I have lost the right to address you by
the name I used to call you in those sweet days of my youth which
I have lost because of my own foolishness. I once came to take you
away with me with the confidence in the old, pure love which I
had for you. I had come to tell you the events in my life that led
me to another woman, and was sure that you would pardon me.
Had I been a little honest and courageous when I had my chance
perhaps I wouldn't have lost you. But no one can defeat his destiny.
Whatever had to happen has happened. I attained all that I had
once hankered for. I spread my wings to reach the sun; not knowing
that the wings that supported me were as fragile as wax. The wings
melted and I fell into an endless abyss. Then an angel appeared in
the form of Vijay Kumar who rescued me. Then I washed away all
my sins, and embarked on the path of truth to make something of
myself. I have written to Abba telling him all that happened after

that. It is likely that one day he might ask you to read that letter. If you happen to read it, I am sure you will forgive my sins. Now all is finished. This is the end of my trial. God bestows His revelation upon me, leaving no space for lies. I beseech you to believe that I never stopped loving you and Bilal even for a second. If you two forgive me, Allah might absolve me. Yours, Qadir.'

Every word struck Zeb's heart like a spear. She wept for a long time.

The letter was still in her hands when Bilal entered the room. 'Why are you still sitting here? Are you all right?'

Without replying or even lifting her head, she held out the letter to him. Bilal took the letter and asked, 'Who gave it to you?'

'Your uncle gave it to me. Your father had entrusted this letter to him.'

Bilal went through the letter and then sat with his back against the wall. He closed his eyes. She warily said to him, 'Why are you silent, my son?'

'So he had written a letter to Abba as well?'

'Did he not tell you?'

'Yes, he let me read it.'

'What did it say?'

Bilal got up, but before leaving, said to his mother, 'Don't get sucked into this quagmire. Leave everything be as it is. There is nothing to gain from it.'

Zeb folded the letter carefully, got up and kept it in her trunk.

Three days had passed since Ghulam Qadir's funeral, but Malla Khaliq was still numb. He moved about like a robot. After reading Ghulam Qadir's letter, he started holding himself responsible for the tragedy. In his sorrow, he had given the letter to Bilal, but then he repented for the mistake. Since that moment he perceived Bilal distancing himself from him. Bilal was his life and soul. He thought if Bilal turned his back on him, he would be left all alone. Malla Khaliq shrank into himself more and more every passing day.

One day, he took his boat out. Bilal rushed to him and said, 'Abba, where do you intend to go to all alone?'

'My son, I just want to exercise my benumbed arms by rowing the boat. I will be back soon.' Having said this, he steered the boat towards the Boulevard. Bilal called out to send Subhan after him, but Doctor Nisar stopped him saying, 'Let him have some time by himself on the lake. The lake may revive and heal him.'

In the meantime, Narayan Joo's boat came from the direction of Dalgate. When Bilal saw it, he said to Nisar Ahmed, 'Doctor Sahib! Isn't that Lala Sahib coming this way?'

'Yes it is!'

'Abba has moved away from him as well and yet Lala Sahib does not complain.'

'He is more than a brother to him. He is more worried about Abba's health than we are.'

Narayan Joo's boat touched the ghat. Bilal and Nisar went to receive him. Both held his hands and pulled him ashore. Noor Mohammad also saw him coming up to the isle, and went to greet him. He said to Bilal, 'Go and tell Abba that Lala Sahib has come. Lala Sahib, he does not come out of his room at all any more. He might come out from the confinement for you.'

'Abba has taken out his shikaarah towards the Dal,' Bilal said to him.

'And you let him go all alone?'

Doctor Nisar allayed his fears. 'It was I who told Bilal not to follow him. I am sure the lake will relieve him of his grief.'

'Doctor Sahib is right, let us sit inside and wait for him.'

Malla Khaliq stopped his boat at the ghat of the Boulevard from where his ancestral graveyard was a stone's throw away. He trudged uphill where his beloved Azi and his youngest son lay in their graves. He had a small bag in his hand. He stopped in the graveyard to catch his breath. After a while he spotted a tall boy dressed in black near Ghulam Qadir's grave, instructing people to erect a gravestone on the grave. It was Sulaiman. The mason and his helper stood aside when Malla Khaliq reached the grave. Reeny was sitting near the grave, a black headscarf obscuring her face. She hurriedly stood up and bowed to Malla Khaliq. Sulaiman also paid his salaam. He was at a loss about how to behave with them in such a situation. Malla Khaliq nodded and then turned to the mason, 'Why did you stop? Finish your task.'

The mason stammered to say, 'I had insisted that I first seek Haji Sahib's permission, and then start the work, but—'

Malla Khaliq held his anger in. He interrupted the mason, 'I am telling you to finish the job assigned to you.'

The mason raised the gravestone. After finishing, he gathered his tools. Malla Khaliq said to him, 'You may leave now. God bless you. Come to me to collect your money. Don't take any money from them.'

The mason and his assistant left as quickly as they could.

Malla Khaliq opened his bag and took out the bulbs of iris from it. He beckoned Sulaiman to come nearer. Sulaiman warily went near him and said in Kashmiri, '*Farmeeviv haz!*' to indicate that he was listening.

Malla Khaliq said, 'I have got some blue iris. Please plant them all around the grave.'

The soil around the grave was still loose. Sulaiman took the bulbs and planted them close to one another. Reeny was standing behind a tree, looking at the grave. Malla Khaliq stood up, took the bucket of water left by the mason, and started sprinkling water on the soil. Sulaiman took the bucket from his hand and watered the iris bulbs. Having finished, he kept the bucket aside. But Malla Khaliq said to him, 'You too sprinkle some water over those flowers that are growing on your grandmother's grave.'

He watered the plants around Aziz Dyad's grave as well. Malla Khaliq then said to him, 'I want to spend some time alone over here, so you can leave.'

Reeny somehow gathered courage and went closer to Ghulam Qadir's grave and Malla Khaliq, but he said to her, 'Please go, please!'

Sulaiman, holding his mother's hand, led her down the slope towards the road.

Malla Khaliq squatted near his son's grave. In utter despair, he said, 'So you did not even give us the trouble of raising your gravestone! All right, let it be so.' Casting a doleful glance at his wife's grave, he grumbled, 'Do you see, Azi, what a fire your darling son has left smouldering in my heart?'

Then he softly chanted the holy verses for the peace of the two departed souls.

Narayan Joo and others were assembled in the drawing room of Gulfam. They discussed the issue which Vijay Kumar had raised when they were at houseboat Glacier. Noor Mohammad said to Narayan Joo, 'Please break your silence. Tell us if it is wise to allow Ghulam Qadir's second wife and son to come here and meet us, particularly Zeb.'

'What is the point in her coming here?' Ghulam Ahmed said. 'What lies here for her? Why should she come to make our wounds ache afresh?'

Doctor Nisar, who had observed how earnest and harmless at heart Reeny was, could not desist from saying, 'Ama Chacha! Such bitterness does not become you. You yourself have seen in Goa what a graceful and humble woman she is. In my opinion she should come for a while to see us here before she leaves for Goa. What do you think, Bilal?'

'What can I say? All depends on Abba's decision.'

All of a sudden it occurred to Narayan Joo that Malla Khaliq had been out for quite a long time. 'We were so absorbed in our discussion that we did not notice that Haji Sahib has been out for many hours.'

Bilal stood up abruptly. 'I will go and find out where he is.' Mukhtar Ahmed also got up. The two called Subhan to get the boat. They left in search of their grandfather. After asking around from a lot of people, they reached the graveyard. They found Malla

Khaliq sweeping the dry autumnal leaves strewn around the two graves with a broom he had fashioned from buck-wheat. They went running to him and took away the broom from his hands. 'What is all this, Abba? When did you get this gravestone erected? We had planned to get a gravestone from Athwajan in a load-carrier. How did you get it here?' Bilal asked him. Malla Khaliq was silent.

'Why don't you say anything?' Mukhtar Ahmed was getting impatient. Malla Khaliq sat down and looked at Qadir's grave. 'He was split into two halves. The other half also had a little right over him. I got angry when I saw him erecting this gravestone, but some unseen force stopped me and I did not stop him. This was perhaps ordained by the Almighty.'

Bilal went silent. For the first time since his father's death, his eyes watered. He calmly said to his grandfather, 'What shall we do with the gravestone that we ordered?'

'Keep it reserved for me,' said Malla Khaliq with a smile. Then he looked at his wife's grave again. Affectionately touching the soil there, he said in a voice choking with emotion, 'I request you to inter me here—'

'Don't talk like that, Abba. Now please come with us; it's getting hot.'

Even after requesting him to get up, neither Bilal nor Mukhtar stood up. Bilal thought that his grandfather, who was looked up to in his fraternity for his strength of character, his larger-than-life presence, who could single-handedly take even the largest barge out of tempestuous tides, who was such an experienced boatman that he made other boatmen feel shy to handle their oars, seemed now like a ripe pear precariously perched on a branch, and could fall down any time. Malla Khaliq looked at Bilal. 'My dear, I know what you are thinking. You are hoping your grandfather will be around forever, holding your hand. But has any mortal lived thus? Only the name of the Almighty has such powers. The boatman who spends his life toiling in the Dal Lake will one day have to lay his oar down and make way for other boatmen to take his place. Thus Malla Khaliq too shall depart one day and you shall wield the

oars. This is an undeniable truth. Now get up, hold my hand for
your Abba is tired.'

Bilal held his left hand and Mukhtar his right and Malla Khaliq
stood up. He released their hands and stretched. He looked at Bilal
and said, 'Thank you! See, just by sharing a few words with you,
the hunch in my back has straightened! You alone are my strength.'

Then he turned to the grave of Ghulam Qadir and said to
himself, but loud enough for Bilal to hear, 'He laid down his life to
end all animosity.'

Having said this, he strode fast down the slope towards the road.

When Bilal and Mukhtar did not return quickly, the family
grew anxious and went out to the isle. Doctor Nisar and Abdul
Razaq called out to the boat that passed the ghat, but Doctor Nisar
said to his father, 'You stay here, we will go and get them back.'
Just then Ghulam Ahmed said, 'There they are; both the boats are
returning.'

Malla Khaliq was the first to climb up the steps. His eyes were
fixed on Narayan Joo who stood in a corner, looking down. Malla
Khaliq said to him with affection, 'Why is our Panditji standing
aloof? Now please forgive this brother of yours.'

Narayan Joo looked at him; his eyes were brimming with tears.
Malla Khaliq hugged him. 'Throughout this storm that overtook
our lives, you have proved to be as pure as gold tested in fire. But
I failed you. Forgive me. For all that you and your family did for
him, I will always—'

Narayan Joo interrupted him, saying, 'No more of these
formalities. Let us go in because an important decision is awaiting
your consent.'

'Bilal Ahmed has already told me. There is nothing to wait for.
The bereaved woman wants to see us before going back, so let her
come. She is not going to live with us permanently, after all.'

When the days of mourning were over, Vijay Kumar and his son
led Reeny and her son Sulaiman to Malla Khaliq's house. Narayan

Joo introduced all of them one by one to Reeny and Sulaiman. Reeny, still clad in black, met them, her eyes brimming over with tears. Sulaiman said, 'No, no, Mummy! You promised not to cry.'

'I'm sorry, my son. You see what it has taken for me to meet them for the first time.'

Mukhta, Zoon, Parveen and Zeb silently shed tears. Then Malla Khaliq entered the room followed by Bilal and Ghulam Ahmed. Reeny pulled her headscarf down on her forehead and stood up to say salaam to her father-in-law. Malla Khaliq responded to her salaam and said, 'Please be seated.'

He too sat down. Reeny was about to say something, but Malla Khaliq said to her, 'My son told me everything about you and himself in his letter. We therefore understand your predicament, and bear no grudge against you. Even if we had had any grudge, it is meaningless now.'

'I have sinned against all of you. But this Sulaiman is his son. He is innocent. He has your blood in his veins. If you just place your affectionate hand on his head once, that would be more than enough for me.'

Sulaiman walked ahead, bowed and placed his head at Malla Khaliq's feet. Malla Khaliq's eyes filled with tears as he held him warmly to his chest. He quivered and tried to hold his tears back. Then he released Sulaiman and was about to stand up, when Narayan Joo stopped him.

'Where are you going?' he asked. She wants to say something to you before seeking your permission to leave. Please sit down.'

Malla Khaliq wiped his tears and sat down again.

Reeny looked towards Vijay Kumar. He opened the briefcase and took out some documents. With her eyes lowered, Reeny said to Malla Khaliq, 'Your son had written his last will. Vijay Kumar will present the will to you because your son had appointed him as the executor of his deed. Being an equal partner in his business, I have already given my assent to his will. When you hear the contents, I hope you will come to know that Qadir never considered himself estranged from you.'

There was a long lull in the room. After that, Vijay Kumar started reading out the will to them, but before doing that he said to Malla Khaliq, 'The will is quite brief. Ghulam Qadir had insisted on getting the deed registered in court before his passing.

"'I, Ghulam Qadir, son of Haji Abdul Khaliq, native of Gagribal, Srinagar, Kashmir, tehsil Srinagar, district Srinagar, now residing at Panaji Goa, state of Goa, in all my senses, solemnly command by this will, that I bequeath all my property and assets, the details of which are given in annexure, 1, 2 and 3, to my esteemed father Haji Abdul Khaliq, resident of Gagribal, Srinagar, and the owner of houseboats Gul, Gulshan and Gulfam. I further command by will that he is authorized to use it in whichever way he likes. My will has the absolute and unconditional support of my wife Reeny Qadir, resident of Daman. Her consent is included in the command of the will.

"Furthermore, I have willed an amount of fifty lakh rupees in the State Bank of India under the account number SB45306 in the name of my first wife Mrs Zaib-un-Nisa, wife of Ghulam Qadir, resident of Gagribal, Srinagar, Kashmir, and I will that she shall be the sole owner of that money.

The Warrantor: Ghulam Qadir'''

The room was submerged in silence. Nobody knew how to react. Vijay Kumar cast a glance at his father. He finally thawed the icy silence. 'He deserves praise for he ultimately proved himself to be a true scion of Haji Abdul Khaliq. Now hand over the will to Haji Sahib.'

'You have put me in a spot. I don't have the strength to bear such a huge debt. My feet are already hanging in my grave and I don't know when I will fall into it. No, it is not possible for me to bear such a heavy yoke. I, a poor boatman, will crumble under the burden,' Malla Khaliq said.

Narayan Joo tried to make him understand. 'It was Qadir's last wish. You must fulfil it. We can sort out other things later.' Then

he turned to Reeny. 'Dear daughter, all this is happening so fast that
he is a bit thrown. So I request you to keep the documents in your
custody and give him some time to think.'

Malla Khaliq's eyes filled with gratitude as he looked at Narayan
Joo. Then he said to Reeny, 'If I call you my daughter, I hope you
will not be offended.'

'Oh, that would mean the world to me, the most precious gift
I have ever got. Having heard these words from you Qadir's soul
must be feeling blessed. I know it.'

'Now you have become a part of our family. Sulaiman too. As
far as land and property are concerned, I never had any interest in
such things. You have to keep the name of the departed soul alive.
This is my prayer; Allah will give you strength and forbearance.'

Reeny said, 'Since we are one now, I have a request to make.
You and Narayan Uncle kindly pay a visit to Goa and see how your
prodigal son has built an empire through sheer hard work.'

'You cannot even conceive how efficient and hard-working he
was. You will have to go there at least once,' Vijay Kumar seconded
Reeny.

'We will surely go there if Allah allows us to. Now you will have
to excuse me. I am very tired and I want to rest. But please don't
leave without having lunch,' Malla Khaliq said.

Malla Khaliq went near Narayan Joo and said, 'Now get up, my
Pandit. You must also get some rest.'

Reeny got up to open the door for them. Before they went out,
she said to him, 'I hope you will have no objection if I spend some
time with Zeb-un-Nisa.'

'Why should I have any objection? Let's leave her alone with
Zeb for some time,' he said to Zoon and Mukhta.

Then Malla Khaliq, Narayan Joo and Vijay Kumar left the room.
Everyone else apart from Zeb also left the room.

It was a strange meeting. A meeting between rivals, destined to
whirl in the same orbit, the pivot in which was now broken. Zeb

didn't know what to say. It was Reeny who finally broke the ice. 'You and your family consider me the biggest sinner, but in all the years that Ghulam Qadir lived with me, he told me just one lie for which I never pardoned him. I wish he had told me that he had such a wonderful first wife in Kashmir pining for him. I would have not married him ever, all my love for him notwithstanding. In his desperation to save me from my crises, he decided to marry me. Oh, I wish you had come there along with him. Oh, I wish—'

Zeb interrupted her, 'I too have many complaints, but what is the point of it? If only he had given me that letter many many years ago, I would have surely forgiven him. I have no grudge against you at all. You don't know how tall and noble you stand in comparison to all of us here. Now he is no more, yet I know that it is again because of him that we have forged such a sacred bond with you that has no name.' The two bereaved women sat there for a long time. When the burden between them had dissipated, Reeny took leave of her.

Noor Mohammad urged her to eat with the family, but Reeny said to him, 'Today I have got so much love from all of you that I really have no need for food. Now, with God's mercy, we will be meeting off and on. I hope the ache of your loss heals soon. I am going away, leaving behind the one most loved by me at the foothills of the mountain. I will keep returning to his grave.'

She called Sulaiman who sat at the prow of houseboat Gulshan chatting with Bilal Ahmed. Both Sulaiman and Bilal Ahmed came near her.

Subhan had already anchored the shikaarah to the ghat. All the family members went to see her off. With a heavy heart, Reeny took leave of them. Wiping her eyes, she sat in the shikaarah with Vijay Kumar. Looking at Bilal, Sulaiman said to him, 'Tomorrow, we will be going back empty-handed. Won't you give me a hug?'

Bilal sadly held Sulaiman in a tight hug and said to him, 'Look after yourself and do take care of your Mummy.'

'Yes, I will,' said Sulaiman.

On the same day in the evening, a huge argument erupted in Narayan Joo's living room, between Vijay Kumar and his son. Vijay Kumar reprimanded his son, 'You refuse to book your return ticket, but that does not mean that I will allow you to stay back here in Kashmir. What avenues will you find here? You have got such a prestigious degree from Switzerland! Was it meant to keep you incarcerated here in these mountains?'

'I trained in tourism! This is considered a flourishing industry across the world. Tell me, is there any place better than Kashmir for managing tourism? If I could in any way serve my homeland, there is certainly no better work to do. Grandpa, why don't you make him see sense?'

'Yes, yes. I understand. It is he who has brainwashed you,' said Vijay Kumar in his rage.

Narayan Joo was about to say something, but Dilip Kumar said to his father, 'Neither he nor anyone else has brainwashed me. I came across many technocrats in Switzerland, Italy and France, who have made great progress in the material sense. But I always found them craving to return to Kashmir. Leave them aside; have you already forgotten Qadir Uncle? Even after becoming such a big hotelier, I witnessed how he pined to return home.'

Narayan Joo could no longer hold himself back. He said to Dilip Kumar, 'My darling, this father of yours is unable to accept this truth. I too faced this very problem over twenty-five years ago when Vijay Kumar had returned after finishing his training. When he told me what he tells you right now, "What lies here to our advantage? There is no space to spread wings and soar in the sky. There are no avenues for progress!" I was rendered speechless, and I could not hold him back. I thought he was right. But what you are saying after having seen all of Europe gives me a fresh perspective. If every son or daughter of Kashmir – Hindu or Muslim – gets proper education and training abroad and then comes back to Kashmir with the resolve to make it a real paradise on earth, then all our troubles will go away. Vijay, I plead for him: give him the opportunity. I, however, swear by my Mother Devi, I have not made any attempt to brainwash him.'

'Listen, Dad, I have resolved to stay here with my Grandpa – come what may! I just need your blessings.'

Vijay Kumar heaved a long sigh. Then he said to his son, 'Okay, you may go ahead. I know nothing is going to change this place. Yet you may give it a try.'

When Malla Khaliq entered Narayan Joo's garden the next day, he found him checking Vijay Kumar's baggage. Seeing him there so early in the morning, Narayan Joo asked him, 'How come Haji Sahib is here so early in the morning?'

'I know Vijay's flight is at ten o'clock and I arrived early so I could speak with him before he leaves.'

'No. I think there is something more serious; I can read it in your eyes.'

Malla Khaliq called his taxi driver in and said to him, 'Rashid Sahib! Please bring that bag here.'

The driver brought a huge bag inside and Malla Khaliq placed it among Vijay Kumar's baggage. 'It contains some almonds, walnuts and some dried vegetables for my daughter-in-law there. Where is Vijay?'

'He is getting ready. Let us go in.'

He took Malla Khaliq into the drawing room. Malla Khaliq looked all around and said to Narayan Joo, 'I don't see Dilip here. Where is he?'

Narayan Joo sat beside him and said with an air of confidentiality, 'There is good news for you. He does not wish to go back to Bombay with his father. And I will not be leaving you alone during the winters henceforth.'

Vijay Kumar came in followed by Dilip Kumar, carrying his father's briefcase. Both of them greeted Malla Khaliq.

'My dear son, will you spare a minute or two for me before you leave?'

Vijay Kumar sat down beside Malla Khaliq on the sofa.

Malla Khaliq took out a big envelope from the inner pocket of his phiran and gave it to Vijay Kumar.

'What is this?' Vijay Kumar asked.

'Please give this to Reeny.'

'But what does it contain?'

'Ghulam Qadir's will. I thought about it long and hard, and then came to the conclusion that I won't be able to bear this responsibility. All this is Reeny's and Sulaiman's. You please return it to them.'

Vijay Kumar said to Khaliq, 'Please try to understand. Your kindness healed Reeny's wounds. If I return these documents to her, she will feel hurt to an extent that you cannot imagine. Please keep the documents with you and let us see what we can do.'

Narayan Joo seconded his proposal. 'Vijay Kumar is right; don't break the poor girl's heart.'

Malla Khaliq accepted their suggestion. He handed over the envelope to Narayan Joo. 'You keep it in your custody.'

'No, my dear friend, I fear greed might blind me. You keep it in your own custody.' Saying this, Narayan Joo put the envelope back in Malla Khaliq's phiran pocket. Dilip, who had gone to fetch the other bag, came in.

'Now let's move, otherwise you will be late. I will drop you at the airport. Then I have to attend to some work at the bank.'

Malla Khaliq feigned ignorance and said, 'Aren't you going along with him?'

'He has been beguiled by this friend of yours,' Vijay Kumar said to end the conversation.

'No, Haji Uncle, it is my own decision. I will not abandon my homeland to go anywhere else. You wait and watch, he himself will return sooner or later,' Dilip said to him.

'They will surely return home. Everyone will return home in search of their roots. But I pray to Allah that no one returns home in the condition that my poor son Qadir did.'

Everyone fell silent at the memory of Qadir. Vijay Kumar's son, nonetheless, changed the subject.

'No more shall my grandpa live alone here. He will not leave his home even in winters.'

'So this year we will enjoy the snow to our heart's content. And then, Haji Abdul Khaliq Sahib, we will see who wins the Nav Sheen bet this time.'

A faint smile appeared on Malla Khaliq's lips. Casting a loving glance at Narayan Joo, he said with a long sigh, 'Yes, that day is not far now.'

When my first novel *Sheen Ta Vatapod* (*Snow and the Bridle Path*) was published in 1987, many of my friends and associates were skeptical, for how could I, who had dedicated the my life to theatre and spent much of my life in the company of dramaturges, switch from drama to fiction, that too so late in life! However, the main reason behind my sudden switch was my realization that drama, despite its strength to influence its audience and stimulate them directly, is finite in scope as it does not overcome the limits of space and time and keep pace with the fast-changing moods of passion, inscapes and transience of reality.

This perception had been lurking in my mind for a long time and spurred me to experiment with the production of long radio serial plays like *Vyath Rooz Pakaan* (*And the Vyath Continued Flowing*) and *Lala Joo and Sons* in Kashmiri. Yet, even after having orchestrated, and then directed such open-ended plays, my mind was not satiated in depicting the latent motives of the characters. Even dialogues and soliloquies seemed inadequate to represent the complex undercurrents that make up the human psyche. I felt that poetry and the novel were the best forms in which the human mind could be unravelled fully. Poetry has been considered divine revelation, but my Creator did not deem me suitable for this faculty. So it was an obvious choice for me to adopt the genre of the novel and this is how *Sheen Ta Vatapod* (translated by me into English and published under the title *Sheen – Snow And The Bridle Path*) came to be. The novel was given the year's best book award from the Jammu & Kashmir Academy of Art Culture & Languages and went on to win the national award from Sahitya Akademi. Soon after publishing this novel, I started writing my second novel.

The outline of this new novel occurred to me in the late 1940s when I rented a small boat at the rate of one rupee per day from the quay of my native place, Chinkral Mohalla, in the city of Srinagar. Taking my childhood friends along, I roved through the Maer Canal of the old city and reached Gagribal in the Dal Lake. It was during this journey that the Dal formed an indelible imprint on my mind, and I took an interest in the dwellers of the Dal. Then, when I reached the college, my brother's business with the tourists strengthened my relation with the houseboat owners in the lake and this interaction continued for years to come. For many years, I even assisted the owner of a couple of houseboats in maintaining their correspondence with various foreign tourists. This experience provided me with an opportunity to understand the family life of the houseboat owners, and their relation to other boatmen and residents of the hamlets in and around the lake. Soon after, my career in broadcasting (first with Radio Kashmir and then with All India Radio) started. It was during that period that in Dachigam Wild Life Sanctuary, I had the good fortune of getting acquainted with a reputed and venerable person – Abdul Samad Kotroo. He owned a chain of houseboats in the Dal Lake. In fact, I was engaged in preparing a documentary there on the rare and pretty inmates of the sanctuary, particularly the Kashmiri stag, known as the hangul. The chief warden of wildlife at the time, Mir Inayat Ullah, had brought Haji Abdul Samad Kotroo along to record an interview for the documentary on the habits and behaviour of various birds and animals living in the sanctuary. Kotroo Sahib was an authority on wildlife in the state of Jammu and Kashmir.

I instantly became an admirer of Kotroo Sahib's sharp and empathetic mind and transparency of heart. Kotroo Sahib's experience of life and his understanding of the local people was immense. This became the foundation stone of our relationship which lasted up to his departure for heavenly abode. My interactions with this exceptional human being and his family members inspired me to write about the lives of the boatmen of the lake who has been mingling the sweat of their toil with the waters of the lake for generations. Being a father figure Kotroo Sahib was venerated by not only the boatmen but also the vegetable growers who dwelled in the marshes around the lake. He had continued the tradition that his father had set – of treating the tourists, who would often come to escape the maddening city life to stay in his houseboat, as his own kith. Similarly, Malla Khaliq is conscientious in his duties of making his guests feel at home. This is how the seed of the novel *Gul Gulshan Gulfam* was sown in my mind and I started weaving the fabric of this novel and writing it.

It was a boon of God that I got acquainted with the proprietors of a big production house of Mumbai – the film-makers Sunil Mehta and Prem Krishen when they had come to Kashmir to shoot their television film *Nai Shirvaani* (based on the Russian short story 'The Overcoat'). When they heard the story of *Gul Gulshan Gulfam*, they were so impressed that they immediately purchased its broadcasting rights from me. This was the genesis of the tele-serial *Gul Gulshan Gulfam*, that became a milestone in the history of the television in India.

The fame of this serial reached even foreign countries in Europe and also the United States where many broadcasting companies telecast it with subtitles, and Kashmiri people, felt for the first time that a beautiful aspect of their social life was portrayed to the world with honesty and empathy. Not only this, the popularly of the series was so impressive, that some hotel owners in Kashmir even changed the names of their hotels, and erected the signboards saying *Gul Gulshan Gulfam*! Some of those signboards are still there – outside the Harwan Gardens, in the Gulmarg bazaar, on the tuck shop at Sona Marg.

Despite having attained so much popularity, I still did not find my creative urge satiated, and my desire to write a full-length novel, as originally started, haunted me all the time. However, after the commercial success of *Gul Gulshan Gulfam*, I got so engrossed in work that I hardly had any respite to pursue such desires. For six long years, I was busy writing the screenplay of *Junoon*, the longest TV-serial of that time. After *Junoon*, my time was taken up in writing other popular serials like *Ghuttan*, *Manzil*, *Saye Devdaar Ke*, *Baaghi*, *Noor Jahan* and many others. But during all these years of relentless work, the desire to complete the novel *Gul Gulshan Gulfam* made me impatient. Two years after that hectic period of my life, I managed to lessen the burden of commercial writing and stayed for two successive summers at my Srinagar residence where my long cherished dream of completing this novel in Kashmiri, my mother tongue, was fulfilled.

The scope of a television series is short-lived and its frame is limited at various levels. Though I had tried my best to present all the characters of the serial in keeping with the cultural traditions of Kashmir, I personally felt that something was lost in the adaptation from the screenplay to the screen and they lacked an authenticity as they did not converse in their native tongue. In the form of the novel, the characters finally embraced their own mother tongue, and they became more solid and natural.

In stimulating me to write this novel, I am grateful to my brother Late Manohar Kaul and my wife Late Shanta Kaul, both of whom are writers as well. They were my unfailing audience every evening to the portions that I wrote during the day. They not only heard me intently, but also scrutinized every detail with honesty and gave me their counsel. I also express my gratitude to the writer Anita Kaul for going through the first draft and tightening it.

I am also grateful to Late Abdul Samad Kotroo who narrated many interesting events of his life to me – especially the incidents were directly related with his vocation, the Dal Lake and the actual life of its inhabitants. His insight proved to be of much help to me in giving texture to this novel. I must record here that it was the powerful portrayals by Parikshat Sahni as the protagonist, Malla Khaliq and Radha Seth who played his wife Aziz Dyad, who added new dimensions to the characters, which I have incorporated in the novel.

Since the TV serial *Gul Gulshan Gulfam* acquired a historical significance, it is appropriate that I convey my gratitude to all my companions whose work contributed to the success of the serial. The title song: '*Muskurati subh ki aur gungunati sham ki/Yeh kahani Gul ki hai, Gulshan ki hai, Gulfam ki*' was written by my dear friend Farooq Nazki. The lyrics rendered into music by Krishan Langoo well-known composer, became tremendously popular and eventually won the Best Title Song Award from Radio, Television Producers and Advetisers Association (RAPA Award) that year. The song is a beautiful synthesis of Kashmiri and Hindi:

Dalaken malaren seemab deeshith,
Aftab coshilan voshila draav,
Wan haaren hund aalav boozith,
Shoka hoth bulbul bagas vanavaan tchav

(Seeing the mercurial shimmering
Of the ripples of the Dal,
The sun rose with a blushed face;
Hearing the calls of the forest-starlings,
The bulbul with full fervour entered the garden, singing songs of love)

This note shall remain incomplete if I fail to express my thanks to my friends, Sunil Mehta and Prem Krishen, the producers of the series, who ignored all the considerations of business and let me have undisturbed freedom in writing the script. I thank Ved Rahi, the director of the series, for having assimilated the true spirit of the script.

This novel, when published in the original, created a stir in the literary circles. Several critics classified it as an epic in Kashmiri literature and there was a demand that it should be translated into English, so that its message would reach readers all over the world, so that they get a feel of the life of these simple boatmen and so that they feel that Kashmir is not only Heaven on Earth but also a real abode of love. So with this desire I was motivated to get the novel translated into English. The search for getting a competent person to take up this work was rather difficult as I wanted him to be a person who was conversant and fluent with both the languages. I was lucky that Professor Shafi Shauq agreed to undertake this mammoth task as he is a renowned litterateur in both the languages. He has kept the local flavour intact. This made my editing easy and I thank him for his work.

I am indebted to Neerja, my daughter, an author herself, for carefully going through the revision and for her inputs. It was she who got in touch with Shri Anuj Bahari of Redink, my agent. This note of mine would be incomplete without expressing my sincere thanks to him for introducing my work to the esteemed publishers at HarperCollins India, who were gracious enough to publish it.

Gul Gulshan Gulfam is the first novel of an epic dimension in the Kashmiri language. Although Kashmiri literature is distinguished for its antiquity and richness of form, the genre of the novel, for various reasons, remained impoverished. In its history of about sixty years, the Kashmiri novel has less than a score titles to its claim. Over the years, however, novels from around the world were translated into the Kashmiri and their availability enriched the understanding of the form.

Gul Gulshan Gulfam is undeniably the quintessential *mahaakaaviya* (prose epic) of contemporary Kashmir. In following the lives of characters belonging to three successive generations of post-independence Kashmir, and paying proportionate attention to the actions and moral choices of each individual living under specific and sometimes limiting socio-economic and cultural conditions, *Gul Gulshan Gulfam* emerges as a novel at the cusp of Indian economic liberalization and about the Kashmiri identity in flux.

What is also unique about this novel is the fact that it was born out a TV script. Before getting published, *Gul Gulshan Gulfam* was tremendously popular as a television serial and the characters had almost become a part of people's everyday lives in the early 90s when it was broadcasted on Doordarshan. This trajectory – from being conceived as a script, being produced episodically in a studio over a period with the participation of the director, actors, lights, setting, etc., then being edited and aired on TV across the country, and in retrospect, being transformed into the form of a novel sheds light on the evolution of the genre. Only Pran Kishore, with his lifelong immersion in the world of theatre, could have written this *mahaakaaviya* and retained its visual element which is crucial to the story.

Giving the story the shape of a complete, comprehensive written text involves being conversed in the rigours of a syntactic mechanism that can render the data gained through observation and intuition into linguistic media and create multi-layered semantic suggestions to carry the narrative, with its complexities of interconnecting plot arcs and an ensemble cast of characters, forward. And though often ignored, post-writing revision involves a different kind of energy from the writer. It is an undeniable feature of literature that its value is commensurate with the amount of labour involved in producing it. And this in turn, in an ideal world, is directly proportional to the amount of labour required from the reader to comprehend and appreciate the text. The novel *Gul Gulshan Gulfam* adequately meets this critical standard.

The tourism industry of Kashmir sets the novel in motion. The characters and events are set against the socio-cultural background that emerged in Srinagar because of an absence of dependable and self-sustaining economy and its parallel dependence on tourism. Many classes of other vocations, like craftsmen, boatmen, *waaza*s (professional cooks) and vendors are intimately associated with this business. It is a culture that has been absorbed by residents who have witnessed unparalleled catastrophes and political upheavals. The want of a sustainable economy, particularly in modern times, makes the urban population vulnerable to accepting the hazards of the tourism industry, as is evidence in cities around the world. To survive as an individual entrepreneur or carry on small-scale family business in the competitive world of tourism could very well imply being able to measure the market value of everything available at one's disposal: labour, housing property, fine arts and crafts, personal peace, ethical mores, conversation, and in certain respects, one's conscience and identity. The values, of course, are determined by an overpowering capitalist motive: to sell and accumulate personal wealth for the uncertain future. The nucleus of this bargain-centric culture is the Dal Lake and its environs, including the Jhelum and the Mughal Gardens, where the story takes place. The picturesque Dal Lake, with its age-old lake culture – which is not just part of the setting for the novel but also assumes characteristics of its own – seems to be somnolently waiting for the good days to return. The houseboats of Malla Khaliq – Gul, Gulshan and Gulfam are stare out emptily over the insulating Zabarwan cliffs.

The underlying motive of the novel *Gul Gulshan Gulfam* is to represent the strengths and the weaknesses of this industry of antiquity through life-like characters. This approach is taken to not simple criticize the system through a story but also to realistically portray with empathy the compulsions and contradictions that various characters go through to fit in or evolve with a quick-changing socio-economic environment. The same dimensions of the novel, nevertheless, has a different import for readers who feel suffocated in the tourist-centric culture of the city (and in turn the story) where every individual seems to have turned into a middleman, and all interactions reduced to economic exchanges. The simulacrum of the city in the novel thus functions differently to the different kinds of readings.

At the centre of the drama is Malla Khaliq, who with help from his lifelong friend, Narayan Joo, the travel agent, depends on making a paltry business of renting out three houseboats Gul, Gulshan and Gulfam to tourists. Taking full advantage of the third person omniscient point of view, Pran Kishore succeeds in depicting the psyches of a host of characters, but it is Malla Khaliq that the narrative voice is closest to. In his immediate actions and responses, both in states of joy and despondence, Malla Khaliq represents the consciousness of a fast-changing locality. He, like a true patriarch, has unwavering faith in his own aplomb and believes that he is the only one who can preserve a certain set of values and principles from the onslaught, and defeat the forces of disintegration. But in states of deep desperation, he becomes a captive of his own dread. He is frightened, his anxiety takes a physical form, he his fears project outwards onto his family through his quick temper. When nothing works, he resorts to prayers.

Narayan Joo acts as a foil to Malla Khaliq, and is also the voice of reason, cultural refinement and equanimity. His role as a benefactor and advisor to the vicissitudes of the lives of others is to show how reason and honesty can restore harmony when everything is out of control. He has suffered personal loss in the death of his wife, yet he symbolizes cohesion, analysis and understanding. In the end, he is rewarded with filial gratitude from his son and all the comforts of life.

A modern epic, the novel encompasses characters belonging to three generations of post-independence Kashmir: the family-centered characters, who hold onto traditions and are nostalgic for an old world order, like Malla Khaliq, Aziz Dyad, Narayan Joo, Naba Kantroo, and Rahim Shoga; the mercenary characters caught up in the swings of the market, like Ghulam Mohammad, Ghulam Qadir, Gul Beg, Parvez and Jane; and finally, a new generation of youth looking for wholesome education and fair opportunities, like Razaq, Vijay Kumar, Dilip Kumar, Parveen, Bilal, Nisar, and Mukhtar. Among all these characters, Malla Khaliq stands tall as a concretion of a firmly rooted and immutable conscience. Qadir, Razaq, Parveen and Vijay Kumar move from one stratum to another and from one state of mind to another. While living in a maze of various economic, political, and social forces, they act towards an illusory freedom that they believe can be acquired with calculation, and are convinced of the efficacy of their actions.

The arrival of a European tourist, going by the name Jane, who rents out the houseboat Gulshan sets off a chain reaction and upsets the lives of Malla Khaliq and his family. Seduced by Jane's charms and promises of monetary gains, Qadir, the profligate son of Malla Khaliq gets caught in the net of smugglers. His association with the hippies, whom Jane introduces him to, drives him deeper and deeper into the quagmire of unlawful activities. On one hand, Qadir and Jane desperately try to evade the police and go into hiding. And on the other hand, Malla Khaliq, Narayan Joo, Bhonsley, Prahlad Singh and Vijay Kumar, attempt to curb the nefarious designs of the criminals operating in and around the Dal. This long hide-and-seek takes a toll on Malla Khaliq's family, particularly Qadir's wife Zeb and their son Bilal. Qadir is finally apprehended by the Mumbai police and Malla Khaliq leaves Srinagar to get to him. Narayan Joo's son Vijay Kumar uses his clout in Mumbai in getting Qadir released on bail. Being remorseful about his illicit dealings and many misdeeds, Qadir is not able to face his benevolent father and loving wife Zeb. With a resolve to return to his family only after washing away all his sins through living a life of hard labour, Qadir disappears again. He goes to Goa and from there to Daman where he helps an ailing hotelier named De Souza, in rebuilding his business. Knowing nothing about Qadir's past, De Souza gets his only daughter Reeny married to Qadir and before his death, bequeaths his property to them.

Qadir, with a complete disregard for his kindred, is driven by his selfish impulses and is forced to leave home. Other characters like Narayan Joo's son, Vijay Kumar, also lives away from Srinagar, aspiring to become successful in a wider world. However, his son, Dilip, returns to the Valley and decided to settle there after gaining a degree in hotel management from a Swiss university. There is also Razaq, a destitute boy, who starts his life as a servant in the houseboats of Malla Khaliq, but then decides to take up his education. He falls in love with his master's daughter Parveen, runs away in dejection when she is married into a rich family, and finally re-surfaces as a police officer and marries Parveen who is divorced from her lecherous husband, Parvez. The movement of the various men, old and young, reflect how economic and social forces determine mobility and migration, and how individuals make moral choices to go or not go against the grain.

Like the other works of Pran Kishore, *Gul Gulshan Gulfam* revolves around a tidy narrative structure so that all other components are proportionate in shape and size the main arc. For every dramatic flare-up that takes place, the author starts with a lull in the foreground, which then snowballs into bigger events by cause and effect. Pran Kishore uses his authorial voice deftly, alternating between stylized modes of omniscience and determinacy of the public uses of language to manage the plot in consonance with the Aristotelian notion of a six-segment pyramidal form. However, unlike the Greek concept of tragedy of necessity, *Gul Gulshan Gulfam*, based on free exercise of choice, is a tragedy of possibility. Qadir's hubris is his delusion of prosperity and his faith in his efforts – legal or illegal. His peripeteia is his willful complicity with Gul Beg and Jane. His fall and suffering finally lead him to the recognition of his tragic errors, his anagnorosis. When the compassion from his father thaws his frozen feelings, the omniscience narration depicts his subjective condition. He confesses all his sins and follies to his loving wife Zeb when he is home again.

Pran Kishore is meticulous in creating the *mise-en-scene* of particular events and the total environment of the novel. The narrative is therefore embedded with cultural referents – *qahwa* (the Kashmiri concoction of full tea leaf, cinnamon and cardamom) and *samovar* (a copper kettle used to boiling qahwa tea leaves), the mention of almonds, saffron, apples, pomegranates, dry morels, *jejyier* (a hookah), *phiran* (a loose outer garment), *kangri* (a brazier with a cover and top of wickers), *nadiry* (lotus stalks) and other items of routine life in Kashmir abounding in the novel are not there without a purpose. Within the limited purlieus of the Dal Lake, the novelist weaves a rich tapestry of Kashmiri culture. He also uses dialogues very consciously, selecting words, accents, variations of speech-rhythms to depict the different dialects for different characters. Though they are all Kashmiri, language of the characters varies from profession to profession. While translating, the variation of dialects and syntax was challenging and I have tried my best to achieve a balance. Translating this epic novel has been pleasant and rewarding, especially since I am deeply involved in the life that has so effectively been presented in the novel.